AMERICAN COUP

EMANUEL CLEAVER II

This is a work of fiction. Names, characters, places, and incidents either are the product of the author's imagination or are used fictitiously. Any resemblance to actual events, locales, organizations, or persons living or dead is entirely coincidental and beyond the intent of either the author or the publisher.

Studio Digital CT, LLC
P.O. Box 4331
Stamford, CT 06907

Story Plant Paperback ISBN-13: 978-1-61188-306-0
Fiction Studio Books E-book ISBN-13: 978-1-945839-41-2

Visit our website at www.TheStoryPlant.com

First Story Plant paperback printing: June 2021
Printed in the United States of America

0 9 8 7 6 5 4 3 2 1

This novel is dedicated to the wise American voter who is inclined not to accept leaders who practice politics without principle; leadership without statesmanship; quotability without believability; and theatricality instead of morality.

Prologue

September 2026

JAY PATTERSON LIMPED FROM THE WASHINGTON MONUMENT TOWARDS THE LINCOLN MEMORIAL. He wore jeans and a torn white cotton shirt—a red necktie wound around his right thigh served as a tourniquet. Glancing behind him, he thought he saw a park ranger walking quickly in his direction. Patterson veered left before the Reflecting Pool and crossed Independence Avenue, then traveled southeast along Ohio Drive. He slumped under the cherry trees near the Tidal Basin, the Potomac River directly before him and the Jefferson Memorial behind him. Perspiring and breathing hard, he wiped the sweat from his brow and, with bloodshot brown eyes, surveyed the sky.

Black thunderclouds boiled up from the horizon, throwing the Potomac and the Jefferson Memorial into deep shadow. A jagged line of lightning etched the sky like a crack in a windowpane, light drops of rain hitting the grass in the small clearing where he'd taken refuge. Patterson had dictated his latest report on President Herbert Chase Hastings into his phone, but the screen was cracked and he couldn't access the Send icon to upload what he'd learned about the controversial resident of the Oval Office to his website at NewzTracker.com. He stabbed randomly at the shattered glass.

"Damn," he muttered, as he lay back in the grass to catch his breath. He had found the information on President Hastings he'd been searching for, and with several states in the Union debating in their legislatures as to whether to secede or not, what he'd discovered might save the country or cause it to fragment forever. If the latter happened, there would be no Lincoln to bring it together again, no Reconstruction, no appeal to the better angels of our nature.

He loosened the tourniquet for sixty seconds and then tightened it again. His mind played back images he had recorded from around the country. Political protests against the current administration raged in major urban centers, causing President Hastings to activate the Loyalty Militia, formerly the National Guard, to patrol cities like Nashville, Cleveland, Detroit, Los Angeles, Atlanta, and dozens more. Hastings' children had been accused of doing business with a foreign power hostile to American interests, but the president had rejected such reports as substitute news.

He imagined empty control rooms of TV networks and news bureaus since all the major news feeds were based on algorithms. Newsroom staffs were at home, huddled around the wall screens in their living rooms, or else sitting in churches, praying that God would spare their side of the political conflict—and crush the opposition in retribution. Even members of the newly formed Congregation of the Heart were gathered in their cinderblock cathedrals across the country, praying for . . . . actually, Patterson didn't know *what* they were doing. Were they praying to a higher power? Themselves? President Hastings? The fledgling denomination, if it could be called that, had figured prominently in some of his reports, but he still hadn't totally figured out the psychology of its flock. Hell, he didn't even know what he himself believed anymore, and pulled a worn black leather Bible from his dirty suit coat. It was true—there were no atheists in foxholes. Agnostics like Patterson, perhaps, but not atheists. He flipped through the pages, sighed, and thought he heard the hoof beats of four extremely angry horsemen galloping down the Mall, but that was either distant thunder, or the agonizing pain in his leg was causing him to hallucinate.

Even now, tens of thousands of immigrants from Mexico were attempting to cross the border, hoping that at least one-half of America would welcome their starved and bleeding bodies into North America. Two-thirds of those storming the southern border were being shot on sight, turning the Rio Grande into a river of blood.

He recalled a scene of a civilian state militia in Montana cleaning out big-box stores of hardware, guns, and food, although they already had plenty of MREs in their bunkers. Wearing camouflage fatigues, they grinned at the cameras as if to say, *"We told you fifteen years ago this day was coming, and damn if society isn't collapsing just like we said on the reality shows."*

A burly man in his forties stopped, faced his invisible audience, held up his middle finger and cried, "Rally the red! The Real Right shall cleanse the earth!"

Patterson grimaced. The weekend warriors had been right, but for the wrong reason, and it was doubtful that they would ever figure out what was really happening.

He had watched events unfold from cities around the world: Moscow, Tehran, New Delhi, Pyongyang, and Beijing. Countries were on heightened nuclear alert. If the two-hundred-and-fifty-year-old experiment in democracy failed, the country would be ripe for attack. Maybe President Revtushenko of the newly reconstituted Soviet Union would realize that he finally had first-strike capability. By the same token, leaders in capitals across the globe believed that Hastings was so self-obsessed and unsystematic in diplomacy and statecraft that he might use the great rift within his country to get his nukes airborne as soon as possible in a September surprise. Indeed, the president had threatened to bomb Pakistan for reasons that weren't entirely clear to his own military advisors. He was a maverick when it came to diplomacy and statecraft, and the doors of missile silos around the world had opened for the first time in decades. Would mushroom clouds soon create hideous blossoms over the homeland? The United States State Department was playing a high-stakes poker game, but no one knew whether the man in the White House dealing the cards was, in fact, a narcissistic nincompoop, as his now-fired Secretary of Homeland Security reportedly referred to him in a meeting that was thought to be safe.

Air Force One had taken off from Wright-Patterson, destination unknown. No press was aboard, and the nation wondered if the president was going abroad, flying to NORAD headquarters in Cheyenne

Mountain, heading to his home in North Carolina, or had resigned. C-SPAN had been off the air for two days, and rumor had it that both Houses of Congress had met in closed session before members returned to their districts. Most buildings in D.C. were empty. Was anyone in charge of the federal government?

Patterson stood and made his way into East Potomac Park, dragging his injured leg across the golf course and driving range. The bullet had passed cleanly through his muscle, and yet his thigh was singing with pain. He collapsed again, grimaced and said to himself, *I used to be considered an elite athlete, so surely I can muster enough energy to stand up and drag myself to safety.* Although he struggled, he was able to stand to his feet and, with excruciating pain, began to navigate to safety. He was vulnerable out in the open, and the stakes were too high to allow himself to be caught.

"No pressure," he said out loud. "It's only the fate of the world that hangs on a few hundred words I want to share with my readers."

He tapped the damaged glass on his phone repeatedly with his thumb—a curious lethargy was settling in, and he knew he had only a minute or two of consciousness left. Suddenly his screen vibrated, the haptic response indicating that he had stumbled across the Send icon.

The thunderclouds were closer, and a heavy rain started falling. Patterson slumped to the ground, barely conscious. Would his story make it to NewzTracker? If it did, would anyone be listening?

As the downpour raged, Patterson's mind closed down, falling into a lucid dream state in which he saw himself at home again with his African American/European father and his Latino mother. They lived in the Southwest section of Atlanta, Georgia, where gangs dominated the neighborhood.

"Jay! Come on, it's time to go!"

"I'm coming, Dad!"

Once in the car, Jay's dad becomes serious.

"Jay, I need to know how you're doing in staying away from the gangs at school. It worries me."

"Dad, they don't mess with me. The toughest guys in the neighborhood treat me like I'm a celebrity. In fact, they come to my games and hold up homemade signs that read 'The Puma from the Projects!' My problem is that they want to hurt anyone who tackles me!" Jay giggles. "I don't hang out with them. When I see them on the streets, I do stop and chat. I don't ignore them or put them down. Dad, you've got to know I have street smarts, and I am the top wide receiver in Atlanta. I can negotiate the streets."

"Okay, son, I'm glad you feel you have the situation under control. I know you've had fights in the past with gang members. Remember the punctured lung? I believe in you, Jay. One day you're going to be the most celebrated wide receiver in the NFL, and even gangbangers are in awe of someone who can rub a sub-4.4 fourty! Just remember you have a wonderful future, son. "

Jay struggles to wake from the dream, and then he clearly hears his father's voice . . . .

"Son! Listen to me, son. You're going to be alright, Jay. It's not your time yet. Just hang on . . . hang on . . . .

Chapter One
August 2026

JAY PATTERSON WAS ASLEEP IN HIS MOTEL ROOM IN BRISTER, ARIZONA, WHEN THE PHONE ON THE CHEAP PINE TABLE NEXT TO HIS BED JANGLED. He reached up with his left hand, his index finger tapping the screen.

"Where the hell are you?" said John Taylor, Chief Editor of NewzTracker.com. "The president's speech at the border has been pushed up two hours. Hastings wants to get the hell out of Dodge before the protesters show up. I should already be getting your feed."

Patterson swung his feet over the side of the sagging mattress and wiped sleep from his eyes. "I'm on it, John. Catch ya later."

He looked at his watch. It was eight-thirty. He could get to the nine o'clock speech if he skipped shaving. Brister was easy to navigate since the border town was little more than Main Street with a feed store, bar, sheriff's office, dry goods store, and a few stucco homes spread across the hardpan for a radius of one mile, a lone traffic light blinking a perpetual yellow in front of the abandoned post office. The sign on the state highway read:

BRISTER
POP: 312

Patterson pulled on his jeans and slipped into his coat with suede elbow patches, a gift from his girlfriend, Sela, who knew of his fondness for the trappings of a lifestyle that was quickly vanishing. His eight-year-old phone did everything he needed, and he wasn't interested in wearing his tech; video glasses and smart fabrics were more hassle than they were worth. He exited his room, put on aviator sunglasses, and marveled at how the sleepy town had come to life because Herbert Chase Hastings, forty-seventh President of the United States, had come to Brister to deliver a major policy speech on immigration, a cornerstone of his campaign in 2023 and 2024. News helicopters crisscrossed the sky as Hastings' faithful—dubbed the Red Republican Legion—filed from buses past security checkpoints into an area the size of a football field next to the guard tower from which Hastings would address the crowd and the nation. Vendors hawked hats and tee shirts with Hastings' trademark slogan of *Reviving The Soul Of America*. The hats and shirts were all Republican red, and anyone wearing a blue shirt or cap was usually bruised and bloody by the time a Hastings rally was over.

Patterson waded through the crowd, had the chip implant in his arm—a begrudging accommodation to what he considered intrusive tech—was scanned by the Secret Service, and slipped into the press pen to the left of the newly-constructed immigration guard tower. He sat on the top step of aluminum bleachers facing the audience and the Rio Grande. He called John Taylor back at NewzTracker to verify that the feed Patterson was providing was live and clear.

"What's the SOB gonna say?" Taylor laughed.

It was a rhetorical question. The White House Communications Office hadn't issued an advance copy of a speech since the inauguration. Hastings was a loose cannon who liked to improvise and play things on the fly. The previous month, he'd given a speech in Baltimore on crime, but had bragged for fifteen minutes on how ingenuity and his knowledge of the laws of physics had helped him shave three strokes off his golf game. He'd segued back to the issue of crime by brandishing a five iron and saying that the police had his permission to beat the hell out of anyone resisting arrest, the implication being that they could use a golf club, Louisville slugger, police baton, or whatever was handy to accomplish the task. Such swift action and strength, he claimed, was the "Roman way." He was also fond of saying that, unlike Rome, his empire would never collapse. All American flags now had the bald eagle—symbol of freedom in America for generations—atop the poles on which they flew. It looked quite similar to the Roman standard, or *Signa Romanum*, after a Republican Congress passed a law changing the design of all flagpoles and staffs from which the colors flew.

Flanked by fifty other reporters, Patterson sat and waited for the appearance of the president. The sky was blue and cloudless, and Jay was reminded of sitting in the now-demolished Georgia Dome on a sunny day, imagining himself running a fly route and hauling in an eighty-yard bomb. He had loved the Atlanta Falcons, "The Dirty Birds," since he was four.

Chapter Two

Red Republican Legion

PRESIDENT HERBERT CHASE HASTINGS SPRANG FROM HIS BLACK LIMOUSINE AND WALKED BRISKLY INTO THE ABANDONED POST OFFICE, WHICH HAD BEEN SCANNED BY THE SECRET SERVICE AND THEN DRESSED UP BY HIS STAFF AS A READY ROOM SO THE PRESIDENT COULD GATHER HIS THOUGHTS AND WAIT TO BE SUMMONED TO THE TOWER.

Hastings was a vigorous sixty-five-year-old. He jogged five miles a day and lifted weights three times a week. He was muscular and fit, and preached frequently at Red Rallies on the benefits of exercise and a healthy diet. He drank three gallons of water a day and claimed to have the prostate of a thirty-year-old man, although he admitted that only his wives could attest to that fact, especially his current spouse, the lovely forty-three-year-old Diane Blair Hastings. While he always laced his speeches with non-political references, he was a smooth and gifted orator who could seamlessly move from one subject to another by using a metaphor that turned his rhetoric back to the topic at hand. He always stood tall and erect, hands braced on the podium as he looked with pale blue eyes at the loyal admirers who came in droves to hear him hold forth. They didn't care whether he talked about his staggering IQ—which he claimed was 156—or jobs. They were enthralled by the presence of what they regarded as genuine greatness. Who else but Hastings would dare compare himself to the Caesars of Rome?

Hastings went straight for the mirror and snapped his fingers. His personal barber and stylist traveled with him wherever he went, and he motioned for the barber to step forward as he gazed into a mirror on the bathroom wall of the post office, turning his head left and right to examine the arc of gray hair, exactly one-fourth of an inch in length, that ran from ear to ear below the crown of his bald head. He fancied it to be a garland of sorts, not unlike the slim crown of oak leaves worn by Augustus and other Roman emperors. As a student of history, he'd read *The History of the Decline and Fall of the Roman Empire* by Edward Gibbon a dozen times.

His barber produced electric clippers, which expertly trimmed the gray garland of hair and then swept down his neck to keep Hastings' skin smooth. It was a weekly ritual.

Hastings left the restroom and entered the old sorting room. His staff, wife, and entourage of relatives, all flanked by the black suits of Secret Service agents, broke into applause. It was spontaneous, although expected by the president. These were his friends and trusted political advisors who had helped him unseat former President Harrison DePeche. Red-meat Republicans had rallied behind Hastings, who had ridiculed DePeche's effort to turn back the federal government to the days of Franklin Roosevelt, job growth, and social contracts. Supply-side economics—trickle down was still the name used by Democrats—had failed for the sixth time since the 1980s. DePeche had wanted to revive the progressive agenda, but his administration had lumbered along like an unwieldy dreadnought ship unable to navigate the seas of governance. Progress had been made, but the pace was too slow, and people were still hurting even though the economic plight of Joe Sixpack had been inflicted by prior administrations. Hastings had won in a landslide, thanks to his Red Republican Legion, which had become a modern political force of ultra-conservatives. The legion whipped citizens into a frenzy with appeals laced with rhetoric of the Founding Fathers. They were part of the larger conservative coalition known as the Real Right, which advocated a purity of government that would make America a shining city on a hilltop, light and salt for the world. Next to referencing the glories of the Roman Empire, Hastings' most frequent quotations came from the Good Book, large portions of which he'd memorized in high school at the Christian Academy of Virginia.

His rise had been meteoric, and as Hastings himself often said to those assembled, *"Not bad for the former head of a tobacco empire whose only government service was two years on the city council of Charlotte, North Carolina."*

"They're ready for you, Mr. President," a staffer announced.

Hastings closed his eyes and pounded his right fist into the palm of his left hand, a ritual performed before every public event, as if he were an athlete about to take the field. In a real sense, he was. According to some in the White House press pool, Hastings had zero interest in policy of governance, and yet he had already begun to speak to aides about a dynasty. He, in fact, understood that he would need to run for re-election on his prodigious personality rather than his tried and tested political agenda. Xenophobia was going over quite well with the Real Right, so he joked to his aides about "giving my people a heavy dose of America for Americans."

Hastings strode from the room, and cheers erupted as he neared the stairway that had been erected so he could ascend the guard tower. At the last minute, he veered away from the portable stairway and began climbing the steel ladder that the guards used. He was, after all, physically fit and always took advantage of an opportunity to demonstrate his strength and stamina. The crowd before him went wild and chanted the familiar mantra of "Hay-stings, Hay-stings!" until the president reached the summit of the tower and stood before the microphone. He stretched his arms over his head as if to embrace the audience, and they reciprocated, as if to embrace their President.

Hastings lowered his arms as the applause died down and began to speak in a slow, measured tone. His voice was especially strong in the lower vocal registers and had a quality that was charismatic, mesmerizing. When he began a speech, no one dared speak for fear of missing a single consonant coming from the mouth of their leader.

"Friends," Hastings began, "I come before you today with humility and gratitude. I come with humility so that I can serve, for the Savior himself came not to be served, but to serve. That is who I am and who I shall remain—your humble servant. And I come with gratitude that you have elected me to be a man who protects you, your homes, and your families."

Hastings spent ten minutes talking of the status of illegal immigration, a solution for which had not been found despite the efforts of previous administrations. He spoke of how he'd once shot and killed an intruder in his North Carolina mansion when a man had sought to murder him and his family twenty years earlier; this was to emphasize his expert marksmanship and the fact that no man or woman alive had ever beaten him at skeet shooting or any athletic contest. This was his sidebar, his foray into the prowess of all things Hastings. And then he made his segue back to immigration after pausing for thirty seconds, which for most speakers would have been deemed awkward and unacceptable, a sign of hesitation. Not so with Hastings. It's all about grand dramatization as imagined by him.

"Marksmanship," he said. "Keeping the enemy in your sights at all times. This tower is similar to the towers along Hadrian's Wall—Hadrian, the great Roman emperor who built a defensive wall across the entire breadth of Britain in the year 122. And that is what we have begun here in Brister, Arizona. Our southern border is one thousand nine hundred and fifty-four miles long, and there shall be one tower for every mile along the Rio Grande from El Paso to San Diego. In each tower shall be stationed a sharpshooter to kill on sight any illegal immigrant crossing into our great nation."

Hastings paused and picked up an M-22 rifle before addressing his audience again.

"Ecce homo!" he bellowed into the microphone. "Behold the man standing on the United States side of the Rio Grande, a man who has just crossed our border illegally!"

A soldier on the ground motioned to the man, who started walking forward before breaking into a run deeper into Arizona territory. Hastings raised the rifle and sighted the man, tracking him through the weapon's scope. The barrel of the rifle followed the illegal for five seconds before Hastings squeezed off a round. The man fell to the ground and tumbled forward. A second shot followed, and the man's body contorted for several seconds before lying still.

"Our new immigration policy!" Hastings declared triumphantly. "Strength, power, marksmanship! These fortifications shall be known as the Towers of Freedom! Others have proposed a wall, and still others have advocated compassion and an open-door policy. No more! We will shoot illegal immigrants dead! No drugs or crime inside our land of plenty. No jobs given to anyone but citizens!"

Applause emanated from the crowd, tentative at first, and then louder when they'd grasped the seriousness of both Hastings' act and the policy it signaled.

Manuel Gonzalez, having been shot by blanks, stood and bowed to the president. He had only been an example of the immigration policy that Hastings wished to enforce.

Hastings paused and put down the rifle. "I am a compassionate man, my friends. The people in Mexico and Central America are God-fearing people, most of whom are Catholics. They finger their beads and eat their crackers at Sunday mass. When they die, they go to heaven. What you see before you is mercy, for Mr. Gonzalez isn't dead, but rather an omen of what shall befall future illegal immigrants should they try to cross the border." Hastings' manner was now soft and subdued. "What we have is a win-win situation. Illegal immigrants will go somewhere else—a nice place, if you will—just not the United States of America!"

The onlookers were now wild with enthusiasm, cheering and waving their red hats—Revive the Soul of America—as Manuel Gonzalez met his wife and children, who had been ushered onto the desert.

Hastings held up his hand, motioning for silence.

"My fellow Americans, I want you to know that, lest there be criticism and lies from the press, Mr. Gonzalez volunteered to be an example of American justice. In exchange, I offered to grant his wife and family citizenship for life. As scripture says, mercy and kindness shall follow them all the days of their lives. My policy is one of goodness and peace and love . . . but no more illegal immigrants!"

The audience tried to surge forward, tried to topple the metal barricades and storm the tower where their beloved President stood, a smile on his features as he once again raised his arms to embrace the crowd.

"Am I right, people?" Hastings said.

"Yes!" came the passionate response of twenty thousand men and women clad in their blood-red shirts and hats. Fathers held their children high in the air to better see the Gonzalez family.

"Am I right, people?"

"Yes!"

"Am I right?"

"Yessss!"

Using the stairs this time, Hastings descended, pausing midway down to wave to his admirers before making his way over to his son standing by.

"Impressive, yes?" he said to his son, his chief advisor.

"As always, Father. Can I get you anything to drink before you leave?"

"No, but I want you to make sure the Attorney General knows what played out here today. I own him and he knows it. He can figure out a way to legally support what was dramatized here today. We have to be willing to shoot these vermin if they're not willing to stay out of our country."

". . . . you mean, if they're not willing to stay out without applying for citizenship, right?"

Silence.

"Dad . . . right?"

"You heard me right the first time! And make sure that the Attorney General understands that I want all children below the age of eighteen separated from their parents at the border before the parents try applying for citizenship. The children are to be held in detention until such time that the parents can be deported. Only then will they be reunited with their parents.

Hastings walked over and entered the presidential limousine, the motorcade ready to speed him away to Air Force One in Tucson.

The First Lady, wearing extra-large sunglasses and a scarf over her long blond hair, had left the gallery reserved for dignitaries and state politicians while her husband delivered his immigration speech. She didn't need to hear the full text of the address or see Mr. Gonzalez enact the drama of death. Her husband's theatrics were predictable and had become boring over the five years they'd been married. At forty-three, Diane Blair Hastings was a beautiful woman who looked to be in her late thirties. Hastings had been married three times before, each wife giving Hastings a child—two sons and a daughter—and after he'd divorced his third wife six years earlier, he'd flown to Scotland to escape her accusations of domestic abuse and physical assault. He'd played a round of golf at St. Andrews, and as he sat and ate an early dinner at the clubhouse overlooking the legendary Old Course, he noticed a group of women engaged in animated conversation. One had been Blair, a fetching au pair who'd looked after the only child of Colin Gallway, Earl of Spitzfaden and master of its imposing castle. The courtship between Hastings and Blair had been a whirlwind, and within a year Blair had moved to Charlotte and become head of market research at Hastings' tobacco company, PB Enterprises. She knew nothing of market research and politely attended meetings, nodded, did interviews, and functioned as goodwill ambassador for the company. Eighteen months after their introduction in Scotland, the two were married. She'd been a smiling, dutiful wife and had acted graciously during Hastings' failed run for mayor of Charlotte.

After having entered the limousine, Hastings glanced with disdain at his wife.

"You left early," he complained. "It's a breach of protocol. You made me look like a damn fool. How can the world take me seriously if *you* can't even sit through a brief speech?"

The First Lady removed her scarf and sunglasses, revealing a black eye, a cut lip, and a purple bruise on her left cheek.

"Would you care to hit me again for my transgression? You were in rare form last night."

Hastings' demeanor changed rapidly, a look of remembrance that exposed his thoughts . . . that he had once again lost control. That had to stop. The wrong people finding out about this could lead to his political demise.

"You are not sorry in the least for what you did. I know you too well to ever think you are capable of actually feeling guilty for physically abusing me. Your concern is only for yourself . . . or, shall I say, your image. I've known that from the beginning. I believe that my own psychological defenses knowing how narcissistic you are is preventing me from becoming pregnant. You screamed at me for not giving you a son, but I'm not to blame. On the more practical side, if the fertility treatments haven't worked it's because I'm forty-three, and you must accept that I can't give you a fourth child. But then again, maybe the real reason I can't is because I can't stomach the idea."

Hastings knit his brows. He could feel his anger growing. He leaned over and stroked his wife's face even though she recoiled instinctively from his touch. "My dear," he said, "have you been taking your pills again? The benzodiazepines?"

"No, *dear,*" she said, putting on her glasses and scarf.

Hastings sat back and folded his arms. "I have no idea what you're talking about. Fertility treatments? I think you're going to have to resume private therapy in the residence. We'll have your psychiatrist brought in discreetly."

The First Lady had been to top fertility specialists in New York City for three years. Despite fertility drugs, artificial insemination, and in-vitro fertilization, she had not been able to conceive. She knew all too well that failure to sire a child made her husband feel like less of a man. While he was a student of the Roman emperors, she regarded him more as a petulant Henry VIII. His endless attempts to gaslight her were transparent and pathetic. It never ceased to amaze her how much he underestimated her.

They didn't speak for the remainder of their journey to the Miami Memorial, where Hastings would deliver a speech that afternoon to commemorate the tragedy wrought by Hurricane Carla in 2024. The city had been erased from the earth by its winds and storm surge.

Hastings, the unparalleled master of projection, knew intuitively how to work the angle of mental illness to his advantage. His predecessor, Harrison DePeche, had been an advocate for mental healthcare, since psychiatric wards and nursing homes were filled with patients shot up with Thorazine, shuffling through corridors like zombies. DePeche's father had suffered from depression and had eventually been hospitalized, only to be diagnosed as schizophrenic. Hastings' response had been to exploit what he regarded as a weakness in the elder DePeche.

"Do you ever wonder why President DePeche was so concerned about mice? They scare him to death. He suffered from mysophobia. Is his son simply a mild-mannered man who never raises his voice? Or is he stoned on antidepressants like his father? Do we want a man suffering from mental instability in the White House?"

The campaign rally cry from then on became, "Depressed DePeche! Depressed DePeche!"

Chapter Three

Good Ole Southern Boys

SENATOR LELAND WALLACE OF TENNESSEE SAT IN HIS OFFICE IN THE DIRKSEN SENATE OFFICE BUILDING. He reached into the bottom left drawer of his broad oak desk and lifted a bottle of Jack Daniels into the air. He got up, produced two shot glasses, and joined his visitor in the sitting area, Senator Tom Chance of Georgia. Wallace was a Republican, Chance a Democrat, but these were good ole boys from the South, and they'd been friends for years. At sixty-six, Wallace was lanky and had thinning gray hair. Chance was a robust fifty-two with dark hair and a tan, and he worked out at the Senate gym every morning beginning at five o'clock. They watched the wall screen as Hastings delivered his speech at Brister, Arizona, before Wallace pressed the remote and brought silence to the room.

"Whaddya think?" Chance asked his colleague.

"I think I want a drink. Simulated murder is a hell of a border policy."

"But not one out of character," Chance remarked.

Chance was one of the most vocal opponents of the president, whom he frequently called mentally unhinged. He was also urging an appellate court challenge to the president's recent executive order lifting restrictions on energy companies—coal, oil, and gas—since Chance believed regulations were necessary to protect the environment. Hastings has had the policy of ignoring climate change completely, saying it was just a Democratic hoax. Yet changes were accelerating much faster than previously warned by scientists, to the extent that there are now reservations being made on transports to Mars from Earth for those who can't breathe the air of Earth any longer. Reservations cost millions of dollars, so what does that say for the future—survival of the monied? Or survival of the fittest?

Wallace poured Jack Daniels into the shot glasses and handed one to the man who sat three feet away. "We drink until the bottle is empty or one of us passes out dead drunk on the floor. While we drink, we tell the truth. No bullshit, no red or blue. A southern code of honor and . . . ." Wallace waved off the end of his sentence as if he were tired, aggravated, or both.

"I have this one," Chance warned with a smile. "I'm younger."

Wallace laughed. "After thirty-six years in this town, I've learned how to hold my liquor. Let's go."

Each took a shot, and Wallace continued as he refilled the glasses. "Does Hastings get re-elected, assuming he survives his term?"

"Depends on the midterms in two months. The House may be up for grabs. I give the president a fifty-fifty chance, although I recently learned that—"

"Dammit, Tom! I said no bullshit. You're playing it safe by giving him even odds. He's a fool, and his mother should have left him on the doorstep of an orphanage after he was born. He would never have risen to power."

Chance squinted and pursed his lips after downing a second shot. "Okay, no BS. The son of a bitch gets re-elected, his pathological narcissistic tendencies notwithstanding. It's what the people want, and it's what they get. He gives the electorate bread and circuses spurting forth from a serious mental illness that masquerades as ego mania, when actually there's no one home upstairs. As a student of history, he play-acts the role perfectly. He knows his lines well enough to act himself right into the Presidency without having any idea what constitutes the position of President of the United States. He gives the Nazi far-right-wingers attention and they adore him as their leader. They could care less that he's not presidential material as long as he gives the far-right attention—just like any other despot in history. And everybody else but the far-right is the enemy. This is how it happened in WWII, and it's playing out all over again."

Wallace paused, his hand shaking a little as he brought the glass to his lips. The tremors had begun two years earlier.

"Sadly, I agree," he said. "I thought he was unelectable, but he's in the Oval even though he just announced that all illegal immigrants will be shot dead at the Southern border.

"Yeh, and he's ordered the Attorney General to make it officially legal to do so—shoot to kill when seen from any of the towers along the southern border. I never thought I'd see this day, and almost wish I hadn't. I bet Percy Beauregard Hastings is smiling down on his son from heaven."

"It's more likely that Percy is looking up from the bottom ring of Dante's Inferno. Hell, Tom, his impersonation of being president is constantly being exposed for what it is—play-acting. He is role playing what he imagines the president to be like based on his knowledge of the Roman emperor Caesar Vespasian, who presided over slaves being fed to the lions in the Colosseum between 70 and 72 A.D. In the President's mind, the slaves are immigrants, and the lions are guns. If he has any hidden motives for being president, other than getting to play the role of an emperor, I don't know what they are. He somehow finds a way to shine a bright light on a character that's larger than life. And I wouldn't be surprised if he sleeps with Mein Kompf on his nightstand for quick reference . . . Roman emperor, Hitler, and the Bible. He's completely insane, and the American people are going along for the ride."

"A remarkable story," Chance said. "The Hastings family. Go figure."

The senators discussed Hastings unlikely rise to power, chalking a large part of it up to megalomania and a public starved for strong confident leadership—the public has no idea that the man is acting—acting out a delusion of grandeur! One has to wonder what will happen when those Americans who are not far-right-wingers realize the truth.

Percy Beauregard Hastings had been the unrivalled King of Tobacco, CEO of PB Enterprises, a company that sold five different brands of cigarettes, as well as chewing and pipe tobacco. The North Carolina tobacco baron was rumored to be worth multi-million dollars until his empire fell on hard times, courtesy of the Great Enlightenment of the 1970s and 1980s, when it was medically proven that cigarette smoking killed people, with lung cancer and heart disease leading a long list of fatal illnesses caused by the carcinogens in tobacco smoke: arsenic, formaldehyde, DDT, carbon monoxide, ammonia, and about forty other deadly chemicals. Tens of millions kicked the habit over the next decade, with sales plummeting further when Dale McCuddy, the grizzled cowboy spokesman and billboard icon for Western Rider Cigarettes, died of lung cancer after telling the nation in jarring TV commercials months before his death that Western Rider was the "gun that shot me." Ironically, McCuddy had delivered a kill shot of his own straight to the heart of the tobacco industry, with sales declining throughout the 1990s. The Surgeon General's warning on every pack of cigarettes grew larger in print, and congress nailed the executives of seven tobacco giants for manipulating the nicotine levels in their cigarettes. Percy himself sat in front of a Senate subcommittee and had taken it on the chin, issuing no statements except for three terse denials that he'd engaged in any such activity. Cigarette sales declined by 30 percent the following year, and continued to fall as the public was educated on how tobacco killed its consumers.

Percy's son, Herbert Chase Hastings, had been Vice President of PB Enterprises. Percy, an outspoken opponent of the federal government's intrusions into the lives of citizens, opposed the regulation of the tobacco industry and many others, from fossil fuels to banking and investment. With his son looking on, as he delivered a speech to the Charlotte Chamber of Commerce, Percy Hastings railed against members of the United States Congress, calling them nothing but slimy, overpaid pimps and whores. Herbert embraced his father's disdain for big government, and when Percy keeled over from a massive heart attack after smoking for fifty-seven years, Herbert Chase Hastings became head of a lethargic PB Enterprises.

In the years that followed, Herbert Hastings continued to sell his father's lethal products, including Western Rider. He once told his Board of Directors of PB Enterprises that they should not worry too much about people smoking because . . . "smoking is a cure for cancer." PB Enterprises, nevertheless, introduced an allegedly safe cigarette into the market, a nicotine-free brand with no harmful chemicals since the "tobacco" was made from vegetable fiber. The cigarette was marketed as a social accessory, a chic way to blend in at parties and social functions. One could go through the motions of smoking and feel sexy and relevant without incurring heart disease or cancer. But there was one problem: no one got addicted.

When he ran for President, Herbert Chase Hastings decided to hand over the day-to-day management of the business to his eldest son, Bradley Hastings.

/

Senator Wallace produced a pack of cigarettes from the vest pocket of his suit coat.

"The real thing," he said. "Nicotine. Strong as hell. I also have cigarettes from France, England, and Russia. They're more potent. Want one? After today's speech in Arizona, I need a smoke."

Senator Chance shook his head. "Never even tried one, not even as a teenager. Listen, about Hastings, I—"

Chance was getting dizzy after eight shots of bourbon. He also began to scratch his arms and legs. "Leland, do you have fleas in here? I feel like my skin is crawling with insects."

"It's the whiskey, son. I *knew* I could drink you under the table! Here, have another shot. Maybe it'll calm your nerves."

Chance smiled tepidly before suddenly grabbing his chest. His face turned red as he slumped to the floor, eyes closed.

Wallace was down by his side in a second, turning his body over, checking on a pulse that didn't exist and trying to resuscitate him. But after five minutes of doing so, he gave up, and called medics.

The medics arrived ten minutes later and took away the body of former Senator Thomas Wilson Chance from the great state of Georgia.

Wallace shook his head and drank another shot of whiskey since he knew that reporters would descend on his office in a matter of minutes. Wallace himself had survived prostate cancer and undergone triple bypass surgery eleven years earlier, and yet it was the younger and healthier man who had crumpled to the floor like wet newspaper.

In a state of shock, he called his wife. "Something isn't right. Tom Chance just dropped dead in my office from a heart attack, and he had a stress test and general checkup just two months ago. Something most definitely isn't right."

He didn't mention the shots of whisky to his wife or to the medics when they took the body away. But certainly they would have to notice the strong odor of whisky around Chance's mouth. An autopsy would be ordered.

God! Chance drank eight straight shots of whisky at my challenge. If he didn't die of a massive heart attack, he might have died from alcohol poisoning. What responsibility or blame should I be feeling for his death?

Chapter Four
Sela & SETI

PATTERSON WOULD NORMALLY HAVE BEEN SHOCKED BY THE SCENE IN BRISTER WERE IT NOT FOR HASTINGS' HISTRIONICS AND THE OUTRAGEOUS STUNTS HE ENGAGED IN ON A REGULAR BASIS. Democrats were suffering from what he termed "Hastings fatigue." America, he thought, resembled a Midwestern carnival where people entered the Fun House and looked at distorted versions of themselves and wondered who or what was staring back at them. The political landscape had become surreal on a daily basis, and every news cycle was filled with an unforeseen turn, a strange and jarring gyration not unlike those caused by creaky rides held together with duct tape and chicken wire. Would a car on the Rocket Ride fly off into the sky at any moment and send its inhabitants hurtling towards the sawdust fifty yards down the midway? People still went to these old-fashioned symbols of Saturday in the Corn Belt, but was it to have fun or tempt fate? And have people now substituted Hastings' Daily Reality Dramas for fun? Or to tempt fate?

President Hastings' previous speeches on Miami were perfect examples. After Hurricane Carla had decimated the city, Citizen Hastings had declared that the unprecedented storm surge and wind speeds were divine retribution for a place that had been a den of sin and iniquity, a formerly great metropolitan area that had become what he called a "nest of gays" that rivaled New Orleans, San Francisco, and other cities with large gay and lesbian populations. It was, he'd stated, "The Home of the Queer."

Now aboard a Boeing 787 with his fellow reporters bound for the Miami Memorial speech, Patterson saw an incoming call from Sela. He switched his phone to text mode so he could communicate with his girlfriend privately.

"Hey you, can you believe what Hastings just enacted before the American public?"asked Sela in disbelief.

"Of course," Jay replied. "How's the country reacting?"

"Hastings supporters, as always, love what Hastings did—after they realized Gonzales was in on the act," said Sela. "But across the nation others are numb. Protests are forming in the streets right this minute, and Arizona's attorney general is filing a motion with the Ninth Circuit Court of Appeals to declare the act of shooting illegal immigrants unconstitutional. The White House Press Secretary, David Wolcott, just issued a statement saying that Gonzales was a willing participant at today's spectacle."

"Wolcott has been an ass ever since he was spokesman for PB Enterprises before Hastings appointed him White House Press Secretary. They're all tainted by being either Hastings' relatives, direct family members, or people Hastings either owes a favor to or is blackmailing."

"Gonzales' wife, Sophia, is publicly thanking Hastings for his kindness to their family, now that they're U.S. citizens."

"In other words, it's another *normal* day in the Hastings Administration. Chaos prevails. Anything else new?"

"Good God! Isn't that enough? Why are you taking this in such stride?" asks Sela.

"Because I'm burned out. I meant, is there anything new at SETI?"

"Just number crunching. Got data from Epsilon Eridani. It's a star ten and a half light years away. Received some non-random radio signals last week. But it was probably a fluke. Only lasted ninety seconds and hasn't repeated."

"Good luck with ET," said Jay, trying to lighten the mood.

"Sometimes I hope we don't find a prolonged signal indicating intelligence."

"Oh, come on, Sela! Who are you kidding? It's your life's work. I know how much it means to you."

"They might be listening to Hastings' speeches," she chimed in. "Can you imagine what they would think of us here on Earth?"

"Certainly not as advanced intelligent life, much less altruistic," Jay was quick to reply. "Look on the bright side. If they're of higher intelligence, they'll simply discount Hasting's speeches for some sort of archaic existence resembling primitive earthworm evolution. Hey, you, pay attention now. I love you," emphasized Jay.

"Love you, too, Jay. You sound exhausted. Get some rest."

Patterson had met Sela when former President Harrison Depeche had been at a ceremony awarding the SETI Extraterrestrial Intelligence Research Center a $125 million-dollar grant that had been part of a much larger piece of legislation funding a mission to Mars scheduled for the 2040s. NASA funding had been slashed dramatically over the years, as had funding for most scientific projects, with Congress and the American people in agreement that money needed to be spent on job creation rather than finding out if ancient microbes were fossilized on the red planet. Harrison DePeche had managed to revive the once-great NASA from its status of monitoring satellites to becoming a visionary agency that was once again launching probes to planets in the solar system and planning the delayed Mars mission.

As for White House Press Secretary David Wolcott, Patterson loathed him. Former spokesman for PB Enterprises, he was a man in his mid-forties who had a silver tongue and had spoken ad nauseam about the federal government's assault on the right of every American to smoke or not to smoke. It was an individual choice, he'd claimed on hundreds of occasions, and while the medical community could say what it wanted about tobacco, the government had overstepped its boundary by siding with medical research. He'd pointed out that alcohol was allegedly linked to heart disease, cirrhosis of the liver, and many types of cancer, and yet it would be a cold day in hell before the government reinstated prohibition. Why, he reasoned, was tobacco any different? He cited research indicating that cigarette smoking relaxed people and that many who lived well into their nineties had been lifelong smokers. Wolcott was unfazed by harsh criticism and smiled whenever attacked at the podium. There was little doubt in anyone's mind that President Hastings had named Wolcott Press Secretary because of his calm demeanor and eloquent oratory about people's right to die from tobacco products.

Patterson put away his phone and settled back in his seat. The flight to Miami would take three hours. He'd learned over the years that he needed to take power naps whenever he could. Otherwise, his blood pressure spiked and he became tired and irritable. The Miami speech would no doubt turn out to be another circus, and he wanted to be ready for the show, regardless of never being surprised, much less shocked anymore.

Chapter Five
House Calls

THE MAN WALKED INTO THE LOBBY OF CIA HEADQUARTERS AT LANGLEY, VIRGINIA, AND WAS ESCORTED TO LEVEL SIX BELOW THE MAIN BUILDING. He was well known in the intelligence community, having been a former overseas case officer in Iraq in his twenties. He rode an underground tram to an adjoining building, where he walked with an armed guard to one of the many computer complexes below "the Company."

The visitor sat at a computer terminal in the bowels of the CIA, turned around to indicate that his escort could leave the room, and then began his task. He could have spoken everything he wanted to communicate, but he chose to use a keyboard to type his message since he presumed that every room in the CIA was bugged for the purposes of internal security.

He had been sending messages to the reporter for the past month. Now he deemed it time to send another to JP.33@newztracker.com. His message was a single word. It would be up to the clever journalist to figure out its meaning. He couldn't be too precise, since the information he wished to convey to NewzTracker's star reporter was always sensitive and usually referenced events that had yet to transpire.

He typed his message and then rose from his seat and left CIA headquarters. He was eager to see just how savvy Jay Patterson was in the days ahead. Would he understand the cryptic correspondence? He thought it likely.

Chapter Six
Hypocrisy

President Hastings deplaned from Air Force One and was taken by motorcade to a spot where the Pérez Art Museum had once stood along I-395. He would be joined by Vice President Cal Quint to commemorate the fifth anniversary since Hurricane Carla had decimated parts of Miami, leaving only the shells of buildings strewn across an area of twenty square miles. Sustained winds of two hundred miles per hour and a forty-foot storm surge had pounded the city for sixteen hours, killing the residents who hadn't evacuated, mostly the poor and elderly. Miami Beach, from Bal Harbor to Key Biscayne, had disappeared first, eroded by relentless gray waves.

In the two years after the storm, parts of the city were bulldozed, and only a small monument had been erected at the location where the president and vice president were now headed. Carla had been the most powerful hurricane ever recorded, and the decision had been made by the governor of Florida, in conjunction with state and federal legislators, not to erect any kind of grand structure to remember the disaster, opting instead to let the bleak, flat landscape be a reminder of what had happened. City and state treasuries, flood insurance, and charitable donations from around the country could not contribute a tenth of what would have been needed to rebuild the city. President DePeche had pleaded with congress for federal assistance money for Miami, but the budget deficit of the United States was too massive. Other coastal cities—mostly small towns—had also been flattened by killer hurricanes over the past few years, and it was becoming less and less feasible to spend billions of dollars to rebuild the communities. The economy of the country was in shambles, and many urban areas were being decimated by storms of crime and poverty that were as devastating as any hurricane.

The president, vice president, and their wives took the stage, shook hands, and hugged. Hastings then moved to the podium and adjusted the microphone in order to address the ten thousand people in attendance.

"My fellow Americans," he began, "we stand at the site of a national tragedy rivaled only by the Civil War, Nine-Eleven, and Hurricane Katrina. Hurricane Carla proved that we are at the mercy of the elements, of God and his wrath when such a cataclysm visits humanity. What are we to make of it? The fine men and women of Miami, displaced or deceased, will forever be remembered on this sacred ground, which by its bleak aspect reminds us of what was lost: a thriving metropolis filled with commerce, children, laughter, cultural diversity, and every element that makes any city in America great."

A voice from the middle of the crowd cried out, "Still think Miami was a nest of gays, you hypocrite?"

Dozens of police officers and Secret Service agents converged on the middle-aged speaker and dragged him away, the crowd parting magically like the Red Sea to allow his removal. Hastings continued without losing his rhetorical cadence, as if he hadn't heard the outcry against his previous statements about the sinfulness of Miami.

"Let us not lose hope, friends, that this great city might yet be rebuilt under my leadership. I stand here today and pledge that before I leave office, new construction will begin on this site and expand outward until the skyline of Miami once again shines like a beacon for the world."

The president spoke for another ten minutes, after which another voice from the crowd interrupted the speech. It was a woman this time who yelled at the top of her lungs. "It's climate change, Mr. President! Why won't you accept global warming as a fact?"

The woman, a young mother holding a baby, was quickly led away from her position. The president didn't take the bait.

Jay watched as the young woman was led away and then he spoke into his recorder as not to forget the event when he wrote up his review of Hastings' speech. He also wanted to be sure and add the latest scientific findings on climate change so hopefully the public will know just how egregious the president's action was.

"I'm just surprised that Hastings didn't order the Secret Service to separate the child from its mother, treating her more as an illegal immigrant. The woman was right, of course. Hastings ignored a massive critical issue of which everyone everywhere was bracing for the worst scenario of climate change the world has ever seen. One would have to live under a rock not to see that summers are hotter, winters are colder, storms much worse, like the one that hit Miami. The Arctic is warming much faster than even scientists predicted, species are becoming extinct. And if that's not enough to worry the world's inhabitants, scientists have recently discovered that Earth is wobbling on its axis and the theory is that Earth has lost its balance due to all the past seventy years of coal mining, fracking, and oil and gas drilling. In the Middle East alone, Saudi Arabia has extracted so much solid earth that it has caused an imbalance of Earth on its axis. We take, take and take reserves from the Earth and give nothing back. It's no small wonder that has resulted in Climate Change. That's just one manner of damage Earth will incur over the next century. We are reaching the point of no return for Earth and its inhabitants. It might already be too late to do anything about a solution to regaining Earth's balance, and one thing is certain if nothing is done. Earth will self-destruct. But does Hastings care? No, oil and gas drilling and coal mining provides jobs, no matter what it does to the Earth. Hastings only cares about his campaign promise to strengthen the economy—and, of course, his image. The emperor has no clothes on. In Hastings mind . . . . God wouldn't dare to cross him.

/

Hastings raised both hands as though giving a benediction. "Let us now bow our heads in prayer for those who lost their lives to Hurricane Carla and for the millions of citizens who were displaced on that fateful night when death struck from the sea."

The audience was quiet for a minute before Hastings proclaimed, "May God bless America."

The president and vice president were driven back to Palm Beach Air Force Base.

Upon arrival, the President requested that he and Vice President Quint be given a moment together in Hanger 3. The two men stood side by side in the middle of the large hanger, their Secret Service details forming a perimeter ten yards away.

Calvin Barkley Quint was a tall man who was a former rodeo rider, a colorful figure who had obtained a Bachelor's Degree in Political Science and decided that he could make more money bull riding and breaking broncos than teaching dull political theory to college students, assuming he went to grad school and earned a Ph.D., which he had no intention of doing. After five years of bruised ribs, he chose to use his knowledge to run for a congressional seat in his home state of Nevada. He won and served two terms in Congress and two terms in the Senate. He was forty-eight, wore cowboy boots and designer suits, and parted his dark brown hair on the side. His warm brown eyes and winning smile had caused voters to affectionately call him Cal. He was quiet, but he was a master at wrangling senators when the majority whip was unable to find the votes needed for a given piece of legislation. "Cal the Vote Wrangler" was his nickname on the Hill.

"Cal," Hastings said," we need to start thinking about re-election. Hell, it's only two years away and I don't see our base holding."

Quint furrowed his brows and folded his arms, deep in thought. After several seconds had elapsed, he spoke with deliberation in his low authoritative voice.

"Mr. President," he said, "we can't count on the evangelical base any longer. Some of them will always be there for us, but not everyone."

"Why is that?"

"Religion, in general, is dying out. Catholic churches are almost empty, partly due to all the sex abuse cases filed against priests. Other denominations aren't far behind. As for evangelicals, many are distancing themselves from us. Your new immigration policy is a good example. Thou shalt not kill has already hit VOXPOP."

VOXPOP, standing for *Popular Voice of the People*, had replaced Twitter, with the popular web service allowing anyone to upload a thirty-second audio file to the popular social media website. Hastings used it daily to preach to his faithful.

"You don't approve?" Hastings asked with an edged warning in his voice.

Quint held up his hands, palms outward, as if to dispel the notion of disagreement with his body language. "To the contrary, Mr. President. A bold statement to be sure. Hell of a move, in fact. Took *cojones*. I'm just pointing out a political reality. Most evangelicals are blue-collar workers losing jobs to the tech industry, and pardon my candor, Mr. President, but your jobs program is failing. Retraining for jobs in the steel industry is now being viewed as a political gimmick and is at an all-time low, and work on extending routes for high-speed bullet trains and infrastructure has slowed. Partners in the private sector have been losing money."

Hastings' face was flush with momentary anger. "DePeche started building the goddamned high-speed rail system but couldn't finish it, and now it's a failed project plaguing *my* administration!"

"True," Quint continued, "and Congress has halted further expansion since the funding wasn't in the budget you presented. Coal is all but dead, farmers are hurting because of the drought last year—a lot of evangelicals live in the Corn Belt, sir—and we're importing more grain than we're exporting."

After the disruption during his speech, Hastings was in no mood to hear about the drought or climate issues which were becoming worse by the day.

"So what the hell do we do, Cal? I know the Bible by heart. I can quote from Deuteronomy, Leviticus, Revelation, the New Testament—even fire and brimstone if I'm of a mind to—and you're telling me that I can't use this to my advantage any longer? Not that I believe in God, which is a fact you're well aware of, but I can't very well try to appeal to intellectuals or scientists, since 73 percent of them are atheists, agnostics, and Democrats. What's the bottom line? What are you telling me?"

Cal Quint smiled and looked his boss straight in the eyes. "You start your own church, sir."

"What are you talking about?"

"Sixty-two percent of the population identifies itself as spiritual but not religious. They believe in a higher power or . . . *something* that they have little interest in defining, not that some don't try. Wiccans, earth-worshippers, and priestesses of Gaia, for example. And then there's the Law of Attraction and a lot of metaphysical talk by New Age motivational speakers who put the individual in the driver's seat. Eastern religions remain popular in the United States, but it's mostly repackaged for western consumption. People can meditate on their chakras or navels or winning the lottery."

"Okay, okay, but how can I sell this to voters? What's the hook?"

"If there's a commonality, it's that people think we're all God, connected through Universal Consciousness because the only consciousness existing is Universal, and your different religions interpret that as God, or what "God" is named in all the different countries of the world . . . or so says my daughter. Very Eastern in flavor."

Hastings nodded, a smile claiming his features. "Doesn't make a hell of a lot of sense to me, but I like it. I like it a *lot*, and I know what to do with it." He turned and motioned to the young woman who was with his Office of Presidential Advance and carried his itinerary in a briefcase at all times. "Get me a speech at a non-denominational church," he ordered. "The sooner the better."

The young woman made a note and backed away quickly.

"Starting a new church is a tall order, Mr. President, but I think you can pull it off."

Hastings laughed. "I'm as charismatic as P.T. Barnum. I can sell ice to Eskimos."

"That you can, sir. That you can."

Quint smiled as the president, surrounded by his detail, walked towards his waiting limousine. It had been a stroke of luck that he'd been a bull rider before entering the political arena. Being a part of the Hastings administration was harder than holding on to a Texas longhorn steer for eight seconds.

Chapter Seven
The Bigger Picture

JAY PATTERSON HAD JET LAG AS HE FLOPPED INTO THE LEATHER CHAIR IN THE LIVING ROOM OF HIS APARTMENT ON SEVENTH STREET IN THE PENN QUARTER OF WASHINGTON, D.C. He'd gotten a new message from his source, whose email designation was LoneWolf777@qmail.com. The leaks and tips had been coming for a month, although he hadn't always known what to make of the terse correspondence from his unknown informant. Two days before the president's trip to Brister, Arizona, Patterson had received a single message: *Hadrian*. He hadn't known what to do with it. Hadrian had been a Roman emperor, and yes, Hastings was a fanatic when it came to Roman history. Hadrian had demonstrated the traits of mercy and humanism, attempting when possible to make peace with opposing factions within the empire. He had built what had become known as Hadrian's Wall to protect the northern boundary of the empire in Britannia to keep out a Celtic sect called the Picts. The message from his source had been brief, but in retrospect he should have been able to interpret its meaning. President Hastings had gone to Arizona to speak of a wall that would keep out illegal immigrants from his empire, and he had spoken of his severe policy of cold-blooded murder in terms of mercy and kindness to the Catholic populations south of the border. It was as if his source had known what the president would say ahead of time, at least in broad strokes.

Patterson suspected that the leaker could be almost anyone in government, from a civil servant in the State Department to a low-level White House staffer who was nevertheless privy to the thoughts and decisions coming from Hastings' inner circle. It could also be someone higher in the pecking order in the West Wing, since rumors of chaos within the White House had plagued the administration from day one.

The new message was one word: *Ikulu*. Patterson had quickly done a search and learned that it was a Swahili word meaning *palace*. A further search revealed that there were 1,037 palaces in countries spanning the length and width of the African continent. Swahili was a Bantu language originating in East Africa, but its various dialects were spoken in almost all countries on the continent.

Palace? Ikulu? Kings, rulers, sheiks, and dictators built palaces throughout the world, and Africa was no exception. Patterson scrolled through the 1.037 palaces in Africa, but nothing unusual presented itself. Perhaps, he reasoned, he was just dead tired. It had been a long day, going from Brister to Miami and back to D.C. His brain was fried, and he needed sleep.

He decided to enlist Sela's help, since the computers at SETI were faster than most and were able to employ wide bandwidths to search thousands of stars at a time, hoping for a few intelligent blips from an advanced civilization. SETI was in Mountain View, California, and he would normally have stopped to see Sela earlier that day, since he'd been in the vicinity, and he missed her. Patterson traveled almost anywhere at the drop of a hat and was therefore able to make their long-distance relationship work. Well, at least most weeks. Sela grumbled occasionally, but he felt she loved him. She was intelligent, beautiful, sexy, insightful, and she admired Jay's commitment to the truth, not to mention his predilection for tradition and all things old and venerable, including love and fidelity. Jay considered it was a start—a good basis for a future together. But something had to change. A long-distance love affair isn't the answer. How could he talk her into moving to D.C. and giving up her career? He knew he couldn't ask her to do that. In this day and time when a couple both have careers, long-distance love relationships pose a real conflict. Jay longed to talk to Sela, tell her his thoughts, his fears, his dreams . . . but he was also afraid it could end things altogether.

Before Jay could meditate on another thought, he fell asleep, his dreams filled with disturbing images of Manuel Gonzalez's body tumbling forward in the Arizona desert, a barren landscape once known as Miami, and a thousand pictures of palaces in Africa. For the past month he'd also dreamt of Lone Wolf sitting at a computer terminal sending him messages. In a recurrent dream, the informant—sometimes a man and sometimes a woman—would turn to him and say, *"I'm giving you everything you need. Use it wisely."*

Everything you need.

The implication of the three words was profound. There was a bigger picture beyond the reporting he was doing, something larger than individual news stories, a picture of which only Lone Wolf was aware. Jay Patterson didn't know what the big picture was, but he wasn't alone. No one in America did.

Chapter Eight
Idealized Prejudice

MAXWELL HART HAD BEEN APPOINTED SECRETARY OF STATE BY PRESIDENT HASTINGS. His confirmation had been somewhat rocky, since although he was a highly decorated four-star general, he was known for his extremist views. He was adamantly opposed to gays and lesbians serving in the military, but then he was opposed to the gay and lesbian lifestyle in general, and believed they were condemned to eternal damnation. When asked to explain his belief, Hart simply replied, "Because the Bible tells me so. Biological appendages and organs exist to be used in the manner nature intended them to be." He had admitted publicly that he disciplined his children with corporal punishment, claiming there was a fine line between valid discipline and physical abuse. He believed in civil rights but was adamantly opposed to what he called a mixing of the races, referring to interracial marriage. While he believed in evolution, given the indisputable fossil record that told a four-billion-year-old story, he rejected the belief that *Homo sapiens* had descended from apes or arboreal creatures with prehensile tails. He invoked a God of intelligent design who had made man in his own image, "not that of a gorilla."

Hart had been a hard ass, a soldier's soldier who had commanded a brigade in the Iraq War and had been investigated for an alleged massacre of over six hundred civilians in Anbar Province. Hart had responded during a formal inquiry that he'd acted on reliable intelligence and that collateral damage was a grim reality of war. He claimed to have destroyed an important command structure of Al Qaeda. The inquiry dragged on for months since, years earlier, he'd allegedly stated that "Genocide isn't always a bad thing." He denied making such a statement and he was exonerated of any wrongdoing in Iraq.

Hart made no attempt to hide that his personal hero was a fictional character, Colonel Kurtz, the savage and insane army officer in *Apocalypse Now,* who was guilty of committing atrocities against the Viet Cong by raising up an army of Montag nard people in the hill country of Vietnam, near the Cambodian border.

"Kurtz had the right idea," Hart once told a reporter, "but his conscience and the chain of command got in the way. In war, you kill the enemy and make them fear you as if you were God Almighty on Judgment Day. Kurtz ultimately mistook his own purity of action for madness, and that was his downfall. He wasn't mad in the least. He was doing his job. Purity and single-mindedness is what a commander needs in the field—a laser-like focus to the point of acquiring tunnel vision. We could have won the Vietnam War in four years were it not for hippies, limited rules of engagement, and politicians who ultimately succumbed to public criticism."

Many critics over the years had doubted Hart's sanity, but he finished his service to America and was held in high esteem by most, though not all, of his peers. He publicly advocated dismantling several arms of the federal government in order to return the country to discipline, spiritual purity, and godliness. The federal government, he believed, was an overgrown, unwieldy bureaucracy that had become corrupted by what he called "a thousand social agendas, unnecessary government offices, and civil servants."

In high school, Hart had attended the Christian Academy of Virginia with none other than Herbert Chase Hastings, and the two had kept in contact over the years. Hart privately acknowledged that Hastings was an educated and intelligent man, but in the general's estimation, Hastings couldn't assimilate and digest facts so that they became useful political tools. He thought in black and white terms, but that was okay. There was a certain purity in Hastings' ignorance—a

Kurtz-like mindset—and that was something Hart could work with. Hastings was a fool, but he was a fool that Hart could suffer lightly in the name of the greater good of the country. When offered a cabinet position, he hadn't hesitated for a moment. For that matter, Hart never hesitated about anything.

Chapter Nine

The Apples Don't Fall Far from the Tree

PATTERSON AWOKE AT FOUR-THIRTY THE NEXT MORNING AFTER SLEEPING NINE HOURS. Feeling refreshed, he got up, poured a cup of strong coffee, and opened his phone to read any stories that had been posted overnight by the mainstream media. His buddy and fellow journalist Beau Bricker had filed an intriguing story with ANPC, the Associated National Press Corps, which was a conglomerate of dozens of news organizations that pooled their resources and reporters much as the Associated Press had done for many decades. Bricker had taken aim at two of Hastings' children, noting that they'd visited the White House clandestinely.

Bradley Tiberius Hastings was the acting CEO of PB Enterprises, a thirty-five-year-old *wunderkind,* known for his business acumen and good looks. Savannah Julia Hastings was a thirty-one-year-old lawyer who was vice president of PB and married to lobbyist Sedge O'Connell. Hastings' third child and youngest son was twenty-six-year-old Todd Augustus Hastings, head of PB Enterprises' investments and its portfolio that extended far beyond tobacco. PB had recently begun to manufacture a private luxury jet to compete with Gulf Stream and Lear Jet. Todd Hastings was also in charge of PB's mergers and acquisitions. Because the tobacco giant's cigarette sales had plummeted severely in a relatively short time, Brad had decided that the company should broaden its portfolio after his father had divested his interests in PB, although how thorough the divestiture had been was an ongoing topic of debate in the press. Nevertheless, PB Enterprises was gaining a reputation as a corporate raider.

According to Bricker's report, which Patterson read while caffeine started the synapses of his brain firing as the sun climbed slowly above the horizon of the nation's capital, the two Hastings children had been spotted entering the Treasury Building after hours on several nights, only to exit the White House the following morning. Bricker noted that a tunnel had been constructed in 1941 to allow the president to leave the White House via the East Wing in case of an emergency attack on the nation's capital. Since then, Bricker noted, a maze of subterranean passageways had been constructed, leading in many directions to allow the president safe egress from the White House without detection. As late as the George W. Bush Administration, a white building with no name mysteriously appeared next to the West Wing over a period of months and was rumored to have a new network of tunnels beneath it, allowing West Wing personnel to escape in case of terrorist attack.

Bricker said that Bradley and Savannah, under heavy Secret Service escort, had also been spotted entering a tunnel at the edge of the Ellipse in President's Park opposite the south lawn of the White House. The tunnel, the report claimed, was normally covered by grass and landscaping, although the area where the president's children were spotted disappearing from view was now surrounded by construction barriers. Bricker alleged that the children had secretly entered the White House on more than a dozen occasions, although the White House Press Office denied any such clandestine meetings between the president and his children. Photographs accompanying the article showed Brad and Savannah entering the Treasury Building, as well as walking beside two uniformed Treasury Security officers through the Ellipse. Since both children were supposedly busy running PB Enterprises in Charlotte, Bricker reasoned, what had they been doing in Washington every few days for the past several months? And if they wished to visit their father, why not use the main entrance?

Patterson knew what Bricker was getting at. Most people assumed that President Hastings was still running PB Enterprises, which could create a conflict of interest depending on his negotiations with foreign governments. Hastings denied that he knew anything at all about PB and said that his children were entirely capable of running the tobacco company on their own. "After all," he'd said, on numerous occasions, "they learned from the best. Me."

/

Later that day, Press Secretary Wolcott asked why Bricker had been "skulking around Washington late at night, strolling down deserted sidewalks or walking through a park at eleven o'clock at night. Was he bored . . . or perhaps lonely, looking for companionship from a stranger? Was Beau a dandy with too much time on his hands?"

When asked what he meant by the term *dandy*, Wolcott shrugged and shot one of his disarming smiles at the press corps.

"Just an expression," he said. "A turn of phrase."

/

Patterson needed to file his own report, one on the Miami Memorial speech from the day before. Whenever home, he preferred to type a copy on his laptop even though it had a voice-activated word processing program. It was another indication that he was fond of older ways of doing things despite his youth. He liked the feel of his fingers on the keypad, each finger pressing a letter and making words, sentences, and paragraphs that he could see on the screen before him. It was like reading a book made from paper and ink. Such books, though sold in limited quantities, had heft when held in the palm of one's hands. A person could smell the pulp from which the paper had been made, could smell the ink and know the craftsmanship that went into producing a hard copy volume.

When Patterson was finished, he revised the piece twice and then uploaded it to the article template at NewzTracker. The opening paragraphs cut to the heart of his story in grand journalistic tradition in order to grab the reader.

NewzTracker.com
August 2026

PRESIDENT EMBRACES MIAMI DESPITE PREVIOUS ATTACKS ON FORMER CITY AS BEING NEST OF GAYS
By Jay Patterson

To have listened to the remarks of President Herbert Hastings as he addressed a crowd assembled to commemorate the destruction of Miami by Hurricane Carla was to have listened to fifteen minutes of prepared text that could have commemorated a natural disaster anywhere in the country.

Hastings remarks were generic: Losing Miami was a tragedy, a great loss, a terrible blow to America. Winds had howled and waves had come ashore with fury. This was the grief expressed by President Hastings, the depth of his emotions, or lack thereof, for a million people who no longer had homes.

Noticeably absent from the president's remarks was any reference to the increased frequency of ferocious Atlantic hurricanes during the last decade, or the belief by 99% of the world's scientific community that such storms are the result of global warming. This is in keeping with Hastings' ongoing silence as to the possible causes of the great drought in the Midwest, which some climatologists fear might create a new Dust Bowl. He also continues to ignore the new scientific findings that the

> origin of the climate change is that Earth has become unbalanced and is wobbling on its axis due to 70-plus years of coal mining, fracking, and oil and gas drilling. The man is so short-sighted in his private concerns that he shows no responsibility for a nation of people.

Patterson then scanned other news sites to see what was being posted. Hate crimes were still on the rise, and protesters demonstrating against the Hastings administration had taken to the streets again. The organization Grass Roots had taken hold organically across America starting the day of Hastings' inauguration, and twenty-five million people had filled the streets of more than three hundred American cities since then. The administration estimated the number of activists to be no more than one hundred thousand.

The rise in crime continued to escalate, and although Hastings advocated an end to violence, he recorded a VOXPOP message urging police to "knock some heads together since protest is un-American."

One article noted that Jimmy Finch, leader of the American Paramilitary Union—an association of civilian state militias—had given several speeches across the country to show that the Real Right and his weekend warriors were still firmly behind Hastings. Candidate Hastings had campaigned with Finch and various militias across the country, engaging in what the APU called "civilian war games." One of Hastings' campaign slogans had been "There's nothing more American than automatic weapons!" And statistics now showed over 297 mass shootings in only the first two-hundred days of the new year, using automatic weapons the murderers bought by simply walking into a gun shop and purchasing. Over two-hundred mass shootings! That's 1.2 shootings per day, 1,219 people injured and 335 murdered. There had been two-hundred school shootings since 2000 and as of the latest school shooting, there is no solution in view. Seems Hastings and the head of the NRA are longtime buddies.

An hour later, Patterson checked the web to gauge the reaction to his article, which had been swift indeed. Press Secretary Wolcott had issued a statement saying that President Hastings had expressed genuine grief over the tragedy caused by Hurricane Carla. As for Hastings' prior remarks about gay and lesbian populations, Wolcott said that the president was merely expressing his strong Christian belief that marriage was between a man and a woman. No denigration of the City of Miami had been intended at any point in time.

President Hastings had gone straight to VOXPOP to condemn the reporter. "Sad, pathetic Patterson is at it again," the president had recorded. "NewzTracker is a failing organization."

Patterson wore the criticism as a badge of honor. NewzTracker was right behind the *New York Times* and the *Washington Post* in online reporting.

Chapter Ten
Chip Implant

JAY PATTERSON GRABBED A LATE BREAKFAST WITH HIS EDITOR, JOHN TAYLOR, AT A GEORGETOWN CAFÉ BEFORE RETURNING TO THE OFFICES OF NEWZTRACKER. They'd discussed the possibility that the White House might revoke Patterson's press credentials since seven correspondents had been ejected from the White House press pool for writing articles that had been construed as critical of the president. Their seats in the White House briefing room had been filled with reporters from small but highly conservative news outlets.

"Why hasn't Hastings already yanked me from covering him?" Patterson asked when seated in his editor's corner office with glass walls.

Taylor, a portly man in his late forties, whose brown beard flowed onto his chest, ran his fingers through thinning hair. "Because, Jay, I think Hastings regards you as somewhat of a challenge. He likes to spar with you, toy with you, like a cat playing with a mouse. You bring attention to focus on him, and he uses that chance every time he can ."

Patterson chuckled. "Before the cat devours the mouse. Isn't that what usually happens?"

Taylor shrugged. "Usually, but you need to ride this train until they ask you to get off. Having second thoughts?"

Patterson shook his head. "No. I may not have a nervous system left by the time Hastings leaves office, but I'm in it for the long haul unless Wolcott sticks a fork in me and tells me I'm done."

Taylor was about to speak when Patterson's phone indicated an incoming text message. It was from Lone

Wolf, the second in two days. As usual, the correspondence was short, the new message reading *Rampling, M.D.* Patterson looked up at his editor. "Does the name Rampling ring a bell?"

"Rampling? Can't say that it does."

Patterson accessed the web and found that there were fifty-nine physicians in the continental United States with the last name *Rampling*. Two were in the Charlotte area. One was an orthopedist, the other a pediatrician.

Taylor stroked his beard, a habit his colleagues claimed made their boss look like an overgrown hobbit. "If memory serves, Hastings dislocated his shoulder a few years back while rock climbing Pilot Mountain in North Carolina."

Patterson nodded. Dr. William Rampling, an orthopedist from Charlotte, seemed like the logical person Lone Wolf was referring to, but what did a dislocated shoulder eight years earlier have to do with the current political climate in Washington? Patterson continued to browse doctors named Rampling, and paused on the entry for Dr. Elizabeth Rampling in Telluride, Colorado.

"A shrink," Patterson raised his eyebrows. "And Hastings has a summer retreat in the mountains near Telluride."

Taylor leaned forward, elbows on the surface of his natural-finish wooden desk. "People have been saying that Hastings is mental ever since his campaign, if not before. I think you should catch a plane for Colorado. In fact, as your editor, I insist."

"Agreed."

Patterson booked a United Airlines flight from Washington to Denver, leaving in less than an hour. The chip in his arm had all the information any airline needed to schedule a passenger—name, address, age, occupation, possible criminal record, and credit card number—and interfaced with an app on his phone. Patterson sprang from his chair, flashed a smile at his boss, and took a subway to Reagan National. He would be in Denver by one o'clock, and then puddle-jump to Montrose Regional Airport near Telluride.

Telluride was a quaint municipality, a former silver mining town nestled in a box canyon in San Miguel County. The town had grown little over the years and had a population of 3,856. Telluride had become even more isolated fifteen years earlier when Herbert Hastings had bought a mountain retreat and dozens of acres surrounding his Colorado home to ensure privacy. These days, the Secret Service maintained a constant presence around the perimeter of Hastings' property, and Telluride still looked as if it were a clean and colorful town from a 1950s postcard.

It was two-thirty when Patterson found the office of Dr. Elizabeth Rampling on West Columbus Avenue. He walked into what appeared to be a small empty waiting room. The furniture consisted of a couch, two chairs, and a table with magazines on fishing and hiking.

"Hello?" Patterson called. "Dr. Rampling?"

There was no answer.

Patterson advanced across the small space and knocked on a door with a gold plate bearing the words *Elizabeth Rampling, M.D.* A diploma on the wall testified to the fact that Rampling had graduated from Boston College and had earned a medical degree from the Duke University School of Medicine. He knocked on the door, which opened three inches from the force applied by the light tap of his knuckles.

"Dr. Rampling?"

He pushed the door open all the way to find a woman lying on the floor, face down, in front of a mahogany desk on the opposite side of the office. Kneeling, he felt for a pulse but couldn't find one. From pictures he'd seen on the web, he knew this was Elizabeth Rampling. He stood and surveyed the room. Rampling's lifeless right arm seemed to be pointing to the wall on Patterson's right, which was a glass sliding door, behind which were several dozen rows of medical charts. It was odd that a doctor would still keep paper files on patients, but some physicians liked to have a hard-copy backup of their computer records since hackers had stayed ahead of the curve of cyber-security advances and regularly breached allegedly secure servers and computers with ease.

Patterson saw three manila folders on the floor and, kneeling again, picked up the files and read the names printed on the tab of each: Hawthorn, Higgins, and Howard. Had someone been looking for a file on Herbert Chase Hastings? Had they found one? Patterson quickly seated himself behind Rampling's desk and saw that since the computer was on, no password would be needed to access the machine—with the screen displaying a list of patients. Whoever had entered the office and taken the files had been in a hurry. This wasn't surprising, since he had already concluded that Rampling had probably been murdered. He manually scrolled through a list of patients with last names beginning with the letter "H" and saw that file #1892 had no name, but rather the word Deleted next to the number.

Rising from the desk, Patterson saw a few drops of blood below Rampling's left arm, which was by her side.

"Good God!"

The chip implant beneath the skin on Rampling's forearm had been removed.

Patterson stood and took a deep breath. He needed to leave since his presence in the office could possibly implicate him in the death, or at the very least, cause him to be detained for a day or two in Telluride. He wiped the manila folders and the desktop's trackpad clean of his prints and left the office, closing the door behind him after wiping his fingerprints from the doorknob as well. He then found an Internet café, and logging on with an alias he used when corresponding with sources—P.W. James—typed a brief message to the police saying that Dr. Elizabeth Rampling was "in trouble."

He got into his rental car and drove out of town. He called his editor, who believed that Hastings was toying with him. Perhaps Hastings was getting fed up with his reporting, after all, and wanted him out of the way. Was he being followed? Was someone trying to frame him for murder? Wiping perspiration from his forehead, he tried to think ahead. He wasn't sure where to go.

/

It was four-thirty when Patterson arrived at Denver International Airport. He hurried into the terminal and purchased a plane ticket to D.C., his reservation registering on his chip implant. He then took a monorail to the bullet train terminal one mile away. Denver was one of the hubs for the high-speed trains, and several destinations were available: Seattle, Los Angeles, San Francisco, Chicago, New York, and Washington, D.C. San Francisco it would be. The city by the bay was near Mountain View, California, the home of SETI. He sent Sela a text telling her to meet him in two hours. After his plane had departed for Washington—if anyone was following him, they might have boarded the flight—Patterson bought a ticket for San Francisco and boarded the train minutes before it left the modern steel-and-glass terminal. He may still have been followed, but he'd done what he could to minimize that possibility. He settled back in the luxurious car and tried to make sense of what had happened in Telluride.

Had Lone Wolf known that Rampling had been murdered? That seemed unlikely, as her body had been warm to the touch and rigor would have set in if she'd been killed before he had received his informant's message that morning.

There was no sign of a gunshot or knife wound, no blunt force trauma to the skull, and no pale blue skin that might have indicated poisoning. He didn't know the cause of death, only that someone had been in a hurry to steal a patient's file and cut the chip implant from the physician's arm.

It seemed more likely that Lone Wolf wanted Patterson to know that President Hastings had consulted a psychiatrist at some point in time. But why? The president's actions were erratic and displayed what many pundits deemed mental instability, but Hastings might have consulted Rampling for any number of reasons. As a reporter, Patterson had quickly learned that it was dangerous to jump to conclusions without hard evidence to back up any theory, but his mind was racing as fast as the bullet train was crossing the desert landscape, which was already being painted the dark blue of twilight.

Patterson decided to use the time to look up Rampling's impressive bio on the web. He saw that she'd been practicing psychiatry for twenty-one years, first in Boulder, and then in Telluride. She practiced general psychiatry, which included marriage and family therapy.

A sudden wave of panic shot up his spinal column, and he shut down his phone. If he'd been sent to Telluride by someone wishing to harm him or sully his reputation, hacking his whereabouts by using the GPS in his chip implant would be child's play. Was someone even now waiting to greet him at his apartment in D.C., thinking he'd been on the Denver flight to Washington? He hated chip implants and the invasion of privacy they represented. He ordered a gin and tonic from the service attendant and looked out the window. He needed to calm down and think.

/

Patterson glanced at his forearm and frowned at what he considered to be the Faustian bargain that was the Web. Early in the digital age, search engines, email programs, and social media sites had routinely gathered information on users in order to target them for advertising by keeping track of products they purchased, their travel destinations, and their likes and dislikes. Nobody had read the Terms of Service, and that held true when the web became active. At first, people volunteered in droves to receive the chip implant, since the Web operated faster if synced with the chip, plus business transactions were approved more quickly, such as Patterson's ticket purchases in Denver. Chips were scanned on-site, or the user's chip could be scanned into a phone instead of a credit card number in order to complete almost any transaction.

By 2020, Congress passed a law requiring all U.S. citizens to receive the chip implant in order to better fight terrorism, despite protests from the ACLU. The argument by the government was that it would be extremely difficult for a terrorist to hide his or her movements given the vast amount of data encoded on every chip. Despite the Non-Intrusive Internet Laws of 2020, most people assumed they could be surveilled but didn't really care. Relinquishing privacy for convenience was an acceptable trade-off, and it had become almost impossible to live in the world without web technology. Despite the non-intrusion laws, Patterson knew that the FBI, CIA, and other intelligence agencies had always played fast and loose with the privacy of citizens, and he wondered if anyone was currently tracking him. It had been established that the government couldn't keep an eye on every individual simultaneously, but it had the capability, in theory, to watch anyone it wanted. Most people didn't dwell on the matter lest they become paranoid.

Riding at two hundred miles per hour on the train's mag-lev rail, Patterson felt quite paranoid indeed.

Chapter Eleven

The Far Right & Then Some

THE PROTESTS BEGAN THE DAY AFTER PRESIDENT HASTINGS FIRED BLANKS AT MANUEL GONZALEZ IN THE HOT, ARID THEATER OF THE ARIZONA DESERT. Gun rights advocates had taken to the streets in Chicago, Philadelphia, Baltimore, Tampa, and a dozen other cities, claiming that if the President of the United States could use a rifle to shoot an illegal, even if the event was staged, then they, too, should have better access to firearms to protect their homes and families. The DePeche administration had succeeded in reinstating a ban on automatic assault weapons, as well as enacting legislation requiring background checks at stores and gun shows. Second Amendment proponents considered the legislation to be an affront to their constitutional rights, and with over 297 mass shootings in the first two-hundred days of this year alone, obviously the ban wasn't effective for those domestic mass-shooters who wanted to go down in history for whatever reason.

Counter-protesters took to the streets, urging that even tighter gun control laws be enacted, given the cavalier way President Hastings had pretended to kill Gonzalez. It set a bad example, they said, and would encourage more people to get guns, legally or illegally, and commit murder in their neighborhoods with little provocation.

The protests quickly escalated into riots, and in the space of sixteen hours, eight people advocating gun control were killed, and over two hundred were brought to emergency rooms for major and minor injuries. Major TV networks pre-empted regular programming to cover protests of a kind that had not been seen since the 1960s.

President Hastings made a brief statement the following day, taking no questions from the White House briefing room.

"We watch with keen interest and admiration in our hearts," he said, "those who have chosen to publicly defend the right to bear arms, and we wholeheartedly condemn the reactionary protests of those who hypocritically oppose the Second Amendment while engaging in acts of violence and savagery. If people like this had been alive during the Revolutionary War, the colonies would still be a part of Great Britain."

To the right of Hastings was his chief of staff and pre-eminent speech writer, the latter looking frightened and on the verge of tears. The chief of staff held up his index finger and drew it horizontally across his throat above the knot in his tie in order to motion that the president should cut his remarks short and leave the podium. The chief of staff wondered if someone had incorrectly briefed him, but then again, he knew this was typical of Hastings to go off-script and make the most outrageous remarks, anything to put the spotlight on himself. The office of president is a stage for his personal performance. That's all.

The president abruptly left the podium and walked from the room, followed by his chief of staff.

"Mr. President, you reversed the facts," the chief of staff said, hardly able to keep up with the brisk pace of the president. "The initial marches were staged by Jimmy Finch and the American Paramilitary Union. Those who were killed and injured were counter-protesters, sir."

Hastings stopped, turned, and stared at his COS. "You're fired!" Walking in the direction of the residence, he then turned to Bailey "Cookie" McKnight, his chief speech writer, and said, "Somebody get this crybaby out of here. Women who cry are weak disgusting creatures."

By that afternoon, Hastings had elevated Senior Advisor Lucille Raines, a thirty-eight year-old woman with shoulder-length black hair, and a former utility industry lobbyist who most of the press corps regarded as ruthless and austere. Before a lid was declared by David Wolcott that afternoon, he read a statement crafted by Raines to the press corps, stating that the president's remarks had been hastily written by Bailey McKnight. The president had not been given the actual facts of the day's events.

At eight o'clock that evening, the president took to VOXPOP to congratulate Jimmy Finch for his deft handling of the protests, which, Hastings claimed, could have cost people their lives under less competent leadership. It was a blessing, he said, that no one had been killed.

Rumors had swirled ever since the presidential campaign that Hastings and Raines were having an affair. They traveled together daily during the run-up to the election, and Diane Hastings was frequently campaigning elsewhere. As John Taylor of NewzTracker had told Patterson, "Diane Hastings can't seem to give the president child number four. Raines, on the other hand, is single, in her early thirties, and still in her child-bearing years. The president likes his women young and fertile."

Taylor wasn't the only one in Washington who'd made this observation.

Chapter Twelve

When the Real Right Needs a Strong Left Clip

SENATOR WALLACE HAD AGREED TO MEET WITH JIMMY FINCH OFF THE RECORD SINCE THE MILITIA LEADER WAS A CITIZEN OF TENNESSEE. Wallace had been a member of the Tennessee Civilian State Militia for years, but resigned his membership when he ran for public office.

"What can I do for you, Jimmy?" Wallace asked from behind the desk in his Senate office.

"I want you to work for the repeal of DePeche's gun legislation. You're a Second Amendment guy like us, so bring something to the floor. We want the right to protect and preserve the proud history of the Confederate Flag, and frankly, we want to quietly fly under the radar of the culture cops as we form a European American society. Why not? African Americans openly sing 'I'm black and I'm proud.' What do they have to be proud about? Now,what about us?"

Wallace shrugged. "Jimmy, I'm sympathetic to the rights of gun owners—always have been—but protests like the one your union staged make it hard for me to do that. It paints gun owners in an unflattering light. Good God, Jimmy! Your men killed eight people."

"Leland, the country has a Republican House and Senate. You and three or four others are all that stand in the way of overturning DePeche's gun legislation."

Wallace stared away from his visitor for a moment before speaking again.

"I'm getting old, Jimmy. Not that I don't have some piss and vinegar left in me, but you're asking that automatic weapons be put on the street again. Who the hell needs that kind of firepower?"

"The Real Right does."

"But your state militias around the country already seem to have found a way to arm themselves with whatever weapons they want, so the gun laws certainly aren't affecting you and your militia, and you need to keep in mind that mass murderers have also had no problem buying automatic weapons, and after this morning, how are you and your militia any different from mass murderers? I'm not going to give you a license to kill any more innocent people."

"The Real Right goes beyond my union, Leland. It extends to average law-abiding Americans across the country."

"And if you got the repeal you're asking for, what then? What difference would it make?"

"It would be a first step."

"A first step to what, for God's sake?"

"The right to fly the Confederate flag. The formation of a White Nationalist Party. Ultimately, we want separate but equal re-established."

"As in Plessy vs. Ferguson?"

"Exactly."

Wallace laughed. "Are you trying to topple the government?"

Finch was not amused. "No. Only to purge it of radical leftist elements. Repeal of gun control legislation is all we're asking for at present."

Wallace was silent as he thought of the radical ideas proposed by Finch. When he spoke at last, he said, "It's too much to take in, Jimmy. You've got to be kidding me."

Finch stood and looked down at the aging Senator. "Leland, I've never been more serious in my life."

Chapter Thirteen

Tracking Device Meets Interference

SELA PICKED UP JAY PATTERSON AT THE TRAIN DEPOT IN SAN FRANCISCO AND DROVE HIM TO HER OFFICE AT SETI HEADQUARTERS IN MOUNTAIN VIEW.

"Do you think I'm being tracked?" Patterson asked as Sela uncorked a bottle of red wine she kept in a locker of her office.

"Never count it out," Sela replied. "As far as I'm concerned, Americans have been tracked for decades, and I regard it as axiomatic that everyone is looked at from time to time. At any given moment, it's a roll of the dice. I think whether people are under surveillance is a function of what they've been saying in emails and on social media. When it comes to journalists, you can take it to the bank that you're looked at once in a while."

"And if one has been critical of the President of the United States?"

"Then you'd better watch your ass, buddy," Sela said while handing Jay a glass of merlot.

"Thanks. I feel better already."

He relayed the events of Telluride, after which Sela wasn't so glib. "Gosh, honey. I didn't realize what has been happening. Now I'm genuinely worried for your safety. I can alter the chip to protect you if you want."

"Chip tampering? That's illegal."

"Yeah, well, you've used some unorthodox means of gathering information in your career as a reporter."

"Guilty as charged."

"We have some great gadgets here at SETI, and we use the same kind of chips as everybody else. I can modify the frequency of a few circuits in your implant so you can't be detected. Your transactions might be slowed a bit, but not much. If somebody is looking for you, sooner or later they'll know you're off the grid."

"I'll take that chance."

Grant passed a thin silver wand across Patterson's forearm, hovering over the implant for a moment. A line of green lights began to blink yellow. When she pushed a button on the tip of the electronic wand, the lights turned solid green again.

"Safe for now," she said. "Your location is now masked."

"Good. I don't want to end up like Rampling. Any thoughts on what *Ikulu* might mean?"

"Let's use Sagan."

"He's been dead since 1996. I'm not following."

"It's a supercomputer that SETI uses. Named after SETI's founder, none other than Carl himself. It's essentially a server farm the size of a football field. Since we search so many stars simultaneously at hundreds of different wavelengths, we need extraordinary computing power. Sagan allows us to survey wide swaths of the sky at once. No one will know we're using Sagan for a simple search."

"Why not?"

"That's another story. First, let's see what shows up for Lone Wolf's second code word, *ikulu*."

The pair took a tram to an adjoining building, the one housing the enormous computer complex known as Sagan.

"This is what I saw in my own search," Patterson said, when they had seated themselves in front of an extra-wide computer screen in a room with dimmed lights. "One thousand thirty-seven buildings in Africa that could be considered to be palatial."

"Let's narrow the search," Sela said. "Sagan, list only palaces in capital cities."

Sixteen results remained.

"Sagan," Sela continued, "list all palaces that have been constructed in the last twenty years."

Six palaces remained—in Kenya, Zambia, Mozambique, the Congo, Rwanda, and Garundi. "Sagan, list palaces constructed in the last ten years."

Pictures of imposing stone structures in Kenya and Garundi remained. They had tall white towers, marble pillars, fountains, and lush gardens surrounding their exteriors.

"List only palaces currently inhabited by a political regime installed in the last five years."

Garundi was now the lone search result.

Sela spoke again. "Display the history of the palace in Garundi."

Patterson and Grant looked at the screen while reading the abbreviated text listed at the beginning of all entries. The construction of Jumba Ogo, translated as the Palace of Ogo, had been completed in 2021. The word *jumba* also meant palace, and the present name of Jumba Ogo had been given the structure when Felix Ogo had been installed as prime minister in 2022.

The pair next read about Garundi and Felix Ogo to see what Lone Wolf might be trying to tell Patterson based on the single word *ikulu*. Garundi was a small African country nestled between Mozambique, Zimbabwe, and Malawi. It was a poor nation formerly ruled by the ruthless dictator Papa Makela, who had portrayed himself as a beneficent prime minister despite murdering his political enemies with army death squads. After ten years of military service, General Felix Ogo of the Supreme Garundi Army staged a coup and bulldozed the home of Papa Makela. Installing himself as the new prime minister of Garundi, he later moved into the sumptuous palace that had already been under construction for Makela.

With a population of forty million people, Garundi was characterized by disease, malnutrition, few educational facilities, and the suppression of women's rights. Ogo's coup had been financed by the sale of blood diamonds to other countries, such uncut diamonds being mined in war zones in order to bribe soldiers to effect regime change. The majority of the population lived in homes made of mud, plywood, or corrugated tin, raising cattle and farming yams since the soil was surprisingly fertile because of its proximity to moist currents blowing in from the Indian Ocean.

Patterson stood and folded his arms. "Nothing here to distinguish Garundi from a dozen other African nations."

Sela kept her eyes on the screen as new text appeared. "Look at this, Jay. Garundi's productivity and

GNP rose by 3 percent last year. That's not typical for an African country that has few natural resources, is mired in poverty and disease, and is under constant oppression."

"It's odd. I'll grant you that. What did you mean that no one would know we used Sagan to do our searches?" Patterson asked.

"This network is protected by numerous firewalls," Grant explained. "We recently discovered four sustained bursts of non-random radio frequencies from Tau Ceti, a star that has five planets in its orbit, two of which are in the habitable zone. The signals are repeating prime numbers, which is definitely not a natural occurrence. Prime numbers are divisible only by the number one and the number itself. On top of that, we were calibrating our dishes at the Allen Telescope Array north of here at the Hat Creek Radio Observatory when we discovered a comet heading to the inner solar system. This was about two years ago. It should reach us in 2036, but it won't be a near-miss as with other earth-crossing objects. Earth has a bullseye painted on it. Either of these discoveries could cause mass hysteria around the world. Aliens? The possibility of extinction of all life on earth? Nations have little time to find a way to deflect Comet JM-2026A."

"That doesn't sound good."

"Not good at all," Sela said. "Meanwhile, let's grab something to eat. We'll get some Chinese takeout and bring it to my apartment."

"Sure."

Patterson thought of the irony of the situation. It was possible that scientists had finally discovered intelligent life in the Milky Way at precisely the time when a rogue comet threatened to destroy most of life on earth as thoroughly as one had eradicated life sixty-five million years earlier, when the dinosaurs had taken a fastball across the plate and been called out by a cosmic umpire. The threat would call for unparalleled cooperation among the nations of the world, with the United States leading the effort. Washington, however, was in turmoil, and President Herbert Chase Hastings was at the center of a political storm that was shaking Washington to its foundation.

Chapter Fourteen
Religion as Politics

PRESIDENT HASTINGS STOOD BEFORE AN AUDIENCE AT THE TEMPLE OF METAPHYSICS IN ANN ARBOR, MICHIGAN, A MEGA-CHURCH DEVOTED TO HEISENBERG'S UNCERTAINTY PRINCIPLE AS MUCH AS IT WAS TO THE CONCEPT OF GOD OR THE DIVINE. Heisenberg's Uncertainty Principle stated that the position of sub-atomic particles was subject to the perception of the observer. New Age metaphysics had brought this quantum cornerstone to the area of spirituality, stating that reality was a function of one's perceptions. The Temple of Metaphysics preached that everyone was a piece of God, and everyone's perception was as valid as anyone else's. The audience of fifteen thousand devotees of higher consciousness was exactly the crowd President Hastings wanted to target to begin building a new religious base for his political party.

The audience wasn't made up of Hastings supporters who made up his Red Republican Legion, nor were they necessarily part of the Real Right, although some members of the mega-church wore red tee shirts and red caps. Many simply wanted a chance to see the President of the United States, while others knew of his fondness for quoting scripture and wondered why he was speaking to a group devoted to New Age spirituality.

Hastings took the stage to warm applause, though not the wild chants he was accustomed to. Hands on the podium as usual, he began his speech. He noticed that Jay Patterson was seated in an area off to the side and reserved for the press.

"Good morning," Hastings began, "and thank you for welcoming me to your beautiful temple of chrome and glass. It's a modern tribute to ancient spiritual beliefs that humanity holds sacred. Christ, the Buddha, Moses, Mohammed, and all great spiritual leaders throughout the ages have emphasized the importance of the inner life and the sacredness of a man or woman's soul. You, my friends, honor that spirit in a most fundamental way."

Some in the audience applauded briefly, unsure of whether such approval was warranted in the confines of a church.

"Sadly," Hastings continued, "the emphasis on a person's spiritual core has been lost in America. We have become a nation that greedily grasps for any shiny bauble, but we do so without attention to the higher consciousness for which our spirits yearn. Indeed, we have lost all ecumenical outreach that should extend from denomination to denomination. My own spirit is made of the same incorruptible essence as yours, and we are all brothers in the heart, regardless of our various belief systems."

People now applauded without reservation since Hastings was addressing the tenets that the temple had been founded on.

"I, for example, have always been Christian, and it was Jesus who said that words betray the heart. A good man brings out the goodness from within his soul, while a bad man summons the evil hidden within his heart. Words, my friends, are outward signs of inner grace, the consciousness that we all share, if you will. We must connect to that grace, to that higher consciousness that is the Universe, for we are all part of what the great poet and philosopher Ralph Waldo Emerson called the Over-Soul. The one is in all, and the all is in one."

The first cheers could now be heard emanating from those wearing red tee shirts, although the crowd as a whole was warming quickly to the metaphysical message of the president.

"It is with humility, therefore, that I announce to you today my allegiance to this higher Truth, this Over-Soul and its transcendental nature that makes each man and woman his or her own temple of worship. We are both the worshipper and that which is worshipped, for we are all God—you, me, and our neighbors. We are the manifestations of a higher power! We are all incarnations of the Divine! The Truth, in its splendid diversity, lies within each man, woman, and child!"

The Temple of Metaphysics was now cheering at decibel levels commensurate with Hastings' political rallies.

"Today, my dear friends, I announce the formation of a new church, which I shall found upon the rock of this speech, and it shall be called the Church of the Heart. You who are assembled here shall be my first disciples and shall go to every corner of this great nation and preach the gospel I give to you today, which is to love yourselves and the God in each and every one of us. Let the words from your heart bring forth goodness and enlightenment as ground is broken for new church buildings even as I speak. Yes, beloved, I have signed an executive order rededicating the country to freedom of worship as outlined in the Constitution, and thanks to benefactors who shall be known to you within the next day or two, these buildings shall grace every state in the union. Thank you, and May the God in all of us bless these United States of America!"

Hastings left the stage to wild applause, red caps tossed in the air while tearful members of the congregation hugged and blessed each other. Many had broken down, weeping and fainting in the aisles. "I love you!" people called to each other. "I love myself and everything around me!"

It would take two hours before the building was cleared and a crew from the temple could clean the pews.

/

Patterson glanced at his colleagues, most of whom were already dictating their reports on the speech. Their articles were flying onto the web at lightning speed and had headlines such as PRESIDENT STARTS

National Religion or President Violates Constitutional Separation of Church and State or President Appoints Himself Savior.

All of the headlines were accurate, Patterson thought as he prepared his own article while a frenzy of weeping worshippers continued to interact on the auditorium floor beneath him. Although Patterson didn't attend church, he'd been schooled for twelve years by nuns who had drummed the Bible and the Catholic Catechism into his mind, and he at least knew the basics of the Judeo-Christian ethic. Hastings had proposed idolatry, the worship of oneself, and in this case, other people.

We are both the worshipper and that which is worshipped, for we are all God—you, me, and our neighbors.

Setting oneself up as God hadn't played out too well for the Israelites, and yet that's exactly what Hastings had done, and he'd used Christ's own words as the lead-in to his pitch for churches to be built by an as yet unnamed benefactor, churches which would apparently preach his own brand of theology that would somehow tap into his Red Republican Legion and the Real Right.

You . . . shall be my first disciples and shall go to every corner of this great nation and preach this gospel I give to you today.

The words had been another paraphrase of the Christian Gospels. Would people really follow Hastings in his mad quest to be a religious leader? Would they conflate Christianity—*I announce the formation of a new church, which I shall found upon the rock of this speech*—with patriotism? A national church would violate the Constitution, and Hastings' words would surely result in court challenges and start a firestorm of debate over the separation of church and state. And yet the president had recently simulated murder in the name of his new immigration policy, with polls showing that 46 percent of the nation approved of his action if it meant protecting the southern border. Patterson thought it likely that many citizens who had spiritual inclinations outside the mainstream of organized religion might buy into the Church of the Heart. Hastings had perverted scripture, and yet people had been moved to tears of joy at the president's declaration, backed by an executive order of religious rededication.

Patterson started to dictate his own article, the headline for which was THE SECOND COMING: PRESIDENT HASTINGS PLAGIARIZES THE BIBLE.

He was on the bus taking the press pool to the airport when he received another cryptic message from Lone Wolf: *TC Autopsy*.

Patterson didn't have to guess the meaning of this latest correspondence. He was to look into the cause of death for Senator Tom Chance. Perhaps Dr. Elizabeth Rampling hadn't been the only person killed in the last two days. Patterson dashed off a text to Sela, requesting that she come to Washington. He would need her sharp mind and technical know-how to find sensitive documents on restricted websites and servers. He wanted to find out what was in Hastings' psychiatric record, which he assumed had been taken from Rampling's office in Telluride, and now he had to investigate the possible murder of Tom Chance.

And if Patterson was honest with himself, he had an ulterior motive for wanting Sela to come to Washington. He wondered if, just maybe, Sela would consider setting up a satellite office for SETI in D.C. That possibility would make his personal agenda for Sela a little more plausible. He knew he had to do something. Sela was everything he admired in a woman he thought he would never find. He wanted Sela close. She represented the only truth in his life of rampant lies he exposes daily in his journalism to the American public. Sela loved revealing truth of the heavens as much as Jay loved revealing truth in political life on The Hill. He swore he would make truth his motto for practicing journalism and he wondered what they could accomplish together as like minds driven to promote truth. Maybe he was being too idealistic, but he had to try and see what Sela thought of his ideas about the two of them forming an alliance of sorts for life. Or was he just lying to himself, unable to face the fact that as scary as feelings are, he loved Sela, and knowing so made Jay feel vulnerable.

Chapter Fifteen

The Hastings Brats' Intrigue

BEAU BRICKER CONTINUED TO FILE REPORTS ON BRAD AND SAVANNAH HASTINGS, WHO WERE BECOMING THE TOPICS OF WHITE HOUSE BRIEFINGS. Bricker had discovered that both Hastings children had visited Iran regularly for the past two years, and since their father had become leader of the free world

they had traveled to Tehran every two weeks, sometimes alone and sometimes together.

Brad and Savannah Hastings had been appointed as advisors to their father after he took office, but Democrats in congress raised holy hell, citing anti-nepotism laws, and the credentials of both children had been revoked after two months. They returned to running PB Enterprises, although they shuttled frequently to Washington and, as Bricker had noted in earlier stories, were evidently entering the White House in a clandestine fashion by using secret entrances. Bricker now posed the obvious question: Were the children still acting as Presidential advisors, and if so,

were they conducting shuttle diplomacy with Iran, a nuclear power since 2021?

During the past decade, Iran had engaged in frequent saber-rattling, threatening to bomb Israel on numerous occasions. It had not only developed a nuclear warhead, but a missile delivery system capable of carrying a payload up to a distance of five thousand miles. Iran was also home to numerous terrorist cells such as the IRF, the Islamic Rebels of Freedom, and other splinter cells that were responsible for terrorist attacks throughout Europe. Technology had allowed terrorist cells to stay two steps ahead of most intelligence agencies in NATO countries, including the United States. The Supreme Ayatollah denied any Islamic involvement in terrorist attacks, but Iranian president Muhammad Al Assad was more bellicose in his attitude towards world events. While denying that his country was behind terrorist attacks anywhere in the world, he

was known to associate with IRF members on a regular basis. He had, after all, been a member of the organization in his youth.

Bricker could offer no proof that Brad and Savannah Hastings had met with the Iranian President, but ANPC had published grainy black-and-white photographs of the Hastings children being greeted outside of government buildings in Tehran by individuals no one could identify. Several senators had suggested that the children be called before the Senate Intelligence Committee and state what their business was in Tehran.

As Bricker pointed out, Brad and Savannah Hastings seemed to be dividing their time between Iran and Washington. Who was running PB Enterprises in Charlotte?

Chapter Sixteen
Garundi, Palaces, and the Bigger Picture

PATTERSON WATCHED THE WALL SCREENS IN HIS OFFICE AT NEWZTRACKER'S WASHINGTON BUREAU. He looked at video streams of Prime Minister Felix Ogo every few minutes, hoping he would see whatever Lone Wolf was attempting to call attention to. Many shots of Ogo showed him dressed in green camouflage fatigues as he inspected soldiers of the Supreme Garundi Army.

Like many third world leaders, Ogo liked to be seen in public, and he could be viewed almost daily as he toured the cattle ranches of Garundi or the country's yam and potato fields. He would talk with the workers, shake their hands, and then smile at the camera, his two clenched fists raised as if to say, *We are a proud and prosperous people working with great dignity.* In broken English, he occasionally claimed that since he had assumed the office of prime minister, "there is no hunger, no poverty. Sickness gone. Garundi strong and stronger." That was his constant reassurance to whoever he believed was watching him walk among his people. "Garundi strong and stronger. Every day, Garundi strong and stronger."

One thing in particular caught Patterson's attention. When Prime Minister Ogo addressed large crowds while standing on one of the many balconies of his palace, he raised his hands above his head, as if to embrace the crowds. The angle of his arms was exactly the same as that of President Hastings when he embraced his followers at political rallies.

Was it coincidence? Patterson wondered. Perhaps, but he continued to note every word and movement of Felix Ogo. The resemblance of the prime minister's body language to that of Hastings was uncanny.

Chapter Seventeen

The Real Right in the Good Ole US of A

SECRETARY OF STATE HART SAT AT HIS DESK AND LOOKED AT REPORTS OF RALLIES AND DEMONSTRATIONS ACROSS AMERICA FOR AND AGAINST HASTINGS AND HIS CONSERVATIVE AGENDA. He'd read reports on what Hastings called his Red Republican Legion and the Red Rallies they attended, and he'd also perused the latest documents about state militias around the country. They were all part of what had become known as the Real Right, though not everyone—certainly not the president—knew how these various threads of growing conservatism were sociologically interwoven.

The important thing was that the Real Right, in all of its iterations, was helping the government to dismantle much of the detritus left from previous administrations. The secretary of education had successfully turned school curricula away from critical thinking and back to the philosophy of repetition and drill used for most of the twentieth century. The Administrator of the EPA had managed to circumvent the few regulations that still existed to protect the environment, enabling carbon emissions to once again rise as the fossil fuel industry drilled for oil in formerly protected reserves off the southern and western coasts of the United States. At Housing and Urban Development, two thousand civil servants had been terminated, and the Housing Secretary played tennis five days a week. Hastings and Hart both believed that inner cities should be left to fail so that gentrification could renew blighted areas and push aside what they regarded as criminal elements of society. Some problems were never going to be fixed, and rugged individualism and laissez faire would fill in whatever fell apart. Hart believed inner cities should be bulldozed, not rebuilt.

Secretary Hart was summoned to the State Department briefing room to receive an update on escalating tensions between Iran and Pakistan. Sunnis were crossing the border into Pakistan in record numbers to escape the Shia-dominated regime of President Muhammad Al Assad. Iran believed that terrorist acts committed in Tehran and other cities within its borders were the result of angry Sunnis seeking vengeance against its government.

Iran was threatening to attack Pakistan for harboring cells of Sunni radicals, but Pakistan had publicly declared for months that no such cells existed, and the prime minister of Pakistan firmly proclaimed that Iran was simply looking for an excuse to attack its neighbor.

Hart listened patiently to the briefing, at which several generals voiced the opinion that diplomacy should be undertaken immediately to prevent a nuclear exchange. Pakistan, a nuclear nation for many decades, was on heightened military alert. The streets of Karachi and Islamabad were almost deserted since the population had been told to stay at home until the political crisis had been averted.

"Sir," said the Chairman of the Joint Chiefs, "the president's children have been visiting Iran on a regular basis. It's been reported in the papers, and my staff verified it this morning."

Hart glared with cold eyes at the chairman. "What in the name of God are the Hastings brats doing in Iran?"

"We don't know, Mr. Secretary."

"There's one other thing you should know," stated the Chief of Staff of the Army. "Right before this briefing, the president uploaded a new message to VOX-POP. He threatened to bomb the crap out of Pakistan."

Hart leapt to his feet, his face flush with anger. "Is that asshole trying to start World War III? Why the hell would he threaten an ally without consulting me or any other chief of staff?

No one around the conference table responded.

Hart returned to his office, where he sat and pressed his fingertips together, silent for several minutes. There had been a time when he himself had been a member of the Joint Chiefs, and he'd recommended bombing Iran in order to destroy its nuclear ambitions. He wouldn't be in favor of doing so now for numerous geopolitical reasons, but why was the president threatening to bomb Pakistan, an ally of the United States? And why hadn't the president told him that his children were regular visitors to Iran? Was Hastings doing an end run around him, or was he just plain stupid?

Secretary of State Hart picked up a large brass paperweight of a soldier in battle and hurled it against the wall to his left, smashing the official government picture of President Herbert Chase Hastings.

Chapter Eighteen
Unsettling Enlightenment

Patterson picked up Sela at Washington Union Station, which accepted high-speed rail traffic, and drove her to his office at NewzTracker. She could have used her tech skills while at SETI in California, but he wanted her by his side. Hopefully, she could use her considerable computer knowledge to research the autopsy of deceased senator Tom Chance. She was a computer savant and could find her way into the back door of almost any system, even if it had an allegedly impenetrable firewall. She was pessimistic, however, that she would learn anything of value about the death of Tom Chance, even though she'd helped Jay gain valuable information for his stories using tactics that were decidedly unorthodox. It still was done in the name of exposing truth.

"The guy died of a heart attack, Jay. It's public knowledge. What are you hoping to find?"

Jay sighed as he poured himself and Sela a cup of coffee. "Whatever Lone Wolf wants me to discover. And no, I have no idea what that might be. There's a terminal waiting for you down the hall. I know you don't like to cyber-snoop, but I think the guy was killed, just like Rampling."

"And I think that reporters are paranoid," she said, finishing her coffee and following Jay to NewzTracker's research room.

Sela looked up articles on the death of Tom Chance and his untimely demise while sitting with Senator Leland Wallace. He'd been taken to MedStar Georgetown University Hospital by medics who had tried to resuscitate him for over twenty minutes. The family had requested an autopsy given that Chance had been in excellent health and wasn't elderly. She tapped the keyboard before her to avoid leaving any voice identification, disguising her keystrokes with a software program that rendered her invisible to all but the most sophisticated IT specialists and their intruder detection programs.

"Here's the autopsy report," she said, after fifteen minutes of navigating documents in the morgue of the hospital. "The cause of death was ventricular tachycardia. Interesting."

"Interesting in what way?" Jay queried.

"V-tach, as it's known, is a type of irregular heartbeat that causes abnormal and spasmodic contractions in the ventricles, which are the larger chambers at the bottom of the heart. It can come on suddenly and cause ventricular fibrillation. If it's severe, it can cause cardiac arrest and death, but Chance had no history whatsoever of any kind of cardiac arrhythmia. For a healthy heart muscle to suddenly go into V-tach and suffer arrest is unusual unless one is subjected to a strong electrical current or some other stimulus. The autopsy shows that there was no occlusion of his coronary arteries, which is usually the cause of heart attacks."

Jay folded his arms and rubbed his unshaven chin. "There was certainly no strong electrical current in Senator Wallace's office—or any other stimulus that would cause ventricular tachycardia. I wonder if—"

"If Elizabeth Rampling died of the same thing? Her body was discovered in an empty office, and that would have legally required an autopsy. With files missing and the chip in her arm cut out, local police would have requested one anyway."

Sela typed for several more minutes before pivoting her swivel chair to face Patterson.

"Rampling's body was taken to Denver Regional Medical Center. The autopsy revealed that she died of a heart attack secondary to ventricular tachycardia. She, too, had no prior history of heart disease."

"Still think I'm paranoid?" Patterson asked.

"I think you believe that the chip caused the heart attack, but I don't see how it's possible. The chips are part information storage devices, part Net interfaces. They use a current that's a hundred times lower than that used by new energy-saving light bulbs."

"Then why was the implant in Rampling's arm removed?"

Sela puffed out her cheeks and shook her head. "I haven't a clue. Maybe she had information on the chip that somebody wanted. Who knows what data Rampling's chip might have had?"

"The information they wanted was the file on President Hastings, not whether she bought Louis Vuitton. She and Chance dropped dead in offices for no apparent reason, and Lone Wolf wants me to pursue this."

"You don't know who Lone Wolf is. Maybe you're being played. Perhaps it's someone in the administration who wants to mess with your head a little bit."

Patterson had considered the possibility, but, as was the case with all newsmen worth their salt, he wasn't going to pass up leads that had thus far checked out. What if Bob Woodward had never met Deep Throat in an underground parking garage? Tricky Dick might have gotten away with the Watergate cover-up. No, he was going to keep investigating.

"Well . . . *this* is strange," Sela said. "According to the report I'm reading, the results from Chance's autopsy were sent to the Office of Government Inquiry. Why would the federal government be interested in what caused his heart attack?"

"It's more than strange," Patterson noted. "I've never heard of an Office of Government Inquiry. Although, there are thousands of federal agencies in D.C. Check it out."

Several minutes later, Sela expressed her findings. "No listing for OGI in a directory of government agencies at the federal level. I'll run a meta-search." Seconds elapsed before Sela said, "All I get is an error message. Can't locate OGI. What do we do next?"

"We find out if Chance's chip was removed as well."

"Good Lord, Jay! The man's dead!"

"His funeral is this afternoon. Viewing continues until one o'clock."

Sela's face turned pale. "I can't believe what you're about to do."

"Believe it. Uncovering the truth is worth it!" Patterson said. "Let's go."

Chapter Nineteen
Implant Ripper at Large

PATTERSON AND SELA CHANGED CLOTHES AND ARRIVED AN HOUR LATER AT THE FUNERAL HOME WHERE TOM CHANCE'S BODY RESTED. A priest was leaving through the front door of the building, meaning that the viewing was over, and the casket would soon be loaded into a hearse and taken to church for the funeral mass. Patterson was well-known among the hundreds of politicians who were attending the services, so he entered the funeral home by a side entrance reserved for employees. He wore a gray suit and sunglasses.

"May I help you?" asked a dignified middle-aged man wearing a dark suit.

"I was at the viewing for Senator Chance and I seem to have gotten lost on my way back from the restroom."

The man smiled politely, speaking with the hushed tone appropriate for a hallway near the viewing rooms. "Ah, I see, sir. Just follow this hall and turn right. That will bring you back to the room where Senator Chance is reposing. Once there, just do an about-face, walk straight to the foyer, and you'll be able to see the parking lot."

"Thank you."

Patterson walked down the carpeted hall until he came to closed doors with a sign that said CHANCE. He opened the door a crack and saw that the room was empty. Behind him, the funeral director was talking to six men, all of whom were obviously pall bearers. He ducked into the room and walked to the casket, which had not yet been closed. Before him was the body of Tom Chance.

Patterson's heart raced, for he knew that he had only minutes, perhaps seconds, before the doors swung wide and the pallbearers entered to take the casket to the waiting hearse. He looked down at the casket, the top lid open, the bottom lid closed over the legs. Patterson lifted Chance's left arm and roughly pushed the sleeve of his coat up to his elbow while turning the arm over. Coarse black stitches had sewn flaps of skin together on Chance's forearm. The chip implant had been removed at some point after the Senator had been taken from the office of Leland Wallace.

Patterson decided that he would pay a visit to Wallace after the funeral was over. He met Sela at the front of the funeral home, told her his plan, and the two got into his car and fell in line with the procession to the church before discreetly peeling away into traffic.

Chapter Twenty

Walls, National Religion & Guard Towers

PRESIDENT HASTINGS STOOD NEXT TO THE SHELL OF A BUILDING IN ALEXANDRIA, VIRGINIA, ITS CINDER-BLOCK WALLS HAVING BEEN HASTILY ERECTED ON A NEWLY POURED FOUNDATION. He was there to dedicate the very first Church of the Heart, and no one but Vice President Cal Quint knew that construction had already begun before the president's scheduled address at the Temple of Metaphysics. Hastings stepped before a podium in front of the structure and adjusted the microphone, bringing it higher to accommodate his height. He then reiterated much of what he'd said at the temple, talking about the god within all human beings and how people would now be able to worship together, but in a fashion that accommodated everyone's individual belief system. It was, he said, the best of both worlds. America would be brought to its knees, he claimed, but only in the best sense of the phrase. The country would again be one nation under God, whoever or whatever that might be. His brief remarks were followed by a chorus of "God Bless America" by a local grammar school choir.

President Hastings thanked the benefactors of the church, the Scarabelli family, which had generously donated $200 million for the construction of similar churches across the country.

/

The Scarabellis were no strangers to politics. John and Patricia Scarabelli, together with John's cousin Nicholas Scarabelli, had originally made their fortune through the coal mines they owned in West Virginia, Kentucky, Pennsylvania, Illinois, and Wyoming. For the past two decades, they had made another fortune from natural gas by using hydraulic fracturing technology, also called fracking, which broke apart shale and sandstone deposits to free up pockets of natural gas. The process polluted the groundwater near most fracking facilities and had been traced to various forms of cancer in a medical tracking study lasting ten years. The water that came from the taps of homes near hydraulic fracturing operations was dirty and smelled bad, and in some locations, it was brown sludge. Fracking had been banned under the last two years of the DePeche administration, but the process was deregulated by an executive order signed by President Hastings within days of taking office. And even now, with scientists on the verge of proving that seventy years of coal mining and oil and gas drilling has resulted in the imbalance of Earth on her axis, Hastings continues to ignore the resulting devastating climate change on Earth, humanity and species extinction, most likely pre-empting our own extinction.

The Scarabelli family had contributed hundreds of millions of dollars to Republican candidates over the years, and in 2020 they had founded the Truth in News Network, or TINN, and critics claimed it was just that, a tin, hollow-sounding version of the day's events from the perspective of the Real Right. If a Republican candidate wanted to get elected to public office, from dog catcher to senator, the road went through the Scarabelli Empire to receive its conservative blessing.

/

As Hastings concluded his remarks in front of the Church of the Heart, he called for a moment of silent prayer for world peace. Later that day, Patterson would write an article noting that the same man who was threatening to bomb Pakistan for no reason was asking that people bow their heads and pray for peace in a troubled world.

As the president stepped off the podium, television cameras pulled back for a wide shot of the scene, allowing viewers to see the bell tower to the right of the partially built church. The tower was a miniature version of the guard tower at Brister, Arizona, and the bell hung in the space where a sharpshooter would normally have been stationed. The dichotomy between the warm, fuzzy amorphous intentions of the Church of the Heart and its military-style bell tower wasn't lost on the Grass Roots movement, members of which daily protested the administration of Herbert Chase Hastings. Thus far, three new Towers of Freedom had been constructed in Arizona. TINN reported that the towers were deterrents that had prevented fifteen thousand illegal immigrants from crossing the southern border, although it offered no facts to demonstrate how it had arrived at the number.

TINN also showed the Gonzalez family shopping at Bloomingdale's in New York City. They were escorted by Secret Service agents.

/

Hastings was alone in the presidential limousine as it drove him back to the White House. He was in a somber mood, since churches sometimes caused him to reflect on his days at the Christian Academy of Virginia. It had been a rigid secondary school with strict discipline. All students dressed in blazer and tie every day, and mornings began with prayer time in the campus chapel. Students were expected to memorize large sections of the Bible each semester. Hastings had failed to do so in his junior year, plus he had been caught smoking Western Rider cigarettes on the sly. He'd been beaten by the headmaster and then locked in a solitary room with no bed for two weeks, where he was forced to eat spare meals while memorizing the entire Book of Psalms and the Gospel of Matthew.

Hastings had never forgotten the harsh punishment. When he was released and sent back to his dorm room, he entered the chapel and walked to the altar, where he spat on the likeness of Christ on a wooden crucifix. If the Christian Academy of Virginia represented God, then he wanted no part of any deity, especially one that was Christian. As brutal as his punishment had been, however, he knew that it had been highly effective in obtaining results. He never smoked again, and his ability to quote from scripture would become legendary at the academy. Hastings decided in later years that physical, verbal, and mental abuses were invaluable tools. They were the means to achieve desired results in both business and his personal life. They were also proving to be assets in his Presidency.

Chapter Twenty-One

When Romance is Just Another Day in Politics

WITH THE FIRST LADY GIVING A SPEECH IN LOS ANGELES ON THE BENEFITS OF DIET AND EXERCISE, A SPEECH THAT ALSO INCLUDED A WARNING AGAINST TOBACCO USE, PRESIDENT HASTINGS HAD A QUIET DINNER WITH CHIEF OF STAFF LUCILLE RAINES. They dined on white wine and lobster in the White House residence. It was allegedly a working dinner, since the two individuals naturally needed to work closely.

"I thought Diane was still nursing the bruises from when she . . . fell down the stairs the other day," Raines remarked as she sipped her Chateau Montelena Chardonnay.

Hastings smiled. "The doctor gave her something for the swelling, and her stylist gave her some cosmetics to cover up the remaining discoloration, which was minor. She's so damn clumsy."

"Indeed," Raines said, eyebrows raised. "Clumsy. It's very rich indeed that the First Lady's chosen cause is health and the dangers of smoking."

"As you know, PB Enterprises now makes nicotine-free cigarettes."

"Which is a dismal failure, my love. I've tried them, and they're nauseating."

"What counts is the image projected by PB. The vegetable-based cigarettes are crap, but the company is moving into new markets. Private jets, coffee, tea, and investments."

Raines paused as the waiter brought the entrees. "Herbert, you really have to walk back your remarks about bombing Pakistan."

"The world could use a few less turbans. What do they do all day? Levitate? Pray to elephants?"

"Walk it back, Herbert."

Hastings took out his phone and called Nick Scarabelli.

"Yes, Mr. President?"

"I'm about to dictate some remarks. Record them and make sure they hit the airwaves as soon as possible."

The president spoke into his phone, saying that cool heads should prevail in the tension between Iran and Pakistan.

"I'll insert these remarks into the speech in which you alluded to nuking Pakistan, sir. I'll sync your dictation with your earlier comments and use footage obtained from other camera angles as well. All other statements will be branded by TINN as cyber lies. You never said them."

Raines looked pleased as Hastings ended the call.

"Shall we retire to the bedroom?" she added when they finished dinner.

Hastings took the soft white hand of his chief of staff and kissed it. "I'm not in the least bit tired. You won't get much sleep, Lucille."

"I'm not here to sleep, Herbert."

Chapter Twenty-Two

Nostalgia for the Past

Patterson sat in his office at NewzTracker, watching the speech Hastings delivered before the Church of the Heart, its ominous bell tower looming in the background as the cameras pulled back at the end. He took out his worn leather Bible and randomly flipped through its pages. The Bible had belonged to his mother, who'd raised him Catholic, but he'd lapsed by the time he reached his early twenties. Priests seemed to be going through the motions as they stood at the alter saying mass. What did all the rules and regulations mean? He'd drifted away from church, smoked some dope, and practiced serial monogamy. Nothing really made him happy until he'd become a journalist, and working at NewzTracker had been a fulfilling and all-consuming career.

Ironically, Sela was a practicing Catholic who never put any pressure on Patterson to attend Sunday mass. She was quite liberal, and yet she loved the old liturgical practices, from the swinging of incense to communion to sitting in an empty church, eyes closed as she fingered rosary beads. When she did so, she looked like a Buddhist transplant, serene and transcendent. He'd tried it on one occasion and hadn't been able to go one minute without checking his phone.

Meanwhile, the world seemed to be flying apart. The divisions in America had deepened, disease and famine were ravaging low-lying countries that had been flooded as sea levels rose. An iceberg the size of Delaware had broken away from the Larsen C Ice Shelf in 2017, and in later years further melting had resulted in large chunks of ice breaking away from Western Antarctica. More countries had become nuclear powers, and in America, rioting and violence in the streets had escalated because of high unemployment. It seemed that God, if such a being existed, had abandoned the world. The Bread Riots, as they were known, had spread to more and more urban areas, and yet even members of the Grass Roots movement seemed to live inside the virtual-reality domains, a cyber world that consumed people regardless of what they were doing. Social networks had become a substitute friend to fill the void left from once having had close relationships with real people. For better or worse, the web had finally connected everyone to everything—yet essentially, nothing but virtual reality. All that was required of human beings to tune out was to stay glued to the screens on their phones and computers.

Maybe that's why Patterson loved the Atlanta Falcons so much and going to the old Georgia Dome to watch a long fly ball float over the brick walls covered with ivy in the outfield. It was real life. Bats were still made of ash wood, and balls from horsehide. The old Georgia Dome was one of the few places where he could lose himself and unplug from the stream of information flowing across the world at any given moment.

Patterson flipped to the passage in the Gospel of Matthew that Hastings had paraphrased.

"Words betray the heart," Patterson said softly. "Words . . . the heart."

What was on the inside of Herbert Chase Hastings, he wondered. If words betrayed the heart, what kind of heart beat within the frame of a man who had poisoned people with both tobacco and venomous political rhetoric? Hastings was opportunistic, and his speech and opinions could shift as swiftly and easily as the engine of an Indie race car. He could shoot Manuel Gonzalez and call it immigration policy, not to mention mercy and kindness for those who might be fired upon in the months ahead, assuming the courts didn't put an end to such lunacy. He was a man consumed with the Caesars of Rome, not the people who had elected him to office, a man whose heart was black and scarred, that prevented disturbing feelings of conscience from rising to the surface.

Patterson closed the Bible and dropped it on his desk. He read the book to impress Sela, but he wasn't finding answers to the deeper question he allowed to swim up into his consciousness from time to time: What was wrong with the world that would cause people to elect for their president someone like Hastings, so obviously unfit to be the leader of a free world.

His reverie was broken when his cell buzzed. It was Bailey "Cookie" McKnight, the chief speechwriter for President Hastings. She wished to speak to Patterson, but not over the phone. Could he meet her at Franklin Delano Roosevelt Memorial Park in an hour?

Patterson knew that McKnight was a member of Hastings' inner circle. He jumped out of his chair, grabbed his coat, and was out the door in less than thirty seconds.

Chapter Twenty-Three

Wayward Children in Over Their Heads

PATTERSON MET COOKIE MCKNIGHT AT THE ROOSEVELT MEMORIAL ON THE TIDAL BASIN. It was a pleasant day, with white billowy clouds overhead, and Patterson sat by McKnight on a stone bench facing the imposing figure of President Franklin Roosevelt seated and swathed in a cape that concealed his wheelchair.

Cookie McKnight was an attractive brunette in her mid-forties. Her hair was shoulder length, her eyes deep blue. Wearing a brown business suit, she stared straight ahead as Patterson slid beside her. The woman looked scared, he thought, and he decided not to launch into conversation. She would have to take the lead.

Several minutes passed, McKnight remaining silent as a breeze blew off the Potomac.

"I'm taking a big risk meeting you," she said at last. "You're a known entity at the White House and not well-liked, although I suppose you already know that. Nobody who is critical of Hastings is liked, and I'm sure you know that as well, but your work is more visible since NewzTracker is a big outfit. The president regards you as a personal enemy."

Patterson was familiar with his reputation, so he let the remark pass.

"I asked you to meet me because I don't think I have much time left in the West Wing," McKnight continued. "I've gently challenged the president regarding what he wants me to put in any given speech, and at first that wasn't a problem. That changed quickly. I'm now told what to write by either Wolcott or Raines, since Hastings will no longer meet with me personally. I write the text, but ten times out of ten the president goes off script, so I'm just going through the motions."

McKnight paused and looked at Patterson for the first time.

"I wanted to be true to my party and also serve my country. I didn't care much for Hastings, but like many, I was naïve and thought that he might actually shake things up in this town and get something done. I was wrong. He's not going to get *anything* done. Not now, not ever. He doesn't care about anyone but himself. This is all about becoming Augustus Caesar. He never thought he could rise this high, but when he saw President Depeche floundering badly, he thought he could pull it off—and he did."

McKnight turned away again and looked vacantly at the Tidal Basin. "When I saw him pretend to shoot Manuel Gonzalez in Brister, I knew I'd had enough. I printed out a copy of my resignation, but didn't hand it in."

"Why not, Cookie?"

"Because I thought I could learn what the bastard is doing at any given moment and tell you about it. I like your articles and opinion pieces. I trust you."

"Thanks. So what *is* the bastard doing?" Patterson asked with the slightest hint of a smile.

McKnight inhaled deeply, as if steeling herself for what she was about to say.

"I presume you've read Beau Bricker's report about Brad and Savannah Hastings and their secret late-night trips to the White House, as well as their trips to Iran."

Patterson nodded again.

"It's all true. Brad and Savannah are escorted into the White House, just as Bricker claimed."

"For what purpose?"

McKnight shrugged. "I can only speculate, but there's a lot of talk in the West Wing to the effect that both children have met with Hamid Abbas Faridoon."

Patterson whistled under his breath. "Shit. Faridoon is highly placed in the Iranian Mafia. What are Hastings' children talking about with the likes of *him*? He's a powerful and dangerous man. I heard he deals in prostitution, opium, hashish, and slavery, with murder as a given."

"That's correct. Although, he's also active in banking and telecommunications. A shrewd businessman, from what I hear."

"Do you have any corroboration on this, Cookie? This is pretty big."

"No, I don't. People in the West Wing are paranoid, but a few of us whisper and talk to each other over dinner or drinks. Everyone's scared of the president except for Raines, Wolcott, and a few others."

Patterson was frustrated. This was a burp, something that got his attention, but he was nowhere near verification, and even if the Hastings children had met with Faridoon, it didn't mean they had any business dealings with the foreign mobster. It was a tantalizing nugget, nothing more.

"I've heard that Hastings has a temper and runs very hot sometimes," Patterson said, steering the conversation in a more general direction.

"That's an understatement."

"There are even rumors that he's physically abusive with the First Lady. Two of his former wives said they were battered."

"I'm not here to talk about the First Lady," McKnight stated with no inflection. "Maybe another time."

Patterson immediately dropped the topic.

"Cookie, have you sent me messages before? You said you like my writing, and I'm curious as to whether or not you've ever communicated with me in a less direct manner."

Was she Lone Wolf?

McKnight turned, a puzzled expression on her face. "Communication? No. Why do you ask?"

"No reason. Newsmen get lots of tips. Will you continue to contact me if you learn anything further?"

"Yes. Beau Bricker has his sources, and now you have one, too—somebody on the inside of the White House. You should get up and leave now. I'll get up in a few minutes."

"I understand," Patterson said as he rose from the stone bench and began walking.

It had been an interesting meeting. Patterson now had information that possibly connected with the stories of Beau Bricker. He found himself looking over his shoulder as he made his way to a Georgetown restaurant to have lunch with Senator Leland Wallace.

Chapter Twenty-Four
Bad Choices with Dire Consequences

Jay Patterson sat opposite Senator Wallace at a small but pricey restaurant on Wisconsin Avenue NW. Patterson ordered a salad and a Perrier. Wallace ordered bourbon on the rocks.

"It's a damn shame I can't sit here and have a cigarette with a good brand of bourbon," Wallace said. "I know they're bad for me, but I'm afraid I've made my peace with the filthy habit. I can look at your football physique and tell that you don't indulge, Jay."

"No, I don't."

"What can I do for you, son? I assume you want to talk with me about Tom Chance, like everyone else. Not that I can provide any relevant information. His legislative accomplishments are a matter of public record, so I'm guessing you want some kind of human interest angle. The real man and not the legislator." Wallace paused as he sipped his bourbon. "Or maybe not. That's not your kind of journalism. You write hard news, not fluff. And I like it. You're not afraid to go after Hastings, and that takes balls."

Patterson smiled politely. "Chance was a healthy man in his fifties. Can you tell me what happened leading up to his heart attack?"

Wallace cleared his throat, a nervous habit he had, and reached a shaky hand for his bourbon as he looked at Patterson beneath bushy gray eyebrows.

"You sound like the Capitol police, but no matter. I'll tell you what I know. We were drinking shots of bourbon and talking about the idiot in the White House. I feel responsible, since I think Tom downed his shots too quickly. Maybe he couldn't handle so much booze. He began to itch before grabbing his chest. Next minute he was dead. God rest his soul. Damn shame is what it is. He had a lot of good years left in him, years that this nation could have used. This country is dying, son, and if you print that, I'll find a way to ruin your career."

"Your words are safe with me, Senator. We're off the record. You said that Chance was itching before he died. Was he allergic to anything?"

Wallace coughed out a laugh. "Not unless it was bourbon."

Patterson ate his salad as the two men chatted about the political climate in Washington and the fact that Hastings had an anemic relationship with Congress, having passed only a single piece of legislation, which was his Jobs for America Bill. The program was tanking badly, and no one expected it to succeed.

"The big tobacco tycoon promised us the sun and the moon," Wallace said, "and he can't get a damn thing done because he thinks Congress is on his payroll. Well, this isn't PB Enterprises. It's the United States of America, and Augustus Hastings Caesar doesn't seem to know where the hell he is. I swear the man hasn't an ounce of presidential material, and doesn't even appear to realize it.

Patterson thanked Wallace for his time and drove back to NewzTracker. He thought of Wallace's words as he weaved his way through traffic. Imbibing a lot of bourbon quickly would likely have caused Chance to pass out like a college kid at a dorm party, not keel over from ventricular tachycardia. It was the report of Chance's sudden itching that Patterson found interesting. He was reminded of the sensation on human skin caused by static electricity, and wondered if chip implants could produce some kind of electric shock. He would ask Sela, who would probably continue to doubt that a small chip could deliver lethal current to the cardiac muscle.

Nursing his bourbon, Wallace remained at the table after Patterson had left. Should he have told the reporter of his conversation with Jimmy Finch, who wanted to repeal DePeche's gun control measures and ultimately start a white nationalist party? Wallace had decided against it. He didn't think Jimmy Finch would be able to start such a party since it had the stench of neo-fascism attached to it, and yet the Real Right and Finch's paramilitary union had definite political clout. Wallace decided that he'd done the right thing not to bring the issue up in conversation with Patterson. It was best to let sleeping dogs lie. Hopefully, Hastings would get booted out of office and Finch's ideas would recede into the background. If Hastings was re-elected, however, that was a different story. All bets would be off, and Jimmy Finch might just get what he wanted.

Chapter Twenty-Five
Sometimes God Must Die

THE CRISIS IN BANGLADESH HAD BEEN BUILDING FOR DECADES. Monsoon rains regularly flooded the country, but rising sea levels had been claiming more square miles of Bangladesh's coast every year since 2027. Bangladesh was a small country east of the Indian subcontinent, and its population was retreating into India to flee waters that were no longer receding. Many islands in Malaysia had disappeared, as had some in the Cook Islands. Some coastal marshlands in Louisiana had vanished forever by 2022, and areas in South America and New Zealand had experienced rising water that made human habitation impossible.

President Hastings sat in the Oval Office with Lucille Raines and David Wolcott. He'd asked his two most trusted senior staff members to join him to discuss a new healthcare proposal.

"Mr. President, we need to talk about your response to the flooding in Bangladesh," Wolcott pointed out. "It's good PR, and it's what the press is expecting."

Raines stayed silent.

"I don't give a good goddamn what the press is expecting!" Hastings bellowed. "Most Americans couldn't find Bangladesh on a map if their lives depended on it, and if voters don't care about it, then neither do I. The issue at hand is healthcare, and that affects people right here in this country. That's what they want to hear about. What has been the Congressional reaction to my Free Market Healthcare Plan?"

"Predictably," Raines said, "they believe that the plan has been tried before. Free market exchanges were set up in all fifty states in 2010, but the plan failed because younger, healthier Americans didn't enroll and therefore didn't enlarge the risk pool for private insurers."

"Yes, yes, I know," Hastings countered with irritation in his voice, "but the exchanges were based on a successful Republican plan in Massachusetts."

"True," Raines pointed out, "but the Democrats have owned that failure on the national level for many years. Do we really want to take ownership of a failed Democratic program?"

Hastings was livid and pounded his fist on his desk. "Americans are ignorant! Nobody but the elderly recall that program. Free market exchanges are a red meat Republican talking point. Competition! It's what this party is about!"

"With all due respect," Wolcott said, "while the people may not recall it, many legislators do, and Lucille's assessment is correct. They don't want to own a failed program."

Hastings stood and ran both of his hands over the shiny crown of his head. "I don't give a damn! I've got to propose some legislation, and this is the debate I want. As long as it doesn't fail until after the next election, I don't care whether people have health insurance or not. It's all about image."

"Your jobs creation program isn't going well," Wolcott said, shrinking back in his chair as he gauged his boss's rising ire. "Do you really wish to work on a legislative package that will be considered strike two?"

The Jobs for America program, or JFA, had been in effect for a year and a half, but it hadn't eased unemployment, although proponents said that it hadn't been given enough time yet.

"The press conference is about to start, Mr. President," Raines stated. "You should probably prepare and get a little makeup."

Hastings left the room with a grimace, Raines and Wolcott following.

/

President Hastings stood at the podium with the Presidential Seal and faced a room filled with the White House Press Corps.

"I'm going to begin today," Hastings said, "by briefly describing my legislative goal over the next year, which will be to enact healthcare reforms and make insurance affordable for all Americans, including the one hundred thirty-eight million people who have lost health coverage over the past nine years."

Hastings had told no one except Raines and Wolcott minutes earlier that he was going to announce a new healthcare plan to the public. It wasn't the first time that Congress would learn of Hastings' intentions along with the press and the American people. For five minutes, he outlined free-market exchanges that would be set up in all states to create competition in the marketplace. No one would be mandated to purchase insurance, and insurance companies would be allowed to offer cheap policies for catastrophic care. Pre-existing conditions would be covered, but a lifetime cap of one million dollars would be placed on every policy in force throughout the country. The legislation, he assured the nation, would be no more than fifty pages long.

"What about Bangladesh, Mr. President?" asked a reporter from the *New York Times*. "Millions of people have been displaced, and over one hundred thousand have been killed in the last week by rising water."

"It's a tragedy," Hastings replied. "Next question."

"Will the United States send humanitarian aid?" asked a beautiful blonde correspondent from the *Washington Post*.

"No."

Several more questions about Bangladesh were asked, but the president said he had no further comment on the issue.

A reporter from the Associated Press, Maryanne Mistretta, asked the president if he thought the flooding was due to climate change.

"Icebergs have nothing to do with the climate or Bangladesh or the price of rice. The *Titanic* hit an iceberg, and not a single person tried to blame that tragedy on global warming. Icebergs have been around for millions of years." Hastings paused, a faraway look in his eyes, before he looked back at Maryanne Mistretta. "Maryanne, have you ever read the Book of Ecclesiastes? It says there's nothing new under the sun, and it's the truth. For millions of years we've had clouds and sunshine and storms and snow. Mankind can no more change the enormous geological processes at work on planet Earth than I could pull the moon out of the sky. No, my dear. Global warming has always been a hoax, an attempt to stop the captains of industry from doing their duty, which is to create jobs. But Democrats don't really want job creation or to help the middle class, because they wouldn't have their bleeding-heart liberal causes any longer."

"To be clear, Mr. President, there will be no aid sent to Bangladesh?" came Mistretta's follow-up. "Sixty-seven countries around the world are sending supplies such as food, water, and medicine."

Hastings sighed and held out his hands in frustration.

"It's survival of the fittest, my dear. Social Darwinism. Nature herself has, with great wisdom, chosen to eradicate certain portions of the population."

Patterson's hand shot up instantly. Hastings, sensing a good sparring match, called on the NewzTracker correspondent.

"Mr. President," Patterson said, "you said recently that God lives in the hearts of everyone. Doesn't he live in the hearts of the people of Bangladesh?"

Hastings paused for dramatic effect before answering. "Ah, it's Jay Patterson, one of my most outspoken critics and purveyor of cyber lies. Jay, my friend, we have to look out for the homeland first."

"With all due respect, Mr. President, you didn't answer my question. Does God live in the hearts of the people of Bangladesh?"

Hastings sighed and braced his arms against the lectern. "Sometimes, God must die."

The president left the room, his last comment leaving a hush over the press corps.

Chapter Twenty-Six

Search for Truth as an Occupational Hazard

PATTERSON PARKED HIS AUTOMOBILE A BLOCK AWAY FROM THE OFFICES OF NEWZTRACKER. As he crossed the street, he heard the sound of an automobile engine revving to his left. A dark-blue sedan was heading straight for him and was accelerating. He started to move forward, but it was too late.

"Jay, you're about to be tackled on the line, and this linebacker is out for blood!

"Dad?"

"Jump, Jay! Jump! Show those bastards who you are! NOW!!"

He jumped into the air and rolled across the hood of the vehicle to avoid a direct impact, falling to the street as the sedan sped away. He wasn't able to get even a partial license plate number. His elbow was sore, but he was otherwise unharmed. He dusted himself off and straightened his coat before hurrying into NewzTracker headquarters. He was met by John Taylor and Sela, who'd heard the screech of tires as the car escaped.

"What the hell happened?" Taylor exclaimed. "Jay, sit down here," and Taylor moved a chair underneath him.

Jay appeared confused, holding his head and muttering to himself.

Sela took Jay's head between her hands. "Jay, you're alright. It's okay." And she wrapped her arms around Jay's shoulders and just rocked him back and forth a few seconds.

Dad, I was back on the field. I was automatically doing what I always did when avoiding being tackled. Dad.... thank you, thank you.... I miss you so much.

Jay raised his head and spoke briskly. "I'm alright ... alright. I just need air. Please, I'm okay."

Both Taylor and Sela stepped away from Jay to give him some breathing room. While he appeared unhurt except for some bleeding from his elbow, it was obvious that he was shaken, wiping away tears. Jay shook himself and stood up, bent over and stood back up, breathing hard still, but coming round to himself.

"Hey, man, you remind me right now of when you used to come off the football field twenty years ago, Jay. Are you sure you're alright?"

"Hit and run. Plain and simple. It was deliberate. I was crossing the street, and the driver hit the accelerator."

"I'll call the police," Sela said.

"I don't know!" Patterson suggested. "If this was somebody in the Hastings administration, then it might be wise to let the incident go. I don't want them thinking they can intimidate me."

Jay was still hearing his father screaming warning to him.

"Like hell!" Taylor said. "If we report this, there'll be a record of it, and the responsible party will be on notice that we didn't think it was a freak occurrence. Two attacks on a well-known reporter would make national news and start a serious investigation."

"I guess you're right," Patterson conceded. "Would you make the call, Sela?"

The police arrived quickly, interviewed Patterson, and said they would file a report. Without a license plate number, they said, there was little they could do; there were a lot of blue late-model sedans in D.C.

When the officers left, Sela sat with Patterson in his office. He related what he'd learned about Chance itching before he'd gone into V-tach.

"You've got to examine one of those chips more carefully, Sela."

She agreed that it would be the prudent thing to do. "Are we safe?" she added. "Since I altered the signal for your chip, nobody should have been able to know where you were just now."

"There are two possibilities," Patterson responded. "Either I'm being tailed the old-fashioned way, or else the chips are capable of doing a lot more than we know. I can't go back to my apartment, so we'll have to stay in a hotel until I can find out what's going on."

"I've found out more about Elizabeth Rampling," Sela said, "but maybe we should go to NASA headquarters here in D.C. I have clearance, and we can use their computers, which are off the grid, just like SETI's. Ever since the comet was discovered, NASA and SETI have been working together closely."

"Okay, but I want to look up one thing before we head to NASA. I want to know what Chance was doing in the days and weeks before his death." And to himself, Patterson thought, *Nasa and SETI are working closely together? That's convenient, so Sela could possibly work right here in D.C. . . . hmmmm . . . .*

Patterson did a search on Senator Tom Chance. Most of what he saw was what he already knew, such as Chance's plan to challenge President Hastings' executive order stating that all gay and lesbian military personnel had to be discharged from the military within ninety days. The order had allegedly been executed at the prompting of Secretary of State Hart, who was adamantly opposed to what he called "the pollution of our troops by those who were genetically flawed from birth." Hart's comments had been applauded by Jimmy Finch and groups that believed in genetic and racial purity.

"Look at this," Patterson said, leaning closer to his computer screen. "Three months ago, Chance went on a fact-finding tour to Africa to ascertain the legitimacy of human rights violations in various countries. His last stops were in Mozambique, Zimbabwe, and Malawi, where he stayed five extra days. All three countries border Garundi."

"Another coincidence?" Sela said.

"I'm not a big believer in coincidences anymore," Patterson stated. "Let's get to NASA and you can show me what you've got on Dr. Rampling."

The two left and drove to 300 E. Street.

Chapter Twenty-Seven
Programmed Nanobots

PATTERSON AND SELA PULLED INTO THE REAR PARKING LOT OF NASA'S WASHINGTON, D.C. HEADQUARTERS, AN EIGHT-STORY, MODERN REDDISH-BROWN BUILDING. Patterson was given a visitor's pass, and the pair was escorted to a computer room after exchanging pleasantries with NASA's Deputy Director for Washington Operations.

Alone in a small computer room in the basement, where heating pipes ran the length of the ceiling above a narrow out-of-the-way corridor, Patterson and Sela dropped their gear and sat at a console.

"Dr. Rampling was your average shrink," Sela began, "who may have been conveniently located when Hastings was looking for a psychiatrist. She was in a small town, and Hastings probably figured he could see her without drawing a lot of attention to himself. This was several years before he ran for office. Other than having a future President for a patient, her practice seems to have been unremarkable, so I looked up her background to see if she was drawn to any specialty within her field. All I found was a keen interest in the research of a Dr. Boyce Rittner, whose work she cited in several scholarly articles she published. She was obsessed with the guy. Rittner was keenly interested in a Taoist concept called the Middle Way, which advocates avoiding extremes of behavior."

"A pretty commonsense notion that would seem to be the goal of all mental health," Patterson commented.

"The one unusual thing is that Rittner dropped out of sight. He closed his practice after being ridiculed by his peers for trying to bring eastern philosophy into mainstream psychiatric practice. He now lives in a community called the Tao Center of San Francisco. His temple is located in Marin City, just north of the city. Not too far from SETI."

"You should check it out," Patterson advised, "but I'm still curious as to whether chip implants caused the death of Chance and Rampling."

"I can use an electron microscope to look at a standard chip used for implants," Sela said. "There's a lab down the hall."

/

An hour later, Sela pushed back the rolling desk chair she was sitting in after examining a chip similar to the ones required to be implanted in the forearms of all Americans. She looked up at Patterson, who'd been pacing the room nervously, waiting for the analysis.

"The chip I examined is outwardly identical to the ones we all have beneath our skin, but it has more raw computing power than Apollo space capsules from the twentieth century. The really interesting thing is that this chip has nanobots on it. Nanotechnology came into its own in 2022 and was already being explored in 2019. Nanobots are microscopic robots that are being programmed to fight cancer and heart disease once they enter the bloodstream. At some point the government obviously started using a second-generation chip."

"Could this kind of chip kill anyone?" Patterson asked.

A woman of science and logic, Sela hesitated and folded her arms. "It all depends on what they're programmed to do. Deliver electrical charges? Theoretically possible. Release nanobots that are programmed to attack instead of cure? Sure, if someone is so inclined."

"It appears that somebody is so inclined," Patterson noted. "It might explain the itching or tingling that Chance felt before he went into V-tach."

"So who killed Chance and Rampling?"

"Hastings comes to mind. Other Presidents have done unthinkable things, such as Nixon and Johnson, both of whom used a great deal of surveillance on political enemies and could twist arms hard to get what they wanted. They've been accused of ruining careers, although how far they went is a matter of speculation. In the meantime, are you up for a little surgery? We need to replace our chip implants and make sure that they're old-style. A car just tried to kill me, and I don't want to suddenly start itching."

"I could encode two chips from the lab here after checking them out. They'll have the same basic info that we have on the ones currently in our arms, only no nanobots. The incision is small, and only a small dermal patch is required to close the wound—assuming you're not hastily sewing up the arm of poor Tom Chance. I'll do it before we leave the building."

Patterson smiled. "I'll put myself into your capable hands. And I'll try to find out more about Hastings' children and any Iran connections they have while you track down Dr. Rittner."

"Did I say I was going to check out Dr. Rittner?" *Hell, Jay's infectious with his love of search for the truth. I'm not an infatuated school girl. I love this man.* "Right! I'm on it."

Chapter Twenty-Eight
All Hat & No Cattle

SECRETARY OF STATE MAXWELL HART SAT IN HIS OFFICE, WAITING TO BE CONNECTED TO VICE PRESIDENT CAL QUINT.

"Hello, Mr. Secretary," came Quint's always-affable voice. "How is the Ship of State holding together?"

"I was hoping you could tell *me*, Mr. Vice President. What are the Hastings children up to?"

"I've asked, Maxwell, and I'm told that they've been going to Iran on business for PB Enterprises. They're apparently peddling coffee, jewelry, and other crap, if I may be candid.

Also a shiny toy called the Slipstream 7000, which is a private jet for businessmen."

"Is there any possibility that they're engaging in secret diplomacy to deal with the tension between Iran and Pakistan?"

"Not that I'm aware of."

"Is there any way you can rein in your boss's VOX-POP rants and threats to nuke Pakistan?"

Quint laughed at the other end of the line. "I believe the president is all hat and no cattle on this one, Maxwell. Sometimes he likes to hear himself talk. I wouldn't worry."

"Thank you, Cal."

Hart hung up and sat forward, elbows on his desk as he reflected on Cal Quint. Why such an intelligent man had run on the ticket with a man like Hastings was a bit of a puzzle. Quint was loyal to the core, and if Hastings ran naked through the streets of Washington, Quint would likely come to his defense with a bit of spin that might even stand a chance of sounding plausible. At the State Department, Hart could at least stay in the shadows and not have to answer for Hastings' more egregious verbal blunders.

It was a burden for Hart to look over the shoulder of President Hastings, but it was a weight the secretary was willing to shoulder. Given the president's black-and-white thinking, he thought he might be able to mold Hastings and his agenda over the long haul. It was paramount that the country returns to a political purity that would essentially reboot the great experiment in democracy begun in 1776. For over two centuries, the principles of the United States had been compromised. Hart intended to change that before Hastings left office.

Chapter Twenty-Nine

Sharks with Blood in the Water

PATTERSON DECIDED THAT HE WOULD CHURN THE WATERS TO SEE IF HE COULDN'T GET A BITE FROM WHITE HOUSE PRESS SECRETARY DAVID WOLCOTT REGARDING THE ACTIVITIES OF THE HASTINGS CHILDREN. After Sela had replaced the chip in his arm, Patterson hurried to the White House briefing room and took his seat in the second row and waited as Wolcott, wearing a dark-blue pinstripe suit, stood behind the lectern, opened his binder, and looked out at the eager faces hoping to be called upon.

Wolcott opened the briefing with remarks about the president's jobs program and his unexpected announcement about healthcare reform, but the questions went straight to current events. Was there still a possibility that the president might bomb Pakistan? Did he stand behind his remarks that Bangladesh was expendable under the doctrine of Social Darwinism? And what did the president mean when he said that God sometimes had to die?

Jay waited patiently as Wolcott, using his trademark GQ smile, deftly handled each question with deflection and non-answers. The man had yet to buckle under the pressure of a growingly hostile press corps that challenged Hastings' bold and unorthodox statements and actions. When he thought Wolcott had finished stonewalling inquiries into presidential policy, Patterson raised his hand to be called on.

"David," he said, "is it true that Brad and Savannah Hastings met with Hamid Abbas Faridoon in Iran?"

Heads in the press corps turned abruptly to Patterson and then Wolcott, not having anticipated the abrupt question and its possible implications.

Wolcott didn't flinch. He showed his pearly white teeth as he glanced down at his leather binder and then at Patterson. He was as calm as when he'd answered questions about lung cancer being linked to Western Rider cigarettes as spokesman at PB Enterprises.

"Jay," he said, "I assure you that Brad and Savannah's meetings with Mr. Faridoon were related to business matters in the PB corporate empire, which is extending its interests beyond safe cigarettes."

Patterson had no follow-up, for there it was, out in the open. The Hastings children had met with Hamid Abbas Faridoon, just as Cookie McKnight had postulated. The White House gossip had been true. Indeed, Wolcott seemed to have been prepared for the question. Patterson had successfully put blood in the water, and he sat back and let the feeding frenzy begin.

Beau Bricker's hand flew into the air like a flag quickly raised and waving in the breeze.

"David," Bricker said, "if these business meetings with Faridoon are about PB Enterprises, why do Brad and Savannah Hastings sneak into the White House at night rather than use the main entrance like every other visitor?"

"Sneak?" Wolcott said. "They simply want to see their father and prefer to stay out of the limelight."

Questions began to fly like snowflakes in a blizzard, the briefing room suddenly filled with palpable energy and pleas to be called on. Were Brad and Savannah secret envoys acting on behalf of the president? Were they in Iran to talk about the tensions between Iran and Pakistan? What kind of business dealings did PB Enterprises have with Faridoon or Iran? How long had the meetings been going on? Had they begun during Hastings' Presidential campaign? Why hadn't the White House disclosed the travel plans of the president's children to a country deemed hostile to United States interests?

Wolcott took it all on the chin, smiling throughout. At last he held up his right hand, palm outward to indicate that he needed to address the onslaught of queries.

"People," he smiled, "you're killing me here. As I've stated, the business trips by the president's children are completely above board. I don't have specific details about talks with Faridoon, but PB is a sprawling company with many diverse corporate interests. I'll look into the matter and try to get answers to your questions. Thank you, ladies and gentlemen."

Within an hour of the press conference, Patterson posted an article on NewzTracker's website, the headline reading WHITE HOUSE CONFIRMS MEETING BETWEEN IRANIAN MOBSTER AND CHILDREN OF THE PRESIDENT. He knew that he'd opened a Pandora's Box for the Hastings family and that reporters would be scurrying to find out everything they could about Faridoon, as well as every place visited by Hastings' offspring for the last two years. And he hadn't betrayed Cookie McKnight by making any accusations. He'd only asked why meetings took place, and Wolcott had played right into his hand.

Patterson had no doubt that all of the leads he was pursuing had a common thread, but the problem was that there are so many to follow. Leaks and rumors were spreading throughout Washington, D.C., with unprecedented speed. He was reminded of an old Beatles song called "Eight Days a Week." He felt that he needed an extra day just to keep up with every news cycle and the information coming from informants.

Later that evening, Maryanne Mistretta wrote an article for the Associated Press. The implications of her piece were far-reaching. Had the Hastings presidential campaign received favors from Iran? Was this why the president wasn't being tough on Iran, a nuclear power that harbored terrorist cells within its borders? Iran had threatened to lob nuclear weapons at Israel and Western Europe on many occasions. Why wasn't President Hastings more actively engaged in opening a formal dialogue with Iran rather than clandestinely sending his children to meet with a nefarious character who, while known to have legitimate business interests, was reputed to be an underworld Mafia figure who had murdered hundreds of individuals? Had Faridoon played any part in the Hastings campaign?

/

Maxwell Hart was apoplectic at the State Department. He called in his deputy secretary and pounded his fist on his desk, his face red with anger, his voice loud enough to be heard by secretaries and receptionists three rooms away.

"Why in the name of God Almighty haven't I heard anything about the goddamn Hastings children meeting with Hamid Abbas Faridoon? I'm the secretary of state, for God's sake, and the president is sending his children to meet with one of the leaders of the Iranian Mafia? Get me the president on the phone! Now!"

An hour later, Hart sat waiting. The president, he was told, was busy and wasn't taking calls.

Chapter Thirty

If It Looks Like a Duck and Quakes Like a Duck—Then It's a Duck

THE TALL FIGURE SELA APPROACHED AT THE TAO CENTER IN MARIN CITY, CALIFORNIA, STOOD ERECT IN A ROCK GARDEN SURROUNDED BY FLOWER BEDS AND TOPIARY. In his early sixties, the man had long hair pulled into a ponytail, his pale blue eyes watching Sela from behind rimless glasses. Wearing a kurta—a knee-length jacket—over churidars—pants resembling baggy pajama bottoms—the man folded his arms and waited for his visitor to draw near. Sela was fairly sure that the garb was Hindu rather than Taoist, but Dr. Boyce Rittner had achieved a definite eastern look, and perhaps that had been his only objective.

"You found me," Rittner said with an expressionless voice. "I take it you're a reporter, and if that's the case, then you know I don't do interviews anymore. I no longer practice medicine, and I'm not interested in meaningless conversation."

"I'm not a journalist," Sela said. "I'm a scientist."

"It makes no difference. I have nothing to say."

Sela took a deep breath as she stopped three feet from Rittner. "You could at least be polite and talk to me for a few minutes. I've flown a long way to see you. Are all Taoists so rude?"

"You're challenging me?"

"It appears that I am."

Rittner broke into laughter. "I like that. I usually manage to intimidate people who seek out the great Dr. Boyce Rittner. I can run most people off in less than three minutes. What's on your mind, Miss . . . . ?"

"Grant. Sela Grant. I'm here on behalf of a reporter named Jay Patterson."

"The journalist at NewzTracker who hassles the madman in the White House? I like him, too. I like anybody, in fact, who gives Hastings a hard time. Let's sit down."

Rittner showed Sela to a stone bench at the edge of the rock garden.

"I'm under the impression that Dr. Elizabeth Rampling was a follower of your therapeutic approaches," Sela said.

"That's correct. She's a dear woman and an excellent clinician."

Sela knit her brows at the psychiatrist's use of the present tense. "I'm afraid that Dr. Rampling is dead. She died of a heart attack. Although, Jay has reason to think she was killed."

"I'm not following. Murdered by heart attack? You're not making sense."

"It's a long story, but she was found dead in her office in Telluride. A patient's file was missing, and Jay believes it belonged to Herbert Hastings."

Rittner nodded slowly. "Elizabeth told me she was seeing Hastings, although I guess it was a breach of ethics on her part, but I believe she was worried for her safety given that Hastings is . . . not a well man."

"Was Rampling drawn to your work because of MCT?"

Rittner frowned, took off his glasses, and rubbed his face. "Yes, she was one of the few practitioners of Moderating Cognitive Therapy. It's nothing more than traditional cognitive therapy dressed up with some eastern concepts, notably one called the Middle Way. I devised it to treat patients with borderline personality disorder. They experience rapid mood swings. They can be paranoid and aggressive one day, and then become tearful victims the next. Quite a bit more complex than that, actually, but that's why I formulated MCT. You say Hastings' file was taken from Elizabeth's office?"

"Yes. Do you believe she may have diagnosed Hastings with borderline personality disorder?"

"I wouldn't have a clue. Although the man is definitely a borderline."

Sela was taken aback at the psychiatrist's frankness. "How do you know that? Was he ever your patient?"

"Goodness, no. I wouldn't consent to see the ass if my life depended on it, but his behavior is commensurate with all of the diagnostic criteria for BPD in the DSM-V, the Diagnostic and Statistical Manual of Mental Disorders."

"Isn't it unethical to reach such a sweeping conclusion without having seen Hastings personally?"

"That's bullshit. If it walks like a duck and quacks like a duck, my dear, then it's a duck. The man's behavior can be seen and evaluated by anyone with access to the news. His presenting symptoms are, as it were, in the public domain. If he chooses to share his pathology with the world, then he'll have to deal with the consequences."

"Nobody has labeled him as a Borderline."

"It's only a matter of time."

"You're the expert, Dr. Rittner. Would you like to be the one who shines the light on the president's disorder?"

Rittner didn't speak for a full minute as he looked around the sunny gardens of the Tao Center. "You're asking an awful lot, Ms. Grant. I'd end up on endless television shows, and I'd become the target of President Hastings. I've worked very hard to maintain my seclusion. Too many of my colleagues believe that borderline personality disorder isn't real, that it's a textbook diagnosis for people who don't fit any other category. Borderline is a pathological narcissistic disorder and is not believed to be treatable. I don't know any therapist or psychiatrist who will treat borderline disorder. They can be dangerous if you get on their bad side. I'd have to renew my professional sparring with them as well."

Sela adopted a pained expression, a plea for Rittner to consider her proposition.

"I've found peace here," the doctor said. "I got tired of patients, interviews, criticism, and all the rest of it. I live in a virtual paradise. I meditate and grow vegetables. Not bad work when you can get it." Rittner paused and sighed heavily. "But there's a disturbed man in the White House. I hear he's threatening to bomb Pakistan, while spouting homespun theology."

"I'm afraid it's all true."

"I'll regret it, but I'll fly back with you and say what's on my mind, assuming NewzTracker will foot my legal bills in case Hastings sues me."

Sela laughed. "I'll talk with Jay, but I think his boss would take that risk."

Rittner rose from the bench and looked down at Sela. "There's only one problem, Ms. Grant?"

"Which is?"

"I don't think anyone cares whether or not the president is mentally ill. The voters sure didn't."

"They didn't have anyone like you to call the president out from a medical perspective."

"That's about to change, Ms. Grant. Shall we go?"

Chapter Thirty-One

Honey Pots & The Presidential Thumb Drive

THE BROTHEL TAPE, AS IT CAME TO BE KNOWN, ARRIVED AT NEWZTRACKER HEADQUARTERS IN THE FORM OF A THUMB DRIVE. It was given to the receptionist by a khaki-clad man from a nationwide delivery service. The return address was from a nonexistent Maryland street. John Taylor immediately sent the contents to Patterson after he'd seen the hour-long video of Herbert Hastings sitting in the main receiving area of a legal New Jersey brothel called the Honey Pot Hideaway. Hastings took a tour of the entire facility, led by Madam Elaine Bravard, who spoke throughout the video with a heavy French accent. The recording had been made eleven months before Hastings ran for president.

"The White House has thus far declined comment," Taylor said.

"Why should we run this?" Patterson asked. "It's outdated and is going to take momentum away from the growing suspicions that the president may have some kind of conflict of interest with the Iranian government. The Brothel Tape will only disrupt the news cycle."

"I hear ya," Taylor said, "but this fell into our laps, and I can't ignore it. There are undoubtedly other copies out there, and if we don't run it, someone else will."

"Whatever. I'll post it with a short statement that states we received it and that the White House declined to comment on what the president was doing there."

"That's all I want," Taylor said before ending the call.

Patterson shook his head. Had the video come from Lone Wolf? Cookie McKnight? Then again, he reasoned, the tape may well have come from the White House itself to intentionally sabotage the story of Brad and Savannah's trips to Tehran.

/

The president responded to the video by saying that he was a committed family man who had no recollection of visiting the Honey Pot Hideaway, although he added on VOXPOP an hour later that he'd always been a wealthy man who was driven to many places by celebrities and those he did business with.

To Patterson's relief, the scandal—a tempest in a teapot—blew over after forty-eight hours. Lone Wolf, however, sent the following message immediately after the Brothel Tape had been posted:

Everything is connected.

/

Patterson wasn't sure how the puzzle pieces fit together, but he would follow the bread crumbs that Lone Wolf dropped in his path, hoping they would eventually lead to a greater understanding of what was happening within the administration of President Hastings. He looked up the Honey Pot Hideaway and found that it was part of a chain of brothels in New Jersey. The owner of the chain was a man named Amos Moffat, who didn't seem connected to anyone of importance, but the brothels were incorporated under the name Paradise and Pleasure, LLC.

A further search revealed that the LLC was listed as an asset of a holding company named Beryllio Enterprises, Inc. Beryllio's subsidiary companies included Far and Wide Real Estate, Good Time Water Parks, and a dozen other corporate entities, including Beryllium Alloys, Inc.

Patterson quickly looked up the corporate filings for Beryllio Enterprises, his eyes opening wide when he saw that the CEO of the holding company was none other than Hamid Abbas Faridoon. The Iranian businessman was also listed as the chief financial officer of Beryllium Alloys, Inc. Patterson paced the room and ran his fingers through his hair. Hastings' visit to the brothel had pre-dated his run for president, and his children were now meeting with Faridoon, a man whose holding company controlled the Honey Pot Hideaway.

Patterson performed a search for beryllium, a chemical element that occurred in crystal and metal form. Beryllium had many applications, and the element and its alloys were used in the construction of aircraft engines, missiles, satellites, mirrors, telescopes, nuclear reactors, and thermonuclear weapons.

Patterson's jaw dropped as he read about beryllium's nuclear applications. Faridoon apparently had his fingers in a lot of pies, and maybe, Patterson reasoned, the other corporations in his holding company were mere diversions from business transactions involving the sale of beryllium. But who was he selling the alloys to? Iran? Nuclear powers? He had no proof that Faridoon was using Beryllium Alloys, Inc. for nefarious purposes, although given the Iranian's reputation for being a mobster, Patterson surmised that the man meeting with Hastings' children had an agenda that was both political and financial in nature. A foreign national was doing business in the United States, had ties with the First Family and was a notorious underworld figure in Iran. To Patterson, it was a news trifecta.

Patterson was about to write an article exposing Faridoon's business interests, but he stopped before typing the story, recalling that Beau Bricker had reported that Brad and Savannah Hastings had been scheduled to leave for an overseas trip the previous day. He punched the number of Dulles Airport into his phone and asked to be connected to the chief tower supervisor and flight controller.

"Beverly Watts here," came a lilting voice on the other end of the call.

"Hi, Bev. This is Jay."

There was silence on the line before the young woman spoke again. "You're the last person I expected to hear from. You're not calling to break my heart again, are you?"

Beverly Watts was a stunning brunette whom Jay had dated prior to going out with Sela. Patterson's demanding hours had torpedoed the relationship, but they had parted amicably.

"Just calling in relation to a story, Bev. The Hastings family keeps three private jets at Dulles. Did the pilot for PB Enterprises file a flight plan in the last day or so? The passengers would have been Bradley and Savannah Hastings."

"I'll check."

A few minutes passed, after which Watts returned to the line. "They were scheduled to depart for Tehran, but they made a last-minute change to their flight plan yesterday afternoon at two o'clock. The plane traveled to Paris instead. It was a Gulfstream 650, which has a range of seven thousand miles. No need to refuel if they wanted to get to Iran, so stopping in Paris or anywhere else wouldn't have been a requirement."

"Interesting."

Patterson realized that the change in flight plan had been made almost immediately after he'd lobbed his question about Faridoon at David Wolcott. The coincidences just kept on coming, although he knew that the change of destination wasn't coincidental at all.

"Thanks, Bev. You're the best."

"I was, and don't you ever forget it," Watts retorted good-naturedly. "Take care, Jay."

Patterson proceeded to type the story, polish it, and then dictate it to his phone before uploading it to the NewzTracker website. The headline read THE U.S. HOLDINGS OF HAMID ABBAS FARIDOON. The article listed the companies Faridoon was associated with and described the uses for beryllium. It went on to relate that the brothel Hastings had visited was under the corporate umbrella of the Iranian, with Patterson suggesting that the president and his family should be more transparent about their business dealings with a possible foreign agent. The piece concluded with the fact that Brad and Savannah had abruptly changed destinations for their trip the previous day.

Satisfied with the piece, Patterson sat back in the chair of his hotel room and clasped his fingers behind his head. He'd made no accusations. He knew, however, that other news organizations would see his story within minutes and begin to ask more questions of David Wolcott. The White House would no doubt feel the necessity to comment. There was an old saying: *Give a man enough rope and he'll hang himself.* Patterson's latest story was more rope.

Chapter Thirty-Two
What a Lovely Web I Weave

The White House Press Office released a statement declaring that the president had been unaware that the Honey Pot Hideaway had been part of the holdings of Hamid Abbas Faridoon. Moreover, the press release said that PB Enterprises, under the direction of Todd Hastings, was conducting business with Beryllium Alloys, Inc. since it was using parts manufactured by the company for its new private luxury jet. Meanwhile, the president, who was on a campaign-style swing through the Midwest to sell healthcare reform, claimed that Jay Patterson was an underhanded journalist who had nothing to do but sit around and look for scandals.

"Sometimes bad things happen to bad people," Hastings said, from the speaker's platform in Des Moines. "I hope Patterson's soul is clean—but of course we know it's not—since we reap what we sow, and God exacts vengeance on the wicked."

Patterson immediately called John Taylor.

"John, the president just threatened me on live television."

"One could construe it as a threat," Taylor admitted. "As usual, Hastings parses his words carefully. All the same, I'd keep looking over my shoulder if I were you. You okay? Any more . . . accidents?"

"No, John. I'm good."

The president later said on VOXPOP that "My children are not criminals."

Standing in his hotel room, Patterson shook his head and laughed. "No one has accused your children of being criminals, you ass—at least not yet."

Chief of Staff Lucille Raines sat in her office in the West Wing. For the president to go on a swing tour touting legislation that hadn't been written yet was madness. He was like a Roman dictator ignoring the Roman senate, but that was his style. She had instructed David Wolcott to issue a release saying that the presidential trip was merely Hastings' way of sending up a trial balloon to see if the idea had any appeal to voters.

Raines ceased writing a memo she'd been working on and stared vacantly at the papers on her desk. She was aware that people suspected she was having an affair with the president. Many in the West Wing noted the way that Hastings' gaze lingered on her for a moment or two longer than was considered proper. He'd always had an eye for the ladies, and he'd shamelessly flirted with her during the campaign. Many believed that Hastings was looking for his next trophy wife, someone who could, unlike Diane Hastings, present him with another child. Though sitting alone, Raines laughed out loud. The last thing she wanted was to marry Herbert Chase Hastings. For the chief of staff, the president was merely a stepping stone to her own political ambitions. She was fairly sure that Cal Quint would one day run for president, and she could think of no one more qualified than herself to be his running mate. The title Vice President Lucille Raines had a certain ring to it, and if she could be vice president, then she could one day sit in the Oval Office.

Chapter Thirty-Three
A Brilliant Hippie

SELA MET PATTERSON AT THE HOTEL AFTER GETTING DR. BOYCE RITTNER SETTLED AT A MARRIOTT IN DOWNTOWN WASHINGTON.

"When do you want to meet with him?" Sela asked.

"Maybe later today," Patterson replied, "but first I want to see if I can get a better look at Garundi."

"A better look? What are you planning? A trip to meet Felix Ogo?" The question was tendered with humor, although Sela had known Jay to go to extremes when pursuing a story. "We can't let Rittner sit on his hands for the next several days while you run to Africa."

"There's more than one way to take a look at Garundi," Patterson said with a Cheshire cat grin. "I want to survey the country by satellite. You know a thing or two about those, don't you?"

Sela placed her hands on her hips and curled her lip to acknowledge the humor she so admired in the journalist she'd fallen in love with. "Yes, but we'd have to fly back to SETI for me to use equipment needed to take a peek at a country on the other side of the world."

"Not necessary. We've got a wizard at NewzTracker that can pull up anything, anywhere, anytime. Now, can I have your full undivided attention? I am feeling very . . . tired all of a sudden. God, you're beautiful!" Jay pulled her to him, onto the bed. "Remind me later, Sela, that I have something very serious to talk to you about."

"More serious than this?"

"More long-term."

Bobby Thibodaux was a throwback to another era. His long dirty-blonde hair was pulled into a ponytail, and he wore jeans, a tie-dyed tee shirt, granny glasses, and a red bandana around his head. He was fifty-two and hadn't been around during the 1960s, but he was a hippie at heart and wore peace medallions and collected vinyl records and CDs at antique stores. He had a Ph.D. in mathematics and a master's degree in computer science. Like Sela, he was tech savvy and was known as the Wizard in NewzTracker circles.

"Look what the cat dragged in!" Thibodaux said when he saw Patterson. Hailing from Lake Charles, Louisiana, he spoke with a Cajun accent. "It's the man our President loves to hate and his lovely bride-to-be, Sela Grant."

"We haven't printed any invitations, Bobby," Sela countered, "but I'll make an honest man of him yet. I'll even get him to go to mass regularly one of these days."

"What brings you here?" Thibodaux asked, seated in an old desk chair tilted at a thirty-degree angle. "I feel lonely and forgotten out here, not to mention unappreciated since nobody's story goes anywhere without me."

"We're interested in your satellite feeds," Patterson explained. "Can you use them to get some high-resolution ground pictures of Garundi?"

Thibodaux sat forward and laughed. "Can my mama cook gumbo? Of course I can, Jay."

The Wizard rolled his chair across the floor and started issuing voice commands to the computers. Within minutes, they saw Africa on one of the wall screens, white clouds drifting over the brown and green continent.

"We're using a dedicated satellite," Thibodaux explained. "It's owned by no one, according to international treaty. Using it comes with only one provision, which is that it not be used for terrorist or military purposes by any government or individual."

"We're just sightseeing," Sela joked.

"Where in Garundi do we want to travel today?" Thibodaux asked.

"The capital city of Rheguto," Patterson answered.

The image on of the wall screen tightened to show the city as it looked from ten miles of altitude.

"Find the palace called Jumba Ogo," Patterson instructed, "and then tighten the shot as much as possible."

The palace came into plain view in a shot that was sharp enough to enable Patterson to see workers tending the lush gardens surrounding the rectangular pool that led to the main gates of the sumptuous residence. The structure itself was square, but it had two enormous wings spreading out east and west from its rear walls. Several dozen courtyards and fountains could be seen on the grounds.

"See what you're looking for?" Sela queried Jay.

"No, but that's the problem. I don't really know what I'm looking for. Bobby, widen the shot and start panning the area around the palace up to a ten-mile radius."

"Your wish is my command," Thibodaux said as he issued more commands to his computer.

The satellite's camera moved slowly across the landscape, showing the city of Rheguto, its citizens leading cattle through the streets and carrying baskets of fruit on their heads as their ancestors had done for centuries. It then showed the countryside surrounding the capital, with farmers working in the fields as they collected yams and other vegetables. Slowly, it worked its way beyond the city limits, revealing only huts and dirt roads cutting through overgrown terrain.

"There!" Patterson said. "Move back a hundred yards!"

Thibodaux reversed the camera's movement before he cried, "What the hell is that?"

"An airfield with two landing strips crisscrossing each other," Sela replied. "I've seen images like these from orbital satellites hundreds of times. One strip is oriented east-west, the other north-south. I count two hangars. It looks like there might be a plane on the tarmac in front of the first."

Patterson craned his head closer to the wall screen, obviously fascinated by what he saw. "This is definitely not Rheguto's commercial airport, which is on its northeast perimeter."

"Agreed," Thibodaux said. "There's a paved two-lane road between the palace and this airfield. It might be a military installation."

"Garundi has no air force," Patterson pointed out, "which is not to say that Felix Ogo doesn't use the field for personal travel."

Thibodaux sat back in his chair, arms folded. "I've seen private airstrips before," he said, "and this one is much larger. Most don't have two runways."

"Zoom in on the shadow that might be a plane," Patterson said.

"Son of a bitch," Thibodaux said. "That's an old turboprop C-130 cargo plane. They haven't been used by most countries for years, but many third world countries scoop up old military hardware and scavenge airplane bone yards like the ones in Arizona and Nevada."

"Looks innocuous," Sela remarked. "A transport could be used for almost anything."

"Which is exactly why it's so intriguing" Patterson said. "Anything covers a lot of territory."

"Suspicious as ever," Thibodaux laughed.

"Suspicion pays my bills," Patterson retorted.

"Ogo's a military dictator," Sela said, "and yet I don't see a single guard or soldier."

"Damn strange," Thibodaux said. "Is this part of a story you're working on?"

"Yeah, although right now it qualifies as deep background and nothing more. Do me a favor, Bobby. Keep some surveillance on this area several times a day and record any activity you see. It's in really good condition, so I assume it's not abandoned. Let me know if you spot anything, even if it's just a Jeep driving around. There's a case of Abita beer in it for you."

"Will do, Jay. Abita's the best damn brewery in Louisiana. But make it Abita Amber."

"You got it."

After clapping Thibodaux on the shoulder, Patterson left so that he and Sela could talk with Dr. Rittner.

"What do you expect to see on those runways?" Sela asked. "President Hastings making an unannounced visit? His children?"

"They're apparently too busy in Iran. What do I expect? The unexpected, love."

Chapter Thirty-Four

This Disorder is Impossible to Hide

PATTERSON WAS IN A HURRY TO GET BOYCE RITTNER ON THE RECORD GIVING HIS ASSESSMENT OF THE MENTAL HEALTH OF PRESIDENT HASTINGS. As a seasoned reporter, he knew he had to take charge of the next news cycle before the White House or another news outlet had the opportunity to do so. The president's psychiatric file had been stolen, and Patterson needed to lay the groundwork for future pieces on the death of Dr. Elizabeth Rampling.

Rittner had shaved, gotten a haircut, and donned a gray double-breasted suit. He looked like a man of science as he sat in NewzTracker's broadcast studio. Patterson wore a suit coat, slacks, and white shirt as he sat opposite the psychiatrist, and the two men went through a sound check.

The lights dimmed and the floor director counted down with his fingers until pointing to Patterson to signal that he was now live. Thirty million viewers would be watching the show, which John Taylor thought might be a game changer in the debate over the competence of President Herbert Chase Hastings.

After introducing himself, Patterson delivered a verbal resume of his guest's medical credentials.

"Dr. Rittner," Patterson began, "what exactly is borderline personality disorder?"

Rittner cleared his throat and clasped his hands in his lap as he sat facing his interviewer. He appeared calm and at ease.

"Borderline personality disorder is a serious mental disorder characterized by mood instability, as well as by low self-esteem, impulsive actions, and unstable personal relationships. Individuals suffering from the disorder experience moments of intense anger punctuated by seemingly normal behavior. The borderline is very narcissistic and can live in denial that he or she has any kind of problem whatsoever. It's a condition for which there is no cure, although there are treatments and medications available."

"Am I correct in saying that you believe President Hastings suffers from this personality disorder?"

"Yes."

Patterson nodded as he glanced at notes on a pad resting on his folded legs, before looking at his guest. "What led you to form such a conclusion, Dr. Rittner? Have you ever seen President Hastings in a clinical setting?"

"No, I haven't."

"Isn't it standard procedure to see a patient in a private session before making such a serious diagnosis?"

"Normally it is, but it's hard to ignore the fact that President Hastings meets most all the diagnostic criteria in the DSM-V."

"Can you describe some of the symptoms?"

"President Hastings constantly engages in *gaslighting*, which is a psychological attempt to make people question their own sanity by feeding them alternate versions of the truth until individuals on the receiving end actually start to believe the lies. Hastings likes the city of Miami one minute, and then condemns it as a city of promiscuity the next. Reality is whatever he wants it to be at the moment. Furthermore, he regards the press as cyber liars even though it can be proven that what he's said or done has been factually reported. Gaslighting is one of the many tools that Borderlines use to control and manipulate people."

"Tell us more about control and manipulation," Patterson prompted.

Dr. Rittner sighed. "Where do I begin? One of the Borderline's most prominent controlling behaviors is *projection*. Their self-esteem is so poor that they usually have no ability to deal with their shortcomings. They therefore project those failings onto other people. For example, Hastings called President DePeche mentally ill, but it's Hastings, beyond any doubt, who is mentally unstable and unqualified to be President. But the biggest example of a Borderline's projection is calling *other* people the controllers and manipulators. That's what Hastings does every day when he calls the press cyber liars.

"Hastings is also, like most borderlines, wildly paranoid. He perceives every honest disagreement with his policies as a threat to himself, so he strikes out in anger and abuses people verbally and mentally when they have the temerity to stand up to his bullying. The paranoia results in the borderline adopting the mindset that he or she is never wrong, never at fault. Has Hastings ever admitted to making a single mistake? No, he fancies himself a Roman emperor, which is as narcissistic as one can get.

"We saw these psychological dynamics at play in the press whenever Hastings went through a divorce. His ex-wives were all accused of being controllers, lazy and worthless women who had somehow abused or betrayed him even though they reported being battered women."

"And all this is done for what purpose, Dr. Rittner?"

"Borderlines need to fill their emptiness. Hastings feeds on power and admiration from others because it's the only thing that gives him a feeling of self-worth. He needs constant approval to fill the void within him. I'm certain you've noticed the ever-attending crowds with red shirts and hats at every speaking event Hastings arranges; he arranges for more than the public realizes. The adoring crowds and support for Hastings is always assured in advance by those doing the president's biding. They're always seated close to the president so as to be easily spotted by the TV cameras, and told to make a lot of noise indicating support. People will do anything to get on TV, so they're preselected right down to the last individual, given the red hats and shirts and told to wear them.

Also, while there's a strong genetic component to the disorder, I suspect that Hastings, like many borderlines, was abused as a child."

Patterson frowned, as if troubled by Dr. Rittner's characterization of borderline personality disorder. "Doctor, you're painting the image of a person who is deeply troubled, so how can a borderline personality rise to the highest office in the land?"

Dr. Rittner took a sip of water from a glass on the table next to his chair and looked at Patterson, holding up an index finger as if the question were of paramount importance.

"Borderlines fall into two categories. High-functioning and low-functioning. It's a grievous mistake to think that people who suffer from borderline personality disorder can never hold a job or experience success. To the contrary, borderlines, because of their extraordinary skill at controlling and manipulating others, rise to great heights in society. Some of the most skilled doctors, lawyers, scientists, teachers, and other professionals suffer from the disorder, although they frequently, but not always, cause chaos in the workplace. Some are considered to be the salt of the earth, pillars of the community.

"It's worth noting that many healthcare professionals refuse to treat borderlines because they attempt to control the very therapeutic process itself. Most borderlines are never diagnosed because they aren't forthcoming about their symptoms and don't seek treatment unless forced into family therapy, which becomes contentious. Borderlines demonize anyone who disagrees with them. In the case of President Hastings, he demonizes Democrats, the press, and members of his own party who believe he's not fit to govern."

"Dr. Rittner, do you have any opinion as to what should be done if a mentally unstable person is currently occupying the White House?"

"I do indeed," Dr. Rittner shot back without missing a beat. "Borderlines deserve competent treatment like anyone else, but no one who suffers from such a severe mental disorder should receive therapy while occupying the Oval Office. What if Hastings feels so insecure one day that he decides to get the praise he wants by launching a nuclear weapon in order to whip the country into a frenzy of misplaced patriotism?"

"Doctor, this has been an illuminating discussion. I look forward to hearing what others have to say about the debate you've opened this evening. Your assessment is sober indeed."

"It's my hope, Jay, that my words will encourage more psychiatrists to speak up about the president's mental health. We have a professional and ethical duty to inform the public about individuals who pose a grave risk to others. Since most borderlines are sociopathic in nature, I feel I've done my civic duty."

Patterson faced the camera a final time, saying, "Send us your thoughts on our broadcast. For now, this is Jay Patterson for NewzTracker dot com."

Patterson escorted Boyce Rittner to a waiting car outside of the studio, but was met by two uniformed officers who forcibly pulled the reporter away from his television guest.

"Dr. Rittner," said a bald, overweight officer, "you're under arrest for failure to comply with federal law mandating that all citizens have a chip implant."

Rittner turned to Jay and unapologetically said, "When I go off the grid, I do it all the way. When I joined the Tao Center, I had the implant removed. No one has the right to know my whereabouts at all times." He winked. "Get me a good lawyer, Jay. That's the deal I have with your boss."

Rittner was driven away by the police, leaving Patterson to question what had just occurred. It had taken less than an hour for someone in the Hastings administration to abduct the only man in the country who had gone on national television to accuse the president of being mentally ill. Patterson had no doubt that a formal White House response would be swift—and vicious.

Patterson froze in his tracks. Rittner had mentioned the spouses of Herbert Hastings, and the word "spouse" had stuck in his mind. He'd completely overlooked the activities of the husband of Savannah Hastings, Sedge O'Connell, the Washington lobbyist who had retained a low profile ever since the election of his father-in-law. Patterson dashed back into the studio and called the offices of Marsh & Brennan, the firm where O'Connell was employed.

"May I speak with Sedge O'Connell please?"

"I'm sorry," a receptionist said, "but he's not in the office at present."

"Do you know when he'll be back?"

"I'm afraid Mr. O'Connell is out of the country."

Patterson sighed heavily for effect. "Gosh, this is an emergency. I'm calling on behalf of Senator Roger Rothstein, and we have a situation that only Mr. O'Connell can deal with. It's urgent."

"Please hold."

A moment later, the secretary came back on the line and said, "Mr. O'Connell will be landing in London within the hour if you wish to try calling Heathrow Airport."

Jay hung up and called Beverly Watts at Dulles International Airport.

"It's Jay again, Bev. Did a Marsh & Brennan jet take off within the last eight to twelve hours?"

"No. I don't think they have one."

"Any PB jet carrying Sedge O'Connell?"

"Yes, a Gulfstream. The flight plan was for Tehran, with a layover in London. You really must be on a hot story."

"Is there any other kind? Thanks."

Patterson ended the call and considered the possibility that the Hastings family was trying to do an end run around the press. What was so important in Iran that even the president's son-in-law would get involved when his children deemed it unwise to travel to the Middle East?

The Hastings clan had upped the ante. He would post a story about O'Connell's visit to Tehran, but he would wait until the private jet had time to land at its final destination, lest Hastings' son-in-law get cold feet and remain in London.

Chapter Thirty-Five
Biding Time

On a personal level, Lone Wolf had many friends and was considered the life of the party, but he had little power in the Washington establishment and received only moderate compensation for his efforts as a government employee. He thought that the appellation of "lone" was quite appropriate.

He thought back to his days in the military and the CIA. He'd been a paratrooper with the 82nd Airborne, an elite Army division out of Fort Bragg, North Carolina, that was considered to be the best trained division of its kind. It was deployed to areas restricted to normal ground troops, and those who had served in the 82nd included celebrities, legislators, and generals.

It was the most strategically mobile division in the entire military.

His distinguished service in the division had quickly earned him a spot in the CIA, and he had been both case officer and station chief, handling valuable foreign assets crucial to national security. He'd been respected by the powers-that-be at Langley, as well as congressmen and top brass in the Army. Back in the day, he'd known the Middle East better than anyone. But what had his service been good for? While he still retained his security clearances, he was nothing but a bureaucrat stuck in the gears of a federal government that was taking orders from a man who governed by recording rants into his VOXPOP account. Lone Wolf was at his desk every morning, like thousands of other civil servants, and mostly what he did was push papers around, a job that wasn't satisfying in the least.

But the term "wolf" was also applicable. Although he was tucked away in an office building a good bit of the time, he knew things that others didn't. A *lot* of things. He still ran into some of his old buddies, and they were quite forthcoming about the life and times of Herbert Chase Hastings. Like a true lone wolf, he was on the prowl. If he could do nothing else, he would bring down the president, whom he deemed to be dangerous to the country. He probably wouldn't get recognition for doing so since his *modus operandi* was to communicate with Jay Patterson and hope that the reporter would do what legislators seemed afraid to do—take on the President of the United States. But lack of recognition was not his present concern. It was results that counted. Maybe somebody would give him a pat on the back someday, but until then, he would keep feeding the NewzTracker reporter whatever he could in order to destabilize the already volatile Hastings administration. As was the case when he was in the Army and CIA, maybe he would once again make a difference in the world.

Chapter Thirty-Six

The Real Right & Murder in the Streets

SELA AWAITED PATTERSON AT THEIR HOTEL ROOM.

"Jay, you have to see this! Quick!"

Patterson joined Sela in front of the room's giant wall screen. A correspondent with ABN, the American Broadcasting Network, was running through the brush alongside Jimmy Finch, who was dressed in camouflaged military fatigues. The correspondent was out of breath while he and his cameraman attempted to keep pace with the militia leader as he raced through a dense pine forest in central Tennessee. The *pop pop pop* of gunfire could be heard in the distance. Finch suddenly dropped to his belly and looked through binoculars at a distant clearing.

"This is one of several civilian war games taking place around the country," the correspondent explained as he glanced at the camera, wearing a Kevlar vest.

"It's one of thirty-six such exercises," Finch whispered. "Leland Wallace has declined my request to introduce legislation repealing DePeche's gun control laws, but the patience of the Real Right and the American Paramilitary Union is wearing thin. Liberals have a stronghold on this government. We're prepared to defend the Constitution. We won't stand by while gays, blacks, Hispanics, and sorry-ass liberals pervert true liberty and democracy."

"It sounds as if your union wants to start a civil war, Mr. Finch."

"We lost the first one," Finch said, "but we won't lose the next."

"Are you going to overthrow the government of the United States?"

"We're going to stand by the side of Herbert Chase Hastings to save it. Call it what you will."

Chapter Thirty-Seven
Caesar's Psychotic Break

PRESIDENT HASTINGS WAS LIFTING WEIGHTS IN THE WHITE HOUSE GYM AS HE WATCHED TINN NEWS ON ONE OF SEVERAL WALL SCREENS. The news report said that more Freedom Towers had been erected along the southern border, and court challenges had failed to halt their construction. Several conservative judges had pointed out that border patrol agents had always been armed with firearms to shoot illegal immigrants who defied orders to turn around or be taken into custody. Since it was illegal to cross the border without documentation, judges said that Hastings' executive order to build towers was merely a more aggressive way of enforcing existing law.

The next report showed Church of the Heart congregations assembling in cafeterias and auditoriums while the Scarabelli family raced to complete dozens of church buildings around the country. There was no prescribed format for the worship, except that all services began with the national anthem. After that, people meditated, sang hymns, listened to lectures on metaphysics, or broke into small groups to share their spiritual beliefs. The Church of the Heart's right to exist had been upheld by conservative judges, who said that the president was merely encouraging freedom of nondenominational worship when he'd established the nebulous congregation.

It was the replay of Jay Patterson's interview with Dr. Boyce Rittner that caused President Hastings to put down the forty-pound weights he was curling. He stormed around the gym, cursing what he regarded as NewzTracker's defamation of his character.

"Damn that son of a bitch Patterson!" Hastings screamed. "And damn Boyce Rittner! Do I not stand on Mount Sinai? Do I not issue the law for all those in the land? Is not my word sovereign? Who are they to challenge me—their Caesar and god?"

Hastings summoned his body man and secretary and gave them instructions to arrange a televised conference for five o'clock that afternoon. He was going to deal head-on with accusations that he had borderline personality disorder, assuming such a condition even existed. He thought it likely that Patterson and the psychiatrist had fabricated the disorder. Borderline personality disorder? He'd never heard of it.

/

Sitting at the head of a conference table, Hastings was surrounded by one of his ex-wives, a psychiatrist, his personal physician, Brad and Savannah Hastings, mega-church pastor Holly Gerard, and Savoy Greene of TINN. Hastings went straight for Patterson's jugular.

"NewzTracker is a lying, despicable outfit, and you can be assured that it will be sued," Hastings said. "Jay Patterson has gone one step beyond most liars in the mainstream media by calling me crazy. He says I have a personality disorder and that I'm mentally unstable. But I sit before you today to tell you that Jay Patterson is the one who is mentally ill, for anyone capable of making up such fiction about me is an unbalanced individual. He has projected onto me his own insecurities and instabilities. I will now ask friends, family, and healthcare professionals to speak to the issue of my mental health. Unfortunately, the First Lady was unable to be present today since she was booked for a speaking engagement."

For the next thirty minutes, the assembly of Hastings backers claimed that the president was a great father, an ever-present friend, and a devout and holy man. The psychiatrist said that he'd examined Hastings and found no indication of any kind of personality disorder. Savoy Greene added that many of the outrageous remarks attributed to Hastings had been invented by news organizations, which he deemed "the devils of journalism." They were liars who reported what Greene called "substitute news."

To close, Hastings rose from his chair, anger in his face, and pointed at the camera with his index finger.

"The devil is the father of all lies. The mainstream media works for the evil one. I will personally defeat NewzTracker and any news outlet that seeks to tarnish my reputation with substitute news."

The floor director indicated that the broadcast was finished. Hastings got up from the table, telling his detail to find some agents and to "get everybody the hell out of here."

/

Patterson watched the speech and then wrote an article citing that President Hastings had demonstrated the very behaviors Dr. Rittner had detailed in the NewzTracker interview. Hastings had projected his own behavior onto Patterson and shown pronounced paranoia and rage. As for the First Lady's absence, she had no speaking engagements scheduled for that day.

Patterson called the federal prison where Rittner was being held since the attorney general deemed the psychiatrist a threat to the president because his diagnosis wasn't based on a clinical examination. Patterson was connected to the director of the facility and listened for three minutes before hanging up, speechless. Dr. Boyce Rittner, he'd been told, had committed suicide, leaving behind a note saying that he couldn't live with the knowledge that he'd damaged the president with such egregious lies.

Another person had been killed to protect the administration. Whether or not it had been ordered by Hastings himself was unknown, but Patterson decided to redouble his effort to find out who was responsible for the murders of Tom Chance and Elizabeth Rampling.

Chapter Thirty-Eight
Wild Card

PATTERSON RECEIVED IMAGES ON HIS PHONE FROM BOBBY THIBODAUX, WHO'D BEEN MONITORING ACTIVITY AT THE GARUNDI AIRSTRIP NEAR JUMBA OGO.

"What am I looking at, Bobby?" Patterson asked.

"Two Iranian fighter jets parked on the tarmac outside the second hanger. I checked the configuration of the fuselage and wings, and they're Iranian—no question about it. But it gets better. They were an escort for another C-130 cargo transport that's now in the first hangar."

"What in the hell are Iranian military planes doing in Garundi?" Patterson asked.

There was silence on the line before Thibodaux answered. "Dunno, Jay. Maybe they're on loan. Like you said, Garundi doesn't have an air force."

"So Felix Ogo just picks Iran out of thin air and requests some fighter jets as loaners? Who the hell is he planning on bombing? No, those jets were strictly for escort purposes, which means that the C-130s are bringing something into Garundi that Ogo regards valuable."

"Any idea what might be in the transports?" Thibodaux asked.

"Not offhand, unless Garundi is importing some of Iran's nuclear technology, courtesy of Faridoon and Beryllium Alloys. But why would Garundi seek to become a nuclear power? Ogo can barely feed his people."

Thibodaux was quick to speak up. "Maybe Iran is using this little out-of-the-way country to assemble more powerful nuclear weapons. It would be a good way to avoid detection."

"Quite possibly, but what further nuclear aspiration does Iran have? Assuming it's ramping up its nuclear weapons development, is Hastings aiding Iran in some way? If so, he's so far into impeachment territory that it makes any blunder made by previous presidents pale in comparison."

"Hastings is *your* beat." Thibodaux laughed. "I'm about to listen to several hours of the Doors, Rolling Stones, and Moody Blues. Bands don't write songs like they used to. Meanwhile, I'll keep watching the airstrip."

"Thanks, Bobby."

Patterson pocketed his phone and wondered why Garundi was so important. The small African country was a wild card in the strange political game being enacted. Since Tom Chance had been in the region shortly before he was killed, Patterson decided to call Jane Levitt, a Chance staffer whom he'd known for five years and who was a good source on what was going on in the Senate. He counted Levitt as more of a friend than a source, since she and her husband often had him over for dinner to talk politics and the Chicago Cubs, the Levitt's being from the Second City. He gave her a call, and the two arranged to meet on the Mall.

/

No one had been appointed to Tom Chance's seat in Georgia, but his staff was still handling daily communications from senators and constituents. Levitt was in her early forties and had black hair that she wore long to draw attention from a waistline that she regarded as a bit too large.

"What's on your mind, Jay?" Levitt asked as the two walked leisurely along the Mall. "Are you going to throw any more grenades at Hastings? The interview with Rittner was riveting, and you've succeeded in getting everybody to talk rather than whisper about the elephant in the room, namely the mental state of our President."

"No more bombshells for now. I wanted to ask you about Tom's visits to Zimbabwe, Mozambique, and Malawi three months ago. I heard he was in Africa to get information on human rights violations. He prolonged his tour and stayed an extra five days. Anything I should know about?"

"He was also there to look into voting irregularities in recent elections for several countries, including the ones you named, but he decided to pay a visit to Garundi, which wasn't on his official itinerary. Tom had heard for a while that Ogo is a merciless dictator worse than Papa Makela. Tom met with Ogo at his palace."

"Jumba Ogo."

"That's the one. Opulent digs. His people barely have food, but like most petty dictators, the man lives in style. Has four wives and eighteen children."

"Did Tom find out anything new about Ogo?"

"That next year's election is pretty much in the bag for Ogo, who owns every official in the provinces of Garundi. Tom recommended to the United Nations U.S. Ambassador that personnel be sent to monitor the election."

"Anything else?"

"Nothing that he mentioned to his staff, although he seemed distracted after returning. I asked him if there was anything he wanted to share, and he said it was just frustration with Hastings, which is the response you get from most Democrats in this town."

"Did he mention anything about an Iranian presence in Garundi?"

Levitt stopped walking and turned sideways, looking at Patterson with a startled expression. "No, he didn't. Good Lord, Jay. Why do you ask?"

"Strictly off the record, Jane, Iranian jets and a couple of old cargo planes were sighted at Ogo's private airstrip in Rheguto."

Levitt nodded, as if relieved. "A lot of African countries receive covert assistance from nations that are both affluent and powerful."

"Thanks, Jane. I'm really sorry about Tom. I only met him a few times, but he seemed like the genuine article."

A tear slid down Levitt's cheek. "More than you'll ever know, Jay."

Chapter Thirty-Nine

All in The Family

PATTERSON RECEIVED WORD FROM BEVERLY WATTS THAT SEDGE O'CONNELL'S PLANE HAD LANDED IN IRAN. He quickly posted a story on NewzTracker stating that the president's son-in-law had traveled to the country after Brad and Savannah Hastings had diverted their jet from Tehran to Paris. Was the president, he asked, using O'Connell to carry on business with Iran, whatever that might be, since his children were now under scrutiny?

Reaction to the news of O'Connell's trip was swift. Marsh & Brennan fired O'Connell within the hour, saying that their firm had no dealings with Iran and that O'Connell had made the unforgiveable mistake of not revealing his travel itinerary, which included a trip to a hostile government.

The White House issued no comment on Patterson's story. President Hastings took to VOXPOP to say what a wonderful, intelligent, and handsome son-in-law he had. He was sure that O'Connell's trip had been made for good reason. He also called Patterson a "scumbag" for publishing yet another piece of substitute news.

By late afternoon, Beau Bricker reported that O'Connell had retained the legal counsel of Shane Donovan, one of Washington's most prestigious criminal lawyers.

Chapter Forty

Who's Running the Country?

PATTERSON'S ARTICLE HAD BEEN ONE MORE ASPECT OF THE *DRIP, DRIP, DRIP* THAT WAS BEGINNING TO THROW SUSPICION ON THE HASTINGS ADMINISTRATION, BUT THE BOMBSHELL JANE LEVITT EXPECTED TO COME FROM JAY HAD INSTEAD COME FROM MARYANNE MISTRETTA. Summarizing Secretary of State Hart's reputation for wanting a smaller government, one that was purified of what he believed to be corrupting liberal influences, Mistretta made the bold allegation that a source in the State Department claimed that Secretary Maxwell Hart was part of a secret group called The Elect.

According to the article, the group allegedly consisted of military brass, legislators, CEOs, entrepreneurs, bankers, and members of the intelligence community. Some were retired, while others were still active in the public or private sectors. Mistretta noted that Maxwell Hart and Herbert Hastings had been schoolmates at the Christian Academy of Virginia. It was unknown whether or not Hastings himself was a member of The Elect.

Mistretta wrote that her source claimed that the present agenda of The Elect was to dismantle as much of the Washington establishment as possible and put into place the radical conservative agenda of the Real Right in the hopes of one day bringing down the two-party system.

By early evening, Patterson's story on Sedge O'Connell and Mistretta's piece on The Elect were being given equal time on television and the Internet in what was being called an explosive news day.

Patterson and Sela were having dinner at a small sandwich shop on the edge of Falls Church, Virginia, when Patterson got a new message from Lone Wolf: *Why aren't you pursuing OGI?*

The implication of the correspondence was clear. The unlisted Office of Government Inquiry might somehow be related to The Elect. Indeed, Patterson thought, maybe the OGI *was* The Elect.

Chapter Forty-One
Investigation Time

SENATOR LELAND WALLACE HAD DECIDED TO BREAK RANKS WITH HIS PARTY. HE COULD CONNECT THE DOTS AS WELL AS ANYONE. The president's children were secretly entering the White House at night and clandestinely meeting with Hamid Abbas Faridoon in Iran, with Faridoon controlling business interests that included the manufacturing of materials that could be used in nuclear weapons. At home, President Hastings was ignoring Iran's bellicose history and threatening to bomb Pakistan. Wallace called for an investigation into the Hastings administration and the Hastings children by the Senate Intelligence Committee. Whose interests, he asked in a brief public address in front of the Capitol Building, were being served by the administration? Those of Iran or those of the United States?

Shortly after his address, Wallace returned to his office. Thirty minutes later, he received a hand-delivered envelope containing a brief message written in cursive on a plain white sheet of paper.

> Dear Leland,
>
> You're a dead man.
>
> Sincerely,
> Jimmy Finch

Wallace wasn't surprised at the terse message. He went outside to smoke, having upped his habit to two packs a day since the death of Tom Chance. He'd expected threats when he'd decided to make his announcement, and he reasoned that if Jimmy Finch didn't kill him, then someone in The Elect might do it. If either failed, then cigarettes would surely kill him one day in the not-too-distant future. Leland Wallace was quite aware that he was a dead man, but he wasn't going down in history on the side of this Administration.

Chapter Forty-Two
History Repeats itself

EVERYTHING IS CONNECTED.

Jay woke up sweating. He couldn't get Lone Wolf's phrase out of his mind, and stories were now breaking with such rapidity that he felt as if the country had passed into Watergate-style territory. Like Nixon, President Hastings was a severely paranoid man who fed on power, only Hastings had much less of an emotional filter than Nixon. How could he pursue a federal agency that didn't seem to exist? He wasn't sure, but if Lone Wolf wanted him to, then he believed there must be a way. He decided to start dialing major departments in the government and ask to be connected to the Office of Government Inquiry. It was the middle of the night, and maybe some sleepy operator will slip up and connect him to a location that's normally off-limits. It was a shot in the dark.

Using a directory of federal agencies, Patterson dialed the numbers of a hundred agencies, receiving a recording for most that related their normal business hours. He then moved on to larger departments, such as Homeland Security. His request to be connected to the Office of Government Inquiry met with the same response each time: *"I'm sorry, but there's no such agency in our listings."*

He tried the FBI and CIA next and received the same response after calling over two hundred departments. Then he tried the Pentagon, but the results were no different. After two hours, he tried the Departments of Agriculture, Commerce, Defense, Education, Energy, Health and Human Services, Labor, Treasury, and Transportation. It was three o'clock in the morning, and he was starting to get punchy and thought he'd try State before falling back into bed next to Sela. He'd left State for last, since Maxwell Hart ran the department and OGI's presence there would have been too obvious.

He made the same request and was told, "Please hold."

Patterson instantly grew alert. Several minutes elapsed. Had he been disconnected?

No, he heard static on the line every few seconds, as if the call was being transferred. After five minutes, a groggy female voice said, "Yes? Hello? Is anyone there?"

Patterson froze and ended the call. The voice on the other end of the line belonged to Chief of Staff Lucille Raines.

After tossing and turning in his bed until six o'clock, Patterson rose and had Sela drive him to NewzTracker's office to meet John Taylor.

"Good God!" Taylor said. "Lucille Raines is somehow connected to this secret agency—perhaps even The Elect itself?"

"She answered the phone, John."

"Is there any chance that the switchboard operator didn't hear your request correctly?" Taylor asked.

"Anything is possible, John, but what are the odds of my accidentally being connected to Raines?"

Taylor sipped his coffee as he sat in the chair normally occupied by Bobby Thibodaux. He was dressed in jeans and a wrinkled white shirt. "Okay, okay," he said, trying to clear his mind. "This means that the autopsy reports may have been sent to the president's chief of staff."

"Maybe," Patterson said. "We don't know how many people work at the Office of Government Inquiry, but I presume Lucille Raines is high in the department's pecking order."

Bobby Thibodaux entered and silently went about his morning routine of checking NewzTracker's transmission system and all of its various computers.

"This is a smoking gun," Taylor said. "Be careful, Jay. You've uncovered something, but whatever it is you discovered could be very dangerous if Maryanne Mistretta's report is accurate."

"Maybe you should request a face-to-face meeting with Lone Wolf," Sela suggested.

"I've made such a request dozens of times. He doesn't reply, which I take to mean a firm *no*."

"Hey, if anybody's interested," Thibodaux said, settling into the chair that Taylor had relinquished, "I've got some interesting images here. They were recorded overnight, since southeast Africa is seven hours ahead of us."

Patterson, Taylor, and Sela stood behind Thibodaux, who indicated that the trio should watch the third screen on his right.

Two men emerged from a private jet, a Slipstream 7000 manufactured by PB Enterprises, parked on the tarmac of the airstrip near Jumba Ogo.

"Zoom in, Bobby," Patterson ordered with urgency in his voice.

A third figure walked down the three fold-out steps of the aircraft. It was Hamid Abbas Faridoon.

Chapter Forty-Three
Only the Innocent Suffer

TODD HASTINGS WAS ESCORTED INTO THE OVAL OFFICE AND SAT NEXT TO LUCILLE RAINES ON ONE OF THE TWO PARALLEL COUCHES IN FRONT OF THE CHIEF EXECUTIVE'S DESK. His father sat on the opposite couch, legs crossed. Todd looked extremely tired for a man in his mid-twenties, and he had dark circles under his eyes. He wore a suit coat with no tie, and he had blue Nikes on his feet, as if he'd dressed hurriedly and wasn't concerned about his appearance even though he was sitting in the White House.

"Dad, sales of Sailor cigarettes have increased by twenty-four percent over the last six months, but PB has expended nearly every dollar in its advertising budget to do it."

Raines touched Todd on the wrist and said, "You should be proud of your efforts. Your task was not an easy one, given the country's initial reaction to Sailor."

"That's exactly right, son!" President Hastings said, leaning forward. "When sales continue to climb, we'll start to turn a healthy profit again. Your grandfather Percy always told me that an empty coffer should never scare a good businessman. It's incentive!"

Todd remained sullen and pulled his arm away from Raines' reassuring touch. He folded his arms and looked through the windows behind his father's desk. "I could use some help from Savannah and Brad. They haven't done a day of work at PB since you took office, Dad."

The President leaned even closer to his son. "I'm thinking of asking Sedge O'Connell to come aboard, since he's no longer with Marsh & Brennan. He could be a real asset, son, and do some of the heavy lifting."

Raines coughed nervously and sat up straighter. "That would be a risky move, Mr. President."

Hastings appeared nonplussed. "I can't get my son-in-law to work for my company? That's preposterous."

"With all due respect, sir, it's not technically your company anymore. Mr. O'Connell also recently flew to Iran, and he'd be under constant scrutiny and might adversely affect PB's image."

Hastings was unmoved, his face showing displeasure at the resistance he was meeting on what he thought was a straightforward solution to his son's problem. "Life is about risk, and so is politics. Sedge has a shrewd business mind and could be a real asset to the company. *My* company, divestiture be damned! I'm still in charge, regardless of what any paperwork says!"

"I agree with Ms. Raines," Todd said.

The president looked at his son and sighed. "I'm going to bring Sedge on as an advisor. He won't be on the payroll—I'll find a way to compensate him for his efforts—and he'll be answerable to *you*, son, although I'd appreciate it if you would at least listen to any suggestions he might have."

The president's secretary in the outer office chimed the phone on his desk.

"Yes, Vera?" the president said.

"Mr. Jimmy Finch is on the line for you, sir."

Hastings rose. "I've got to take this, so please give me the room, son. And don't worry. Things at PB will be fine with you in charge."

Todd left, and President Hastings turned to Raines. "Lucille, did you put this call on my calendar today?"

"I told Finch that you might have a few minutes, Herbert. You need to keep your base happy, and Finch is no small player. His paramilitary union accounts for forty percent of the Real Right."

Raines exited the Oval Office as Hastings sat behind his broad desk and pushed a button on his phone.

"Jimmy! Good to hear from you! What can I do for you today?"

The president had a good idea what was on the mind of the indomitable Mr. Finch, but for the next five minutes he listened patiently to the militia leader. Finch wanted to increase the frequency of his union's weekend training maneuvers and didn't want the federal government to interfere. He also wanted permission to send convoys through major metropolitan areas. Would the president back him, he asked.

"Of course, Jimmy. You and your weekend soldiers have the right to bear arms. You'll have the backing of the National Guard, which I'm renaming the Loyalty Militia by executive order, meaning loyalty to the country and the Constitution, of course."

Hastings hung up as Raines was escorted back into the office.

"Lunch, Herbert?" she said.

"Of course, my dear. I'll tell Vera to notify the kitchen."

"By the way, Herbert, you never told me if you smoked cigarettes as a young man."

"In my teens and twenties, but when I began my exercise regimen decades ago, I quit. Hell, the damn things kill people."

Chapter Forty-Four
The Elect

SECRETARY HART WAS UNCONCERNED ABOUT MARYANNE MISTRETTA'S ARTICLE NAMING HIM AS THE HEAD OF A SECRET ORGANIZATION CALLED THE ELECT. In point of fact, there were more secret societies in Washington, D.C., than anyone could imagine, and more than a few past presidents, legislators, and cabinet members had belonged to them. Secret societies were nothing new in a town that largely ran on secrecy. Transparency in government was an illusion that candidates talked about from the stump, but Washington was steeped in mystery and always had been. The American public was naïve to think otherwise.

Mistretta, of course, had wanted to drum up a conspiracy theory, and there was nothing new about that either. JFK had allegedly been shot by Cubans, the mafia, the CIA, and a dozen other factions that Hart couldn't remember. And there was still buzz about testing facilities such as Areas 51, 64, and 73, where high-tech aircraft and stealth technology had been developed over the years. Little gray men with big heads? Ridiculous. As far as Hart was concerned, Mistretta could pursue her conspiracy theories all she wanted. It was no secret that he and Hastings had attended the Christian Academy of Virginia and that both men held ultra-conservative views. If Mistretta wanted to dress up the obvious with a bit of cloak and dagger, then let her have at it. She was no more than a fly buzzing about, a minor nuisance that would eventually go away and be forgotten.

Chapter Forty-Five

A First Lady Who Can't be Bought

Diane Hastings sat in a room of the Renewed Springs Center, a rehab facility outside Oakton, Virginia. The three buildings of the center, where rooms cost ten thousand dollars a day, were nestled among trees that made it invisible from the road a half-mile away. The doctors had reduced her daily dosage of benzodiazepines, which was ironic since the First Lady had not been taking any tranquilizers or sleeping pills when her husband whisked her off in the dead of night to receive treatment for a nonexistent addiction. She took the few pills given her, pushed them to the side of her mouth with her tongue, and then spit them out and flushed them down the toilet when the nurse left.

She'd been a fool to marry Herbert Hastings, but he'd been a rich and powerful man who'd swept her off her feet and flown her to brunch in London and dinner in Paris on the same day when their courtship began. It was only after several months of their intense relationship that she noticed that her soon-to-be husband was paranoid and seemed to take offense at seemingly innocuous remarks. She'd dismissed the behavior as something to be expected from a CEO who was constantly criticized. His temper had also concerned her, but reporters were always pushing microphones in his face and asking him questions about PB Enterprises. They'd had no respect for his privacy. Only later did she learn that Hastings was suffering from a mental disorder, the name of which she'd been unaware of until watching Jay Patterson's interview with Dr. Boyce Rittner. She'd been battered for years and now understood that her husband was a cowardly abuser who took out his own insecurities on his wife.

The First Lady's personal secretary, Audrey Dickerson, entered the suite. Dickerson was slender and, with Cherokee ancestry, had high cheekbones, dark skin, black hair, and almond-shaped eyes. She occupied an adjoining room at the center. She and the First Lady had been friends when Blair lived abroad, and had been the logical choice for a personal assistant.

"Is there anything I can do for you, ma'am?" Dickerson asked.

"Did you have the Brothel Tape delivered to Jay Patterson?" the First Lady asked.

"Yes."

"Did he post it to NewzTracker?"

"Yes, ma'am. It didn't gain much traction. It was, after all, eleven years old."

"I'm not worried. I'll have other surprises for Herbert in the future."

"Yes, ma'am."

Mrs. Hastings appeared exasperated.

"Audrey, when we're alone, you can call me Diane. *Ma'am* is protocol when we're around others, but not behind closed doors."

"I know, Diane. It's just that I'm worried I'll make a slip in public."

"Don't worry about it. You know, Audrey, that Herbert underestimates me. He doesn't know that I have ways of compromising his image as well as his Presidency."

"I've been wondering when you're going to make your move."

Diane Hastings smiled.

"When the time is right, Audrey. When the time is right."

Chapter Forty-Six
Run a Diversion

For the sake of safety, Patterson and Sela had moved to a house in the Virginia countryside owned by John Taylor. In his mind, Patterson went over recent events, while Sela talked with a colleague at SETI.

"Penny for your thoughts?" Sela said when she'd completed her call. She was worried about Jay. She knew he wouldn't tell her to what extent he was concerned about his safety. But all she could think about was any possibility that Jay could be killed like the other three through triggering of the chip embedded in his arm even though she had successfully converted his patch to a previous version than the new chip nanotech version that had triggered the murder of now-three victims? But the psychiatrist didn't have a chip in his arm and we didn't write into the text that he was forced to have one inserted. Do you want me to? The thought still terrorized her.

"I'm on overload," Patterson said. "Hastings is breaking every political rule in the book and thumbing his nose at the country, the press, and Congress. It's like playing whack-a-mole. Every time I start to pursue a lead, another one pops up. I think Hastings enjoys screwing with people's heads."

"That's what Rittner was getting at," Sela observed. "Hastings craves attention at any cost, and the cost is chaos. Borderlines don't have to plan how to create chaos. Chaos happens as a result of Hastings' craving to be the center of attention, and his paranoia."

"True, but I feel like my job is similar to yours."

"In what way?" Sela saw no parallel between their occupations.

"You're looking for a single signal while searching through endless numbers of stars. Me? I'm searching for a common thread among myriad details that don't appear to be connected, at least on the surface."

"What does your gut tell you?"

"That I have to connect the dots I have, starting with the murders. That should grab people's attention in a big way, and after that I'll capitalize on people's attention on homicide in order to work the Iran angle of the story. Like a football play, I'm going to use misdirection. While everyone's looking left, I'm going to run right and see where I can break through the opposition when they least expect it."

Sela looked admiringly at Patterson and kissed him on the lips. "If anyone can make sense of all this, it's you." She winked. "Besides, I'm praying for you. Prayer is pretty powerful. It's mankind's greatest underused resource."

"I'm agnostic, if you recall. I believe in the Atlanta Falcons."

"We'll see if you still are when you figure out the political puzzle of the decade. As Hamlet said, *There are more things in heaven and earth, Horatio, than are dreamt of in your philosophy*."

Patterson shook his head and laughed. "Now you're throwing in Shakespeare to make me a believer."

Sela patted him on the chest. "I can't make you into anything. It's above my pay grade. Free will rules."

"Oh, in that case . . ." He pulls her down to sit on his lap . . . "I am just exercising my free will. Now let's see whose will is stronger?"

/

Patterson worked on his article for two hours. The headline was the most provocative he'd written in a long time: WAS TOM CHANCE MURDERED?

In the body of the article, Patterson started with the obvious.

Chance and Rampling had died suddenly from arrhythmias brought on by ventricular tachycardia, and both mysteriously had their chip implants removed from their arms. Chance had been a vocal critic of the president, while Rampling had been in possession of a file on President Hastings, a fact borne out by Dr. Boyce Rittner before his alleged suicide even though his handwritten suicide note contradicted his strong feelings against the president. Moreover, he said new chips had the capability of releasing nanobots into the bloodstream, small biological mechanisms that could cure or kill. In short, he concluded that there were two explained deaths and one unexplained death whose only commonality was the administration of President Herbert Hastings.

Patterson heard quickly from John Taylor after sending the article to NewzTracker.

"I'm afraid I'm going to have to block this one, Jay. It's too incendiary."

"The article doesn't allege fact," Patterson countered. "It only poses a question, which is followed by irrefutable details."

There was silence on the other end of the call.

"This is going to cause a shit storm," Taylor warned. "You may not come out and say it, but you're very close to accusing the President of the United States of murder."

"No, I said that the Hastings' administration is the only thing all three of the deceased have in common."

"But you're—"

"Look, John, I did your Brothel Tape story, and I'm calling in a marker. We can't bury three deaths that can only be explained by homicide. In the good old days of journalism, this story would have already hit the newsstands. If we run this, the bodies will undoubtedly be exhumed, and there will be an analysis of what was in their bloodstreams. If I'm wrong about this, I'll hand in my resignation."

Taylor was silent for over a minute. "Very well, Jay. But I pray that you're right, or lawyers will be calling me in short order."

"Don't worry, John. Sela says she's praying for us both."

The connection was suddenly terminated. "I don't think John believes in God, either," Patterson said as he turned to Sela. "By the way, what have your colleagues told you about the signals from Tau Ceti?"

"They've resumed, and not only are prime numbers being broadcast from a distance of twelve light years, but they're now being received every ninety minutes. There's someone out there, someone intelligent."

"I'd sure like to believe that."

Chapter Forty-Seven

I'm a Borderline? What's a Borderline?

"HOW IN THE HELL DID ANYONE FIND OUT I SAW RAMPLING?" PRESIDENT HASTINGS BELLOWED WHILE LEANING AGAINST THE EDGE OF HIS DESK. The Oval Office was in shambles. Bronze statues had been hurled across the room, gouging plaster from the gently curving walls. Stately pictures and portraits hung crookedly or lay on the floor. Sofa cushions first stabbed with scissors had been tossed across the room, and bookshelves had been cleared of their contents in one fell swoop of Hastings' fury.

"I've checked with senior staff," Wolcott replied, "and no one seems to know."

"That's not an answer, goddammit!"

"Was the First Lady aware of your visits to Dr. Rampling?" Raines asked.

"No! It had to be that snooping asshole Jay Patterson!" Hastings said, the veins in his temples pulsing with anger. His fists were clenched into tight balls, as if he wanted to fight. Wolcott and Raines stood ten feet away, not far from the entry to the office.

"What was in the file, Mr. President?" Wolcott queried.

Hastings banged his fist down on the edge of his desk, sending several files skittering across the floor. "How the hell do *I* know? Doctors never show what they're writing in your file. I went to see Rampling because I was having trouble sleeping and needed some pills. PB was taking a nosedive, and I was under a lot of stress. We were losing a million dollars a week. But Rampling wouldn't just write out a prescription. No, she wanted to explore my anxiety, and, like all shrinks, talk about my childhood and my parents."

"Did Dr. Rampling ever diagnose you with borderline personality disorder?" Raines asked.

"No! She said my stress came from . . . well, I don't recall the exact words she used. Mood instability, I think. The bitch also said I was paranoid. Said I didn't want to take responsibility for my own actions, which is what *all* psychiatrists tell their patients. Was I moody or paranoid? Hell yes, but I was running the largest tobacco company in the country, and I was taking flak from every side. I sure as hell *was* moody, for God's sake!"

"I'll tell the press that you consulted with Dr. Rampling about a sleep disorder," Wolcott said in an even voice. "It's the best damage control we can muster at present."

"People are calling me a murderer, David."

"Give us the room," Raines said to her colleague. Wolcott left as Raines approached the distraught Hastings, who was pacing back and forth in front of his desk, clenching and unclenching his fists.

"Herbert, this will all blow over. Your base remains loyal, and no one is going to believe that the President of the United States is a murderer. Stop and take a deep breath. You've got to compose yourself."

Hastings stopped in his tracks and inhaled deeply, his muscular chest thrust forward against his crisp white shirt and expensive silk tie.

"I am invincible, am I not!"

"You are, love, and always will be. You're Julius and Augustus and Tiberius. You are the personification of power. No one can take that away from you."

The president stood straight and smiled at his chief of staff.

"What would I do without you, Lucille? You're my anchor and guiding star." He embraced her and held her tightly for several seconds. The two then kissed passionately, Hastings' hands sweeping across the back of Raines' blue silk blouse. "I love you, Lucille."

Raines backed away and smiled as she gazed into his eyes. "I'll ask housekeeping to clean up the office.

I'll say that the door blew open during last night's thunderstorm and that items were scattered about."

"You think of everything," the president remarked.

Raines smiled. "That's very true. Everything."

Chapter Forty-Eight
The One Apple That Fell Far from the Tree

PATTERSON AND SELA HAD PURCHASED NEW PHONES USING CASH SO THAT THE SALES TRANSACTION WOULD NOT HAVE TO BE PROCESSED BY THEIR CHIP IMPLANTS. They used fake IDs and registered the new computers under the names of Gail Gunderson and P.W. James.

"This should help camouflage us a little longer," Sela noted.

At Taylor's house in Virginia, the first thing Patterson did was look up Todd Hastings.

"This guy looks awful, Sela. He's only twenty-six, but he looks forty. Looks like he hasn't slept in days."

"And your point is?"

"Brad and Savannah are AWOL, so that leaves this poor sap in the driver's seat at PB. I think the pressure is getting to him. He could use a shoulder to cry on—in the form of female companionship, that is."

"Oh, no, Jay. I'm not going to hang out with the dude."

"Well, I can't very well walk up to him and start asking questions. I'm on the White House shit list. Just send him an email and ask if you can speak with him. Although be sure to attach a glamorous picture of yourself as bait. Tell him you're a freelancer and that you're doing a piece on the health benefits of Sailor cigarettes. They seem to be gaining some popularity, and I doubt that Todd would turn down an opportunity for some good PR. If he's hurting as badly as I think, he'd accept an invitation from a beautiful young woman in a heartbeat."

"An intelligent species circling Tau Ceti is trying to talk with us, and you're willing to farm me out to a son of the president who peddles vegetable cigarettes."

"Please? But then again, if he so much as touches you . . ."

"Ah . . . well, that should have been spoken a little sooner. Seems to me you're all to willing to use my expertise.

"Yes, when I think about what I just said. There's so much at stake, damn it! I'm sorry. I'm not yet used to having you with me long enough that I can separate myself as a reporter from myself who loves you, Sela. But if he touches you or tries to compromise you in any way, another old football play comes to mind and he'll be out of commission for a long time."

Sela ran her fingers through her hair. "The things I do for love," she said. "What am I expecting to hear from young Mr. Hastings?"

"Anything he wants to tell you."

Todd agreed to meet with Sela in the early afternoon. She caught a shuttle to Charlotte and approached the young Hastings at an outside café. He smiled when he saw her and waved her past his security detail.

"Thank you for seeing me on such short notice," Sela said. "I'm Gail Gunderson. I do freelance work and thought you might have an interesting story."

"Because I'm the president's son, no doubt. Are you a stringer with the *Charlotte Times*?"

"No, and if you have any hesitation about talking to me, please let me know."

Todd Hastings looked down in the mouth. He wasn't dressed like an executive, and he reminded Sela of a boy who'd just lost his puppy.

"No, I'm happy to talk with you, Ms. Gunderson. Maybe some honest press about PB Enterprises would help right now."

"How does it feel to be running such a large outfit like PB?" Sela asked.

"Technically, Brad and Savannah are in charge, but they're . . . ." Todd paused, choosing his words carefully. "They're busy with other matters. Sedge O'Connell is being brought in to see to the day-to-day running of the company." Todd had a faraway look in his eye as he watched pedestrians on the other side of the street while he spoke. "O'Connell was a lobbyist, not a businessman. His former firm worked for Big Pharma as well as companies that manufacture food additives. You know, all those complicated chemical names printed on the side of boxed and canned foods." Todd suddenly refocused his gaze and looked at Sela. "Gee, I'm sorry, Ms. Gunderson. I must be boring you."

"Don't worry about it. And call me Gail. I hear that PB is doing business with Beryllium Alloys."

"Beryllium makes parts we use in our new Slipstream 7000 private jet. It's a beauty. Perhaps you'd like a ride in one sometime."

"Perhaps."

"I've put in a lot of work on expanding PB's portfolio, but my main task has been to make Sailor cigarettes—that's our new nicotine-free brand—more palatable and therefore more competitive. It was a lot more challenging than overseeing routine buys from Beryllium Alloys, or monitoring the new lines of PB clothing, herbal teas, and jewelry that Savannah and Brad are selling."

"They've met with Hamid Abbas Faridoon, haven't they? Caused quite a fuss, from what I've read."

Todd rolled his eyes. "Faridoon? Yes, but I wish they'd stay away from him. Faridoon was a silent partner in PB Enterprises years ago, but he got out when cigarette sales started plummeting. I'd prefer not to talk about Faridoon, if you don't mind. Or my father. I'm not a politician."

"Then tell me about Sailor cigarettes," Sela said, leaning forward to demonstrate her interest in the product. "I don't smoke, so I'm afraid I'm at a disadvantage."

"Sailor is starting to take off. The tobacco plant is a member of the *solanaceae* family of botanicals. Some of these plants are well known, like tomatoes, potatoes, and other vegetables. Some are deadly, like belladonna and mandrake root, which contain alkaloid poisons. Some even have nicotine, just like tobacco. But many in the family that *don't* have nicotine are genetically similar to tobacco. Our chemists refined Sailor so that the leaves we now use in the cigarette have a high genetic compatibility with tobacco, and the higher the genetic similarities, the closer we get to the taste of real tobacco. That's why Sailor has enjoyed increased sales recently."

"And it's safe?"

"Completely. Nothing in the cigarette stimulates any neurotransmitter in the brain the way tobacco does, like dopamine or acetylcholine."

"May I quote you?"

"Sure, since I'm not telling you about our proprietary blend of leaves that enhances the flavor of our product."

The two chatted about what Todd called the new era of safe cigarettes. He also said that PB Enterprises would reclaim the greatness achieved by his grandfather, Percy Beauregard Hastings.

"That's quite a story," Sela said. "Thanks for your time."

"Uh, would you like to meet again?" Todd asked. "Maybe for drinks or dinner?"

"Gee, I've got a boyfriend, Todd, but otherwise I'd jump at the chance."

Todd Hastings looked crestfallen. "It was nice meeting you. Call anytime."

Sela smiled and left. She didn't believe that she'd obtained any useful information, but maybe her impression that PB didn't seem to be involved in any kind of illegal activity would be valuable in its own right. Jay would be the judge of that.

Chapter Forty-Nine
The Emperor Has No Clothes On

HERBERT CHASE HASTINGS WAS ALONE IN THE MASTER BEDROOM ON THE SECOND FLOOR OF THE WHITE HOUSE RESIDENCE. His wife was across the hall, and for the first time in their marriage she looked angry rather than scared, a sign that she was standing up to him. Had he lost control over her? Would she dare divorce him while he was a sitting President? It would be a disgrace and impugn his manhood.

He opened the door of the walk-in closet to his left and looked at himself in the full-length mirror. He was dressed impeccably, and he smoothed the fringe of hair encircling his bald head—his Roman garland befitting an emperor. But he quickly withdrew his hand and took a step back.

"Everyone's lying about us," he said to his reflection, his tone fearful. "Reporters make up stories and spread them to the entire country. They're all lies. What's happened to us?"

Hastings' body began to tremble. Maybe it was more than Diane he'd lost. Maybe the entire country was losing faith in his leadership. But how could that happen? He'd worked his way up the ladder, learning the tobacco industry by walking through the fields and inspecting the plants with his father's crop manager. And he'd learned the business side of PB, pouring over spreadsheets for hours at a time and sitting in on board meetings conducted by Percy, the old war horse who claimed that power was the only thing worth attaining in life.

"We have enemies," Hastings said. "Some even want us to resign. What do we do?"

Tears rolled down his cheeks as he lowered his head and sobbed.

"This is our administration, our kingdom. We're their lord, their good shepherd, and yet they wish to crucify us."

His reflection didn't answer.

Hastings' eyes glazed over as he stared again into the mirror. He was lightheaded, but in a pleasant kind of way. He felt as if he might float right off the floor. The image staring back at him from the glass wore a toga and garland of oak leaves. He, Herbert Chase Hastings, was Emperor of the United States of America. He could do anything he wanted. He had legions of soldiers who would follow him—his Red Roman Legion. They were voters and weekend warriors and red-meat Republicans. They were the Real Right, and they would follow his dictates. He was afraid of no one.

He closed the closet door and pounded his right fist into the palm of his left hand. Yes, it's true. How could he have doubted. He felt more empowered than ever. He would lead, and the nation would follow him. Those who didn't would pay a heavy price.

Chapter Fifty
Macbeth Doth Murder Sleep

PATTERSON MET COOKIE MCKNIGHT AT THE SMITHSONIAN AIR AND SPACE MUSEUM. They strolled through the Human Spaceflight exhibit, space capsules from the Mercury, Gemini, and Apollo programs suspended above them. Large panels on the walls showed photographs of the capsules when they had drifted through the darkness of space in the 1960s and when the Lunar Excursion Module had landed on the moon in 1969.

"Cookie, I've got to find out what Brad and Savannah are talking about with Faridoon. I've reached a dead end. I can't talk to the children—no journalist can—because they're too insulated, and I doubt they'd have anything truthful to say even if I could get an interview. Do you have any idea at all what this Iran connection might mean?"

"I'm afraid not, Jay. The entire West Wing is in damage control mode since Hastings' Presidency is one catastrophe after another except to the Real Right." McKnight paused and smiled. "Which makes this an opportune moment to find the answers you're looking for."

"What do you mean?"

"A lot of the staff are secretly against Hastings because they feel he's making them look bad, but they're too frightened to resign. There's one staffer in particular who has it in for Hastings, although I can't name names. I have reason to believe that the staffer is building a case against Hastings and may eventually go public."

The pair had arrived at the Space Shuttle *Discovery*, which they circled as they spoke.

"But who knows when this person might release any damning information he or she might have?"

Patterson asked. "It may not come out for months or years, if at all."

"If I can gain access to the individual's files for a few minutes, I could see if there's one on Faridoon and copy it."

"I'd appreciate it, Cookie, but don't put yourself in danger."

Cookie pointed at the space shuttle. "That's danger, Jay. Me? I'm a staffer. What's the worst that could happen? I get fired."

Patterson shook his head. "I'm afraid a lot worse could befall you, Cookie. A lot worse."

McKnight said nothing. She knew that someone had tried to run over Patterson near NewzTracker headquarters.

"A point well-taken. I'll be careful."

/

Cookie McKnight walked through the halls of the West Wing. It was late at night, and a few lights were still on in some of the offices that gave the executive branch its lifeblood. But the hum of activity was far below the frenetic pace that was usual for the wing. McKnight walked slowly towards the door of the staffer she believed was growing more disillusioned with the president by the day. A desk lamp spilled yellow light into the hall as she walked past the doorway, glancing to her left. The office was empty.

McKnight walked to the end of the hall, intending to turn around and retrace her steps. She had a thumb drive in her pocket that would hopefully copy a file about the Hastings family's connection to Faridoon. Before she could turn, however, two hands grasped her by the shoulder and spun her around. It was the president. Her breath suspended in her chest, her heart raced as Hastings looked into her eyes, his face just inches from her own.

"You're here very late," the president whispered.

"Yes, Mr. President."

"And what exactly are you doing?"

"I was working on your speech on healthcare reform." Cookie swallowed hard. She had never seen such a wild-eyed expression on the chief executive's face.

The president turned his head slightly and grinned, his hands still firmly grasping his speechwriter's shoulders. "You're looking for leaks, aren't you?"

"Well, I was just—"

"Tell me the truth," the president said, shaking McKnight hard.

"Yes, sir," she lied. "I was."

The President exhaled, his breath assailing his captive's nostrils. McKnight realized that he'd been drinking, although he wasn't drunk

"Good. I was looking for leaks, too. There are too many of them, Cookie. There are people who want to bring us down, but we can't let that happen, can we?"

"No, sir."

"If you find anything, let me know."

Hastings released his employee and walked away slowly. He was dressed in a gray suit, but McKnight had never seen the President behave so strangely. She didn't know if he was sleepwalking or had suffered a psychotic break. She hurried from the West Wing, fearing another meeting with the president.

She called Jay from her car and told him of the strange encounter with Hastings and that she hadn't been able to retrieve any file.

"He reminded me of Macbeth roaming Inverness Castle, touched and perhaps mad," McKnight said.

"*Macbeth doth murder sleep,*" Patterson said, repeating the famous line of Shakespeare's play. "Macbeth wandered around in a daze after murdering King Duncan. Perhaps Hastings is more than just a borderline. We have three unsolved murders, and I wouldn't put anything past him. Thanks, Cookie. Don't worry about the file for now."

McKnight thought she detected disappointment in Patterson's voice, but she'd done all she could. She drove home, shaken by what had transpired. Could the president really be a murderer? Jay Patterson seemed to think it might be a possibility. She did as well.

Chapter Fifty-One
Negotiations with an Enemy Nation?

PATTERSON'S DISAPPOINTMENT DIDN'T LAST LONG. He turned on the wall screen in the living room of John Taylor's Virginia home and saw that the major networks were broadcasting a conversation between Faridoon and the Hastings children. It had been what Cookie was looking for, only Beau Bricker had obviously beaten her to the punch. The recording was audio only and was brief, but the content was magnetic.

> **Bradley Hastings**: How far have operations progressed?
> **Faridoon**: The first stage is nearly complete.
> **Savannah Hastings**: And the next stage?
> **Faridoon**: We're close. Very close.
> **Bradley Hastings**: Are you going to be able to go the distance?
> **Faridoon**: As promised. The country will be . . . [static] . . . storm . . . [static] . . . and rivals . . . [static] . . . decimated.

The recording lasted no more than fifteen seconds, but it was enough to make Patterson's mind race as it searched for possible interpretations. Were

Faridoon and the Hastings siblings talking about nuclear weapons? Were they referring to the stages of a ballistic missile that could go the distance that could reach Tel Aviv, Islamabad, or New York? Was a nuclear attack the operation which the parties had discussed?

The snippet of voices was unsettling, and Patterson turned off the wall screen after listening to commentaries by political and military analysts. Perhaps he'd been right—Beryllium Alloys was supplying parts for a nuclear weapon, and the Hastings administration was somehow complicit.

Patterson thought of his conversation with Cookie McKnight moments earlier.

Macbeth doth murder sleep. Why was Hastings wandering the White House in a daze? What had the man done to make him into the zombie-like form Cookie McKnight had encountered? Was he preparing to start a nuclear holocaust across the face of the earth?

It's what Dr. Boyce Rittner had predicted.

Chapter Fifty-Two
Gone Rogue

HASTINGS AWOKE THE FOLLOWING MORNING FEELING TIRED AND LETHARGIC. He'd had bad dreams during the night, dreams that he'd been sitting in the imperial Roman throne chair when thousands of angry citizens rushed him, seeking to depose him. Insults and accusations had been hurled his way, but he realized that these mercurial images had been dreams, nothing more. He nevertheless called his secretary and asked her to summon the vice president to the White House. He needed the reassurance that only the calm and measured Cal Quint could deliver.

Before beginning his daily schedule, the president sat down to breakfast alone, since his wife no longer shared meals with her husband. Using a remote, he switched on a wall screen as he ate so that he could see what new lies had been published about him overnight. The lead story caused him to drop the spoon carrying blueberry yogurt to his mouth.

The anchor of ABN was announcing the resignation of Secretary of Defense Daniel Montgomery, who had made a public statement early that morning calling the president an idiot who was unfit to be commander in chief. A decorated Iraq War veteran and former Nebraska Senator, Montgomery said that the president rarely consulted him on foreign policy and didn't appear to be interested in the deployment of American troops. He could no longer serve in an administration, he said, over which a dark cloud hung, especially when it came to secret talks with Iran, about which he had not been informed.

"Whether Brad and Savannah Hastings are talking about jewelry or jets or nuclear proliferation, they have no business negotiating with Hamid Abbas Faridoon or the Government of Iran," Montgomery asserted. "As much as I'd love to protect this country from the acts of a madman, I can't do so if the president is going to engage in tobacco diplomacy. If the president and his family couldn't run PB family Enterprises successfully, how can he deal with foreign governments?"

President Hastings stood and screamed. "Where is Cal Quint, for God's sake? Get him into the Oval Office as soon as possible!" "Goddammit!" Hastings yelled, sweeping his breakfast dishes onto the floor.

"They're calling me a murderer, Cal. They say I'm mentally ill." Hastings sat behind his desk in the Oval Office and drummed his fingers on the hardwood surface before him. "And this whole Iran thing! PB is making jets and selling them to businessmen like Faridoon. Case closed. All this is bad enough, but now Montgomery is resigning and calling me an idiot in front of the entire nation. You know Washington better than anyone in my administration, Cal. You go on the Sunday morning talk shows and defend my honor—and don't think I'm not grateful."

Cal Quint sat facing the president. He crossed his legs and appeared, as always, outwardly calm. People said that if you were trapped in a burning building, Quint was the person you'd want by your side. He would find a way to safety without showing the slightest hint of panic. People evaluated him in the same way when it came to politics. He was unflappable and always managed to weather uncomfortable questions and situations, coming out on the other side as a statesman who was never tarnished by scandal. He was well-liked, and people thought he was the kind of gracious man that every public servant should be. People said that he carried a smile in his pocket.

"What kind of damage control should we do?" Hastings asked.

"None," Quint said. "Don't respond to the deaths of Chance and Rampling, or to allegations that you have borderline personality disorder. Same for Iran. No comment on down the line. Let the news cycles play out. People have short memories."

"But Montgomery's resignation makes me look bad, Cal."

"I agree, Mr. President, but you should simply make a public statement thanking him for his service to the country, and express regret that the two of you have come to a parting of the ways."

Hastings shook his head. "I can't stonewall *everything*. I've got to be proactive."

"True, which is why you're going to change the news cycle entirely."

Hastings knit his brows and leaned forward. "I'm listening."

Quint exhibited a troubled look on his face. He folded his arms and took a deep breath, frown lines wrinkling his always-tanned forehead. "What if I told you that a small group of Sunnis have indeed formed a terrorist cell in Western Pakistan and are sneaking back into Iran and threatening to blow up the country's nuclear facilities on the Gulf of Oman with a suitcase bomb? Iran may be our enemy, but if radical Sunnis want to detonate a nuclear device, it threatens the entire region and possibly the world. Steering currents could carry radioactive fallout across the oceans."

"I get the same briefings as you every morning, Cal. Have I missed something?"

"Possibly. The conflict between Sunnis and Shias has always been tense. I'm just saying . . . what if I told you that this were the case?"

"It would give me the leverage I need to put Pakistan on notice that they have to control radicals and terrorists within their borders in order to prevent a nuclear nightmare."

Quint's tense facial expression relaxed. "Exactly, Mr. President."

"Are you saying that I should again threaten to bomb Pakistan?"

"Whoa, there," Quint said. "First you issue a severe warning to Pakistan, mentioning surgical airstrikes might be used to take out the terrorist cells if Pakistan chooses to ignore the problem. If they refuse to heed your warning, however, then you may have to change your rhetoric."

"Lucille told me I had to walk back my threats against Pakistan."

Quint tilted his head and raised his eyebrows. "Tactical situations change, sir. That's why intelligence briefings are issued daily. No one is saying that we're going to nuke anybody, but the United States can't allow terrorists to threaten global security. You can also say that you don't believe that Iran can handle the threat on its own, given the religious infighting that has existed between Sunnis and Shias for generations."

Hastings nodded. "Plus people won't think I'm giving Iran any kind of preferential treatment."

Vice President Quint smiled. "You'll change the topic of conversation in the country, which is what you need now that Montgomery has thrown you under the bus."

Hastings looked frustrated. "Cal, DePeche tried to explain the chain of command to me regarding military operations and nuclear strikes, but I confess that I still don't understand it all."

"Not to worry, sir. Major military operations go from you through the secretary of defense, down to commanders with the Unified Combatant Command, sometimes known as the Combatant Commanders in the Field, such as CENTCOM or PACCOM. When it comes to the question of a nuclear strike, you confer with the secretary of defense. If he disagrees with you, you can fire him and then appeal to the deputy secretary of defense, and then on down the chain of command at Defense—the secretary of the Army, the secretary of the Navy, the secretary of the Air Force, and so forth. It's a court martial offense for them to disobey military orders from the commander in chief. Sooner or later, you'd find a junior officer to obey your orders, but I'd always like you to confer with me first on military action of any kind. You should never explore the nuclear option except in case of dire and irrevocable circumstances."

Hastings nodded.

"Sir, did you understand my last statement? Once you give the command to launch a nuclear missile, it can be almost impossible to reverse the decision."

"Yes, Cal. Almost impossible. But the Pakistan scenario . . . it almost sounds too good to be true. Will this really do the trick?"

"I'm only saying, Mr. President . . . what if I were to tell you about an active terror cell in Pakistan?" He paused. "What if?"

"Cal, you've put my mind at ease. Damn everything that Patterson, Mistretta, Bricker, and the rest of the liars are saying. We're going to take the bull by the horns."

"Something I did quite literally many times in my youth, Mr. President. The trick is not to be afraid of the bull. You have to let him know who's boss when you get in the ring. You're head of the rodeo, sir. I suggest you do the same."

After Quint left the Oval Office, Hastings sat motionless. He felt on top of the world, and laughed out loud. Had he ever *not* been in charge of everything? No, there was nothing to worry about. He was still the emperor—Augustus, Julius, and Tiberius. No one would wrestle power from his grasp.

/

The president recorded a VOXPOP that simply said, "Pakistan, you'd better watch out. Might makes right." The upload caused a furor among legislators and diplomats, demanding to know what the president was talking about. He seemed to be contradicting his earlier retraction that no action was being contemplated against Pakistan. After conferring with the president and vice president, Lucille Raines decided that Press Secretary Wolcott should issue a statement in the press briefing room.

Wolcott explained that a well-organized group of Sunni terrorists was operating out of Jiwani, west of the port of Gwadar, and that it was suspected they were targeting an Iranian nuclear facility just across the border. A carrier group had been sent to the Gulf of Oman since the president, who would monitor the situation closely, would not allow terrorists to threaten any nuclear facility because of religious infighting. Wolcott said that no nuclear strike was being contemplated, although, he added, all options were always on the table for the commander in chief.

/

Secretary of State Hart was livid.

"Does Hastings just make this shit up?" he asked the deputy secretary, who had been hastily summoned. "I have no knowledge of any kind of Sunni terrorist organization in Western Pakistan. Who the hell is in charge at Defense now that Montgomery is gone?"

"Deputy Secretary Newman. I've already spoken with him. He signed off on the carrier group pretty fast. He's always been a hawk, and said that the movement of ships to the Gulf was merely a show of force."

Hart closed his eyes and rubbed his face with both hands. "Montgomery had the right idea in leaving, but I'm not the kind to resign. Hastings could start a nuclear conflagration within twenty-four hours."

Five minutes later, Hart spoke with the Chairman of the Joint Chiefs of Staff, General William Sutherland.

"Maxwell, he's gone rogue," Sutherland said. "We asked the president to show us the intelligence behind his order to send a carrier group to the Gulf of Oman. He said he was the commander in chief and didn't have to justify his orders with me. Technically, he's right. As you know, the Joint Chiefs' is an advisory board. We can't order missile strikes, send troops into battle, or cause a single rifle shot to be fired. Although Hastings is the first president I know of not to consult the Joint Chiefs on something this big. Like me, I'm betting you haven't seen any intel either."

"No, Will. I haven't. Apparently no one has."

"Maybe it's time to act. I met with the other Joint Chiefs, and they're ready to speak with the Combatant Commanders in the Field to see if they're willing to defy a direct order from the SOB."

There was a long pause on the line before Hart voiced his opinion. "Not just yet, Will. That would technically be treason."

"Not if he's unfit."

Hart sighed deeply. "I've discussed this with Quint on more than one occasion, since he would have to relieve the president by invoking the Twenty-fifth Amendment. He doesn't want to go down that road, given the popularity that Hastings still enjoys among his base and the Real Right. Given the situation that's brewing, however, I think we have to keep all options open. If Hastings gives the orders for an airstrike—or worse—I want you to be ready to speak on a moment's notice with the combatant commanders. Whatever decision Hastings makes, it currently has to go through the deputy secretary of defense or, in the case of a nuclear strike, the National Military Command Center at the Pentagon. If he decides one way or the other, call me. If he enters the White House Situation Room, I want the duty officer to alert me."

"Understood, Max."

Hart settled back in his chair after the call and looked at a row of pictures on his wall, each showing him shaking hands with former presidents. He'd never known anyone like Hastings before. The man had clarity of purpose and a resolve that Hart had always wanted to see in the executive branch of government, but his mind was like a watch spring wound too tightly. It could pop at any moment and cause the hands to go spinning around madly. He still hoped that Hastings might remain in office so the government might be cleansed of undesirable elements and returned to the purity of intention—the elegant simplicity of governance—conceived by the Founding Fathers. Hart, however, was beginning to think that he might have to cut bait and run. If the time came, he hoped he could convince the fiercely loyal Cal Quint to invoke the Twenty-fifth Amendment. The life of every creature on the planet might depend on it.

Chapter Fifty-Three
Strange Bedfellows

BRAD HASTINGS WAS QUICK TO RESPOND TO THE TAPE OF HIS CONVERSATION WITH FARIDOON. He said that the "operation" referred to was simply supplying various kinds of mechanical parts, to be delivered in "stages," to the PB Aircraft Assembly Plant in Durham, North Carolina. He claimed that he and his sister had discussed how far the Slipstream 7000 could go without refueling—would it be able to go a "distance" of eight thousand miles nonstop?—and that it was an aircraft that would "devastate" the other companies and take the private jet industry by "storm," thus giving rivals such as Lear Jet and Gulf Stream serious competition.

Patterson watched the statement with some degree of consternation. Had his story collapsed? Everything Brad Hastings said made perfect sense and explained the remarks on the tape acquired by Bricker. And there was the conversation between Todd Hastings and Sela to consider. The president would naturally be expected to give his son-in-law, Sedge O'Connell, a role in PB Enterprises after being dismissed from Marsh & Brennan. And if Sailor cigarette sales were improving because the company had tried to imitate the taste of tobacco, then all of the conspiracies floating about came to nothing. There was no "there" there. Perhaps he had been chasing shadows. As Sela had suggested more than once, maybe he was being played by the White House. Maybe Lone Wolf was a close ally of the administration, supplying him with misinformation to make NewzTracker and other media outlets look foolish—to make them into cyber liars—which would effectively feed right into the ongoing narrative of President Hastings. Even the strange events in Garundi could be explained by the simple theory that sometimes two very different countries become strange bedfellows in order to enhance their mutual, if somewhat different, interests.

And yet Patterson wasn't convinced that the remarks on the tape were innocent allusions to the Slipstream 7000. He had no proof, but Brad and Savannah had altered their travel plans when it was discovered that they'd met with Faridoon, and there were many other companies that could supply PB Enterprises with parts made from beryllium and its alloys. No, Patterson was sticking to his guns. Something was amiss.

He decided to see what else he could find out about Jumba Ogo, and conducted a fresh search on the palace, looking this time into the construction of the mansion. He saw cranes, bulldozers, and backhoes moving mountains of earth and lifting heavy stone blocks into place. He zoomed in for a closer look at the construction equipment and noted that the writing on all of the heavy machinery was in Farsi, the language of modern Iran. He sent a copy of the images to a staffer at NewzTracker, requesting a translation of the linguistic symbols.

The reply was illuminating. The Farsi indicated that the equipment was owned by the Tehran-based National Iranian Construction and Development Company. Patterson had expected the company to be another subsidiary of Hamid Abbas Faridoon, but it was state-owned.

Later pictures of palace construction during the years after Papa Makela had been overthrown, showed Jumba Ogo near completion. The workers were clearly Middle Eastern. Shots of the dedication showed Felix Ogo standing in the center of a dozen Iranian businessmen. The group was assembled in what appeared to be one of the lush gardens of the palace. To the immediate right of Ogo were Mahmoud Madani, Iran's Deputy Foreign Minister of State, and President Muhammad Al Assad. A close-up showed Hamid Abbas Faridoon in the background on the far right. This wasn't surprising to Patterson, as the Iranian mafia had not operated independently from the official state government for decades. Only with the blessing of a president and his ministers could the mafia conduct its business, with the government taking a sizeable cut from mafia activities. The implication was clear: Iran had finished the palace for Felix Ogo, who obviously couldn't have afforded to build such a sumptuous residence even with money from blood diamonds or the over-taxation of his people.

Patterson wondered yet again what Iran, Garundi, and Herbert Hastings had in common, and it struck him that, while blood diamonds couldn't have financed a palace costing billions of dollars, the traffic in such conflict gems still represented small fortunes for those who defied resolutions issued by the United Nations Security Council seeking to ensure that diamonds entering the international market had not financed violent rebel movements. The Iranian mafia would not have any hesitation in dealing in blood diamonds, and it was widely known that Hezbollah and other terrorist organizations orchestrated their flow into Europe. Felix Ogo had already used such diamonds to finance his coup. As for President Hastings, a narcissistic and power hungry man whose family tobacco empire had fallen on hard times, he might be expected to line his pockets with money from illegal gems. Indeed, Savannah Hastings had added a line of jewelry to the portfolio of PB Enterprises. Despite efforts to screen diamonds for legitimacy, it was difficult for even seasoned gemologists to certify that a polished, cut gem was illegal.

Patterson sent Bobby Thibodaux a message asking him to look for signs of smuggling, such as armed convoys going into or out of the palace. Diamonds could be hidden in almost any kind of container, large or small, but the telltale signs of diamond smuggling were guards, frequent shipments of various goods, and armed soldiers traveling in caravans of jeeps and trucks. The most Thibodaux could hope to spot would be something out of the ordinary, but the Cajun technician had a keen eye, and not much went unnoticed by a woodsman who liked to hunt, trap, and fish.

Chapter Fifty-Four

A Presidential Order Defied

UNTIL RETIRING A DECADE EARLIER, PROFESSOR JOSHUA ROLLINS WAS A PROFESSOR EMERITUS AT UCLA. He'd grown restless giving guest lectures to people who regarded him as a pop icon because he'd written several books on science and astronomy and had discovered the first exo-planets in the galaxy of Andromeda. Despite his fame and shock of gray hair—he was known as Josh to the general public—he'd longed to do real science again rather than make the late-night talk show circuit. He'd therefore volunteered to work at SETI, which was always looking for talented men and women to augment their staff since funding was spotty from year to year.

Rollins had seen the signal data from Tau Ceti with his own eyes, and he believed that such a message from an extraterrestrial civilization was meant for all mankind, not a single country or a covert element within its government. It was, he thought, the most significant discovery made since *Homo sapiens* had learned how to use fire. The news of intelligence beyond the solar system belonged to the world.

Although SETI and NASA had received instructions from various intelligence agencies not to reveal any data on extraterrestrials or the comet, he hastily assembled a dozen local reporters at his home in Mountain View, California, telling them that he had important scientific news to share. There were two TV cameras among the small gathering, and he stepped onto his driveway and addressed the reporters. What he said shocked the world. His statement, no longer than five minutes, spoke of the Tau Ceti signals and

Comet JM-2026A, which would impact earth in 2044. His words were picked up within a matter of minutes and went viral across the Internet. Scientists gave hasty press conferences, urging world governments to cooperate in finding a way to safely deflect the comet's trajectory using any number of means that had been discussed since the late 1990s. Citizens went out into their streets and backyards that night and gazed into the sky. What awaited them? Doom? Conquest? If the comet could be deflected, maybe the extraterrestrials orbiting Tau Ceti would have the key to world peace or ending cancer.

Many fundamentalist Christians ran through the streets proclaiming the Second Coming and the end of the world. Time had run out for planet Earth. The fulfillment of this biblical prophecy, they said, was only ten years away.

Mankind went to bed that night, unsure of the future and its place in the cosmos. What became obvious to all were two missing icons of current contemporary society on Earth: the Universal Quest for Truth and the human race united in Universal Peace. Patterson was doing his share in searching for truth, and while Sela's work with SETI brought news of a comet threatening a collision with Earth, the news also brought the need for all the countries and people inhabiting Earth to join in unified peace in working together to deflect the comet from Earth. Even the cryptic communication to Earth from Tau Seti brought the hope that communications with another world in the cosmos could possibly benefit humanity in ways humankind can't seem to help itself.

Chapter Fifty-Five
To Hell with Your Constitutional Rights

HERBERT CHASE HASTINGS WAS FURIOUS. How was it that no one had informed the leader of the free world about a comet or extraterrestrials? The answer was quite simple, he reasoned. Nobody trusted him to handle news that affected the entire world. He was an erratic Borderline, and many within his own administration believed he was psychologically unfit to be commander in chief. And while all presidents had their detractors, Grass Roots wasn't just criticizing him. They had the audacity to laugh at him and call him a buffoon.

His first reaction was to take to VOXPOP to accuse the lying press of having nothing better to talk about than little green men landing on the White House lawn in flying saucers, not that any news outlet had run such a story. Lucille Raines told him that he had to make a statement, given the shocking nature of the revelations provided to the press by Rollins. It was his job, she pointed out, to prevent panic in the nation and around the world. She gave him remarks prepared by Bailey McKnight, but Hastings wadded them up and threw them to the floor. "I'll speak from the heart," he told his mistress.

/

Hastings looked out over the briefing room with supreme confidence. "We've all heard the interesting speculations of Professor Joshua Rollins, and let me state unequivocally that the idea of extraterrestrial life is nonsense. Jesus Christ came to save mankind, not some creatures on Mars or circling a star called Tau Ceti. What SETI has discovered are radio signals that are being interpreted as intelligence, but there's an old saying that if you sit a monkey down in front of a typewriter, statistical odds predict that sooner or later he'll type some meaningful sentences. That's what we're dealing with—a statistical anomaly. All we have is a few blips and bleeps on someone's computer. As for the comet, it's nothing more than a Democratic scare tactic to force countries of the world, many of whom are our enemies, to sit down together and, in the long run, reach agreements that go far beyond any defense against a rock that is supposedly hurtling in the direction of Earth. I won't be taken in by their ploy."

Hastings called on a reporter when he'd finished his remarks.

"Mr. President, the signals from Tau Ceti are non-random and are being sent in the form of prime numbers."

"The Bible doesn't mention prime numbers. Next question."

Patterson put up his hand, not expecting to be called on, but the president went straight for his nemesis in the press.

"Well, well, well, if it isn't my friend Jay Patterson, who alleges I'm crazy. What's on your mind, Jay? What kind of lies are you going to write today?"

Patterson ignored the sarcasm. "Sir, NASA released a picture of the comet this morning that clearly shows the image of JM-2026A. NASA is an agency that is part of the executive branch of government," Jay snidely informed the President.

Hastings shook his head with a sarcastic smile. "Jay, your reporting is so bad that were it not entertaining, I would kick you out of here myself, and don't think I'm not man enough to take you on. I've looked at pictures obtained by TINN, and Nick Scarabelli himself assures me that the NASA picture was photoshopped by Democrats working at SETI. I therefore fired the NASA administrator this morning right before this briefing. I've ordered his deputy not to send any signals into space, since I've heard that many scientists wish to reply to the phantom communication. I'll sign an executive order today that will extend this ban to SETI and all Americans, including universities and research facilities."

Patterson threw his hand into the air.

"What is it now, Patterson!"

"If I'm not mistaken, Mr. President, that would be an outright violation of the First Amendment."

"To Hell with your constitutional rights!" To Hell with everyone's constitutional rights!

Hastings paused for dramatic effect after holding up his hands to indicate that he was cutting short any further question and answer time.

"Ladies and gentlemen, the real danger to the world is Pakistan, which is harboring jihadists who seek to gain access to nuclear facilities in Iran. My focus as commander in chief is on these extremists, and I won't take my eye off the ball."

President Hastings abruptly left the room.

"He's taken his populism to galactic proportions," Beau Bricker whispered to Patterson. "Literally."

"Maybe aliens really *do* need to land on the White House lawn and give us an ultimatum," Patterson said. "Either we achieve peace, or there will be hell to pay. Michael Rennie in *The Day the Earth Stood Still*."

"I'd laugh," Bricker retorted, "if it wasn't the truth."

Chapter Fifty-Six
Far Right with Blinders On

SECRETARY MAXWELL HART HAD ENOUGH CLOUT WITH NASA AND THE MILITARY TO BEGIN WORKING ON A SOLUTION TO DEFLECT COMET JM-2026A. The universe had thrown Earth a curve ball, but NASA and private research had been working on numerous ways to deal with earth-crossing asteroids and comets. There was time to formulate a strategy, covertly if necessary, with the help of scientific think tanks and the military.

As for aliens, Hart wasn't interested in whether they existed or not. SETI was a reputable organization, and the signals were probably legitimate, but interstellar space travel was not considered possible by most scientists. No big-headed extraterrestrials would be knocking on the door any time soon—maybe never.

Hart rather liked Hastings' response to the news issued by Josh Rollins. The United States needed to get on with business, and he had a government to downsize and cleanse. This was no time for international outreach or a rousing chorus of "Kumbaya."

Chapter Fifty-Seven

Here a Plant, There a Plant. Everywhere Tobacco Plants

PATTERSON STOOD NEXT TO BOBBY THIBODAUX IN THE NEWZTRACKER TRANSMISSION ROOM.

"I've got good news and bad news," Thibodaux said. "The bad news is that I can't see any suspicious activity in Garundi that would indicate the movement of blood diamonds. We already know that Ogo used such diamonds to finance his coup, but unless you want to fly over there and search through the bushes, you're not going to find much."

Patterson nodded. "I know, Bobby."

"The good news is that I've seen plants driven out of the palace."

"Doesn't sound terribly important."

"Au contraire. What I saw were tobacco plants, my friend."

"Seriously?"

"I kid thee not. I had to zoom in with extreme magnification and then compare what I saw with info on the web, but there can be no doubt. The plants' root balls are tied in burlap sacks, and hundreds of them were conveyed from the palace to the countryside."

"Is Ogo growing the plants in his gardens, perhaps for personal use?"

"I scanned the palace grounds thoroughly. I can't find any tobacco plants in the gardens."

"Bobby, you have to—"

"I know. Keep scanning the countryside and palace. I'm already on it. You think PB is behind it?"

"If it isn't, I'll buy you the entire Abita Brewery. Meanwhile, what else is going on in the world? It's getting hard to keep up."

"Behold," Thibodaux said, motioning to several wall screens he'd activated.

Grass Roots had mobilized in several cities in order to protest the president's stance on the comet and signals from Tau Ceti. Protesters in other cities carried signs demanding that President Hastings submit to a psychiatric evaluation.

Along the southern border, thirty-four Towers of Freedom had been erected, and twenty-six illegal immigrants had been wounded or killed as they tried to enter the country.

Bangladesh had been decimated, but the United States Ambassador to the United Nations stated that the U.S. was declining to participate in humanitarian aid to refugees now settled in nearby countries, a relocation that was creating overpopulation, disease, and crime.

Patterson found all of the images troubling, but those on the last wall screen struck him as the most disturbing because of the bigotry and xenophobia displayed by Jimmy Finch and his Tennessee militia. Finch was standing on a platform, talking to a crowd of two thousand militia sympathizers.

"We stand behind President Hastings!" Finch said through a bullhorn. "I, too, don't believe in alien life in the galaxy, but . . . ." He paused to select his words carefully. "But if they *do* exist, they sure as hell won't look like us or be the same color. They won't be white, red-blooded Americans. If they ever try to land here, we'll shoot 'em on sight."

"I think I'm going to be sick," Patterson said, sitting in a chair adjacent to Thibodaux's.

"You'll get through it, Jay. Get out there and do your job. A free press is the only thing standing between the United States as we once knew it and a police state. Not that I'm putting any pressure on you."

Patterson got up and left the shack. He walked like a man on a mission.

/

Patterson again listened to the brief recording of the conversation between Faridoon and the Hastings' siblings. The operation they spoke of, he realized, might have something to do with growing tobacco in Garundi, and it might well involve the stages of growing the plants, resulting in taking the tobacco market by storm. But in what country? Sailor cigarettes were marginally more popular than they had been, but no one in America was getting addicted to the proprietary blend of leaves used by PB Enterprises. According to Sela, Todd Hastings had been convincing in his assertion that Sailor was truly nicotine-free. Moreover, he didn't seem to be complicit in any kind of wrongdoing and had no connection with Iran or Garundi.

Patterson shook off his misgivings. Felix Ogo was moving tobacco plants around his country, and Patterson felt certain that Hastings and Faridoon were involved with the African dictator. But in what way? A White House cover-up was in progress, and if he could find out what it was, it might be big enough to bring down Herbert Chase Hastings. But if he made a false accusation, his own career would be at an end, and Hastings, a delusional man dangerous to the country under any circumstances, would go unchecked. Everything rode on the next moves he would make. Damn it! Why was the truth eluding him? The latest clue would not leave him alone . . . *Everything is connected!*

Chapter Fifty-Eight
Lung Cancer: A Bygone Age?

LELAND WALLACE WAS SHORT OF BREATH AFTER CLIMBING THE STAIRS OF HIS TOWNHOUSE, AND IT WASN'T THE FIRST TIME. He was a smart man and knew there were several medical explanations for his symptom. It could be stress, but despite the insanity in Washington since the inauguration of Herbert Hastings, Wallace had weathered many storms and wasn't prone to panic attacks. It was more likely that he had heart disease, lung cancer, or emphysema—or all three. He would get a checkup and learn what he presumed would be grim reaper news.

But he loved smoking almost as much as he loved bourbon. In fact, one without the other was almost unthinkable, and especially in this administration. He considered smoking and bourbon to be one of his last simple joys in life. He sat down and opened a pack of his favorite Russian cigarettes. Lighting one, he drew the smoke deeply into his lungs, where he let it swirl so that the chemicals could enter his bloodstream more thoroughly, and then exhaled, sending a plume of blue haze into the air before him. He loved everything about the act of smoking—lighting the tip of the cigarette with his gold lighter, inhaling, letting the stimulants in the tobacco infiltrate his brain, and exhaling with satisfaction as he waited in anticipation of the next puff.

Wallace had cigarettes from almost every country that manufactured them. He enjoyed comparing the strengths and flavors of different blends. Yes, he loved cigarettes as much as bourbon, which was saying a lot. They were to die for.

Chapter Fifty-Nine

Impromptu Meeting with the Elect

PATTERSON, WHO LIKED TO JOG IN ORDER TO DEAL WITH THE STRESSES OF HIS JOB, WAS RUNNING ON A QUARTER-MILE TRACK OUTSIDE WASHINGTON, D.C. He felt good if he could get in three miles a day, which he found cleared his head and sometimes even produced epiphanies about leads he was following. He was on his fourth lap when two men in dark suits raced onto the track directly in front of him and pulled him towards a black van, its sliding door open, his toes dragging in the grass as his chest heaved in an effort to catch his breath. Wheezing, he was stunned when his head crashed against the metal frame on the opposite side of the van as the door slid shut and locked. A wire mesh separated him from the driver and his companion.

He rubbed the bump on his head, which throbbed from the impact with the side of the van, and tried to open the back door, but it, too, was locked. He tumbled left and right as the vehicle made sharp turns—left, right, left again—and looked through the mesh to see if he could catch a glimpse through the front windshield of where the men were taking him. The van was accelerating—Patterson estimated they were doing eighty—and he saw they were now in the countryside. They passed red maple, sycamore, and white oak trees, and the state highway ahead looked empty.

Thirty minutes later, the van slowed and halted. Facing sideways, Patterson prepared to throw his body forward in anticipation of the side door sliding open, but as he lurched into the sunlight, the two men who'd abducted him caught him in mid-air, and he was quickly blindfolded by two additional men. He was dragged forward and his hands were put in iron cuffs at the end of two long chains, his arms raised above his head and spread wide as he was hoisted into the air. Creaky gears sounded in the distance, and judging by the smells around him, he guessed he was in a barn. Hanging four feet above the ground, Patterson dangled helplessly in darkness, his shoulder muscles singing with pain as he struggled to breathe.

"You ask too many questions," one of his abductors stated. The voice was low and scratchy, as if the speaker had scraped his vocal chords with two packs of cigarettes a day for years. "Your occupation is a dangerous one."

"Who . . . are . . . you?" Patterson said, gasping for air as he struggled to get the words out.

"We serve The Elect," the second abductor said. He was much younger and spoke dispassionately, as if he might be a CEO seated at the head of a conference room filled with his management team. "You may have heard of us, thanks to Maryanne Mistretta. She's another fine journalist who asks too many questions. That's why we need to make an example of you."

"You read the Bible, don't you, Patterson?" It was the harsh voice of the first man again. "You've been observed carrying a worn leather copy wherever you go."

"What of it?"

"You no doubt know that Christ hung on the cross for several hours before he died from what many forensic experts believe was asphyxiation. The poor man couldn't breathe after six hours. He also probably went into shock and cardiac failure."

Patterson heard the men talking further, but after fifteen minutes he began to hallucinate. He saw blurry images swimming before his eyes. The lifeless body of Dr. Charlotte Rampling lay on the floor below him; Sela was replacing the chip in his arm; Iranian jets landed on an isolated airfield; and brown military trucks carried tobacco plants out of Jumba Ogo. Scenes ran together in his mind, disjointed and out of order, like the frames of a surrealistic film.

"Jay? Jay, look at me, son"

"Dad? How can I be looking at you? Am I dead?"

"Not quite. But you're close, son, I want you to listen to me. Jay, you were one renown football player, remember? You were offered millions to join multiple NFL Teams—number one NFL Draft pick. Do you remember what happened next, Jay? Ever since high school, and long into college, you showed signs of being a great journalist and writer. All the awards and acknowledgements!

"Dad, I remember . . . . Dad, I love you. Are you really here? I do, yes, I do remember. But writing was just for fun then. I fell in love with Bernstein and Woodward's work in the Nixon Watergate affair. So I decided to major in journalism. The deciding factor was when I went to an Atlanta Falcons game and saw half my idols in wheel chairs. I decided I would much rather break a story than incur multiple concussions."

"That's you, Jay. You're a seeker of the Truth. That's my boy!

"Dad! Dad! Don't leave me!

"It's not your time, Jay. I'll be here when it is. Uncovering the Truth will set you free and give the world's people back their freedom to choose. You have a mission, Jay. Don't forget that.

He strained to bring air into his lungs, but the weight of his body pulled his torso down so that his diaphragm couldn't expand. Beads of sweat poured down his face and limbs as his body tried to cool itself. He was moments away from unconsciousness when the chains suspending him grew slack and his body fell to the ground.

He heard the clanking of chain links and a loud *thud*, which was the full weight of his body impacting the earthen floor. He lay on his left side, legs curled, arms extended above his head and to the side, pulling his right shoulder backwards. His hands had been freed from the iron cuffs.

It was the first man who spoke. "You were never in danger of death, Mr. Patterson. It would have looked suspicious to have another death follow those of Tom Chance and Elizabeth Rampling. It is a warning only. If you do not desist in your present inquiries, you will die in an apparent accident, and I assure you that no questions will be asked. Good day, Mr. Patterson."

The prisoner heard the wide wooden barn door slam shut. Everything was darkness, and Patterson tried to straighten his limbs, but the pain was too great. He blacked out within seconds.

Patterson wasn't sure how long he'd been unconscious, but when he came to, his head throbbed as he tried to move his arms and legs, and rise to a kneeling position. Removing his blindfold, he squinted even though the rays of sunlight penetrating the slats of the old barn were weak. As he looked at old harnesses, buckets, and shovels scattered about, he heard a car door slam outside the barn. Had his abductors returned? He staggered to his feet, every joint in his body aching, and limped to a point behind a bale of hay.

The barn door creaked open, and light from the late afternoon sun slanted across the yellow straw.

"Jay? Are you in here, Jay?"

It was the voice of Cookie McKnight.

Jay stood as erect as his sore muscles would allow. "Over here."

"My God, what happened?" Cookie cried.

Patterson related his abduction and how he'd been hoisted into the air by what he suspected was an old pulley used to lift bales of hay to the loft. "How did you know I was here?"

"We've had you watched. We feared something like this might happen."

"We? Who is we?"

"Grass Roots, of which I'm a member. The actual leadership of Grass Roots is an underground organization since protest in America isn't safe. Some of our members have disappeared and never been seen again, so organizers fly low under the radar. There is one other member of the movement in the West Wing, but if our identities were known, we'd probably be killed. We need to get you to a safe house we operate in Virginia."

"No," Jay said, massaging his wrists. "They said this was just a warning. It'll be more dangerous if I drop out of sight altogether. I'll hold off on publishing anything else for the time being, but I have to be free to move around and do my work."

Fresh in Jay's mind were every word his dad had said to him. He wasn't hallucinating. If other worlds can communicate with us, why not other dimensions in time and space as well?

Sela was distraught and hugged Jay as tears streamed down her cheeks.

"I'd tell you to stop investigating Hastings," she said, "but I know you need to do your job. Do you know who did this?"

"Four men, one of whom said they were from The Elect. It looks as if Maryanne Mistretta's piece was accurate. Somewhere tucked away in the federal government is a group that goes by that name, and they apparently don't like people looking into their activities or those of the president."

"What's your next move, Jay?" Taylor asked.

"I'm going to try to find out names of The Elect—or the OGI. I presume they're one and the same."

"Sounds dangerous," Sela said, knowing she was stating the obvious.

"I'm going to look through some archives at the Library of Congress," Patterson said. "If I can't use a library, then I'm pretty well done in this town anyway."

Chapter Sixty
Which Way is Out of the Oval Office?

DIANE HASTINGS HAD REMAINED IN THE BEDROOM ACROSS THE HALL FROM THE PRESIDENT'S MASTER SUITE ON THE SECOND FLOOR OF THE WHITE HOUSE RESIDENCE, REFUSING TO SHARE HER HUSBAND'S BED. Hastings declined to speak with his wife, and gruffly moved past her in the hallway each morning, at times mumbling *"Bitch"* under his breath.

Her friend and personal assistant, Audrey Dickerson, stood in the White House office of the First Lady. "You asked for me, ma'am?"

"Yes. I thought we'd watch NewzTracker together. I trust you sent my new recording to their offices."

"This morning."

The First Lady had friends in the White House, friends who were loyal only to her, not her husband. She wasn't yet finished with Herbert Chase Hastings. In fact, she was just getting started. She had her own Secret Service detail. If Hastings wanted to harm her further now that she no longer allowed herself to be in the same room with him, she had men in black suits to protect her.

/

For obvious reasons, John Taylor didn't assign Patterson to post or comment on the recording received from the same nonexistent Maryland address from which the Brothel Tape had come. The recording showed President Hastings and Lucille Raines having a quiet, intimate dinner in the White House. The quality of the recording wasn't good and it had obviously been made from a phone left in record mode on a table in the corner of the room, but the two figures in the frame were undeniably Hastings and Raines.

As the evening progressed, Hastings leaned over and kissed Raines. Moments later, he took her by the hand and led her away.

/

At the next White House press briefing, David Wolcott was quick to point out that the quality of the recording was poor due to the placement of the phone and its distance from the president. He claimed that the meeting between Raines and the president had been a working dinner. Furthermore, the president had simply leaned forward to emphasize a remark—pure body language—but his lips had not touched the skin of his chief of staff. At the end of the meal, he'd extended his hand to motion to Raines which way she should go. The president, Wolcott said emphatically, had never held the hand of Raines.

Moments after the briefing, the president said on VOXPOP that "This is another lie. It probably comes from Pants-on-Fire Patterson. Besides, what I do is nobody's business."

Chapter Sixty-One

In the Depths of the Library of Congress

PATTERSON HAD NO WAY TO CONNECT THE OFFICE OF GOVERNMENT INQUIRY WITH THE ELECT. OGI and Raines were somehow linked, but this told him nothing of the secret organization Mistretta had written about.

The Library of Congress housed more than sixty-eight million books on shelves that, if laid end-to-end, would span 1,284 miles. It had gone through its first wave of digitization in 1990, but by 2018, only 10 percent of the vast collection had been converted to digital format. In 2026, the percentage was approaching 50 percent. The entire operation was fairly conventional, and the nation's congressional library still operated with protocols from past generations, with much of its holdings available only in hard copy format, a fact that gave him optimism that he might track down a reference to OGI in some dusty file that had long since been forgotten on a back shelf in a seldom-used room of the facility. The retro feel of the library appealed to his Luddite sensibilities.

Wearing dark glasses and a floppy Indiana Jones hat, Patterson went to the Main Reading Room located in the Thomas Jefferson Building across from the Supreme Court. He asked a young male librarian where he could find information on the Office of Government Inquiry. The librarian did a quick search and said that no such office was listed in the collection's electronic files.

"May I look in your old card catalog?" Patterson asked.

He was led down a corridor to a room that was twenty yards long and lined with old wooden card catalogs, ten for each letter of the alphabet. Six librarians were on duty in the room, he was told, should he need further assistance.

Patterson began his search with the obvious. He ran his index finger across the wooden catalogs until he came to the letter "O," and then found drawers that listed entries beginning with *Office of Government—* After a few minutes, Patterson concluded that there must be at least ten thousand agencies starting with these words, and most were obscure federal departments that no one had likely ever heard of, such as the U.S. Office of Government Statisticians or the U.S. Office of Government Receipts. The names were so generic that he couldn't hazard a guess as to what duties most of the federal agencies he saw referenced might have been charged with executing, despite brief descriptions of their functions. The entries spoke of a huge federal bureaucracy, although a majority of entries were for offices that dated back fifty to a hundred years and had been closed for decades or incorporated into other federal agencies. The one thing that all entries had in common was that their three-by-five index cards listed the dates on which the offices were created and closed, the directors of the offices, and what their duties were—usually cryptic and written in government-speak.

Patterson at last came across the card he was looking for.

> The U.S. Office of Government Inquiry
> Inception: 1947
> Department Head: General Wilson Wyler, Department of Defense
> Mission Statement: To gather relevant data for commander in chief
> Clearance: Eyes Only
> File: 167421

That was the extent of the information on the card, but Jay was nevertheless taken aback. "Eyes Only" was a security clearance term indicating that very few people were allowed to read a document, even within a specific agency of the intelligence community. In the case of the Office of Government Inquiry, this wasn't surprising, he thought, since the mission of General Wyler, whoever that might have been, was to relate certain information directly to the president. In 1947, the commander in chief would have been Harry Truman.

Patterson jotted down the file number and took it to one of the librarians in the catalog room, asking if he could be shown the file. The librarian returned empty-handed ten minutes later, causing Patterson to believe that he'd stumbled over something that had raised a giant red flag. The librarian, he thought, might be on the telephone as soon as she walked away, telling someone that there had been an inquiry about *that* file. Instead, the librarian returned and told Patterson that he should follow her to a room where she had brought the entire file on a rolling metal cart.

"It's a large file," the short young woman said. She smiled and seemed eager to help. "Please make yourself at home, and leave the documents here when you're finished so that I can re-shelve them properly."

Patterson looked at six dusty white cartons filled with brown file folders. He transferred the cartons to a metal table and opened one labeled "1 of 6."

He glanced at red-stenciled letters on all of the cartons, which read *Declassified 2020*, and took off his glasses and began to peruse the documents in a folder that contained the first entries. The office had been created in 1947 as part of the Department of Defense. The Soviets, under the direction of Stalin, had begun a nuclear program based on Russian spying on the Manhattan Project, which had developed the atomic bombs detonated over Hiroshima and Nagasaki. By 1947, the Russian nuclear program was in full swing, with the first successful detonation of a Soviet nuclear weapon occurring in August of 1949 at Kazakhstan. President Truman had been given regular updates over and above what his generals were given, since the commander in chief was wary of the extent of power that had been unleashed over Japan. Patterson read several memos in which Truman told his staff that the atomic bomb wasn't a toy to be used anytime the United States wanted to win a war. The National Military Establishment was formed in 1947 to replace the War Department, and the NME was renamed the Department of Defense in August of 1949, the same month that Russia completed its first test of the A-bomb. More memos referenced what had quickly become known as the Cold War, a term first coined in 1947 by millionaire Bernard Baruch, an advisor to Harry Truman.

Patterson sat back, amazed at the material in each subsequent folder. A lot of things had happened in 1947. It was the year that the Central Intelligence Agency had been created, since Truman deemed the CIA necessary to gather intelligence on Soviet activity during the Cold War.

As he continued paging through the documents in the folders before him, he realized that the OGI had gathered information on a lot more than nuclear weapons and the Cold War. In 1952, UFOs had been spotted in daylight over the Capitol Building in Washington, D.C., and Truman had demanded an explanation of the strange lights that had been photographed and reported in newspapers around the country. Air Force generals denounced the lights as "aerial phenomena."

Patterson began leafing more quickly through the files, as there was too much information to assimilate in one sitting.

President Eisenhower and his military advisors had been greatly alarmed by the Soviet satellite Sputnik, believing that the Russians would soon be able to drop nuclear weapons on the United States from Earth orbit. Sputnik had been launched in 1957. In 1958, Eisenhower created NASA, and the space race was on.

Truman and Eisenhower had also been concerned about a small country in Southeast Asia called Vietnam, which had been colonized by the French beginning in 1859. Both Presidents had sent military advisors to the country, and their successor, John F. Kennedy, also believed that if Vietnam fell to Ho Chi Minh and the communist factions there, a domino effect would ensue that would result in all of Southeast Asia falling under the spell of China and the Soviet Union.

When it came to President Kennedy, the folders Patterson was reading had thousands of files and memos on his assassination, the Warren Commission, and whether or not Lee Harvey Oswald had acted alone. Presidents from Lyndon Johnson to Gerald Ford had secretly expressed misgivings about the Warren Commission's conclusion that Oswald had been a lone gunman.

The files contained enough material to occupy historians for decades. Thousands of pages had been devoted to the McCarthy hearings, Nixon's communist witch hunt of the 1950s, the Vietnam War, Watergate, the energy crisis in 1976, terrorism, and economic recessions. File 167421 also contained dossiers on the private lives of senators and congressmen—dossiers with salacious material that, if released, would have created political, economic, and sexual scandals that would have caused many public servants to resign or be indicted and imprisoned. Over the years, intelligence gathering had taken a decidedly personal turn.

Patterson moved to the last folder in carton number six. The penultimate page of the last file folder contained another brief entry.

> The U.S. Office of Government Inquiry
> Discontinued: 1977
> Department Head: General Forest Whitcomb
> Prior Mission Statement: To gather relevant information for the secretary of defense
> Clearance: Eyes Only
> File: 167421

Patterson noted that the mission statement had changed. Between 1947 and 1977, information was being gathered for the secretary of defense, not the commander in chief. But there was one more page in the file. It was the most revealing of everything he had read.

> The U.S. Office of Government Inquiry
> Reconvened: 1982
> Department Head: General Reed Thompson

Mission Statement: To orchestrate the agenda of the State Department
Clearance: Etiam Electus
File: 167421

The Office of Government Inquiry was now under the State Department, not the DoD, and the clearance had gone from "Eyes Only" to *Etiam Electus*, Latin for "The Elect." The mission statement for OGI was to carry out the agenda of the State Department, but what had been the agenda in 1982?

Patterson thought back to his American History courses in college. In 1982, newly elected President Ronald Regan had said in his inaugural address that "government is not the solution to our problem; government *is* the problem." During his administration, President Reagan advocated a limited role for the federal government, which included lowering taxes on the wealthy and deregulating industries to allow for economic growth. The decades following the Reagan administration had witnessed Republican presidents and the GOP advocate Reagan's vision of a leaner, less obtrusive federal government. Maryanne Mistretta's article claimed that Secretary of State Maxwell Hart wanted to downsize the federal government and eliminate some of its bureaucracy. If Mistretta's source was to be believed, it seemed plausible that *Etiam Electus* still existed and was the twenty-first century grandchild of the vision first articulated by Ronald Reagan.

Patterson thought of the dossiers on the personal lives of those in government he'd seen in the files before him. Had the OGI, now known as *Etiam Electus*, been responsible for ruining the lives of countless Americans? He hadn't seen any evidence that the dossiers had been used, but perhaps actions against individuals had been kept off the books. He himself had been taken by members of The Elect to a rural farm and strung up like a common horse thief in the nineteenth century. And Senator Tom Chance and Dr. Elizabeth Rampling were dead.

The latter point brought up a troubling possibility, which was that *Etiam Electus*—OGI—was using its considerable internal power within the government to protect Herbert Chase Hastings, a mentally unstable man who was proposing the most radically conservative agenda of any presidential administration in American history.

The more immediate question was what he was going to do with the information he'd uncovered in the old cartons, which looked as if they hadn't been opened in years. He thought back to the last scene in the classic *Raiders of the Lost Ark*, in which the Ark of the Covenant had been quietly pushed down a long corridor in a warehouse of enormous size, where it would ostensibly be forgotten.

Patterson had uncovered his own version of the Ark, a collection of politically explosive documents that could shake Washington as much as President Hastings was doing. He would talk with John Taylor about what to do next. If he published an article on what he'd found at the Library of Congress, he would surely be apprehended a second time.

And most likely, killed.

Chapter Sixty-Two
All the Dots Connected

John Taylor and Sela sat in the editor's office at NewzTracker headquarters, listening to Patterson describe the files he'd discovered at the Library of Congress.

Taylor couldn't suppress a laugh. "So in this digital age when virtually nothing is secret any longer and satellites can record the last argument I had with my wife, Jay finds an old file and a yellowed piece of paper that has incriminating evidence on Hart, Raines, and maybe the President. Go figure."

"Since we know that OGI and The Elect is the same organization," Patterson said, "it's safe to assume that Raines and Hart have seen the Chance autopsy report."

"Probably," Sela said, "but it doesn't necessarily mean that they had anything to do with the murders."

"But it *does* mean that The Elect were aware of the murders, and very quickly,"

Patterson said. "The autopsy reports were sent to OGI, and that only happens if somebody made a request for the medical documents. Why else would the hospitals have sent the results anywhere but to local law enforcement agencies?"

"And nobody puts in such a request unless they're expecting to find something," Taylor added. "That speaks directly to prior knowledge of what would happen to Chance and Rampling."

Taylor's secretary handed him a dozen phone messages, which he quickly leafed through as the trio spoke.

"Someone named Jane Levitt called for me five times in the last two hours," Taylor remarked. "And two of these are for you, Jay. Know anyone by that name?"

"She's a staffer at Tom Chance's office."

Patterson grabbed his phone immediately.

"Jane?" he said when the staffer answered the call.

"Thank God," Levitt said. "Chance's widow brought the second autopsy report to the office this morning, the one based on the exhumation of Tom's body. She wasn't quite sure what to make of it and was hoping we could decipher its technical jargon. We all regard her as family."

"What did the report say?" Patterson asked, switching his phone to speaker.

"We only had a few minutes to look at it, but the report said that nanobots had been found in large concentrations in Tom's heart muscle. The bots knocked out the two points on the heart that conduct the electrical signals that make the chambers contract: the sinoatrial node and the atrioventricular node. His heart went into V-tach very quickly. How did nanobots get into his bloodstream?"

"The government is now using second-generation chip implants that carry nanobots," Patterson replied. "They can be programmed to do just about anything inside the human body."

"Programmed?" Levitt said, her voice strained. "Are you telling me this was indeed intentional?"

"I'm afraid so, Jane. You said that you only got to see the report for a few minutes. How come?"

"Men in dark suits burst into the office flashing badges and said the report was confidential and had been sent to Mrs. Chance by accident. They snatched the papers from my hand and left in quite a hurry."

"Badges? What agency were they from?"

"I couldn't really tell, although one man said he was from the Secret Service."

Patterson spoke, thinking out loud as much as talking to Levitt. "Autopsy reports in many states can be accessed by the general public. In some states and in D.C., such reports are available to immediate family members and to law enforcement agencies if they suspect a crime has been committed. Mrs. Chance had a right to see that report, but she was obviously followed."

"So it probably *was* the Secret Service," Levitt said.

"I doubt it. They don't have jurisdiction to investigate such cases. My guess is that they were from The Elect, just like the men who held me captive in Virginia."

"The group that Mistretta wrote about?" Levitt asked.

"Jane, let me get back to you," Patterson said abruptly, dodging the question. "Thanks for the heads-up."

Patterson looked at Taylor and Sela. "John, this has to get out, but not under *my* byline or I'm a dead man."

Taylor nodded. "I'm going to write the piece myself. We have hard evidence that says a secret organization exists and that they received both autopsy reports, the first of which indicates that Chance was murdered by programmed nanotechnology. I'll check with the authorities in Denver to see if they found the same thing when Rampling's body was exhumed. I'll also write that an unnamed NewzTracker source traced the organization to the White House Chief of Staff."

"The shit's gonna hit the fan when you name Raines and Hart as recipients of a report on the murder of a senator," Patterson noted, "as well as a psychiatrist who was in possession of a psychiatric file on Hastings."

"If the shit doesn't hit the fan when you're working a big story," Taylor said, "then it means you're not doing something right. I'm going to order private security guards to watch our offices twenty-four-seven."

"I'll keep hammering on Iran and Garundi, and hopefully Lone Wolf will keep feeding me info."

"Lone Wolf says, *everything is connected,*" Sela reminded him.

"According to Jane Levitt," Patterson said, "Chance visited Ogo and Garundi three months before his death. I'm willing to bet he was killed for something he saw while he was in Africa."

Silence descended upon all three sitting in the NewzTracker office at the stark possibility that Hastings or Hart, or both, might soon be implicated in numerous murders by headlines about to break in less than twenty-four hours

"Okay, everybody," Taylor said. "Let's get to work."

Chapter Sixty-Three

What Tobacco Plants?

After his meeting with Taylor, Patterson went to his office down the hall, while Sela drove to NASA's D.C. headquarters to catch up on work and gather the latest news on Comet JM-2026A and the signals from Tau Ceti. He turned on three of his wall screens and scanned each one until he saw news footage coming from Garundi on a network devoted to international news. The BBC was doing a piece on economic development in South African countries. Patterson watched Felix Ogo riding a Jeep through fields as he inspected farming operations, an activity he engaged in daily so as to be seen mingling with his people. Patterson sat forward as he saw Ogo's Jeep slowly making its way through a wide field, only the crop wasn't yams or potatoes. Behind the dictator were mature tobacco plants.

"Holy hell."

Patterson performed a search for all African countries growing tobacco and saw that Tanzania, Zambia, Zimbabwe, Malawi, and Mozambique all grew the crop in abundance. Garundi wasn't included in the list.

Patterson looked at the BFNS report for ten more minutes as he hastily scribbled the names he saw on green road signs, as well as any numbers indicating the distance to nearby townships. He then grabbed his coat and headed down to the basement.

/

"We're looking for tobacco fields," Patterson said excitedly.

Bobby Thibodaux shook his head. "I've been following the trucks carrying the plants from the palace, and they ride into the jungle. You can't grow tobacco under a forest canopy, and I can't scan the entire country."

Patterson took out his notes and placed them on the desk of NewzTracker's computer wizard. "I just saw Ogo on TV as he rode through tobacco fields in his jeep. I wrote down what was on some of the road signs so we could get a fix on exactly where he was."

"Signs? Now you're talking!" Thibodaux said excitedly as he pulled up a map of Garundi on the wall screen and zoomed in on major and minor roads crisscrossing the country. It took him less than ten minutes to find the roads that Patterson had the presence of mind to note as he'd watched his wall screen.

"Well?" Patterson said expectantly.

A minute elapsed as Thibodaux triangulated a location based on three of the coordinates Patterson had provided.

"Well, if that don't beat my mama's homemade tomato sauce," Thibodaux said. "It's a tobacco field tucked away like a gator hiding in the grass on the edge of a swamp." He zoomed out so they could see three square miles of countryside. "The tobacco field is surrounded by trees on all sides, and adjoining fields are definitely being used to grow yams and other crops."

"Scan an area for twenty square miles and see if you can spot a similar pattern of trees that divide growing areas into yams and tobacco," Patterson instructed.

Thibodaux maneuvered the satellite camera providing the images of Garundi, and leaned back in his chair.

"I spot twenty different fields," he said. "The tobacco fields aren't recognizable unless you're actively looking for them and use the right magnification with the satellite camera."

After a two-hour search of the entire country, Thibodaux spotted another thousand tobacco fields.

"Ogo has camouflaged the fields on purpose," he asserted. "There's no reason to spread them out in such a fashion when, as a dictator, he could have appropriated any parcels of land he wanted to centralize crop production. This is a far more time-consuming and expensive method of cultivating tobacco."

"Unless you have foreign governments footing the bill," Patterson pointed out.

"True," the technician said as he rubbed his chin. "This pattern also explains why I couldn't detect where the trucks were going. While searching the countryside, I've noticed that trucks disappear under forest canopies and then appear loaded with yams, potatoes, and other vegetables. I also saw machinery in the tobacco fields just now, which is unusual inasmuch as cultivation of other vegetables seems to be done by hand, oxen, or wooden plows. A pretty low-tech operation nationwide when it comes to their declared cash crops."

"Where are the cultivated plants being taken?" Patterson asked.

Thibodaux smiled. "Let's follow the trail, Sherlock."

An hour later, the wizard had found nothing.

"There are thousands of roads winding through Garundi," Thibodaux noted. "If Ogo can keep movements to the fields on the down-low, I suspect he can do the same when it comes to moving trucks *away* from the fields carrying harvested plants."

"Zoom back out and look for thoroughfares where the roads from the tobacco fields intersect," Patterson suggested. "It's like those old newspaper puzzles, where you have to trace the way out of a complicated maze with a pencil. Lots of dead ends, but there's always a way out."

"A low-tech approach," Thibodaux noted, "but sound. Better than asking a computer to use algorithms to solve the problem."

"I'm a low-tech guy," Patterson commented. "Seek and ye shall find."

Thibodaux outlined all roads going to or from the tobacco fields in red. Roughly half led to the palace. The rest he changed to blue and then followed them with a cursor imposed on the graphic.

"I've isolated six routes," Thibodaux announced. "All are part of the country's national highway system. Five lead east, but one goes to northern Garundi."

"Follow that one first," Patterson said.

Thibodaux traced the northern highway and then folded his arms. "We have a winner, ladies and gentlemen! Behold. When I zoom in, we can see nothing less than a factory with large red letters painted on the side: Persian Dynasty. The logo beside it, large as life, is a pack of cigarettes with a few of the filtered cancer sticks poking out of the top. I guess his secrecy stops here."

"Like all dictators," Patterson said, "he's got an ego ten sizes larger than the average human. He's probably selling cigarettes within his country, and that means that the Persian Dynasty Blend is no secret."

"Persian Dynasty?" Thibodaux said. "Iran used to be called Persia."

"You noticed."

"Too bad you can't get a carton of those cigarettes. I don't smoke anymore, but if I did, I would put them on my shelf as a trophy—a reminder of how truly great I am at my job."

"Great indeed," Patterson said, "and I probably owe you enough Abita Beer to keep you buzzed for the rest of your life. But I know exactly where I can get a carton of Persian Dynasty right here in D.C. Meanwhile, find out where those other five national highways lead."

Thibodaux continued to chat about how he also deserved a raise, not noticing that Patterson was already out the door.

Patterson left a little rubber in the small parking lot as he peeled out, headed for the office of Senator Leland Wallace, a man who enjoyed smoking as much as life itself. He also had a collection of foreign cigarettes.

Chapter Sixty-Four
The Real Stuff

Leland Wallace returned to his office from the Senate floor after casting a vote against Hastings' tax reform bill that would give large businesses an enormous tax break while making up the revenue by raising taxes on low and middle-income families across America and by gutting programs like Medicare, Social Security, health research, emergency services and education. Although half of the Republican majority in the Senate and House of Representatives privately detested the President and had obstructed much of his legislation, they nevertheless put on brave faces when interviewed by the press and stated that Hastings had been the choice of the people. When it came to "starving the beast"—cutting social programs—Republicans seemed to detest President Hastings a little less. Wallace was sorting through memos when he was told that Jay Patterson was waiting to see him.

"Hello, Jay," Wallace said as Patterson was escorted into his office. "You're not on my schedule, but I'd rather talk with you than a bunch of my friends who are going to give me hell because I just helped torpedo a piece of Hastings' legislation. It was a close vote, but the tax bill was defeated, thank God."

"Thank you for giving me the time, Senator. You're a smoker, if I recall."

Wallace looked perplexed at the strange segue into his thoroughly enjoyable but lethal habit.

"You know I am, son, and a heavy one at that. I'd recommend it to everyone if it wasn't a practice that landed people six feet under. But surely that's not what brought you here today."

Wallace had no intention of mentioning that he'd been short of breath lately and that it was almost certainly due to cigarettes. He didn't want anyone's pity, not now and not when he himself was six feet under, which might be sooner rather than later.

"Actually, it's *exactly* why I came by today," Patterson confessed. "You have cigarettes from around the world, don't you?"

"I do indeed. I'm not sure if it's legal to have some of the brands I keep in my collection, but I have them, nevertheless. I have connections, shall we say, who are able to procure cartons from international markets. I should have taken up stamp collecting or golf, but I got hooked at an early age, thanks to people like that bastard Percy Beauregard Hastings. The boat sailed for me a long time ago. I know they have pills and gum and patches these days that can make it easier to quit, but I enjoy it too much."

"Do you ever smoke Persian Dynasty?"

Wallace turned up the corner of his mouth in a good-natured grimace, as if to tell his visitor that he surely already knew the answer to his question.

"Persian Dynasty? Now that is a damn good cigarette. Not the strongest tobacco blend around, but it's up there. It gives a man the right kind of kick when he inhales, and it tastes good, too. That's the daily double, son. Strong and good-tasting on the palate."

"So it's not mild like, say, Sailor."

Wallace broke into a laughter, which in turn caused him to experience a thirty-second coughing fit. He cleared his throat, wiped his eyes, and answered the reporter. "Sailor? That's a smoke for young adults who want to go through the motions. I tried a couple the day they went on sale and never lit one again. Worst tasting cigarette I ever had in my mouth. Garbage."

"I've heard that PB has improved the flavor and that Sailor is now very close to the taste of real tobacco."

"Close, as they say, only counts in horseshoes, son. I want tobacco, not some vegetable leaf. Besides, I wouldn't pay a nickel to PB Enterprises even if they made the best cigarette in the world. They used to, meaning Western Rider. But now? I wouldn't put money into the hands of Hastings' empire if someone put a gun to my head. In fact, I wouldn't buy *any* of PB's new products. I have no intention of enriching Brad or Savannah. Not only are they the offspring of the biggest fool to ever sit in the White House—and there have been many—but they seem to have a fondness for Iran."

A look of disdain crossed the senator's face.

"You can tell a lot about folks by the company they keep," Wallace remarked. "I have nothing against anyone from the Middle East, but an Iranian mobster? That's a different story."

Patterson nodded. "It will be interesting to see how the story about Brad and Savannah develops."

"By the way, did you ever find what you were looking for in relation to the death of Tom Chance?"

"He was murdered. You'll read about it within the next day or so. Although I ask that you remain silent until my editor puts the story onto our site."

"Murdered? It's what I figured. A damn shame is what it is, but I'm not surprised. I knew something was wrong when he grabbed his chest and keeled over. And Jay?"

"Yes, sir?"

"Nail the bastards who did it."

"I'll do my best, Senator. May I have a carton of Persian Dynasty in the meantime? It's for a story I'm working on. I wish I could say more, but I'm not at liberty to go into details."

Wallace asked one of his staffers to get a carton of Persian Dynasty cigarettes from the storage closet in the outer office. Patterson left and drove to a drug store and bought a carton of Sailor before heading to an independent lab that tested anything suspected of containing harmful or carcinogenic substances. He requested that the two brands be analyzed and compared with one another. He was beginning to wonder if PB Enterprises was genuinely out of the tobacco business. *Real* tobacco.

Chapter Sixty-Five
Civil War

LED BY JIMMY FINCH, A CONVOY OF VEHICLES OWNED BY THE TENNESSEE CIVILIAN STATE MILITIA ROLLED THROUGH THE CLEAN, MODERN STREETS OF NASHVILLE. Finch drove one of several Jeeps wearing his weekend combat fatigues, waving to pedestrians who stopped to look at the unexpected caravan. A convoy of troop carriers purchased from Army surplus outlets carried over a thousand members of the self-proclaimed state militia. Canvas-covered supply trucks brought up the rear, as if they were part of a well-executed military operation.

The event was covered by the American Broadcasting Network. A female correspondent from ABN ran up to the lead Jeep to speak with Finch when the caravan halted in the central business district between a convention center and an arena.

"Mr. Finch!" the young female African-American reporter called, her camera and sound men trailing behind her. They stopped by the side of the Jeep, panting to catch their breath. "I'm Jenny Warner. May we have a word?"

"Of course, darlin'. I have all the time in the world to make a statement."

The reporter glanced over her shoulder to make sure her crew was in place. The sound man nodded that they were live.

"There are similar caravans rolling into Memphis, Chattanooga, and Knoxville," Warner said. "Are you taking over these cities? Or perhaps, even the entire state?"

"Ms. Warner, we're just making our presence known."

"Mr. Finch," Warner continued, "the governor of Tennessee says that you don't have permission to stage any kind of paramilitary exercises on municipal or state property."

"Does it look like we're engaged in any kind of military exercises, young lady? Do you see us running through the streets or firing any weapons?"

"No, sir, but all of your men are heavily armed. If I'm not mistaken, they're holding automatic rifles."

"It's our constitutional right to bear arms, and we've rented the convention center over your shoulder for a meeting of our membership over the next two days. We're also holding conventions and rallies in the other cities you mentioned."

"The governor says that he'll call up the National Guard to force you to leave the city," Warner stated.

Finch laughed out loud. "Honey, there's a new sheriff in town, and his name is President Herbert Chase Hastings. I received his personal permission to stage these maneuvers, and if you look around, you'll see that the National Guard, now known as the Loyalty Militia, seems to be supporting our presence here today."

Warner turned abruptly, as did her cameraman, to see vehicles of the renamed National Guard rolling onto side streets and flanking Finch's civilian brigade. They, too, had Jeeps and troop carriers, but they had tanks as well.

"We're here to make a statement that conservatism is here to stay," Finch said. "Voters elected Herbert Hastings, who is going to stand for core American values and make this country into what our Founding Fathers envisioned. He's going to revive the soul of America, Ms. Warner. And I'd like to thank the Scarabelli family for their donations to the American Paramilitary Union. They've given us twenty-five million dollars to help buy new equipment, uniforms, guns, and ammo."

TINN crews were now on the scene, standing on every street corner, interviewing members of both the paramilitary forces and the Loyalty Militia. They had obviously known the event was forthcoming. Many TINN reporters were asking troops to step down from their carriers and pose for the cameras. The soldiers were more than accommodating, smiling as if they were part of a homecoming parade to celebrate a great military victory. As the men in fatigues began to pose and mingle, it became increasingly difficult to distinguish between the civilian militia from the Loyalty Militia.

Jimmy Finch stood in his Jeep and motioned for the figure beside him to stand as well.

"Despite this overwhelming show of patriotism today here in Nashville," Finch said, "I want to inject a personal note into these events, and that's to announce my marriage yesterday to Holly Gerard, pastor of the Green Falls mega-church in Los Angeles, California. Holly, I should add, has been named by President Hastings as pastor of the National Congregation of the Church of the Heart because of her experience running such a large organization in California and her national and international outreach."

Holly Gerard was a petite forty-two-year-old woman with short black hair and a slim figure. Tabloids claimed that she'd had numerous plastic surgeries and that her smile was that of a beauty pageant queen rather than that of an ordained minister. Jenny Warner circled the Jeep and held her microphone next to Gerard, who had stepped from the vehicle.

"Ms. Gerard," Warner said, "the president isn't allowed to actively participate in the running of any religion since it's a violation of the Constitution. Do you have any comment?"

Gerard, wearing fatigues that matched those worn by the members of the American Paramilitary Union, smiled as she replied. "President Hastings merely made a recommendation for the purpose of renewing America's spiritual values. Have our hearts become so hardened that a president can't openly express his faith?"

"What are your plans for the Church of the Heart?" Warner asked, "And why are you dressed in a military uniform?"

TINN reporters and cameras had rushed helter-skelter to the Jeep to get shots of Finch and Gerard and to record the pastor's response.

"I'll be in charge of church enrollment," Gerard explained, "as well as day-to-day operations of the church and the drafting of official doctrine for the congregation."

Warner looked confused but recovered quickly. "When President Hastings formed the church, he said that he was honoring the Divine in everyone and that his mission was an ecumenical outreach. He made no mention of a doctrine or membership. Are you saying that the average American isn't free to worship at any Church of the Heart in their cities and towns?"

"Everyone is welcome at our churches, but we have to maintain security in these times of domestic and international terrorism."

"What kind of security are you talking about?" Warner asked.

Gerard frowned and held out her hands in frustration, as if the answer was self-explanatory. "I know it's difficult for the liberal media like those at ABN and other outlets of substitute news to understand, but we have to think of America first if we're going to revive its soul and help our president keep his campaign promise. We naturally can't let any Muslims into the church since so many are homegrown radicals or working for worldwide terrorist organizations. The terrorist activity in Pakistan could very well become commonplace in our own backyard. We'll also be taking a hard look at other minorities as well. Additionally, we'll screen for members of the Grass Roots movement, since it seeks to overthrow the government by violent protests. As far as liberal Democrats are concerned, they'll have to undergo careful vetting. Those who oppose President Hastings are opposed to liberty, freedom, and democracy."

Warner was determined to get a straight answer to her question. "But what kind of security measures will be taken by the Church of the Heart?"

Finch stepped out of the Jeep and stood by Warner's side. "As pastor of the congregation, Holly has appointed me as security chief for all churches in the country. The bell towers, as you might have observed, are constructed to resemble the immigration guard towers along our southern border. The bells will be removed and armed guards will be stationed in their place at every church. And that, Ms. Warner, is all we have to say for now."

Finch and Gerard then devoted their attention exclusively to reporters from TINN.

Ten blocks from where Finch and Gerard granted interviews to TINN, five thousand members of Grass Roots marched to the heart of Nashville's central business district. They carried signs such as *No Neofascists In America* and *Impeach Herbert Hastings*.

The protesters had marched five blocks before they were met by members of the Loyalty Militia and ordered to turn around. Wes Brockton, the leader of the march, showed a sergeant his permit to peacefully protest, but he was nevertheless instructed to make his followers disband. They would not be allowed, he was told, to advance any farther. "Go home," ordered Sergeant Don Mortensen.

"This is outrageous!" Brockton called out. "We have a right to free speech!"

"Shouting won't be tolerated," Sergeant Mortensen countered. "You've committed a hostile act against the United States of America."

"You're out of your mind!" Brockton shouted, waving his right arm forward to indicate that Grass Roots protesters should proceed towards the CBD.

Grass Roots renewed their progress towards the heart of Nashville, but troops in olive drab pushed them back, some protesters hurling themselves at rapidly-forming lines of the Loyalty Militia. Grass Movement members lay on the street, stunned and bruised as tear gas canisters were lobbed into the dense throng of protesters filling the streets behind them. Some managed to get through as they covered their noses with the collars of their shirts. Shots rang out, and some of the protesters fell to the ground, wounded or dead. Others began to run for side streets, hoping to reach the central business district by another route, but soldiers with the Tennessee Civilian State Militia, having heard the shouts and gunfire, had deserted their troop carriers and moved to flank positions, anticipating that Grass Roots would seek different paths to the arena and convention center.

More gunfire erupted, and tear gas wafted through the streets of downtown Nashville.

An hour later, sixteen members of Grass Roots were dead and seventy-six lay on the streets, wounded. Jimmy Finch and Pastor Holly Gerard stood in their Jeep, pleased at the great victory they had achieved. The Loyalty Militia and the American Paramilitary Union had prevailed in stopping those opposed to President Hastings. Finch smiled at the smell of gunfire and battle in the air. Gerard bowed her head and audibly thanked the spirit of God in all people for wielding its terrible swift sword against those who sought to bring down the United States of America.

Chapter Sixty-Six
God is a Republican

PATTERSON WATCHED THE UNFOLDING DEBACLE IN NASHVILLE ON HIS LAPTOP. America had been taken in by the Church of the Heart, which had, not surprisingly, been manipulated by Hastings to become an important segment of his political base as well as a new and highly organized part of the Real Right. Holly Gerard, a well-known televangelist, had pimped herself out to serve a political agenda, not that precedent hadn't been set by other televangelists who believed that God was a registered member of the Republican Party. A verse of scripture came to Patterson's mind: *Render unto Caesar that which is Caesar's, and to God that which is God's.* It described perfectly the blurred boundaries between church and state exacerbated by the unconstitutional Church of the Heart, but it had added meaning given that President Hastings fancied himself a modern-day emperor of Rome.

Patterson continued to watch the violence in Nashville as members of Grass Roots were beaten and kicked. There was no federal or state authority to hold the Loyalty Militia or Jimmy Finch's men in check. There was anarchy in the streets, and Patterson wondered if Hastings felt so threatened by bad press and a growing debate over his mental instability that he had personally unleashed Finch's state militias on the protesters to warn those who opposed him that he would resort to violence in order to silence the escalating criticism of his administration. If so, would nuking Pakistan be next on his list of things to do to prove that he was not to be challenged, that he was a man who wielded absolute power?

Patterson turned, closed the laptop, and thought about the coincidence of Grass Roots being assembled in large numbers just blocks away from Nashville's CBD at the exact moment when Finch's state militia had rolled to a stop between the convention center and the arena. Grass Roots was active in hundreds of cities across America, and on any given day it protested dozens of Hastings' policies, statements, and decisions. But they couldn't have just shown up in Nashville by accident, Patterson reasoned. They had to have known ahead of time that something big was going to take place in Nashville and other major cities in Tennessee. He could think of only one way they could have known when and where to assemble. Cookie McKnight was a covert member of Grass Roots, which had by necessity turned from an organic movement to one that needed to orchestrate its many marches and protests. But McKnight had mentioned that someone else in the White House was also a member of the movement. And then there was the West Wing staffer who was allegedly building a case against Hastings and his mad tenure as leader of the free world. For that matter, McKnight had told him that more and more of Hastings' inner circle were turning against him. Any one of a dozen people might have tipped off Grass Roots that Finch was bringing his troops into Nashville as a show of force to intimidate those who would challenge the President. But who?

Patterson leafed through his Bible looking for another scripture passage, one that he thought was appropriate—and frightening. It was from the Gospel of Matthew, words spoken by Jesus of a time of great tribulation. He read the words aloud. "So when you see the abomination of desolation spoken of by the prophet Daniel standing in the holy place, then let those who are in Judea flee to the mountains."

Herbert Chase Hastings was an abomination to the country, a man living in the White House, a place that the American people had deemed to be almost sacred since its construction. But there was, Patterson thought, a deeper meaning to the passage. Hastings and Gerard were taking Hastings' political agenda of violence, hatred, and bigotry to the people in the name of God, placing the president's perverted ideas into the domain of religion.

Leland Wallace had said it best. The country was dying, and it seemed as if civil war might be on the horizon if Jimmy Finch, together with a new political base, took over more states in defiance of gubernatorial orders to vacate state and municipal property.

Patterson took a deep breath. Would he be able to expose illegal activity on the part of President Hastings before things got out of control—before cities across the nation became battlegrounds?

If Finch expanded his troops into other cities, there would be precious little time to stop the madman in the White House.

Chapter Sixty-Seven
Unhinged

Secretary of State Hart wasn't pleased with the reports airing on every major news outlet. U.S. fighter jets were flying over the Arabian Sea, paralleling the coasts of Pakistan and southwest Iran. The F-45s were flying at a distance of twelve nautical miles from the coast in order to honor the territorial waters of each country, but their flight paths made it clear that they were hugging to the sovereign limit of each country as precisely as possible.

Deputy Secretary of Defense Newman stated that the planes were engaged in military training exercises and nothing more, although he added that Pakistan should take notice of the strong military presence of the United States in the region. "The United States will not tolerate the presence of terrorist training camps or staging areas for terrorist activity in any nation, especially when explicit threats have been made against nuclear facilities inside of any country."

NATO allies were puzzled and alarmed by what Deputy Secretary Newman called military training exercises and asked the United States Ambassador to the United Nations for an explanation for what they regarded as the blatant and bellicose nature of the operation over the Arabian Sea. The prime minister of Great Britain and the chancellor of Germany stated publicly that their intelligence gathering agencies showed no terrorist activity within the borders of Pakistan.

The Congressional leadership of both the House and the Senate said that the President had briefed them on the military operations, but had been given no specifics. The information given to them, said a Democratic senator, had been limited to what the press was reporting and that the briefing had taken all of five minutes. "It was nothing more than a formality," he said. "For that matter, no briefings are required for routine training exercises. The whole thing makes no sense."

Republican Senator Paul McFarland said, "The country needs unity in a time of crisis. U.S. troops have been deployed and possibly put in harm's way. Shame on anyone who doesn't get behind freedom and the flag."

The ABN Nightly News anchor noted the contradiction in statements, saying that routine training exercises by the military did not constitute a crisis.

Hart switched channels on the wall screen in his office and watched news on the takeover of downtown Nashville and the alliance between the Church of the Heart and the American Paramilitary Union. The riots in Nashville had lasted for twelve hours and were being compared to the 1968 protests staged at the Democratic National Convention in Chicago. The death toll was still rising.

"Hastings is overplaying his hand," Hart said to himself. "The country can't be downsized and cleansed of its political sins if it's plunged into civil war. As for fighter jets flying near Pakistan and Iran, it's an insane move."

Hart paused at his use of the word *insane*. He had no doubt that President Hastings was mentally ill, and all efforts to get Vice President Quint to rein in his boss had failed. He was running out of options, and called the Chairman of the Joint Chiefs. General Sutherland took the call immediately.

"Will," Hart said, "it's time we ask the Pentagon and the commanders in the field to defy the president's orders."

"I've already talked with all of them, Max. Nobody is willing to commit treason. I appealed to them personally, but they said they intend to follow the chain of command."

"And what if Hastings orders a nuclear strike?" Hart asked.

"Newman said he's not sure what he personally would do. The same goes for the secretaries of the Army, Navy, and the Air Force."

"You're . . . not sure?"

"That's correct."

Hart hung up abruptly. Matters were quickly getting out of hand. Hastings was not proving to be the malleable puppet he had counted on. Before his inauguration, Hastings had promised Hart that he would accept the counsel of his top advisors since he had no military experience and was coming from the private sector, with an eye towards handling the economy and domestic issues.

Hart, normally a calm individual under any circumstance, rose from his desk and looked at pictures of heroic battles throughout history. There had never been a military coup in the United States in its long and glorious history, but several of his former colleagues in the military—generals and admirals—had contacted him privately to ask about the intentions of President Hastings. Some stood behind their commander in chief. Others felt that the republic was on the verge of collapse and had recommended that the president be forcibly removed from power if the vice president couldn't be persuaded to invoke the Twenty-fifth Amendment. Hart was now considering the ramifications of such a move and recalled his hero from *Apocalypse Now*, Colonel Kurtz. Did he—Secretary of State Maxwell Hart—have the same purity of purpose that the infamous colonel had demonstrated?

He knew the answer to his own question. If Hastings was going to turn America's streets into a battleground using state militias, a coup of sorts would already have been undertaken, for the rule of law would have been violated and the Constitution would have become a mockery. If blood was going to be shed, it might as well be in the name of preserving the Union. And yet there was only one way to stop Hastings with a coup. Surgical airstrikes would have to be undertaken against the Loyalty Militia—what an odious name, Hart thought—and Jimmy Finch's state militias. Street fighting wasn't an option. The troop strength of the National Guard—its proper name—and the state militias could match conventional U.S. ground forces if it came to fighting urban battles in the cities of America. The country would be destroyed.

But whose side would Cal Quint be on if a coup became necessary? Who would fill in the vacuum of power? If not Quint, then a military man would have to step forward and assume the role of President until the rule of law had been reestablished. Hart deemed himself to be that man.

Chapter Sixty-Eight
Divesting Morality

THE INDEPENDENT LAB TOOK ONLY A DAY TO ANALYZE PERSIAN DYNASTY AND SAILOR CIGARETTES. PATTERSON STOOD IN TAYLOR'S OFFICE, READING THE RESULTS. He shook his head before handing the report to his boss as he sat in an overstuffed chair in the corner, curling his leg over the right armrest.

"PB is once again selling the real thing in Sailor cigarettes," Patterson said, "which means that their increase in profits lately is due to slowly reintroducing nicotine into its blend. People are getting hooked. The lab report says that there is a genetic match between the tobacco in the different brands of cigarettes that is beyond any statistical probability. The exact same leaves used for one brand are being used for the other."

Taylor scratched his head, put the report on his desk, and looked at his lead reporter. "Looks like Todd Hastings is out of the loop," he said, "Sela says the guy is distraught and overworked and appears convinced that some variety of harmless plant leaf is responsible for the uptick in sales of Sailor."

"Todd gives the Hastings family plausible deniability and explains why they left such an inexperienced young man in charge of the entire operation," Patterson said. "Brad, Savannah, and the President are obviously making the big decisions." Patterson picked up an unopened pack of Persian Dynasty and examined the fine print beneath the brand's logo, which was a sultan's palace surrounded by palm trees.

"Manufactured by Silk Road Enterprises," Patterson said. "I wonder if—"

"If Silk Road is a subsidiary of Faridoon's holding company," Taylor said.

"Exactly, but it's a foreign company and wouldn't be listed in the online database of the Securities and Exchange Commission."

Patterson moved to a desktop in Taylor's office and performed a search for Silk Road Enterprises. It was listed as a subsidiary of Beryllio Enterprises and described as a company dealing in spices such as cayenne pepper, coriander, cumin, fenugreek, saffron, garlic, and cardamom, all used in traditional Iranian cuisine.

"I'm stumped," Taylor said. "Same tobacco leaves, different companies. And Silk Road isn't listed as being in the business of selling cigarettes."

"But it's public knowledge that PB has enlarged its portfolio over the past year," Patterson said as he continued to search the Internet. "Mergers and acquisitions are a matter of public record. They're listed with the offices of secretaries of state as well as state securities regulators. I'm looking through North Carolina listings."

Several moments elapsed before Patterson grinned at his editor. "There. I found it. There was naturally no merger between PB and Silk Road, or the latter wouldn't still be listed as a corporate entity. But PB conducted what is called an asset purchase of Silk Road, meaning they bought various assets of the Iranian company. PB Enterprises acquired two of Silk Road's buildings, some of its real estate, and machinery."

"What kind of machinery?" Taylor asked.

"I'm not sure, but I bet that whatever it is was flown to Garundi on a C-130. I'll check with Bobby. He saw some heavy machinery in some of the tobacco fields."

"If what you're saying is true, then we have direct links between PB, Iran, and Garundi."

"I'd bet my career on it," Patterson said. "Bradley, Savannah, and Sedge O'Connell have been doing business with the Iranians, and it doesn't have a damn thing to do with nuclear technology. It's about tobacco and cigarettes."

"But Brad and Savannah would be responsible for anything PB does," Taylor pointed out. "Hastings divested before he took office."

"The only thing Hastings divested himself of is his sense of morality," Patterson shot back. "Take it to the bank, John. Our President is running this scam in order to get back into the business of addicting Americans to cigarettes and making his tobacco empire great again."

"Are you going to publish this?"

"No. I have to finish connecting the dots. If I post too early, the Hastings family might shut the entire operation down. When I finally publish, the operation involving all three countries has to be actively up and running."

"Do you want me to put someone else on this, Jay? I mean, you were strung up in a barn and given a stern warning by The Elect."

Patterson shook his head. "This is *my* story, John, and I'm going to see it through to the end. I admit that it's risky, but that's the problem with America today. Nobody wants to speak truth to power. I'm not going to bail on this."

Taylor smiled. "It was a rhetorical question."

But Jay was already out the door. *I'm on it, Dad. The Truth is everything connected . . . all the dots connected.*

Chapter Sixty-Nine
Do American Citizens Care?

JOHN TAYLOR'S ARTICLE ON THE CAUSE OF DEATH OF TOM CHANCE AND ELIZABETH RAMPLING CAUSED AN INITIAL STIR, ESPECIALLY BECAUSE THE AUTOPSY REPORTS HAD BEEN SENT TO THE ELECT, OTHERWISE KNOWN AS THE OFFICE OF GOVERNMENT INQUIRY, A MYSTERIOUS AGENCY LINKED TO LUCILLE RAINES. Taylor laid out all of Patterson's methodical research and the details on nanobots found in the heart muscles of the victims. There was outrage among Democrats and the Grass Roots organization, but a flash poll revealed that fifty-six percent of Americans felt that the entire story was too far-fetched. Thirty-three percent had no opinion on the claims made in the article, while only eleven percent believed that President Hastings, Secretary Hart, and Chief of Staff Lucille Raines should be investigated in relation to the deaths. TINN claimed it was substitute news and that NewzTracker was becoming desperate, resembling a tabloid more than a respected news organization.

/

Deputy White House Press Secretary Grant Schneider stood in for David Wolcott, who,

he said, had the flu. He stated that no one at the White House had received any information, let alone autopsy reports, on the deaths of Senator Tom Chance or Dr. Elizabeth Rampling. Furthermore, he informed the press corps that Lucille Raines had received no phone call in the middle of the night and belonged to no secret organization, which he said was more in keeping with science fiction than reporting the news. Finally, he said that Chief of Staff Raines was recommending to the Justice Department that an investigation be conducted into the wild accusations made in the latest NewzTracker article, which she regarded as libelous and posed a threat to the president, since it had the potential to inflame readers or prejudice them against his leadership.

/

Democrats seized the opportunity to call for the Attorney General of the United States to appoint Special Counsel to investigate the President on his possible involvement in the death of Chance and Rampling, as well as his possible ties with Iran and Hamid Abbas Faridoon. They also believed that President Hastings had violated the Constitution by encouraging the formation of the Church of the Heart, granting civilian state militias equal footing with the National Guard, and for deploying the National Guard in a matter unrelated to a national emergency.

The Attorney General was swift and terse in his response. He stated that he would not commit resources, manpower, or millions of dollars based on the absurd allegations made by a single news outlet that believed in a secret organization, surely concocted by the liars at NewzTracker, who had allegedly given Harry Truman information on flying saucers. As for murder by nanotechnology, he said such a plot more properly belonged in an episode of *Star Trek*. As for Bradley and Savannah Hastings, the Attorney General said that the Hastings children had adequately explained their business interests in PB Enterprises' new Slipstream 7000. And the National Guard, he said, was still the same fine reserve force of the United States Army, regardless of what name it had been given, and had merely been present in Nashville to handle the unlawful assembly of five thousand members of Grass Roots.

The Attorney General took no questions after his statement.

John Taylor sat in his office with a sullen look on his face. His article hadn't caused the outcry he'd anticipated. If President DePeche had been even remotely implicated in a murder scandal, Republicans would have demanded that Special Counsel be appointed and would have recommended impeachment before an investigation had even begun. Everything Hastings was doing, in fact, would not have been tolerated in the DePeche administration. He would have been ousted long before his full term had run its course. Maybe Dr. Boyce Rittner had been correct. Maybe nobody really cared anymore what their government was doing. They had, after all, elected Hastings, and most of his base was sticking by the man despite the egregious nature of his actions.

The country has lost its moral compass.

Chapter Seventy

Playground Rule: If You Hit Me, I'll Hit Back!

PRESIDENT HASTINGS WAS APOPLECTIC AT TAYLOR'S NEWS REPORT. He was the President, and the liars were going after him anyway. He'd been told by one of his many lawyers after he'd won the election that a sitting President couldn't be indicted for anything. He was above the law. But now NewzTracker was attempting to link the White House to murder.

He walked around his office, doing deep breathing exercises to relax. Hastings liked to think his nerves had always been steel, but since criticisms had continued to mount with each passing week against a man who prided his imperial image, he had grown irritable and angry and far more paranoid that his image was being pulled apart.

"I'll let the news cycle play out, just as Cal advised me to," he said aloud as he began to walk around the office, holding to the oval contour. "Pakistan will get everybody's attention. All of this will blow over, just as Cal said it would. He knows what he's doing."

Hastings stopped. He *had* to do something. *He had to.* Yes, he would use VOXPOP and let people know how he felt—make his enemies scared of him. He dictated a brief message: "NewzTracker is murdering the Truth. Shame on Patterson and Taylor for their lies. Their days are numbered."

He wanted to dictate more, but he checked himself. He'd experienced a momentary lapse in judgment. He'd forgotten that he couldn't allow himself to react.

"But I have to hurt *someone*," he said as he resumed his pacing. "I've been attacked, and I have to show people who's in charge just like I showed God that I was in charge when I spit on the crucifix in high school . . . . not that I believe in God anymore."

He thought back to the times when his father had schooled him on how to handle criticism. Percy Hastings had been proactive and had taught his son that he should always fight back—and fight back hard. Power was its own end. It made people respect you. It was the key that unlocked all doors, from wealth to pleasure. Herbert Hastings had secretly tortured some of his classmates in high school, and in business he'd been ruthless in running PB Enterprises. He'd stepped on anyone who'd gotten in his way, had put other companies out of business, and hired and fired people with caprice. The key to power was to make people fear you, to criticize and denigrate and mock. To abuse them, if necessary, but one *always* had to land a punch. Julius and Augustus had sent legions of soldiers to their deaths to preserve their empires. *Their* empires. They had executed enemies and imprisoned those who opposed them.

His breath came hard and fast as he walked around the Oval Office again and again.

"Maxwell always understood these principles, even in school. He was a ruthless general who didn't care whether or not he killed civilians in a campaign. His only objective was to get the job done. It's why I nominated him. It's why I nominated Montgomery, but he turned on me and called me an idiot."

No comment, Mr. President. Let the news cycles play out. People have short memories.

"Yes, Cal, you're right, but I have to find a way to respond, even if it's indirectly."

Hastings went to his phone and called Lucille Raines, ordering her to his office at once before he resumed his pacing around the office of the Chief Executive of the United States.

"I'll hurt someone. Yes. I won't react to the article, but I'll make my enemies feel pain. That's the rule, is it not? If someone abuses you, then you abuse *them*—or others. You abuse whoever resembles the offending party. Show power. Show power. I know. I'll send a nuclear submarine to Pakistan called the USS Hastings! I'll show everyone who's in charge!"

Hastings knew exactly who he would hurt—bleeding heart Democrats and those who counted on them to provide a free lunch. He would hurt people in need, people who were liars and manipulators, people who didn't work or pull themselves up by their bootstraps. If he, Herbert Chase Hastings, forty-seventh President of the United States, could work his way up to becoming the head of PB Enterprises and then the leader of the free world, then others should be able to pull their weight. When people attacked you, you inflicted pain, regardless of who got in the way.

It was about power and who was left standing when the battle was over.

As Lucille Raines was shown into the Oval Office, Hastings quickly morphed into the confident man on display at his rallies and public appearances.

"Lucille, I want you to draft executive orders. Insurance will no longer cover pre-existing conditions, and emergency room visits will no longer be covered for those who get their healthcare through trips to the ER. People wouldn't get sick to begin with—wouldn't have pre-existing conditions—if they practiced the kind of healthy diet and exercise regimen I adhere to every day. As for those who pop into the ER whenever they have the sniffles, they're lazy and don't work. They deserve whatever illnesses they get."

"I agree with your policies on paper, Herbert, but we need to go about this with a legislative—"

"My mind is made up, Lucille. We'll juggle some numbers at Health and Human Services if we have to, and be sure to run the language of the orders you draft by the Attorney General so we have some kind of constitutional or budgetary basis on which to take these actions.

"Very well, Herbert," Raines said with a smile. "I love it when you're forceful. It's when you're at your best. You're due at Andrews to board Air Force One, with wheels up in two hours. It will be a short flight to Nashville. Good luck at the convention."

Hastings took Raines in his arms and hugged her tightly before kissing her softly on the lips.

Hastings felt strong and energetic as he stood in the dressing room of the convention center in Nashville, where he would address an arm of his Red Republican Legion, as well as the Tennessee Civilian State Militia. The Loyalty Militia had cordoned off the center for an area of several blocks, and Grass Roots had been denied further permits by the mayor of Nashville to stage protests in the city since he would not, he said, allow them to spill more blood in the streets. The mayor claimed that one-third of the protesters who had tried to reach Jimmy Finch's caravan had been armed with weapons, all of which had been confiscated, but he refused to show them to the press.

Hastings stood before the mirror, his imperial image staring back and reminding him not to address Taylor's report or any matter pertaining to Iran. When it was time for him to go before the decidedly friendly crowd, he pounded his right fist into his left palm as usual and sprinted onto the elevated stage and stood behind the podium. He held up his hands as was his custom, but the spring in his step caused journalists to compare the president's body language to that of Rocky Balboa.

Seated behind the president on either side were Brad and Savannah Hastings, Sedge O'Connell, Jimmy Finch, Holly Gerard, and the mayor of Nashville. Noticeably absent were Senator Leland Wallace, Todd Hastings, and the First Lady. Because of thunderous applause, the President couldn't begin his speech for ten minutes.

When he finally began, Hastings spoke with the same confidence he'd exuded at Brister, Arizona. "Ladies and gentlemen, I have an important announcement, one you will have the privilege of hearing for the first time."

A hush of anticipation fell over the convention center.

"I met with the FBI yesterday," Hastings continued, "and I can now verify what I have long suspected. Not only has it been proven that members of Grass Roots are anarchists, but many of them are terrorist sympathizers.

Many of these unpatriotic Americans who were taken into custody by the Loyalty Militia and the Nashville Police Department have confessed during interrogation that they have strong ties to the Sunni terrorists in Pakistan. Yes, dear friends, the crisis on the other side of the world has come to our shores, and I'm ordering that all nuclear power plants and government agencies receive round-the-clock protection from the Loyalty Militia in order to stop homegrown terrorism."

Chants of "No more roots!" echoed throughout the great hall as the President stepped back from the microphone and looked over the sea of his admirers as they, with one voice, expressed outrage and hatred for the Grass Roots organization.

When he resumed, Hastings said, "Ask yourself, my friends: Why do these protesters spend so much time in the streets? Don't they have families or jobs? No, friends, they're lazy, leeches on the great society of America, which is why, as of today, I am curtailing their access to healthcare by executive order. Today, my fellow Americans, we begin to—how shall I put it?—cut the grass!"

The chants in the hall changed to "Cut the grass! Cut the Grass!"

Furthermore," Hastings said, "I'm ordering that all Grass Roots members be put into internment camps if they are found to have any ties to terrorism. I want them off the streets so that mothers and fathers can take their children to school in safety, free from bloodshed and riots. There will be no more school shootings after this! Our children will finally be safe!"

Red caps were tossed in the air, and the heavy leather boots of Tennessee Civilian State Militia troops created the sound of thunder as weekend soldiers stamped their heels on the concrete floor of the auditorium.

Hastings held up his hands, motioning for silence. He then wandered from the topic of politics, knowing that he could segue back to a new topic with the kind of rhetoric that had gained him the presidency.

"Everyone knows I like to keep fit, and I swim a hundred laps a day if I don't jog five miles. I guess I could walk on water instead, but I want to keep fit."

The crowd erupted into laughter as Hastings smiled, turning left and right so as to connect with all sections of the convention center.

"But seriously, friends, I was swimming the other day and thought of how Our Lord walked on the water one night. Can you imagine it? Jesus' feet hovering over the turbulent waves? What a spectacle that must have been. But the prime minister of Pakistan—Yasir Rafiq? I don't think so, friends. Rafiq is granting aid to terrorists from outside Pakistan, but I'm warning him right now that unless he takes immediate measures to dissolve the terrorist camps in his country, he will face the wrath of the United States of America."

Hastings paused for another outburst of applause, and then continued his speech. He had brought his rhetoric from swimming to Christ to Pakistan, and he wasn't finished. He knew that his words were going to homes all across America, and it was time to scare the living hell out of as many people as he could while appealing to God in the process.

"Christ asked St. Peter to step out of the boat and walk on the water with him, and I'm up to that challenge. I can do it. Rafiq can't. I defy the storms raging against America as I grasp the Lord's hand in partnership against all enemies of our nation."

Many in attendance were fainting from their frenzied enthusiasm and had to be escorted from the main hall of the center to first aid rooms. Others were giving each other high fives as they whooped and hollered and applauded. They had come to hear tough talk, and Hastings was delivering up his particular brand of red meat to his Red Republican Legion, a pride of lions hungry for divine retribution against the enemies of America, foreign or domestic.

"I'd now like Church of the Heart Pastor Holly Gerard to conclude our meeting with a moment of prayer," Hastings said.

Gerard stepped up to the lectern and bowed her head, which caused a ripple effect in the center as people removed their red hats and lowered their heads as she spoke.

"O Divine Over-soul of these United States of America," she said, "I ask you to bless Herbert Hastings, the greatest president this country has ever known. And I ask you to bless the brave warriors in this convention center and those ensuring our safety on the streets outside, for no greater love hath a man than to lay down his life for his brother. In the words of the Book of Psalms, I beg of thee, O Lord, to destroy our enemies and crush them with your vengeance. Let them know that you alone are the Lord God most high, a God to be feared, a God who will exact retribution on all who defy you and your servants, such as your humble and obedient child, President Herbert Chase Hastings. And finally, Lord, bless the Church of the Heart, that it may not be a sanctuary for the godless and heathen among us who prowl like ravenous wolves to destroy your precious flock. May you defeat them as you defeated pharaoh and his chariots, killing all who stand in the way of people seeking the light of your salvation. I humbly ask this in the name of the Divine. Amen."

People raised their heads and cheered as President Hastings left the stage to a crescendo of applause. No one cared that God was now both Christian deity as well as the amorphous divinity that Hastings asserted lived inside of every human being on the planet. The Grass Roots movement had been conflated with Muslims and terrorists. God was whoever or whatever Herbert Hastings said he was on any given day.

In the Presidential limousine, President Hastings sat calmly as he watched people on the sidewalks waving to him. He had his energy, vitality, and momentum back. He felt better than he had in weeks. His image was restored, and thus, his confidence.

Chapter Seventy-One
Presidential Conflict of Interest

Bobby Thibodaux appeared pleased with himself as Patterson entered the room.

"I've got the videos you've been waiting for," he stated proudly. "Take a look at the cargo coming out of the C-130s on the airstrip near Jumba Ogo."

Patterson stood behind Thibodaux's chair and watched as the wizard of NewzTracker replayed images he'd captured over the past twelve hours. Crates had been unloaded from the cargo planes, letters stenciled on their sides reading *PB Select Seed—Charlotte NC.* In videos of a second and third C-130, heavy machinery was unloaded from the rear cargo hold. In plain view were tractors, crop sprayers, and combine harvesters.

"I've better resolution on the tail of the planes because of the angle at which the pilots stopped them on the tarmac. You can plainly see the horizontal bars of green, white, and red of the Iranian flag. Damn hard to see even with high res satellite imagery. The writing on the equipment is also Iranian. It's owned by Silk Road Enterprises."

"PB and Iran are engaged in a joint tobacco growing operation in Garundi," Patterson said. "Unbelievable."

"It gets better," Thibodaux said. "The machinery is taken on flatbed trailers to the tobacco fields we previously saw. The trucks carrying the crates of seed packets go straight to the palace. I scanned its gardens for the umpteenth time—there are over five dozen—and stopped looking for tobacco plants. Instead, I saw these."

Thibodaux brought up images of rectangular frames in the gardens. "Those are hot beds," he said.

"It's where the seeds are planted and incubated until they germinate and grow into plants large enough to be taken to the fields. There's a lot of machinery tilling the soil in those, by the way, to prepare for planting."

"The stages of an operation," Patterson said. "It's what Brad and Savannah were talking about with Faridoon. I'm guessing that the next stages are to increase the export of the tobacco grown in Garundi. The operation, to paraphrase Faridoon, would take any rival companies by storm. PB's competition would be decimated. Do you know how the tobacco is exported?"

Thibodaux looked insulted. "They don't call me a wizard for nothing. One road, as we saw, goes to the Persian Dynasty factory in Garundi. The other five lead to port cities on the east coast of Africa. Maputo, Nacala, Pemba, Mozambique, and Mombasa, to be exact."

"It's a big world, Bobby. Do we know the destinations of the ships carrying tobacco from those ports?"

"I could track the movements of ships, but it would take weeks to see where each departure ended up, assuming I could isolate the various ships being loaded in their respective African ports. So I worked backwards. I used a satellite in geosynchronous orbit over the Eastern Seaboard of the United States and zoomed in on the PB plant just outside of Charlotte. The cigarette factory that manufactures Sailor cigarettes receives shipments from Norfolk, Baltimore, Wilmington, Charleston, Savannah, and Jacksonville. Those port cities all had ships with registries corresponding with the East African port cities I just mentioned. It's our smoking gun, pun intended."

"Great work, Bobby."

"Are you ready to get Abita to make me a majority shareholder, because I have icing on the cake?"

"There's more?"

"A little extra. It's called lagniappe in Louisiana. The shipments going from the Eastern Seaboard ports to the PB factory outside Charlotte all have escorts."

Patterson slapped his forehead. He knew what was coming.

"The eighteen wheelers bringing tobacco to PB are all accompanied by Jeeps and troop carriers of civilian state militias from North Carolina, South Carolina, and Georgia. The logo on all of these escort vehicles indicates that they're part of the American Paramilitary Union."

"Holy crap," Patterson uttered. "Iran is helping PB to grow tobacco in Garundi. Felix Ogo takes a cut of the harvested plants and makes Persian Dynasty in his country, which is why there's been an uptick in his economy recently. The rest of the tobacco goes to the United States and ends up at the PB plant and is used in Sailor cigarettes—with a little help from Jimmy Finch."

"Sounds like an awfully expensive operation," Thibodaux noted. "How can PB turn a profit?"

"As you already noted, with help from Iran."

"What's in it for the Iranian mafia?"

"Probably a cut of the profits, but it has to be more than that. As you say, such a worldwide operation would be really expensive. My guess is that Iran is footing a large part of the bill in order to receive some type of political favor in return."

"Which is why President Hastings is hassling Pakistan instead of Iran," Thibodaux said. "Does it have to do with allowing Iran to further develop nuclear technology?"

"That's what comes to mind. If Iran can develop more powerful warheads and missile delivery systems, it could threaten any place in the world."

"And now?"

"It's time to run this by John and then share it with the world."

"Stay away from barns," Thibodaux said, the humor fading from his voice. "You and Sela need to be careful."

Patterson knew that publishing again was risky, but he'd pursued the story, and finally knew what was behind the Hastings family relationship with Iran and Garundi. President Hastings was thumbing his nose at any number of laws, but he was enriching himself by working with a foreign government, not to mention endangering the health of America by replacing Western Rider with Sailor. And he was doing so while sitting in office. He was in clear violation of the emoluments clause of the Constitution.

Patterson would be careful, but he would publish—and under his own name.

Chapter Seventy-Two
Legitimate Blackmail

President Hastings arrived at the White House, signed the executive orders drafted by Raines, including those he'd announced in Nashville, and went upstairs to his bedroom to freshen up. He was surprised to see his wife standing in his suite, waiting for him with a smile. It was shaping up to be the perfect end to a perfect day. Diane had probably seen his magnificent performance on television, he reasoned, and was again attracted to his raw sensuality and lust for power. He would take her and ravish her before he got back to work. His heart belonged to Lucille, but one woman had never been enough for his sexual appetite. He approached her with open arms, but she stiffened and stepped back.

"Stay right there," warned the First Lady, her features hardening.

"What's going on?" Hastings asked.

"Tear up the executive orders, Herbert," she said, her eyes fixed on her husband's stare. "All of them. The ones on healthcare and those pertaining to Grass Roots. There will be no interrogations and no internment camps. In fact, you'll sign no more executive orders at all without my permission."

"Are you mad? I believe you need to return to the Renewed Springs Center for a lengthy stay. You're obviously not well."

He stepped forward to grab her, but she put her arm out, palm against his chest, and pushed him away.

"Do I have to teach you a lesson again?" he asked.

"A lesson? I thought it was a body double who had taught me what you call a lesson."

"You lousy bitch!" Hastings screamed. "I'm the president!"

"Tear up the orders, or I'll release the video that was secretly made of you standing in front of your full-length mirror, talking to yourself while imagining yourself to be a Roman emperor. If anyone questions whether or not you're mentally unstable, the video will assuage their doubts. You're a borderline personality, Herbert. A sociopath. You have no conscience."

"Give it to me, or I'll kill you. Right here. Right now. I'll make it look like a suicide."

"I've sent a copy to a trusted individual and told that person to release the video if anything happens to me—or if you don't destroy the executive orders you had Lucille Raines draft."

Hastings, his face red, lunged at his wife. His hands were poised to seize her by the throat and squeeze until she could no longer breathe.

The First Lady held up a slender, black rectangular electronic device and pushed a red button on its surface. Two Secret Service agents immediately entered the bedroom. Hastings immediately released his hands from around his wife's throat, but not before the two agents saw what was happening.

"Is everything all right, ma'am?" the first young man, dressed in black, asked.

"Well, Herbert?" the First Lady said. "Is everything all right?"

Hastings stood erect and straightened his tie. Clearing his throat and forcing a smile, he turned to face the agents.

"Yes," he said. "Everything's fine. I merely stumbled."

The President approached his wife and whispered in her ear. "You win—for now."

The First Lady brushed past the President, walked across the hall, and entered her own bedroom. The two agents stationed themselves outside the suite, one on each side of the door.

Hastings closed the door to his own room, breathing heavily. He would kill his wife, but not yet. When the time was right, he would hire someone to make it look like an accident. She'd crossed a line, and he would not allow her to go on living while possessing any kind of leverage against him.

He smiled at himself in the mirror. The image smiled back, giving Hastings all the validation he needed.

Chapter Seventy-Three

Truth and Consequences

COOKIE MCKNIGHT OPENED THE MESSAGE ON HER PHONE. IT WAS UNSIGNED, AND THE TEXT WAS BRIEF.

> Ms. McKnight:
>
> Release this video if any harm should come to the First Lady, or if the President releases any further executive orders on any matter. Otherwise, show it to no one.
>
> A Friend

Cookie watched the video attached to the message, and her first impulse was to contact Jay Patterson immediately. The video constituted strong evidence that the President was mentally ill, perhaps even psychotic, and it totally validated Jay's interview with Dr. Boyce Rittner. She was about to forward the message to Patterson's NewzTracker address, but stopped and withdrew her hand. She didn't know who the sender was, although she thought that the disgruntled staffer in the West Wing, the one gathering evidence against the President, was the logical candidate, for who else would have such access to the First Family?

Otherwise, show it to no one.

She wouldn't jeopardize what might be a larger plan to bring down the President, but she would keep a close eye on Hastings and the First Lady.

Chapter Seventy-Four
Delusion of Power

WHEN UNITED STATES AIR FORCE F-45 HORNET FIGHTER JETS FLEW OVER GWADAR, INVADING THE SOVEREIGN AIRSPACE OF PAKISTAN, AN EMERGENCY SESSION OF THE UNITED NATIONS SECURITY COUNCIL WAS CONVENED AT THE REQUEST OF FIVE OF THE EIGHT PERMANENT MEMBERS OF THE BODY ENTRUSTED WITH SECURING PEACE AROUND THE WORLD: GREAT BRITAIN, FRANCE, CHINA, THE SOVIET UNION, AND GERMANY.

Echoing the news briefings given by Deputy White House Press Secretary Schneider, U.S. Ambassador Allison Barnes declared that the flyover had been for the purposes of reconnaissance since ground intelligence indicated that the terrorist training camp near Gwadar was growing in size and appeared to be preparing for a raid in Iran. Temporary and permanent members of the Security Council demanded to see proof of the camp's existence, but Barnes said that the United States Department of Defense wasn't in the habit of sharing sensitive intelligence that might compromise future military operations.

The Security Council drafted a resolution condemning the actions of the United States military. Pakistan had scrambled Mirage IV-E fighter jets to patrol the area and ward off further incursions into its airspace. Prime Minister Yasir Rafiq stated that Pakistan and the United States were fast approaching the brink of war. The Pakistani Ambassador to the Security Council had provided aerial reconnaissance of land within two hundred square miles of Gwadar to prove that no Sunni terrorist camps existed in the area and added verbally that no such camps existed anywhere in Pakistan. TINN said it had analyzed the footage and found proof that the video had been doctored by the Pakistani government.

President Hastings' comment on VOXPOP was to the point: "Rafiq is a liar. The UN is still a paper tiger. Beware, Pakistan!"

Many Americans began converting their basements into fallout shelters, stocking their homes with canned food and bottled water.

Chapter Seventy-Five

Nicotine in Sailor Cigarettes? No! Really?

DEPUTY PRESS SECRETARY GRANT SCHNEIDER MADE HIS USUAL OPENING STATEMENT BEFORE TAKING QUESTIONS FROM THE PRESS CORPS. The statement dealt exclusively with Patterson's article alleging that PB was once again selling nicotine-laced cigarettes in the United States while partnering with Iran and Garundi in the growing of tobacco in Africa.

"PB has not merged with Silk Road Enterprises," Schneider stated flippantly, his face a study in disdain as he addressed a press corps that he clearly detested. "PB engaged in a purchase of certain Silk Road assets, such as farming equipment that was obviously sent to Garundi by mistake. Also, PB sold crates of tobacco seeds to Iran and Garundi over the past two years since PB doesn't use real tobacco in Sailor cigarettes. It was merely selling off its inventory. It's really as simple as that."

Beau Bricker nearly jumped from his seat as he asked the first question. "How do you account for the fact that thousands of packs of Sailor cigarettes have been analyzed by labs around the country since Jay Patterson's story broke, and they were all found to contain high levels of nicotine and are identical to the tobacco blend used by the Persian Dynasty brand?"

Schneider sighed, as if aggravated that he had to explain anything pertaining to Patterson's report.

"Regrettably," Schneider said, "nicotine found its way into many packs of Sailor recently as a result of experimentation to make Sailor taste more like real tobacco. The same kind of seeds that were sold to Silk Road for its Persian Dynasty brand were used to cross-pollinate a new type of plant from the *solanaceae* family of botanicals. Chemists at PB found a way to grow hybrid plants that tasted just like tobacco, and laboratory tests showed that no nicotine was contained in the new blend. An internal PB study, however, indicated that the manufacturing process was flawed and the company has issued a recall of all unopened packs of Sailor."

Bricker was quick with a follow-up. "Todd Hastings, who claimed he was in charge of the new blend, said that he was unaware of any kind of hybrid experiment, only that new plants were being used in the manufacture of Sailor."

"Todd Hastings is only in charge of PB's expanding portfolio," Schneider claimed. "He has taken a leave of absence from PB to research new market concepts, with Sedge O'Connell now heading day-to-day operations at PB under the direction of Brad and Savannah Hastings. I can't speak for what Todd might have said or meant."

Maryanne Mistretta was next to raise her hand. "Grant, NewzTracker published videos that show the movement of tobacco from fields in Garundi to cargo ships on the African coast. Shipments can also be seen in Mr. Patterson's report that show cargo arriving on the Eastern Seaboard and then proceeding to the PB factory outside of Charlotte. The ships all sailed from ports on the east coast of Africa."

Schneider bowed his head as he braced both of his arms against the lectern. When he looked up and spoke, his tone was demeaning and sarcastic.

"Did anyone actually see where the ships in Africa went? For that matter, does anyone know what was aboard the vessels that unloaded cargo that was shipped to the PB facility in Charlotte? Has anyone seen even a single tobacco plant at the North Carolina factory? PB Enterprises is a large company that has invested money in many new products and technologies."

"Why would new products be shipped to a tobacco factory?" a reporter from ABN asked.

"For a lot of reasons," Schneider said brusquely.

Other questions were hurled at Schneider in rapid succession, ranging from the possibility that the president or his staff had committed murder, to the worldwide condemnation of America's bellicose attitude toward Pakistan and intelligence claims that it couldn't confirm. Schneider dismissed them all as substitute news and said he would answer further questions when the press had something meaningful to ask. With that, he exited the briefing room.

Chapter Seventy-Six
Covering Tracks

Sitting at his basement terminal in the CIA, Lone Wolf grew concerned that his previous messages had not been completely erased. The possibility of his having left a trail haunted him, as discovery would not only endanger him but would jeopardize the entire project.

He spent an hour using various algorithms to see if he could find some faint trace—some echo—of the messages he'd sent to Patterson. If anyone traced the private communications to him, he'd be sacked in a New York minute. Sure enough, he found his messages hiding on a CIA server in Sydney, Australia, as well as the main computer complex at Langley. How they'd gotten there was a mystery.

He knew that Patterson's girlfriend was as tech savvy as they came, a woman who could listen for faint whispers of intelligence from distant stars. For Sela Grant, finding his digital echo might be child's play if she put enough time into it. He would therefore have a little fun and use a different algorithm to send his next message. He would make it appear that his communication had originated from multiple locations, and keep Patterson and his gifted girlfriend busy if they tried to find out who he was.

He sent his two-word message and then logged out of the system. He was satisfied with Patterson's reporting—and that of NewzTracker in general—which had been accurate despite the White House's continued denials of facts posted to the news website. Republicans were starting to distance themselves from their party leader, and Americans were slowly but surely losing confidence in a man who they now believed should never have assumed the highest office in the land.

Lone Wolf was about to leave the building when he was approached by a stunning blonde in her early thirties. She had green eyes, fair skin, and a figure that drew his attention immediately.

"Excuse me, sir," she said. "I have to ask you to follow me. You've just sent a communication that my department has intercepted. My orders are to forward it to the Office of Government Inquiry."

Lone Wolf frowned. He should have never used a new algorithm. He'd underestimated the savants at the CIA.

"Is that really necessary, Miss . . . ."

"Masters. Melanie Masters."

Masters, who spoke with a sultry voice, exuded confidence as she made eye contact with him. "Given your prior service to this agency, however, I can perhaps see that the message isn't reported to OGI, although I'll have to ask you to refrain from sending any further communications from our terminals."

"That's very kind of you, Ms. Masters. What about the other members of your department. Can I trust that they will all be so discreet?"

Masters smiled. "I'm the only one who intercepted your communication, and as far as I'm concerned, it never happened."

Lone Wolf nodded. "We have a deal."

Masters stepped forward and shook Lone Wolf's hand before disappearing into a hallway connected to the main foyer of the CIA.

When Lone Wolf was seated in his car, he opened his hand and looked at the paper Melanie Masters had slipped him when she'd shaken his hand. It contained her name, address, and telephone number. He laughed loudly. It had been years since any woman had been so brazen. He was usually the one who initiated flirtations. It had made his day.

Chapter Seventy-Seven
Secret Passages

PATTERSON, SELA, AND TAYLOR HAD WATCHED THE WHITE HOUSE PRESS BRIEFING AT NEWZTRACKER HEADQUARTERS.

"You basically accused the President of murder," Patterson told John, "and I accused him of working with two foreign governments to line his pockets while lying about his cigarettes. Is anything going to stick?"

"Maybe not," Taylor replied, "but we told the truth and made our point. The country is divided, and Hastings' popularity couldn't get much lower, although some of his base is still sticking by him. There are renewed calls by Democratic congressional leaders for the Attorney General to investigate the murders of Chance and Rampling. As for Iran and Garundi, congressmen on the talk shows are asking for investigations by the Senate Intelligence Committee and the House Committee on Oversight and Investigations. And this morning Beau Bricker released a leaked email from Raines to Savannah telling her and Brad to lay over in Paris instead of proceeding to Iran. A lot of congressmen want Raines, O'Connell, and the Hastings children to testify."

Patterson's phone indicated an incoming message. It was from Lone Wolf. It read: *There's more.*

Patterson threw his hands into the air. "Why doesn't this man just come out and tell me what he's getting at?"

"Plausible deniability," Taylor answered. "It's how Woodward and Deep Throat worked in the seventies."

Patterson, who appeared distracted, suddenly froze. "I know who the White House staffer is who's assembling dirt on Hastings. It's Wolcott. He doesn't have the flu. I'd bet money on it. He just suddenly disappeared from sight."

Patterson called Cookie McKnight.

"Cookie, how much does Wolcott know about what NewzTracker has been publishing?"

There was a pronounced pause on the line. "What makes you think that David is the one who I was referring to?"

"It's a no-brainer, Cookie. He's the one building a case against Hastings, gathering info to bring him down. But first, why?"

The sigh on the other end of the call was audible. "David has been challenging Hastings more and more. The President has been flying off the handle whenever David disagrees with him. While at PB, David took a lot of flak from Hastings over the years, and he was doing so as press secretary as well, which has been a thankless job. How can you give a coherent answer to what the President does? How can you explain away madness and sound even remotely credible? David wanted to steer the President to a more centrist position on any number of matters, and the same can be said for a lot of people in the West Wing."

"How much does Wolcott know about Chance, Rampling, Iran, and Garundi?"

"I honestly don't know, but as former spokesman of PB, he would know quite a bit. He kept in touch with top-level management there. As for Chance or Rampling, I believe Wolcott knew whatever Raines did."

"We have to get into his office and copy his entire hard drive and see what he has. I can't wait any longer to get the entire story, and neither can the country. But why are you speaking of Wolcott in the past tense?"

"Because he killed himself, Jay. His body was discovered thirty minutes ago at his Georgetown home. I think he was ready to go public with whatever he had, but . . . I don't know. I guess he got scared." Cookie paused. "I don't think it's possible to get into the White House. I heard that Hastings gave the order to crash the entire place."

Patterson knew that a crash meant that no one got in or out of the building at 1600 Pennsylvania Avenue. In the event of a crash, the Secret Service sealed all entrances and exits to the White House. It was usually done because of a security breach.

"David's office will be locked and sealed within the hour," McKnight said, "but I presume not before they remove his computers."

"Then we've got to move now," Patterson said with urgency.

"How will we get in?"

"The same way Brad and Savannah do. Through tunnels. Meet me in fifteen minutes at the Ellipse in President's Park."

Patterson ended the call.

"Jay!" Sela cried. "You can't just sneak into the White House. Please! There's got to be another way."

"I wish there was, Sela. Wish me luck."

Patterson left before Sela could respond.

Sela decided that she would, for the tenth time, try to trace the messages from Lone Wolf.

Chapter Seventy-Eight
The Lady has Pluck

Audrey Dickerson entered the First Lady's office. She thought that Diane Hastings, seated behind her desk, looked calmer than she had in months.

"That was quite a feat," Dickerson commented. "You blackmailed the president and got away with it. No executive orders. What's your next move? You are, after all, the leader of Grass Roots. Is there any message I should relay to the state organizers?"

The First Lady smiled. "Tell them that it's safe to take to the streets again. I trust that your lines of communication with them are still open."

"As always."

/

Diane Hastings reflected on her marriage. Her husband had grown more erratic and petulant with each passing month after their marriage. He had become paranoid, irrational, abusive. He put words in her mouth—would gaslight her until she'd questioned her own sanity. He wouldn't allow her to express opinions no matter how innocuous they were. She entered therapy, but remained fearful for her safety since he would threaten her weekly, at times slapping and cursing her. Out of fear, she'd consented to undergo infertility treatments, hoping that she might appease her husband if she could present him with a child. With each successive failure by fertility specialists, Hastings' abuse of her—physical, verbal, and mental—had grown worse.

When her husband decided to run for president, she asked for a divorce, but he threatened to kill her, and she had no doubt at the time that he could find a way to do it. She decided to bide her time until the campaign was over, since she deemed that, as a political outsider, he had no chance to win a national election to the highest office in the land. When he won, she was numb for a week. She was tired after a grueling campaign during which she'd plastered a smile on her face day after day as the candidate was flown in his chartered jet to multiple states, dragging her to one rally after another. The abuse resumed within a few weeks of their moving into the White House. Each time he was mocked or criticized for his lack of experience and rookie political mistakes, he'd taken it out on her, his wife.

She'd grown to hate her husband long before he ever took office, and when she saw that the Grass Roots movement had organically grown across the country beginning on Inauguration Day, she decided to use her most trusted friend and advisor in the world, Audrey Dickerson, to help coordinate the fledgling movement, offering them advice on how to expand their protests and get under Hastings' skin, feeding them his schedule since she was privy to his travel plans. She'd also known what slogans should be used on their signs because she knew what aggravated him the most. The more she could get the movement to provoke him into making foolish statements, the more she thought he might one day be impeached. Over the months, she'd communicated with state organizers through Dickerson while retaining her confidentiality, offering them advice on what issue to protest each day since the one thing her husband hated more than anything else was being kept off balance. Grass Roots had done a splendid job of controlling the news cycle, protesting one issue when Hastings had tried to focus attention on another. She'd sent protesters into Nashville when she learned that Jimmy Finch wanted to flex his muscles there.

Her assistant's words interrupted her reverie.

"I take it you heard about Wolcott," Dickerson said.

"Suicide."

"We should get to his office. I heard that he has compromising information on the president stored on his hard drive."

"We can't let Herbert get that drive," the First Lady said. "He'll destroy it. Wolcott probably accumulated as much damaging evidence on him over the years as I have. Let's get to his office."

The pair stopped by a Secret Service agent in the hall outside the First Lady's office in the East Wing.

"The White House has been crashed," he stated. "No one goes in or out."

"Thank you," said the First Lady, who turned to the two men in her regular detail. "Do I still have access to the West Wing?"

"Yes, ma'am."

The First Lady looked at Dickerson, and the two women proceeded through the residence, hoping to get to David Wolcott's office before the president or anyone he'd delegated for the job.

Chapter Seventy-Nine

Crash the White House

PRESIDENT HASTINGS HAD BEEN INFORMED OF WOLCOTT'S DEATH BY LUCILLE RAINES. She immediately advised her boss to crash the White House so that no one could leave the premises with anything belonging to Wolcott, especially the computers and documents in his office.

"He knew too much," Raines said. "I should have known something was up when he began calling in to say he had the flu.

"Don't beat yourself up about it, Lucille," Hastings said. "You made the right call to crash the White House. We'll go to his office personally and confiscate his computer."

The two were walking to Wolcott's office in the West Wing when Raines' assistant approached them. "You're needed in the Situation Room immediately, Mr. President."

"Thank you," Raines told her assistant. "We're on our way to the Situation Room. Make sure that a guard is stationed outside his office."

The President and Raines went to the Situation Room in the basement of the West Wing.

Raines' assistant looked puzzled. Where was a guard supposed to be stationed? Raines hadn't specified the office of anyone in particular. He assumed that the chief of staff wanted an extra guard outside the Oval Office since the White House was being crashed, so he requested that a uniformed Marine join the existing complement of guards outside the president's office.

Chapter Eighty
Tunneling

McKnight met Patterson at the Ellipse and gave him gray pants and a white work shirt with the name and logo Capitol AC and Heating Inspections. She also provided him with a metal tool case with the same name and logo. Patterson put his equipment into the kit before he hastily changed, with McKnight facing away, and then stashed his own clothes into the bottom of the large case.

"The company does all the air conditioning and heating work for federal office buildings," McKnight said, "including the White House. And here—you'll need a visitor's pass."

"Thanks, but where the hell is the entrance to the tunnel?" Patterson said.

McKnight looked around. "There's a barricaded section on the other side of the bushes behind us. It looks like the same place I saw in Beau Bricker's report about Brad and Savannah's secret trips into the White House."

Patterson climbed over what was a typical barricade used for crowd control and dropped to his knees. It was early evening, but there was still enough light to see the ground clearly. He saw only green grass. He methodically moved his hand across the lawn until it encountered a metal ring folded downward so that it was flush with the ground. He lifted it and saw that a square patch of grass and dirt four feet wide had been dislodged. Putting it aside, he motioned for McKnight to join him. She straddled the barricade and knelt beside him.

Patterson removed a narrow-beam flashlight from the tool case McKnight had provided. "There's a ladder that goes straight down for about fifteen feet. Ready?"

"Yeah. We don't have much time."

"You go first," Patterson said, "and I'll follow so that I can put the sod back in place."

Two minutes later, Patterson and McKnight stood at the end of a concrete tunnel that stretched far into the distance.

"Let's hope Bricker knew what he was writing about," Patterson commented as they started to walk forward.

The ceiling of the arched tunnel measured seven feet from the floor, so there wasn't much clearance. The space was narrow, and they walked single file for ninety-eight paces, after which they stood in front of a blue wooden door with an ordinary knob.

"The damn thing is locked," Patterson moaned. "It's pretty low-tech, but without a key, I don't see how we go any farther."

McKnight reached into the tool case and grasped a hammer. "Then let's take a low-tech approach."

She raised the hammer in her right hand and brought it down on the metal doorknob, which fell to the floor with a *clank*. It took several seconds for the echo in the tunnel behind them to fade.

Patterson inserted the index and middle finger of his right hand into the round hole where the knob had been and was able to slide the metal bolt to the left, after which he pulled the door open. Before him was a brick stairway lit by a single tungsten bulb protruding from the wall.

"It looks more like the entrance to a cheap hotel," McKnight commented.

Patterson motioned for his companion to follow him as he quietly ascended the stairs. They curved to the right after twelve steps and then rose twelve more. They now stood before another door. This one opened via a numeric keypad.

"I and about twenty others in the West Wing have a code for keypads," McKnight said. "It's 94382765. Here's hoping."

She entered the code, and the door opened.

"That was too easy," Patterson commented.

"True, but remember that this door isn't supposed to exist. It's not on any schematic of the White House."

"You go first," Patterson said. "Your face is known inside the White House."

McKnight led the way into a wide corridor with arches in the ceiling every ten feet. "We're in the sub-basement of the East Wing," she said. "There's a tunnel one story up connecting the East Wing and West Wing. It was built in 1950 when the interior of the White House was rebuilt by Truman. It's a maze down here. Follow me."

Patterson and McKnight climbed the stairs and were moving to the west when they ran into a uniformed Secret Service guard, a gold badge on his pressed white shirt. "Sorry, ma'am, but we're asking people not to move around too much right now. And who is *this* gentleman?"

McKnight acted frustrated and put her hands on her hips. "Can't you read? He's here to fix the air conditioning. In case you haven't noticed, it's a bit warm in here. Even the President complained a little while ago. Mr. Arnold is checking the ductwork and needs to look at the electrical switching junctions below the residence."

"I'm sorry, but—"

"I'm Bailey McKnight, chief speechwriter for the president, and I'm late for a meeting with him."

"Sorry, ma'am. Go right ahead."

Patterson and McKnight continued through the tunnel to the West Wing, passing other guards who made no attempt to stop them as the speech writer rambled on about where the electrical equipment in the sub-basement was located.

"You sound like you know what you're talking about," Patterson whispered, his lips barely moving.

"I do. Everyone who works here has to know the layout of the entire complex in case of an emergency. There are endless basements, sub-basements, and egress tunnels. The White House is a far bigger complex than anyone imagines. When we get to the West Wing, you need to start talking to me using a lot of technical language. Make it look like you're absorbed in your job."

They walked another five minutes and approached military guards at the entrance to the main sub-basement of the West Wing."

"The M-60 switching circuits are drawing way too many amps, ma'am," Patterson said as he stood by a Marine in dress blues. "If I don't find the current surge, this entire place will be filled with smoke in less than two hours. You can't have this kind of voltage imbalance without risking a fire. Do you have any idea how many amps are bleeding from the main coils under the residence, which feed directly into the conduits in this wing?"

McKnight held up her laminated ID so the Marine could see her, although she was reasonably certain that he recognized her. He nodded imperceptibly, and the two entered the West Wing.

"Nice job," McKnight said. "Straight ahead and then we take a left."

Patterson took out a voltage meter from the tool case and looked at it as he walked behind McKnight. "I think we're near the problem," he said, "but I'll have to check a wall socket to see if there's an overload."

They passed guards, none of whom seemed suspicious of the uniformed workman. Most of the West Wing staff were in their offices, clearly visible through glass partitions that separated them from the hallways. They'd been through crash drills, and most simply hunkered down and stayed at their desks as usual, absorbed in whatever was on their computer screens.

"In here," McKnight whispered.

The lights in David Wolcott's office were on, and McKnight closed the blinds so no one in the hall could see them, and then closed the door. "You'll have to hurry. We may only have minutes."

Patterson glanced around quickly to see if Wolcott's desktop was the only computer in the office. He saw no other, but he noted spectacular photographs on the walls of star clusters and galaxies. Sela, he thought, would have approved of the décor.

Patterson booted the PC on Wolcott's desk and sat down in the leather chair facing the screen. He took an external jump drive from the tool case and inserted it into a side port. Not surprisingly, the PC was password protected.

"Hurry," McKnight said.

"I can't get into his system. I'm going to have to use a portable decryption device."

Patterson produced a rectangular mini-computer—smooth, black, and slim—and connected it to Wolcott's PC. He then typed some keys and stared at the screen.

"Okay, I'm in," he said sixty seconds later. "Damn—there must be a hundred thousand files here. I can't fit them all onto a portable drive."

"Think of something fast," McKnight advised. She could see the shadows of figures passing through the hallway as she stood at the blinds. "I'll be surprised if someone doesn't knock on the door very soon."

"I'll have to copy everything straight to the decryption computer. It's not made to hold this much information either, but it's my only option."

Patterson typed more commands on Wolcott's PC and waited. "Download's in progress."

Three minutes passed, then five. "The transfer's complete," Patterson said. "Let's hope that what we're looking for is on here."

"If not," McKnight said, "then we went to a lot of trouble for—"

The door suddenly opened, and Patterson looked up to see the First Lady and Audrey Dickerson. Diane Hastings glanced from McKnight to the repairman.

"I escorted this gentleman here to do some electrical work," McKnight explained. "He traced the problem to several offices in the West Wing, ma'am."

The First Lady and Dickerson entered and closed the door.

"You're Jay Patterson," the First Lady said.

Patterson stood and bowed his head slightly as he put the drive and his portable computer into the tool case. "That would be me, Mrs. Hastings."

"I don't have to ask why you're here," the First Lady said. "I presume it's for the same reason I am. Did you get what you came for?"

"Yes, I believe I did," Patterson replied.

"Then you'd better leave," Dickerson suggested. "Do you have a way out?"

"We were going to use the tunnel from the East Wing to the Treasury Building," McKnight said. "Just like Brad and Savannah."

"I'll go with you," the First Lady said. "With a crash on, you'll find it a lot harder to get out than however you found your way in. Follow me. Audrey, stay here and see if you can find somebody to remove Wolcott's hard drive. Have it taken to my office."

Two Secret Service agents entered and told the First Lady and the others to leave. "We have orders to seal this office," the first said. "Everybody out, please."

Patterson and McKnight followed Dickerson and the First Lady to yet another sub-basement in the East Wing and paused in front of a steel door that could only be opened by pressing the right sequence of buttons on an alphanumeric keypad that McKnight wasn't used to.

"On the other side is a zigzag tunnel built in 1941," the First Lady explained, "but it's been updated. I could turn on the lights, but it's best to use your flashlight. Mr. Patterson, I hope you're able to accomplish your task with the material you've gathered, but you mustn't quote me as saying that."

"I understand, Mrs. Hastings."

The First Lady entered the alphanumeric code and gave them keys to unlock doors and gates at the end of the tunnel.

Patterson and McKnight navigated the 761-foot long tunnel rapidly, walked up a flight of stairs, and found themselves in an alley adjacent to the Treasury Building. To their left were basement windows, and some of the lights inside were brightly lit.

"We could have taken a few branching tunnels we just passed to enter the building itself," McKnight explained, "but that naturally would have presented a few extra problems. I have to get back into the White House, which as you recall, is crashed. My sudden disappearance might raise some questions, if it hasn't already. Here. You need to get to this address in Virginia. It's the safe house I mentioned that's run by Grass Roots. I'll have John and Sela pick you up, but stay here until you see them drive up."

Patterson looked at McKnight as she turned to go. "Thanks, Cookie. None of this would have been possible without your—"

"Thank me by writing a great article and exposing Herbert Chase Hastings for the dishonest man that he is," McKnight said.

Patterson smiled broadly. "Consider it done."

McKnight disappeared down the steps and into the tunnel.

Patterson changed back into his street clothes and walked down the dim alley that led to the street. As he neared the sidewalk, he peeked left and right before stepping onto the pavement. A few cars passed by, but traffic was light. He decided there was no threat and that he should make himself visible in the twilight so that John and Sela could see him. Walking down the sidewalk a few paces, he felt a sharp sting in his right thigh, the sting quickly turning into a burning pain as he fell forward onto the pavement. His pant leg was wet, warm blood trickling from his wound. He looked up in all directions to see where the shot had come from, but he saw no one. Attempting to get to his feet, he saw a car brake suddenly and was relieved that help had arrived.

"Hey, buddy," an unfamiliar voice called, "you'd better not stop in a bar the next time you head home from work."

"I'm not drunk! I've been shot!"

The car window was raised as the car sped into the evening, which was growing a deeper blue by the minute. The horizon was a mixture of orange and crimson, and a crescent moon hung in the sky above the White House. Patterson thought it odd that he could stop to appreciate the beauty of the evening, but realized that everything was moving in slow motion. The cars on the street were crawling along as if they were in a school zone. He was growing dizzy, and each time he tried to stagger to his feet, he ended up back on the ground.

"Jay!"

Was someone calling his name? If so, the voice seemed far away—miles away, as if it were at the end of a long tunnel. Tunnel? Had he just been in a tunnel?

"Jay, over here!"

He saw Sela and John Taylor running towards him, although their movements were, like everything around him, in slow motion. An SUV was by the curb, its doors open and the engine running. He felt himself lifted up under both arms, but another shot rang out before his friends could put his body safely into the vehicle. The bullet missed, skipping off the concrete sidewalk with a sharp *ping*.

And then he was in the SUV, with Sela by his side in the rear seat as Taylor hit the accelerator, the vehicle speeding away from the Treasury Building.

"I seem to have gotten into a spot of trouble," Patterson said weakly. "My tool case. Where is it?"

"I threw it in the cargo well," Sela replied. "Hang on, Jay. We're going to an address provided by Cookie."

Patterson smiled weakly. "Good. I could use some sleep."

He closed his eyes as the SUV drove into the night.

/

Jimmy Finch, sitting in a van across from the Treasury Building, had missed Patterson due to poor visibility. Twilight was the worst time to squeeze off a shot and hit a target. He'd aimed for Patterson's chest and couldn't believe that he'd been off the mark by so much, but a bus had rumbled past, shaking the asphalt on the street—and the van as well. His second shot had been at a *moving* target and hadn't come close.

He swung into traffic and followed the SUV that had retrieved the wounded body of Jay Patterson, enemy of the president, enemy of the country. He would simply follow them to their destination and try again.

The SUV was going eighty, and Finch pressed the accelerator of his van, weaving in and out of traffic since Patterson's driver changed lanes frequently. Ahead, the Interstate branched into three directions, but Finch could clearly make out the red taillights of the SUV as it moved into the far left lane. It appeared headed for the exit to Maryland. Finch maneuvered the van into the left lane, but at the last minute the SUV veered wildly to the right and disappeared into traffic that was flowing onto an off ramp. It was too late. He would have to kill Patterson another time.

Chapter Eighty-One

They can't open fire on us—can they?

PRESIDENT HASTINGS SAT IN THE WHITE HOUSE SITUATION ROOM WITH LUCILLE RAINES, HIS NATIONAL SECURITY ADVISOR, DEPUTY SECRETARY OF DEFENSE NEWMAN, GENERAL WILLIAM SUTHERLAND, AND THE OTHER JOINT CHIEFS.

"What am I looking at?" Hastings asked as he gazed at the large monitor on the wall at the end of the room.

"Western Pakistan," Sutherland said. "The three blue triangles are our F-45 Hornets. The six red triangles represent Pakistan's Mirage IV-E jets, which they scrambled when our jets incurred on their airspace.

"It's reconnaissance," Hastings declared. "What's all the fuss about?"

Sutherland tried to remain calm even though he would have liked to shout his answer.

"Sir, we have no right to be in their airspace at all. It has been perceived as a hostile act against the Pakistani Government."

Hastings waved dismissively at the display. "Tell them we don't mean any harm and that we're just taking some pictures."

"It doesn't work that way, Mr. President," Sutherland said. "The Pakistani Government is insisting that we leave their airspace immediately, or they'll open fire."

Hastings looked perplexed. "Can they do that? Is it legal?"

"Sir, it's the United States that is in violation of International Law, not Pakistan. May I ask who gave the order for jets to enter Pakistani airspace?"

"Deputy Secretary Newman relayed my order for reconnaissance to Pacific Command," Hastings replied.

Newman shrugged and sank lower in his chair. "Following orders," he muttered.

"With all due respect, Mr. President," Sutherland said, "Pakistan has the right to defend itself."

Hastings sat up straighter, glanced at Raines, and folded his arms. "Not when they're breeding terrorist cells within their borders."

"Sir," Sutherland said, "no one has ever seen such camps. I implore you, Mr. President, if you have any such proof, please produce it now before this situation gets out of hand."

"Too late," said Admiral Tyler Bidwell, Chief of the Navy. "They just shot down one of our Hornets. Two left."

"What are your orders, Mr. President?" Sutherland asked. "I recommend we disengage."

"I agree," Raines said.

"Fire on the coordinates I provided the commander of PACCOM!" Hastings barked.

"Our pilots have scanned those coordinates," Sutherland countered. "They see nothing there."

Bidwell sat forward in his seat. "A Mirage just went down. It's a dogfight."

"Mr. President, you may have just initiated a state of war," Sutherland stated.

Hastings glared at everyone in the room. "Am I the only patriot here? I'm your commander in chief!"

No one in the Situation Room answered.

"Stand down, Mr. President," Raines said. "Recall our fighter jets."

Hastings set his jaw and narrowed his eyes to menacing slits. He wanted to hit someone, to harm his military advisors.

"Very well! Recall the damn jets. But this isn't over, people. I will have Rafiq on his knees begging for mercy before this is over."

Hastings stormed out of the room. On the monitor, the two remaining blue triangles drifted back over the Arabian Sea. The Mirage IV-E jets didn't give chase.

The Pakistani government published aerial photos of the dogfight, which were broadcast on major networks around the world. A state of war, military analysts said, was a possibility the United States needed to be prepared for.

Chapter Eighty-Two
Progress of Science Wins Out

JOSH ROLLINS WAS WORKING A LATE SHIFT AT SETI WITH A CREW THAT KNEW HIM WELL AND TRUSTED HIM. Twenty young astronomers sat at their computer stations, looking for what they called "patterned signals" from thousands of stars, while a team of ten had been assigned to monitor the signals from Tau Ceti.

The signals from Tau Ceti were still being received every ninety minutes, although each time the signals repeated, another prime number was added to those previously transmitted. Rollins sat calmly at his station and took control of a single satellite dish miles away at the Allen Telescope Array. With a few keystrokes, he changed the dish's mode from RECEIVE to SEND. He was about to disobey a direct order from the Hastings Administration, but world leaders and the scientific community were already engaged in vigorous debate as to what type of reply should be sent to an intelligent civilization 12.5 light years away. It was only a matter of time before another country sent the signal, but Rollins believed that, given Hastings' posture towards Pakistan and the possibility that World War III might end all life on Earth very soon, the signal needed to be sent sooner rather than later. Even if President Hastings' actions destroyed mankind completely, the intelligent beings orbiting Tau Ceti would know that their signals had been received and processed—that the advanced creatures on the third planet from the sun were not so arrogant as to ignore such important communication.

Rollins gave the satellite dish a series of commands to transmit prime numbers to Tau Ceti every ninety minutes. He sat back, satisfied that he'd done what was right and moral. No one, not even the President of the United States, had the right to dictate the actions of the entire world.

Rollins left his station to get some coffee, and then sat down again and sorted through data coming from a hundred stars known to have exoplanets. He would make a public announcement when the transmissions to Tau Ceti had the chance to go through several cycles over the next few days. He might be arrested, but the scientific community would be proud of him. He wouldn't be some old stodgy professor emeritus any longer. He was back in the game.

Chapter Eighty-Three

Far-Right Paramilitary

JIMMY FINCH TURNED OFF THE WALL SCREEN HE WAS WATCHING. HE KNEW AMERICA WAS ON THE BRINK OF WAR, WHICH MEANT THAT PEOPLE WERE AFRAID. Stocking up on canned goods and bottled water would do nothing to keep them safe from nuclear radiation, but he realized that people always took whatever measures were at their disposal, even futile ones, when faced with horrific circumstances. Not much had changed since the 1960s, when American school children had been forced to undergo duck and cover drills, crouching under their desks to allegedly protect themselves from the blinding flash and subsequent radiation of a nuclear attack.

Finch also knew that image was everything, something he'd learned from carefully observing the Hastings presidential campaign. Style always trumped substance. For this reason alone, he knew that he could now make a bold move with the American Paramilitary Union. People regarded his union of state militias as an extension of the National Guard, especially since events in Nashville. A poll had revealed that a majority of Americans didn't know what the Loyalty Militia was, although most assumed it was part of the Army. The same poll indicated that almost all citizens believed that the American Paramilitary Union was a branch of the American Armed Forces.

Finch used his phone to give orders that militias roll into twenty-five state capitals in the same fashion as he'd taken the Tennessee Civilian State Militia into Nashville. They were to make their presence known in the streets without engaging in any kind of military activity. People would be comforted to know that what they perceived to be the federal government was nearby should missiles start raining from the sky. If the operation was as successful as he anticipated it would be, he would order militias to make their presence known in the remaining twenty-five states.

Finch had waited for this moment for twenty years. The time had finally come when his weekend warriors could flex their muscles.

Chapter Eighty-Four
Decoding Encrypted Files

Jay Patterson lay comfortably in bed at the safe house provided by friends of Cookie McKnight, a couple who belonged to Grass Roots. The bleeding from the wound had stopped—the bullet had apparently missed arteries, nerves, and tendons—and he was feeling stronger, although his leg throbbed if he tried to stand. He'd slept well, and the rest had helped him recover his strength.

For most of the night, Sela worked on the computer which Patterson had used to copy the contents of David Wolcott's PC. At noon, she turned to Patterson, who was resting in a recliner in the living room of the spacious Virginia home and shook her head.

"All of his files are encrypted," she said, "and I can't get any of my software to decrypt them. Maybe you need to take this to Bobby Thibodaux."

"No time," Patterson said, "and I'm sure that the entire office is under constant surveillance. It's up to you."

"I'm out of ideas."

"I saw a lot of photographs of space on the walls in Wolcott's office," he said. "I'm guessing he's an astronomy buff. If so, he may have been following developments at SETI. Have you tried decrypting the files using binary numbers?"

Sela shook her head and laughed. "That would be too easy. Nobody would use something so simple to lock down a file . . . which is precisely why he might have used it. Let me give it a shot."

Sela continued to work on the computer, which she had placed on the coffee table.

"Damn," she said. "It's working."

"O ye of little faith," replied Patterson, smiling at Sela.

"Getting religious now that you're injured?"

I don't think it's religious I'm getting, locking eyes with Sela.

An hour later, Patterson and Sela were reading files that Wolcott had made on Herbert Chase Hastings. It covered the time period from the presidential campaign to the present, a few days before Wolcott had committed suicide.

"An incredible story," John Taylor said, looking over their shoulders. "It explains everything."

Patterson learned that Tom Chance had confronted President Hastings after returning from Garundi. Prime Minister Felix Ogo and his staff had totally misunderstood Chance's reason for visiting their country, believing him to be an emissary of the president on strictly private matters pertaining to PB Enterprises and the Hastings family. Hastings had declared that it was all a misunderstanding when the senator had spoken of the elaborate operation to grow tobacco in Africa in order to profit both Garundi and PB Enterprises.

Chance had spoken with Secretary of State Hart in person to relay what he'd learned in Garundi, and despite giving a seemingly sympathetic reception, Hart gave his ever-present bodyman/fixer, Lucky, an ominous sign by pounding on the left side of his chest, which meant that Chance should have a heart attack. So Chance was killed, the death made to appear to be the result of a heart attack. As leader of The Elect—*Etiam Electus*—Hart was in control of a wide network that extended throughout the government, including military brass, civil servants, elected officials, and more than a few CEOs of major corporations. Finding someone to carry out his directives was never a problem.

But Chance had also learned from Ogo that Wolcott himself had been put in charge of the operation because of his familiarity with PB Enterprises and the tobacco business in general. With Hastings having formally divested his interests in PB, Wolcott knew that Brad and Savannah were the logical people to help insulate the President from any accusations of wrongdoing, and he'd told them to expand PB's business interests into other areas, such as manufacturing the Slipstream 7000 private jet. The more PB diversified, he reasoned, the easier it would be to bury illegal contacts and business dealings with Iran and Garundi.

The initial stages of the operation had gone well, and the tobacco had been introduced slowly in selected test markets for Sailor cigarettes. But Hastings had been decimated by the failure of Western Rider and checked with Wolcott a dozen times each day to gauge the success of the clandestine operation. He'd become obsessed with rebuilding the empire of his father, and according to the decrypted files, Hastings had been unable to accept the financial decline of PB. In fact, he couldn't accept failure in *any* area of his life. Wolcott realized that Hastings' pathology was dictating his every decision, from growing tobacco in Africa to running for president, to conquering the many women he had married or had affairs with. He was never satisfied with anything but absolute power, and Wolcott, who'd been aware of his boss's visits to Dr. Charlotte Rampling in Telluride, had called Maxwell Hart, Hastings' longtime friend from high school, to discuss the president's mental instability. The White House press secretary feared that Hastings might do something irrational that could threaten the security of the nation or the entire world. Expressing concern, Hart had promised to look into the matter. In actuality, the secretary of state decided to bury any discussion of the president's mental incompetence by having Dr. Elizabeth Rampling killed and Hastings' file removed from her office.

Wolcott had taken his case to Raines even though he was aware that she and Hastings were lovers. She catered to the president's whims most of the time, but tried to check his more irrational statements and moves to save him from embarrassment. Although Wolcott had begun to suspect she wanted to preserve some dignity for the administration since she herself had lofty political ambitions. Raines had advised him to give the president a wide berth on most issues, but Wolcott had committed the unpardonable sin of challenging Hastings on several key matters, even though he'd tried to do so with great respect. The president had grown increasingly hostile towards his press secretary, causing Wolcott to shrink from doing anything but relaying the administration's positions from the briefing room. But Wolcott had grown angry, having been the public voice for PB Enterprises, which had entailed fielding questions on Western Rider, a product that had been proven by hundreds of studies to cause cancer and heart disease. He'd taken it on the chin year after year for Hastings, who didn't seem appreciative of all the PB spokesman had done.

Once in the White House, Hastings seemed to have no sympathy for the job that he, Wolcott, had to do each day as he defended the growing irrationality of the president's remarks and political decisions. He had begun to document everything he knew about Hastings, keeping a record of both his personal and political actions, past and present. The files Patterson was reading and listening to made it clear that Wolcott was planning on taking his story to the American people and had already contacted literary agents with an eye for making his private diary entries into a tell-all biography of the president.

"What about Iran?" Sela asked. "How does Faridoon play into all of this?"

Patterson continued to examine the copious material David Wolcott had committed to voice and word files. For the first time, he understood what Lone Wolf had meant when he'd said, *There's more.* An even bigger story lay beyond the tobacco operation in Garundi.

The entire operation had been proposed by Hamid Abbas Faridoon. The Iranian mob, with the blessing of President Muhammad Al Assad, would foot the bill for the operation in Africa, although PB had purchased certain assets from Silk Road Enterprises, such as farming equipment, when the operation wasn't proceeding as quickly as Brad and Savannah would have liked. Iran's involvement in the affairs of PB was contingent, however, on Hastings' willingness, should he be elected president, to turn a blind eye on Iran furthering its nuclear ambitions. Iran now sought to develop better missile delivery systems and more powerful nuclear warheads. Hastings had told Faridoon during many meetings in European cities that he always played to win, but that many pundits and polls were predicting that his election was a long shot, even with large infusions of cash from the Scarabelli family. Faridoon had replied that Iran, through the Iranian mafia, would be able to deliver as much cash as needed to fund Hastings' run for highest office in the land.

It was agreed that PB Enterprises would expand into products beyond tobacco so that any meetings between the Hastings children and Faridoon could be explained in terms of mutual business interests. It was decided that PB would invest much of its net worth into the Slipstream 7000 jet since the company anticipated new revenue from Sailor once nicotine had been reintroduced into the PB's cigarettes. It was at such meetings between Brad, Savannah, and Faridoon that the mobster delivered nearly a billion dollars to the Hastings children to help get their father elected President. With creative bookkeeping, Wolcott himself laundered the money through PB to the campaign of Herbert Chase Hastings, making it look as if Hastings was funding his own run for the White House. President Harrison Depeche, already seen as a weak leader, was outspent three to one and lost the election to Hastings.

The last file that Patterson read indicated that Wolcott had felt great remorse at the actions he'd taken on behalf of Herbert Hastings over the years. He felt that he'd imperiled the country and had been complicit in murder. The weight of his crimes was too great to carry, and he'd said, *"I don't know how much longer I can live with myself."*

"But consorting with a foreign power to become president," Taylor said. "That goes far beyond anything imaginable, even for a man like Hastings. He allowed Iran to buy him the election. The Founding Fathers must be turning over in their graves."

"A pathological borderline's narcissism and need for control supersedes any rational action," Sela observed. "The end justifies the means."

"According to Wolcott," Patterson continued, "there was another reason Hastings accepted Faridoon's deal, one deeply rooted in Hastings' pathology. Faridoon told Hastings that Iran's goal was to one day obliterate Israel, which Hastings found especially appealing because Christ had been a Jew. Wolcott recounts an episode in which Hastings was physically abused by the headmaster at the Christian Academy of Virginia, an event that Hastings never recovered from. He felt betrayed by God, and in his later years he privately denounced his belief that Christ was anything but a historical figure. He began to hate the very concept of God, although he spouted scripture to help get himself elected. To Hastings, Israel represented a strong Judeo-Christian ethic that he found repugnant. In Wolcott's estimation, Hastings would have taken the Iranian deal regardless, but the idea of having Israel nuked was icing on the cake."

Taylor stood erect and folded his arms, considering what Patterson had explained.

"When Hastings formed the Church of the Heart," Taylor speculated, "he saw yet another way that he could torpedo religion by degrees, especially Christianity. The church would not only serve as a new political base, but he would have the opportunity to draw people away from their various denominations."

"Reasonable speculation," Patterson agreed. "And remember that Percy Beauregard Hastings was solidly against big government, and he passed his political views to his son. Hastings had numerous reasons—political, economic, religious, and psychological—to want to be president. But now it's time to give America the complete story of their forty-seventh president and how Iran provided his path to power."

"Can the nation survive such a story?" Sela asked.

"Can it survive *without* the story?" Patterson retorted. "I'll begin writing the account after a cup of coffee and a couple of pain relievers."

"You're in no shape to do this," Taylor said. "Let me write it."

"Not this time, John. It's mine, and it needs my stamp on it since I have a large following.

Chapter Eighty-Five
Bucking Bronco

LONE WOLF HAD BEEN IN BED WITH MELANIE MASTERS FOR TWELVE HOURS. HE AND HIS WIFE RARELY SPOKE ANYMORE, AND SHE WAS AWARE THAT HE'D HAD SEVERAL DALLIANCES OVER A PERIOD OF MANY YEARS. He wouldn't be missed at home no matter how much time he spent with the alluring and sexy computer analyst from the CIA.

"How did you learn to do such things in bed, Mr. Vice President?" Masters asked, panting from their latest bout of lovemaking.

"Well, honey, I worked as a cowboy for a while in my youth. I learned how to stay on top of a bucking bronco for a long time, and I've tried to stay in shape ever since. I just have . . . staying power, I suppose."

The lovers burst out laughing.

"Won't you be missed by the president and others within the administration?"

Quint laughed again. "Hell, they don't call me except for photo opportunities, state funerals, and campaign rallies. The vice presidency is the sorriest job in the world. As a comedian decades ago said, I get no respect. I have a great title, but I live in the shadows."

"And so you're Lone Wolf," Masters said, propping her head on her elbow as she lay on the sheets, looking down at the prostrate form of Cal Quint.

"That I am. A rogue. A voice howling in the wilderness."

"You were certainly howling just now," she joked.

"Not to worry. My Secret Service detail knows how I roll. No questions will be asked. Now then, how about some more howling?"

Masters lay down as Quint turned and took the young woman in his arms.

Chapter Eighty-Six
Bringing Down the Curtain

THE FIRST LADY STOOD IN THE OVAL OFFICE IN MID-AFTERNOON.

"I have something to tell you, Herbert," she said with no affect in her voice. "Something important."

"Oh, good God! Now what? Have you or one of your minions been sneaking around the White House again? I don't have time for your bullshit. Get out."

"I'm leaving you, Herbert. I'm going to file for divorce based on the grounds of spousal abuse."

Hastings looked up from the papers on his desk, disbelief etched on his features. The blood drained from his face as he tried to speak, but the words didn't come. Finally, he stammered, "Y-you can't. Wait until I leave office."

"That could be anywhere from two to six years away," the First Lady countered. "I'm not willing to wait that long and live as your prisoner in the meantime. You can't stop me. I have a Secret Service detail, and there are people in possession of a great deal of information about you. The recording of you impersonating a Roman emperor for starters. There are also people who have David Wolcott's personal file on your dealings with Iran and Garundi."

"You're bluffing," the President said. "I had the office sealed off, and I'm told that you and Dickerson were escorted from the room before you had time to copy anything."

The First Lady shrugged. "Whatever you say, Herbert. The point is, you're not going to hurt or intimidate me. As for the political consequences of our divorce, I'll be delighted if I prevent you from having a second term."

Hastings rose from his chair and pointed to the door.

"Would you please leave, Diane. I have work to do."

The First Lady left, after which Hastings walked to the middle of his office and fell to his knees, his head buried in his hands. What was he going to do? His wife would make him look like a fool. He stood, deciding that he would get TINN, Savoy Greene, the Scarabelli family—whoever it would take—to manufacture damaging news on Diane, preferably something that indicated she was a longtime drug abuser and that she'd recently stayed at a rehab facility. TINN could also fabricate a few extramarital affairs with no trouble. He would beat her yet.

But Hastings felt abandoned, vulnerable. People didn't leave him. He left *them*. That was the way it always worked. He started pacing around the room, his breath shallow, his forehead sweaty. He called for Raines, but she wasn't in the White House. He called for Quint, but he was nowhere to be found, which wasn't surprising since he had an annoying habit of not responding to a summons.

"I've got to do something," he said.

He stood motionless in front of his desk for more than ten minutes. And then he decided what action he would take. He left the Oval Office, headed for the Situation Room.

/

The operations officer on duty was Major Clifford Farnsworth of the U.S. Army. He immediately rose to attention, clearly surprised by the unannounced entry of the president. Farnsworth was a youthful thirty-two years old and had close-cut brown hair.

"Major," Hastings said, "connect me with Deputy Secretary of Defense Newman. Immediately."

"Yes, sir."

"And get me the Deputy Director of Operations at the Pentagon while you're at it."

"The War Room?" Farnsworth asked, his voice breaking.

"Do it."

"Should I call General Sutherland and the other Joint Chiefs, Mr. President?"

Hastings smiled and sat in the chair at the end of the long conference table. “No, Major. Just do as I asked.”

“Perhaps I should get Strategic Command in Omaha on the line, sir.”

Hastings sat forward, his hands clasped on the table as a dozen wall monitors flickered on both sides of the room. “Do I have to call in a replacement, or are you going to place those calls?”

“Right away, sir.”

“Good, Major. You and I are about to change world history.”

Chapter Eighty-Seven

The People Have a Right to Know the Truth

PATTERSON DICTATED THE STORY HE HAD GLEANED FROM THE MATERIAL HE'D FOUND ON DAVID WOLCOTT'S DRIVE. The shocking news that Iran had helped put Hastings in the White House would be available for everyone in the world to read. He'd worked the story, played detective, been hit by a car, abducted by *Etiam Electus*, and been shot after sneaking into the White House, but he'd found what he'd been looking for. Democracy had been compromised and perverted by a mentally unstable president who had placed the electoral process in the hands of a hostile foreign power.

"You're in no condition to go out there," Taylor reminded him for the tenth time. "The story is useless if you collapse before you can send it."

Just get me back to NewzTracker HQ," Patterson countered. "Finch's militias are on the move, one of our fighter jets was shot down by Pakistan, and people are talking about secession and civil war. If Hastings is as mad as we all believe him to be, the entire world may be hours away from destruction. I think my life is worth the nine billion people on the planet."

"You're writing the story, but let *me* go out and get it transmitted."

"Your chip implant says you're head of NewzTracker. You wouldn't make it. Stay close, and when I'm done, you can drive me back here and I'll lay low."

Patterson struggled to his feet and kissed Sela square on the mouth, and passionately. "If we get out of this alive, will you marry me? I'd get down on my knee, but it's shot."

Holding back tears, Sela nodded, stunned, "Yes, Jay, I will marry you," she said. "So I have a husband when our child is born . . . albeit, somewhat late. The marriage, that is."

Stunned into speechlessness, Jay stared at Sela's face.

"Jay, damn it, come on!" hollered Taylor holding the door open and out of ear shot.

Patterson and Taylor left, headed for the Newz-Tracker offices.

Chapter Eighty-Eight
The Point of No Return

"DEPUTY SECRETARY OF DEFENSE NEWMAN IS ON THE LINE, MR. PRESIDENT," MAJOR FARNSWORTH SAID. Despite his training, the major was trying his hardest to be calm and collected. The tremor in his voice was barely perceptible, but definitely there. "I also have you patched through to Lieutenant Charles Jamison at the National Military Command and Control Center. The War Room."

Hastings wasted no time. His thoughts were on his wife's announcement that she was leaving him, which would be a personal humiliation as well as a political blow that could hurt him badly in the polls. True to his pathology, it was time to retaliate against Pakistan, his wife, liberals—anyone who opposed his wishes. Cal Quint told him to change the news cycle, and that's exactly what he intended to do, only in a grander way than his vice president could have ever envisioned.

Hastings spoke with resolution, his nerves rock steady.

"Deputy Secretary Newman," he said, "what are your targets in Pakistan?"

"Targets, sir?"

"*Nuclear* targets. Major cities."

There was a pause on the other end of the call, followed by Newman's voice, which spoke with hesitation. "Uh, Islamabad, Karachi, Lahore, Quetta, and Hyderabad."

"What about Gwadar?"

Another pause followed, and it was clear that Newman didn't know the answer to the question and was conferring with others in the War Room."

"It's a low-priority target, Mr. President, but one of our nuclear submarines in the Arabian Sea has the coordinates for Gwadar. Sir, what are your intentions?"

"To end the terrorist nightmare in Pakistan," Hastings replied as he surveyed his nail cuticles. He decided that he would have to change to a different manicurist. It was so hard to find the right people to do a job sometimes. "Deputy Secretary Newman, it is my intention to launch nuclear strikes at the cities you mentioned, including Gwadar. Do you concur with my decision?"

This time there was no hesitation on the line. "No, sir, I do not."

"You're fired," Hastings said. "Get me the Secretaries of the Army, Navy, and the Air Force."

"They're already assembled in the War Room," Newman said.

Secretary of the Army Henry "Champ" Beckwith was a lean but muscular man who had a spine of steel. He was usually quiet, but when he spoke, his commands instilled fear in his listeners. By comparison, Secretary of the Navy Steven Poke was a soft-spoken man who smiled frequently and loved to socialize at parties. Secretary of the Air Force Benjamin Bates wore round, rimless glasses and always seemed to be gazing at some distant point so that those engaged in conversation with him thought he wasn't listening to them. In actuality, he absorbed every nuance of every word spoken in his presence. He was bald, and his demeanor had merited him the nickname Stoneface.

"Secretary Beckwith," President Hastings said, "do you concur with my decision to launch?"

"No, sir," said the resolute voice of the secretary.

"You're relieved," the President said. "Admiral Poke," the President continued, "do you concur with my decision to launch?"

"No, Mr. President."

"You are relived as well. Secretary Bates, do you concur with my decision to launch?"

A minute elapsed before Hastings received his response.

"I concur, Mr. President."

Hastings smiled. "Very well. Lieutenant Jamison, are you prepared to receive the 153-character code to verify my identity?"

"Yes, sir."

Hastings began to read from the laminated card he carried at all times, known as the Biscuit. "FLOORPX-DEDICATEENGLANDHOUSEFDFGMOUNT . . . ."

"In the name of God, Mr. President!" Admiral Poke cried. "Stop this madness!"

". . . JKLAMPREADORWAGONYTUSTAMP . . . ."

Chapter Eighty-Nine

Mushroom Clouds on the Horizon

As Secretary of State Hart was driven to the White House, he told his driver to run as many red lights as he had to, not that the streets of Washington, D.C., were crowded since most people were at home, waiting to see if a mushroom cloud was going to appear on the horizon. After the dogfight between American and Pakistani jets, both countries had issued statements declaring that any further hostile action would be considered an act of war. The country was nervous, and the growing presence of the American Paramilitary Union in many cities was making liberals feel uncertain as to who was in charge of the country. The streets of D.C. and many cities had little automobile or pedestrian traffic.

By pressing a button on his phone console, Major Farnsworth had alerted Hart that the President had entered the Situation Room. It had been part of Hart's personal failsafe measure to ensure that Hastings didn't attempt to launch nuclear missiles on his own—should he ever figure out the protocol.

The White House was still a mile away, and Hart tried to reach Vice President Quint repeatedly, but the vice president wasn't responding. He was, Hart thought, probably holed up somewhere, screwing another sweet young thing that had caught his attention. And yet he was one of the few people that President Hastings seemed to trust, and maybe the only person who might be able to talk his boss off the ledge if he were considering military action against Pakistan or some other country.

"Dammit, Quint," Hart said aloud. "Take the call, for God's sake."

The driver announced that the vehicle was about to enter the main gate of the White House.

Hart took out a beta blocker, popped it in his mouth, and chased it with a sip of bottled water. He felt his blood pressure climbing, and he needed to be as focused as he'd been on the battlefield. If Hastings had entered the Situation Room, it hadn't been to shoot the bull with Major Farnsworth. The President most definitely had something on his mind, and in all likelihood that *something* was Pakistan.

Hart tried Cal Quint one last time before exiting the vehicle as it pulled to a stop. It was a sorry world, Hart thought, when a smiling, laid-back ex-cowboy might be the only hope of preventing World War III.

Cal Quint was irritated that Hart was blowing up his phone. He finally decided to answer, but wasn't shy about showing his displeasure. "For Christ's sake, what?"

"Get your ass to the White House Situation Room!" Hart said, almost screaming. "The President just walked in with no prior warning, and the duty officer secretly alerted me to his presence. Do you know what this is about?"

Quint hesitated. "It's probably about Pakistan, Max. Tell the President to chill out and that I'm on my way. Tell him that his buddy Cal has new information and that he needs to calm down. Put it in exactly those terms."

The line went dead.

Quint turned and looked at the lovely naked body of Melanie Masters.

"Sorry, honey," Quint said, "but I've got to go into the office."

Masters looked up at her lover as he quickly put on his white shirt and trousers. "Do you have to save the world from the actions of your boss?" she giggled.

Quint smiled as he tightened the knot of his tie and grabbed his suit coat. "Something like that, darlin'. Keep the bed warm for me, okay?"

The vice president walked out of the room and ordered his detail to take him to the White House.

Chapter Ninety
For the People

JOHN TAYLOR RAN INTO A ROADBLOCK NEAR THE WASHINGTON MONUMENT. The Loyalty Militia told him to turn around and go home since the Washington D.C. Metropolitan Police Department wanted the streets cleared. Taylor nodded, threw his SUV into reverse and drove a block before pulling over to the side.

"I guess this is where you get out," he said to Patterson.

Patterson nodded. "I'll go around the troops and keep to the side. Nobody will see me."

"Good luck, Jay."

"Thanks, John. I'm going to need it."

Patterson headed toward the Lincoln Memorial, but saw a park ranger walking quickly toward him. He veered toward the Tidal Basin and stopped between the Jefferson Memorial and the Potomac River. Dark clouds were moving in fast. If he didn't get to the office and find Bobby soon, he would collapse and he wouldn't be able tell the nation that Iran had bought the last presidential election for Herbert Chase Hastings.

He had adjusted his tourniquet several times, but he was beginning to feel weak again and knew time was running out. He wondered if he was on a fool's errand. The world was coming apart. People wanted to live—that much he believed—but if crisis was averted in the next several hours, did anybody care about their government anymore? Yes, President Hastings was mentally ill, but voters had listened to his hate-filled rhetoric and elected him, nevertheless, because they favored his bluster and tough talk over the controlled, intellectual manner of President Harrison DePeche.

Patterson had remained an optimist and thought that maybe—just maybe—the American people would be shocked by his report and demand that their legislators hold the Hastings Administration accountable for its actions. But as Sela had noted, the nation might not be capable of absorbing news that the electoral process for the highest office in the land had been tainted by money from a foreign power. People might lose hope in the system altogether. Perhaps they would actually favor secession over remaining in a Union that was as corrupt and dark as the heart of Herbert Hastings.

Patterson knew he had to try. The free press, though denigrated by the President, had saved the country from more than one constitutional crisis by shining the light of truth on corruption. And, after all, Patterson had a mission, sent from on high by a dad he missed dearly every day since his had died. A free press was a safeguard that the Founding Fathers themselves deemed absolutely necessary to the democracy they had crafted. His dad, a man of the turbulent 60s, had taught him that and had nurtured Jay's love of writing and entry into the world of journalism. This mission of journalistic Truth was for his dad—for his country.

As the black clouds rolled in, Patterson's thumb fumbled across his phone's broken screen. He felt a sudden vibration as he slumped to the ground, his vision failing. He'd done his part. What happened next was out of his hands.

/

John Taylor had backed away from the Loyalty Militia blockade, turned onto 14th Street, driven south, veered left onto Ohio Drive SW at the Thomas Jefferson Memorial, and was moving south in the heavy downpour. He slowed as he paralleled the golf course and maneuvered the SUV onto the driving range. Up ahead, he saw the limp form of Jay Patterson. He pulled up, threw the vehicle into neutral, exited the SUV and knelt by the side of his longtime friend. He was alive. After inserting his hands under Patterson's armpits, Taylor lifted the unconscious form of Patterson, dragged it to the open passenger door, and with great effort, situated the rain-soaked body in the passenger seat and secured it with a seatbelt. Climbing back into the driver's seat, Taylor hit the accelerator.

"No!" he cried.

The tires dug into the wet sod of the golf course, the rubber spinning in a rut that only got deeper as Taylor gave the vehicle more gas.

Exiting the SUV, Taylor opened the rear hatch, tore off the tops of two pieces of luggage, and wedged them in front of the rear tires. Back in the driver's seat, he applied gentle pressure to the accelerator. The SUV lurched forward, slipped back, and then forward again. It was free of the mud. Slowly, the NewzTracker editor guided the vehicle back onto Ohio Drive and drove the way he came. When he reached 14th Street, he breathed a sigh of relief—until he saw flashing lights in his rearview mirror. A police cruiser was approaching from the rear. Taylor gunned the engine and drove two blocks at sixty miles per hour. He braked, turned left, right, and left again. He wasn't sure where he was because of the blinding rain, but a few minutes later he found an on-ramp to the Interstate.

He headed for the safe house in Virginia, wondering if Patterson's transmission had been spent. He would know soon enough.

Chapter Ninety-One

Round the Bend & Over the Edge

PRESIDENT HASTINGS CONTINUED TO READ THE IDENTITY VERIFICATION CODE FROM THE LAMINATED CARD HE HELD IN HIS HAND. The look on his face was one of pride and satisfaction. General Sutherland believed the President exhibited an almost gleeful sense of retribution, although he couldn't fathom the man's emotions. What need did he have for revenge?

"We're going to bomb Gwadar, Islamabad, Karachi, Lahore, Quetta, and Hyderabad," President Hastings announced.

"I am vehemently against this attack," Sutherland reiterated when Hastings had finished his verification code, "but why not go after the target you believe is dangerous, which is Gwadar, rather than all of these other cities. For that matter, why not use conventional weapons? Why are you intent on starting a nuclear holocaust that could spread throughout the world and eradicate all mankind?"

"Because the terrorists are operating with the sanction of Rafiq and his entire government. Terrorists must be taught a lesson once and for all. Global terrorism will be wiped from the face of the earth, and I, Herbert Chase Hastings, will have been responsible for curing the world of a cancer that has been allowed to linger for too many decades in the modern era. I promised in my campaign that I would put an end to terrorism, and I intend to honor that campaign pledge today. Right here, right now."

"You're insane," Sutherland proclaimed. "Literally and metaphorically."

The President faced General Sutherland directly, a calm smile on his face. "You don't have the constitutional authority to stop me, General. I'm the commander in chief, the supreme military authority of the United States. I am obviously better versed in military strategy than any career brass in this room or at the Pentagon, and I intend to use my superior intelligence to take swift action against a scourge upon the earth."

A sober voice spoke through the audio speakers in the Situation Room. "This is the War Room, Mr. President. Lieutenant Jamison here. Teams stationed in missile silos in the Midwest and aboard a submarine in the Arabian Sea are now going through their two-man protocols to verify your command."

"How much longer until they launch?' the President asked.

"A matter of minutes," Jamison answered.

General Sutherland took a deep breath and lunged toward the President. "You stupid bastard!" he screamed. "I'll kill you with my bare hands if you don't rescind your orders immediately!"

Major Farnsworth took out his sidearm and held it with both hands, his arms outstretched as he aimed the pistol at General Sutherland. His hands shaking, he momentarily aimed the weapon at the president before sighting General Sutherland again. He wasn't sure what he should do. He'd alerted Secretary of State Hart, but he hadn't shown up. He decided that he would follow the orders of the president. Farnsworth looked at the digital clock on the wall, its red numbers counting down the time until launch. There were four minutes and forty-eight seconds left until nuclear missiles were airborne. Armageddon was close at hand.

Chapter Ninety-Two
What Now?

JOHN TAYLOR LOOKED ON AS HIS OLD SCHOOL FRIEND, DR. ARMAND JELLICO, EXAMINED PATTERSON, WHO LAY IN BED AT THE VIRGINIA SAFE HOUSE. Dr. Jellico was assisted by a nurse who had brought a small chest of medical supplies.

"What can you do, Armand?" Taylor asked.

"I'm going to give him fluids. Nurse, hang a banana bag."

"What's that?" Sela queried.

"Sodium chloride, multivitamins, thiamine, folic acid, and magnesium sulfate. I'm also going to give him a wide-spectrum antibiotic intravenously. I'd like to give him a blood transfusion as well. What's his blood type?"

"A-positive," Sela replied.

The nurse shook her head. There was no A-positive in the medical chest.

"That's all I can do for now," Jellico stated.

Taylor and Sela left the room while the nurse set up the IV tubing.

/

Taylor and Sela watched scenes from around the world on a wall screen in the living room.

"Is this how it's going to end?" Sela asked.

"I don't think anyone knows the answer to that question," Taylor replied grimly. "D.C. is ground zero, which is why so many people have left."

Sela pointed to the wall screen, noting that Air Force One was airborne. "Hastings is leaving as well?"

"He can launch from Air Force One," Taylor pointed out. "It's a flying command center every bit as sophisticated as anything at the Pentagon or in the White House Situation Room, although . . . ."

"Although *what*?"

"There are two planes that carry the designation of Air Force One. They often travel together so that a potential enemy never knows which plane the president is on. Hastings may or may not be on board the one that just took off."

"Why would the White House order one of the planes into the air if the president isn't aboard?"

"To make Pakistan think that Hastings isn't in D.C. Under normal circumstances, not that any of this is normal, a president would be on his way to Cheyenne Mountain. Hastings may be betting that Rafiq will go after him personally, rather than the entire country. I don't think Rafiq has the stomach for this, but Hastings has backed him into a corner. He has to defend Pakistan—to do *something*. What worries me is what the rest of the world will do. Once the first nuke is launched, what actions other nuclear powers might take is anyone's guess. North Korea and the Soviet Union may see this as an opportunity to annihilate the United States since it will be the aggressor."

Dr. Jellico appeared in the doorway.

"Jay should be fine," he said. "He's young and in good shape. He'll need more extensive care once he's free to move about again. A day or two in the hospital wouldn't hurt."

"Can we talk with him?" Sela asked.

"My pat answer is, make it brief, but it really doesn't make any difference as long as you don't wear him out."

The nurse exited Patterson's room as Sela and Taylor entered.

"Jay," Sela said as she stood next to the bed where Patterson lay, "I traced Lone Wolf's signal. It came from the CIA, even though he tried to make it appear as if it was coming from multiple sources."

"So who is our mystery person?" Patterson asked.

"I tapped into footage from a surveillance camera in the main parking lot at CIA headquarters, which also shows the entrance to the main complex at Langley. Focusing on the days when you received communications from Lone Wolf, there was only one person of note who was always at the CIA whenever you received a message from Lone Wolf. It was Vice President Cal Quint."

"Why wouldn't he use one of the CIA's secret entrances?" Taylor asked.

"Why should he?" Patterson countered. "He obviously didn't think he could be traced, and if memory serves, he used to work there."

"But he's an outspoken advocate of Hastings," Sela pointed out.

"It's his job to defend the President," Patterson said. "If he'd been critical, he would have been fired a long time ago. He obviously is a lot more politically astute than people give him credit for. I think he's been angling for the office of president ever since he accepted the position as Hastings' running mate. He knew Hastings was a loose cannon and mentally unbalanced. He wanted me to take down the president for him."

"What do we do now?" Taylor asked.

"Did my story get out?" Patterson asked.

Taylor shook his head and folded his arms. "It can't have, or it would have been on every major network by now. Bobby might be able to figure out what happened, but I can't locate him. He disappeared, which is what most people in Washington have done in the last day or two."

"No," Patterson said. "He's not the kind to desert his post. He probably saw that the office was being closely watched by *Etiam Electus* or one of the militias, and snuck away. God only knows where he's hiding, but I'm sure he'll be in touch. Meanwhile, we wait."

Patterson dictated a second report, after which Sela tried to upload it to the NewzTracker website.

"It won't upload," she said. "Something is blocking the signal. I tried sending it to my Gail Gunderson account, but it won't upload to that either. Somebody is actively searching for this report and intercepting it."

"For now," Patterson said, "the report isn't going to get out."

Chapter Ninety-Three
Lone Wolf Aborts

MAXWELL HART BURST INTO THE SITUATION ROOM TO FIND MAJOR FARNSWORTH AIMING A PISTOL AT GENERAL SUTHERLAND, WHO HAD BACKED AWAY FROM THE PRESIDENT.

"What are you doing here, Max?" Hastings asked.

"Farnsworth alerted me that you were in the room. I gave him orders to notify me if you entered. There's a button on his console that can silently alert any cabinet member that the president is in the Situation Room."

Hastings sat in the chair at the head of the conference table. "You're too late, Max. The birds will be in the air in less than five minutes."

The door to the Situation Room opened again, and in walked Vice President Cal Quint. "Mr. President," he said, "it looks like you've done a fine job, but may I have a word with you alone in the hall? Time is of the essence."

Hastings rose and followed Quint into the corridor outside the Situation Room.

"Mr. President," Quint said, "You've made your point and shown your staff and military advisors who's boss. And the world will know that Herbert Chase Hastings is a force to be reckoned with. By this time, satellite reconnaissance will have told most governments in the world that both Pakistan and the United States are preparing to launch nuclear weapons. Satellites monitor missile silos twenty-four seven, and they can surely tell that something is about to happen in the next few minutes."

"Yes!" Hastings said enthusiastically. "It's positively glorious."

"Sir, all you have to do is declare victory and there will be no need to go through the actual launch."

"Declare victory?"

"Yes, sir. Just issue a statement saying that the terrorist camps near Gwadar have been destroyed by our F-45 Hornets."

"No, Cal. It's all so clear now. This is what the world needs. The nuclear radiation will purify the world, and the United States will never be challenged again. Yes, there will be a great many casualties from the radiation, and a large percentage of the world's population will die, but my administration will be seen as ushering in a new age for mankind."

Quint glanced at the gold watch on his wrist. He had less than two minutes to change the president's mind.

"Unfortunately," Quint resumed, "the United States will take one or more direct hits and become uninhabitable within fifty years. Long before then, most societal structures will start to break down. You won't have a country to govern, sir. Go back inside, rescind your orders, and then declare the greatest military victory in the history of the country."

Hastings looked at Quint as precious seconds ticked away.

"You always understand the big picture, Cal. By God, it'll work. I'll be the most famous man in the history of the world."

"You will, sir, but you need to move quickly."

The two men returned to the Situation Room.

"Cancel my orders," the President said. "I've just received word that the terrorist training camp in Pakistan has been destroyed."

Sutherland glanced at Quint, who shook his head slightly, indicating that it was best not to ask for an explanation.

"Stop the damn launch!" Hastings exclaimed. "There are only fifty-six seconds left."

"Sir," said Quint, "you have to give the verification code to stop the launch. Read the code from the Biscuit. Quickly!"

"The what?"

"The Biscuit is the laminated card you're holding. You have to read a separate code to stop the missiles. Please hurry, sir."

The President located the code and began reading it to Lieutenant Jamison at the Pentagon as General Sutherland breathed a sigh of relief.

Major Farnsworth put his sidearm back in its holster and sat down, wiping perspiration from his brow.

The President left when the immediate threat had been averted. Quint, Hart, and Sutherland, however, remained to see if Pakistan, too, would stand down and whether or not other nations would close the doors of their missile silos.

"The ass doesn't even know that a crisis still looms over the world," Hart commented.

"Quite true, Mr. Secretary," Quint said. "I guess you and I will have to nursemaid the situation for the next few hours while the president takes his victory laps in front of a mirror."

Hart's eyes widened. "That's the first time I've ever heard you speak ill of the President."

"It may not be the last," Quint said. "I suspect that you and I will have to talk in the days ahead."

"Indeed," Hart said.

Chapter Ninety-Four

Unofficial Pilot on Decoy Angel

PATTERSON WAS CHECKED INTO THE EMERGENCY ROOM AT THE GEORGETOWN MEDICAL CENTER AND DECLINED TO BE ADMITTED AS A PATIENT. He was given prescriptions for antibiotics and pain relievers after telling the physician that he had an important story to pursue. Taylor was driving Sela and Patterson back to the safe house when Sela received an incoming message.

"Anything important?" Patterson asked.

Her fingers played on the keypad for several seconds, her eyes widening as if she couldn't believe what she was seeing.

"It's from Bobby!"

"Where is that crazy-ass Cajun?" Taylor asked.

Sela looked up, mouth agape. "He's on Air Force One. It's headed for Cheyenne Mountain."

Taylor glanced quickly at his passengers before speaking. "How in the living hell did he get aboard the—"

"He says it's a long story. I'll read what he's writing."

"He's our wizard, is he not?" Patterson said.

"Bobby says that he's on the decoy Angel," Sela continued.

"Angel?" Patterson said.

"Angel is another name for Air Force One," Taylor explained. "As I told Sela, there are two of them."

"He says that Hastings is still in Washington."

"Does he know where my story is?" Patterson asked.

Sela paused while she sent and received communication from Thibodaux.

"Bobby says he's working on it. He says that all he knows at present is that Jay's transmission was intercepted—he doesn't know by whom—and never made it to the web."

"How the hell could that happen?" Patterson asked. "No one could possibly have known what I was sending out."

"It will remain a mystery for now," Taylor observed, "and the only one who can solve such a conundrum is on Air Force One. We may *never* know the answer."

"Why not?" Patterson asked.

"Because it's only a matter of time before somebody discovers who he is and has him arrested."

Patterson shook his head as he popped a pain reliever. "All of our work was for nothing. I don't think the country can hold together for more than a day or two."

"It looks bad," Taylor agreed, "but—"

A black Escalade approached from the rear. An arm appeared from its passenger-side window. It was holding a gun.

Loud *pings* could be heard ricocheting off the asphalt road. Someone was attempting to shoot out the tires of Taylor's SUV.

Chapter Ninety-Five

States Secede from the Union

Jimmy Finch stood on a street corner in Nashville, Tennessee, with his bride, Holly Gerard. He put his arm around her waist and squeezed tightly.

"The American Paramilitary Union has successfully taken eighteen state capitals," he said. "Our troops are in thirty other states, and twelve have voted to secede from the Union. It's still only a vote and doesn't mean that any state has formally declared its independence, but it indicates that people are willing to move forward in making this a new nation."

"President Hastings just announced that the terrorist camp in Pakistan has been destroyed and that nuclear war has been averted," Gerard said. "Won't things go back to normal? I mean, he just saved the damn fucking country."

"A female preacher who curses?"

Gerard rolled her eyes.

"Nothing is going back to normal, Holly. Hastings can't rule without my approval. He gave me permission for these maneuvers, and perhaps he didn't understand just how strong we are. The only way to get us off the streets in all fifty states would be to open fire, and that's not going to happen. No, I'm hoping for secession."

"Are there any terms you would accept?" Gerard asked.

"The creation of a white nationalist party that is equal in weight to the other two political parties. Then I'll talk turkey. I can't lose either way. Secession guarantees that such a party will be formed since there would be no one to stop me. I will naturally be its leader. Eventually, I intend to become president of the nation, whatever it might be called. Trust in Herbert Hastings for now. He took the genie out of the bottle, but he still wants to stay in power. That's okay with me. It'll work to our advantage to have a popular man like him running the show a while longer." Finch winked. "Trust in Hastings, honey."

"And God?"

"Whose God?" Finch laughed. "Yours? Mine? The spiritual nonsense worshipped by the Temple of Metaphysics and the Church of the Heart?"

Gerard smiled. "I see your point. It doesn't make a whole lot of difference."

"Why not?"

"I'm spiritual but not religious. I was never really interested in who or what God was."

"You little spitfire. I love you."

The husband and wife kissed before Finch looked up and made sure that guards were stationed on every corner. Everything was going as planned.

Chapter Ninety-Six
Big Brother

LUCILLE RAINES AND MAXWELL HART STOOD AT THE LARGEST SERVER FARM IN THE COUNTRY. Located beneath the Pentagon, it was easily the size of four football fields. It was where the federal government monitored the communications of citizens and transactions processed by the chip implants in people's forearms. Data was collected on virtually everyone, although the algorithms of Big Brother, as it was known at the Department of Defense, were such that only certain information was filtered from the vast volume of data collected every second of the day, and sent to computer analysts for further prioritization. All information, however, was available if someone sat down and actively searched for a given bit of data.

As secretary of state and head of *Etiam Electus*, Maxwell Hart was more than familiar with the operation of Big Brother, and members of The Elect had free and unfettered access to the server farm whenever they wanted. Certain members, of course, such as IT specialists, routinely monitored the vast server array, looking for certain keywords that had been programmed into the system for the purposes of tripping what The Elect benignly called "an information alert."

A technician met Raines and Hart and introduced himself.

"Good morning," said Colonel Robert Syzmanski. The Army colonel was dressed in his full uniform of khaki suit and tie, complete with medals and military decorations. He was fifty-two, had a crew cut, and wore black-rimmed glasses.

"You called my office," Hart said. "You have information that the Office of Government Inquiry might find useful?"

Yes, Mr. Secretary. We do. If you and Chief of Staff Raines will follow me, I'll take you to a terminal where you can see what we found."

The trio walked a distance of thirty yards to one of a hundred rooms that opened to the corridor that ran on all four sides of the farm.

"One of my teams intercepted a signal," Colonel Syzmanski explained. "Would you like me to play the transmission for you?"

"Yes, please," Raines replied.

It was the news story by Jay Patterson, the one he'd uploaded in East Potomac Park.

"Someone tried to post another story almost identical to this one to an account owned by an individual named Gail Gunderson, which we believe to be an alias or pseudonym. We blocked it."

"May we have the room?" Hart requested.

"Certainly," Colonel Syzmanski said before leaving.

Hart and Raines watched the report two more times before commenting.

"So we've been *formally* accused of murder," Raines said. "How could this possibly happen, Max? No one was taking the stories of Taylor and Mistretta seriously, but Patterson has uncovered everything."

"Patterson is clever, Lucille. The late-night call you received when someone asked for the Office of Government Inquiry was no doubt from the intrepid Mr. Patterson."

"His report about the murders of Chance and Rampling is quite accurate, Max. You ordered that both individuals be terminated with nanotechnology, and there it is in his report."

"Wolcott left me no choice," Hart said, "when he told me that Chance had been snooping around Garundi, and also that the president was sounding unhinged, for lack of a better term. I didn't know about the tobacco operation prior to Wolcott's call, but I didn't think it would present a problem, at least not until I learned that Hastings was doing business with Faridoon. I had no idea that Iran was funding his operation or that it had delivered the Hastings campaign large amounts of cash, ensuring the president's electoral victory."

Raines nodded. "I didn't know about Iran either, although I suspected something was up with Brad and Savannah when they started coming into the White House through the tunnel system. Later, when it was reported that they were traveling to Tehran, I asked Herbert what was going on. He said it was all about the Slipstream jet."

"He may be crazy," Hart declared, "but he's one determined bastard. Still, doing business with Iran was a rookie move. It's further proof that he knows nothing about the geopolitical climate of the world, as if we needed further proof after his saber rattling against Pakistan."

"Does he stay in office?" Raines asked.

"I'll have to talk more about that with Quint, but I would say that Hastings remaining in the Oval Office is looking doubtful. We have time to make a decision as long as we keep Patterson's report from ever hitting the Internet."

"The membership of *Etiam Electus* shall want a vote of its primary thirteen members as soon as possible," Raines commented.

"I believe they'll do what you and I recommend," Hart said. "What's your own opinion, Lucille?"

"I think Herbert needs to go."

"I'm inclined to agree, although I originally thought that having Hastings in the White House would be useful in attaining the goals of *Etiam Electus*. He was the ideal Manchurian candidate."

"We'll have to terminate Patterson once and for all," Raines said, "as well as Sela Grant and John Taylor. They'll continue to try to publish their report, and sooner or later they'll succeed."

"I'm already on it. I dispatched a team to try to kill the three of them while they were traveling together. They do so a lot, and I've arranged further attempts until I know with certainty that all three are dead. A car accident won't produce any suspicion."

"Agreed."

Hart and Raines left the server farm.

Chapter Ninety-Seven
Incognito

SELA AND PATTERSON DECIDED TO GO TO SETI HEADQUARTERS IN D.C. TO USE THE SATELLITE ON THE ROOF IN ORDER TO GET IN TOUCH WITH BOBBY THIBODAUX AGAIN. John Taylor's vehicle was now known to *Etiam Electus*, and they all three barely escaped being murdered when someone tried to blow out Taylor's tires.

Patterson and Sela went to a junkyard and bought an old Chevy Malibu for a hundred dollars cash. The couple sat in the dusty vehicle surrounded by axles and chassis from other automobiles, and realized they had no key to start the Chevy. Patterson reached under the steering column and pulled away a piece of plastic.

"What are you doing?" Sela asked. "This car is already beat up pretty badly, and you're peeling away more parts?"

"I'm hotwiring it," Patterson explained. "A very old trick. If I can find the ignition and battery wires and touch them together, I should be able to start this old bucket's engine."

Five minutes later, the engine coughed and sputtered before turning over.

"My God!" Sela cried. "It sounds awful."

"We'll put some gas in it and I'll add a couple quarts of oil. That should do the trick."

"My implant still says I'm Gail Gunderson," Sela said. "Let's get to a private room at NASA and I'll try to reach Bobby using the same frequency he contacted us with from Air Force One."

After several failed attempts, Sela was able to get in touch with Thibodaux, who was still aboard Air

Force One. He said the plane was on the tarmac at the airfield adjoining Cheyenne Mountain Air Force Station.

Jay," Thibodaux said, "your report was intercepted by a hacker team at the server farm beneath the Pentagon. It's called Big Brother. I managed to upload the report to the plane before we landed. You wouldn't believe how many electronic toys Air Force One has. If I was of a mind to, I could probably call up the U.S. Geologic Survey at the South Pole and ask them what the temperature is today. From this room on the plane, you can launch anything from firecrackers to nuclear weapons. Did I mention that the plane also has two kitchens and an operating room?"

"How did you get on board, Bobby?" Sela asked.

"I knew the transmission tower wasn't going to be safe, so I figured I'd get the hell out of Dodge like everybody else, but since you were investigating Hastings, I thought I'd do it in style. I got a haircut, shaved, and—how shall I put it—appropriated a uniform from an Air Force officer at Wright-Patterson. It was in his locker. He wasn't on duty, but he normally flies aboard Air Force One and works here in the command center. It was rather easy to come aboard since this is a decoy and people were in a big hurry to get this bird off the ground. They had orders to leave, plus everyone thought that Washington was about to disappear beneath a mushroom cloud. Essentially, I saluted and walked on board, no questions asked."

Patterson wasn't surprised by Thibodaux's accomplishment, given the resourcefulness of the NewzTracker technician, as well as the chaos that had reigned over the nation's capital for the past forty-eight hours.

"Can you send out my story?" Patterson asked. "Can you get it on the Net?"

"Sure, but it could be traced too easily, and I don't want to spend the rest of my life at the federal penitentiary in Leavenworth. I hear prison food is pretty bad."

"Can you send it to the vice president?" Patterson asked as he maneuvered the old vehicle he'd purchased.

"Hell yeah. Air Force One has several dedicated lines that go straight to the VP. A piece of cake."

"Do it, Bobby, and the sooner the better. Erase it when you're done so there's no trace of it."

"Consider it sent. I'll get back in touch when I can safely terminate my little charade."

The call ended and Patterson bought two quarts of motor oil at an auto parts store. The couple then took the car to a drive-thru burger joint to get some food.

"Will the vice president know what to do with the report?" Sela asked.

"He wanted me to have all of this information, and he apparently has computer skills. Then again, I'm not sure if *Etiam Electus* will intercept it a second time regardless of its format now that it knows what's in my article. Call it a Hail Mary pass."

"Getting religious on me *again*?"

"You're carrying my child and my dad's grandchild. I owe my existence right now to my dad"

"But, Jay, your dad is dead, isn't he?"

"I thought so. But I heard from him at critical moments. You say you have transmissions from another planet . . . so just maybe there's hope yet for truth to come to planet Earth. Sela, I don't think we have all the truth of the universe. I'm not arrogant enough to think that we know everything there is to know, and that Earth is all there is. In fact, at this point in time, I think we here on Earth must appear naïve when it comes to knowing how the universe operates—much less after mortal life on Earth, or on other planets and solar systems.

Chapter Ninety-Eight
Delusions of Grandeur

President Hastings, feeling invigorated by what he was claiming as his victory over Pakistan, boarded Air Force One and flew to Atlanta, Georgia, where he would address a crowd of his Red Republican Legion. According to flash polls taken after his announcement that he had single-handedly averted a nuclear crisis and delivered a blow to terrorism that might spell an end to jihadists around the world, Hastings believed he had considerable political capital, and he intended to spend it as soon as possible. It was a chance to give his administration an infusion of patriotic rhetoric and inflict serious damage to his opponents, especially those in the press.

He was met at the airport by Jimmy Finch, who rode with him in the presidential limousine to the auditorium where he would deliver his address.

"Mr. President," Finch said, "twenty-one states have voted to secede from the union, and more are expected to join them. There has been no final ratification by any of the state legislatures yet, but it's only a matter of time."

"Can a state really secede from the Union?" Hastings asked.

"Not legally, but leaving the Union means that a state is no longer bound by the Constitution. There will be fighting in the streets, of course, but as commander in chief, you could lessen the bloodshed if you support our cause and agree to be President of a *new* union. You can help make the transition a lot easier."

Hastings thought of how Cal Quint had reassured him that claiming victory would be an enormous plus in his attempt to keep a firm hold on the reins of the country. Quint hadn't mentioned secession, and Hastings trusted his vice president.

"Jimmy, I gave you permission to flex your muscles and stage maneuvers. I told you it was okay to roll into cities across the land in order to show you were a force to be reckoned with. I assumed that it would also be a statement of your support for my administration."

"It can be, sir."

"But I didn't give you permission to dissolve the goddamned country! It's going too far."

"Are you willing to help form a white nationalist political party? Would we have your endorsement?"

Hastings paused and rubbed his chin uneasily, unsure of how to answer.

"In time, Jimmy. But not yet. Such a move would have to be phased in gradually. I'm in perfect agreement with your stance on white pride and the inferiority of all other races, but I can't run for president on such a platform. It would be too risky. We'd have the backing of the Real Right, but the rest of the country wouldn't fall in line. No, we need to lay a lot of groundwork. It could take years to attain the kind of goal you're seeking. Years!"

"Then with all due respect, Mr. President, I see no choice but to secede. I and my followers aren't willing to wait that long. We've been silent for decades, but now is the time for action. If you're defeated in the next election, which is always a possibility, the American Paramilitary Union may never have another chance to take this step. I've stood beside you, Mr. President, when others chose to criticize your actions and try to bring you down. I'm calling in a marker. Without the backing of my men and their sympathizers, you won't get re-elected."

"But we just defeated Pakistan," Hastings said with frustration.

"And I congratulate you, Mr. President, but that's part of a much bigger picture. It's time to crush minorities, gays, and many other undesirable elements of society."

"For God's sake, Jimmy! I'm the leader of the United States of America, not the Confederacy!"

Finch laughed. "What's in a name, sir?"

Chapter Ninety-Nine
In the Right Hands

VICE PRESIDENT QUINT WAS EATING BRUNCH WITH MELANIE MASTERS AT A PRIVATE RESIDENCE HE MAINTAINED IN D.C. WHEN HIS PHONE CHIRPED A PRIORITY EMAIL ALERT. He opened the message and frowned. "Well, son of a bitch. It's from Jay Patterson."

Masters shrugged. "I couldn't even speculate."

"I suspect it was intercepted by some folks who would rather remain nameless. Let me read through the report and see what my friend has to say."

"Patterson is your friend?"

"In a roundabout kind of way."

"I want to get back to bed," Masters complained after Quint had finished reading the article.

"All in good time, darlin'. I want you to send this out on the Internet."

"From here at the CIA? That's a bit risky."

Quint sat and reflected on what he should do. He'd sent the reporter information on Hastings for a while, and Patterson hadn't let him down. He'd figured out everything—and then some. He couldn't let the reporting go to waste. Too much depended on it.

"I have a better idea," he said at last. "This is a NewzTracker story, and it should be sent from their server."

"NewzTracker is probably under heavy guard by either the Loyalty Militia or Jimmy Finch's troops. I doubt we could get in."

Quint threw his head back and laughed. "Honey, I'm the vice president. I know how to ride an ornery bull, and this is the biggest rodeo of my life. Let's go. I'll get in—trust me."

The pair left in the vice president's motorcade, headed for Chevy Chase Village, Maryland.

Chapter One Hundred
Lethal Ambition

LUCILLE RAINES SAT IN HER OFFICE AFTER RETURNING FROM THE SERVER FARM AT THE PENTAGON. She pondered the events of the past several days and glanced at the autopsy reports for Chance and Rampling. Maxwell Hart had been thorough and methodical, and but for the cleverness of Jay Patterson, the murders would have never come to light. Hart had been left with little recourse but to protect the president using the severest of measures.

It was another document that claimed her attention, however: the psychiatric file that Dr. Elizabeth Rampling had kept on Hastings. She noted that Hastings had battered his ex-wives and poisoned his children against them. He'd been a master at gaslighting, projection, and manipulation. Outwardly, he was a wealthy, powerful, and successful man. On the inside, he was empty and desperate for people's approval. He could be socially gregarious and the life of the party, a man who exuded confidence and enjoyed many friends. Within, he still looked for scapegoats to punish for various childhood traumas, especially his abuse at the Christian Academy of Virginia. He had been diagnosed by Rampling as having borderline personality disorder.

The question Raines now considered was whether or not she would make it public. If *Etiam Electus* voted to remove the president from office, there would be no need to validate the opinion of Dr. Boyce Rittner by leaking Rampling's file. If Hastings was allowed to stay in power, that was a different matter. The thirteen members of *Etiam Electus* would meet to vote soon, and she, of course, would vote for Hastings' removal. She'd always thought her time to shine—to become the vice president for Cal Quint—would come when Herbert had finished his second term. It now looked as if Hastings wouldn't even finish his first. But would Quint name her as his vice president? Of course he would. As a member of *Etiam Electus*, she was aware of the many marital infidelities Quint had committed over the years, including his latest with Melanie Masters. She had all the dirt she needed to become the vice president.

Chapter One Hundred One

Telling the Truth to One Who Cares

"I FEEL HELPLESS JUST DRIVING AROUND," SELA SAID. "Do we wait indefinitely to see whether Quint received your report from Bobby?"

"No," Patterson replied. "I'm going to tell my story to Leland Wallace so that somebody within the government knows the entire truth. He's a man of honor, and he'll believe me."

Patterson aimed the Malibu at the Dirksen Senate Office Building and donned his Indiana Jones hat and aviator sunglasses. Ahead, he spied a roadblock comprised of soldiers from the Loyalty Militia.

"Sela, get into the back and pull down the rear seat, which will allow you to crawl into the trunk. I think I can get us through the checkpoint up ahead, but they may be looking for you as well."

Sela complied with Patterson's request as he turned on the radio, found an oldies station, and cranked up the volume. He rolled to a stop on Delaware Avenue and waited as a soldier in olive drab approached the vehicle. His nametag read Lieutenant Willow.

"Please pull over, sir," Willow said. Willow was in his late forties, lean and muscular, and stood with hands on his hips.

"Anything wrong, Loo-tenant?" Patterson said, affecting a southern accent.

Willow glanced at a picture he held in his hand and then at Patterson. He bent forward and looked in the back seat of a car.

"Lookin' for something?" Patterson asked. "I ain't got no drugs, at least not in the car."

"Could you turn that music down, sir?"

"It's just the Rolling Stones. Good song, huh? Satisfaction?"

"I said to turn down the music."

Patterson turned the radio knob on the dashboard to his left, but only a little.

Another soldier walked towards the vehicle. Colonel Louis Drake was older, had a slight paunch, and ears that lay flat against his head, causing his face to look rectangular.

"Anything wrong here?" Drake asked.

"This guy won't turn down the music," Willow said. "Sir, would you step out of the car, please? We're looking for someone, and I'll have to ask you to remove your hat and sunglasses."

Patterson saw that the picture Willow was holding was a photo of himself.

"Aw shit," Patterson complained. "Just like the song says—I can't get no satisfaction . . . Loo-tenant."

"Wait a second," Drake said, as Jay was in the process of opening the door. "Where are you going, son?"

"Over to the Lincoln Memorial if I can ever find it. I've been drivin' around these crazy streets for an hour. I want to see where the March on Washington was. You know—1963 and Joan Baez, Martin Luther King, and Peter, Paul, and Mary."

Drake stepped back and laughed.

"Let this poor bastard through, Lieutenant. He's one of those dropouts. Used to call 'em hippies. Let him enjoy his nostalgia and get stoned. Who the hell cares?"

Willow waved Patterson through, and the Malibu crept forward until the Loyalty Militia was in his rearview mirror.

"Come on out," Patterson called to Sela. "We're almost there."

Back in the worn passenger seat, Sela shook her head and grinned. "I know you like old things, but this was way over the top."

"Indiana Jones and the Rolling Stones will never go out of style," he said. "And my dad told me, neither will Martin Luther King!'"

Colonel Drake got on his radio and asked to be connected with Secretary of State Hart.

"Hart here. What do you have, Colonel?"

"I just waved Jay Patterson through our checkpoint, Mr. Secretary. You asked to be notified. He's traveling in an old Chevrolet Malibu. I suspect Ms. Grant was in the trunk."

"What about John Taylor?"

"Unsure whether he was with Patterson, who was dressed in an old hat and pretending to be a hippie. We could have detained him, but you said you had other plans for his termination."

"That's correct. Thank you, Colonel."

Drake wondered if he would see the morning news and learn that a Chevy Malibu had been in a terrible accident. He didn't much care. He disliked reporters, dropouts, stoners, liberals, and hippies. They were all worthless in his estimation, a weight pulling down the conservative elements of society.

Chapter One Hundred Two

Uploading to NewzTracker & Out to the World

VICE PRESIDENT QUINT AND MELANIE MASTERS ARRIVED AT NEWZTRACKER'S OFFICES, WHICH WERE UNDER HEAVY GUARD BY THE CIVILIAN STATE MILITIA. Secret Service agents got out of the lead vehicles of the motorcade, followed by the vice president and Masters. The troops of the civilian militia seemed perplexed that such an imposing caravan of black vehicles was arrayed in front of the building. Many of the soldiers raised their automatic rifles slightly and stepped towards the Secret Service agents.

"Hi, boys!" Quint said as he surveyed the area.

"And who might you be?" asked a man in his late thirties, with a mullet haircut, and light-brown camouflage fatigues.

"The vice president of the United States. And who are you?"

"I'm Sergeant Joe Griffith, platoon leader of the Virginia Volunteers," the man said proudly. "How do I know you're the vice president?"

Quint turned to Masters. "See? Nobody recognizes me unless I'm on television next to the President. It's a thankless job." He turned back to Griffith. "Joe, how many people do you see traveling around in a black limousine with a motorcycle escort and a Secret Service detail? By the way, there's a satellite overhead recording everything we say and do, and snipers can be here within ten minutes."

"Well, I guess you make a point," Griffith said with a slight southern drawl.

"Exactly," Quint said, extending his hand, which the sergeant took and pumped. "Joe—may I call you

Joe?—you and your men here are doing a fine job. Fine indeed. It's good to see

that there are still some Americans who aren't afraid to get down in the trenches and get dirty to serve their country."

"Thank ya, sir. Just doin' our job. May I ask what your business is here? I know you're the second honcho of the country and all that, but I have strict orders from Jimmy Finch himself to keep everyone away from this location."

"Call me Cal, and I'm here to . . . . hey, Joe, excuse me a minute, but have you ever been to the rodeo? I was a bull rider before I got into politics, and I have two tickets for you and the little lady to go to the Real West Rodeo Show tonight in D.C. I'm busy, so would you like those tickets? A gift from the vice president?"

The expression on Joe Griffith's face turned from suspicion to the smile of a small child on Christmas morning. "Gosh, that would be swell. Thank ya, Cal. My old lady positively *loves* horses."

Quint winked. "Glad to hear it. Now here's the deal. I and my assistant have some business inside. Hush-hush stuff. National security. So we need to get in there and have a look around."

"You want us to go in first and shoot up the place?" Griffith asked.

Quint slapped the sergeant on the shoulder and chuckled. "That won't be necessary, Joe, but thanks for the offer. Just guard it while we're inside and don't let anyone in, okay?"

"You can count on me, Cal. The Virginia Volunteers won't let you down."

Quint and Masters entered the building, after which the vice president turned to Masters. "Work your mojo, Melanie. Get that Patterson article onto the web."

She inserted a portable drive on which the article was stored into one of Bobby Thibodaux's terminals. The transfer and conversion took only a few seconds.

"It's been uploaded to the NewzTracker website," Masters said. "The article is going out to the world at this very moment."

"Melanie, I could take you right here and now if we had more time, but let's get back to my private residence and watch the news unfold while we're in bed. I don't want to start howling with the diligent Sergeant Griffith right outside the door."

"More bull riding and bronco busting when we get to your place?"

"You can count on it, sweetheart. The rodeo is in town tonight, and I'm not talking about the one I gave Joe tickets to.

The lovers kissed and left the building. The motorcade left the area quickly. Joe Griffith stared as the last vehicle disappeared from sight.

"Pretty nice fella," he said. "And to think he's the vice president. Don't that beat all."

Chapter One Hundred Three
A Senator's Gift to Truth

PATTERSON AND SELA WERE MET BY LORETTA VELAZQUEZ, THE CHIEF OF STAFF FOR SENATOR LELAND WALLACE.

"I'm sorry," Velazquez said, "but the senator has been hospitalized for congestive heart failure and emphysema. He's at Georgetown Medical Center."

"Ms. Velasquez, I need to see the senator, and it's urgent," Patterson said. "Will you come with us so that I can be assured of being admitted to his room? I count Leland as a friend, and I think he'd want to hear what I have to say."

"He's very fond of you, Mr. Patterson. I'd be happy to go with you."

/

Leland Wallace was in a private room with security guards posted at the door. Velasquez told them that Patterson was a regular visitor of the senator, and after he was checked for weapons on his person, he was admitted to the room, where Wallace, who was asleep, was receiving oxygen. Plastic tubing from an IV bag coiled downwards into his forearm.

Wallace opened his eyes and looked at Patterson. The faint trace of a smile crossed his face as he tilted his head to the side.

"Let this be a lesson, Jay. Never start smoking, because the damn things will kill ya. I'm another Dale McCuddy, killed by Western Rider and a dozen other brands over the years. I have no one to blame but myself, but this isn't the way I wanted to go out."

Patterson touched Wallace's hand gently. "Hang in there, my friend. You may pull through yet. I came here to tell you about a story I wrote that got lost in the shuffle. It's important that you know what's in it."

"You mean the story that's running on television now," Wallace said as his bloodshot eyes focused on the wall screen opposite his bed.

Patterson turned and saw his face narrating the story that he'd written and filmed after being shot. "Well, it seems that Bobby got the report to the vice president, who had the good sense to send it out through the NewzTracker website. Quint has been my informant, Leland."

Wallace, Velasquez, Patterson, and Sela watched the report from beginning to end.

Fighting a coughing fit, Wallace pursed his lips and frowned. "So the bastard got himself elected with help from the Iranian mafia and government. A damn shame is what it is. Can't say that I'm surprised, though. Hastings is an unprincipled and immoral man. I hope he gets locked up for life."

"We can certainly hope," Patterson gave a forced smile as he looked at the weak form of Wallace. "I should be going now so that you can get some rest."

Patterson realized that Wallace didn't have long to live despite the idle encouragement he'd offered upon entering the room. He no longer needed to confide the details of what he'd learned since the story was running now, although he was glad that Wallace had gotten to see the piece.

"Hold on a minute," Wallace said with a weak voice. "I'm an old man and I'm dying, but I have something for you. Take my phone. It's my gift to you. I secretly recorded sixty-eight senators and congressman over the past year confessing that they hate Hastings' guts even though they publicly support his insane rhetoric and policies. There's actually a lot more on the recordings than that, though. You'll see what I mean and know why it's important. Publish it when you think the time is right, my friend."

"Thank you, Leland," Patterson said as he picked up the cell phone. "Take your pain meds and try to relax."

"I'd rather bourbon, son."

Back in the Chevy, Patterson drove out of the hospital parking lot and pressed the accelerator. A cloud of blue exhaust spewed from the Malibu's tailpipe. He glanced at the odometer, which read 376,000 miles. *The car has staying power*. He only wished that he could say the same for Senator Leland Wallace.

Chapter One Hundred Four
Stroking His Red Herd

PRESIDENT HASTINGS WAS FORCED TO CUT A DEAL WITH JIMMY FINCH TO PREVENT SECESSION BY THE STATES. He assured Finch that Harrison DePeche's gun legislation would be repealed, by executive order if necessary, and that the Confederate flag could fly freely in any state of the Union. A white nationalist party would be formed, although the president would not formally endorse it until he was ready to leave office. In return, Finch agreed to return control of the states to their governors, the troops of the American Paramilitary Union leaving major urban areas to return to their private rural encampments.

Hastings felt he had scored yet another victory, and he listened carefully to the voices he heard speaking in his ear, the voices of Julius and Augustus and Tiberius, telling him of his greatness and assured place in history. And then he heard Julius himself speak.

"You deserve nomination for the Nobel Peace Price for what you have accomplished. Bring it up in the next cabinet meeting."

"That's exactly what I'll do!" Hastings responded.

Having seen Patterson's article, the president now felt Patterson had no way to stop his triumph. He took to the stage, and after speaking of his great victory over Pakistan, as well as dealing a death blow to terrorism around the world, Hastings decided to address the NewzTracker report. Hastings looked out over his Red Republican—no—his Red Roman Legion before him, all of whom now knew he was a god, the man who had saved humanity from nuclear Armageddon. He tried to speak several times, but had to stop because of the chants of "He-ro! He-ro! He-ro!"

"Thank you, dear friends and fellow Americans," the president said at last. "Before I talk to you about a new tax bill that I will be sending to Congress, I want to say a few words about the article by Jay Patterson, the most dishonest journalist in the country. He's a liar and a disloyal American. It's time I tell you that I was secretly working with the intelligence community to prevent Iran from advancing its nuclear weapons program any further. I and my children, Brad and Savannah, entered into talks with the despicable Hamid Abbas Faridoon in order to gain information that will be invaluable in protecting the Middle East from any military posturing from Iran. While the threat in Pakistan was very real, the threat from Iran was equally as dangerous, and it, too, has been averted. The world is a safer place today than it was yesterday."

The crowd swallowed every syllable of Hastings' speech, convinced that he was truly a commander in chief who had done more than any other modern president to battle terrorism and avert nuclear proliferation. Red hats were tossed into the air like so many pieces of confetti.

"My growing tobacco in South Africa is nonsense, of course, and has been explained by my new White House Press Secretary, Grant Schneider. As for Jay Patterson, he may be smoking something himself, but it sure isn't regular cigarettes, if you take my meaning."

The crowd laughed at his clichéd humor.

For the next sixty minutes, the President touched on numerous topics. He spoke of his admiration for Jimmy Finch and the American Paramilitary Union and the fine work it had done over the past several days, helping the Loyalty Militia to keep the streets of America safe during the tense moments when Yasir Rafiq had, he claimed, threatened to nuke America out of existence. Furthermore, the American Paramilitary Union had prevented chaos by keeping the terrorist sympathizers of the Grass Roots movement in check. The protest movement, he promised, would soon be disbanded altogether and declared illegal by executive order.

Hastings left the auditorium and rode back to Air Force One, thinking of the means he would employ to kill his wife. She'd forbidden him to issue any further executive orders, but he would issue several more in order to keep his promises to Finch and the American people. It would take time, but he would find a way to put her six feet under.

Chapter One Hundred Five
From the Sacristy to Being Saved

PATTERSON AND SELA WERE BEING CHASED.

"I don't think my little hippie impersonation fooled the soldiers at the checkpoint," Patterson confessed.

A black SUV was gaining on the Malibu as it roared down the Interstate. Patterson changed lanes frequently, but the engine of the Chevy couldn't get the old heap of metal to go faster than seventy miles per hour. The SUV was doing ninety.

Sela's seatbelt buckle became unattached, and she was thrown against Patterson as he maneuvered the vehicle from lane to lane.

"We need to get to surface streets!" she cried. "We'll never outrun our pursuer, so you need to come up with a different strategy. Besides, I'm not so sure that the door won't come off its hinges so that I'll go flying out of the car entirely."

Patterson's response was to take the next exit and hit the brakes. They didn't respond until he pumped them several times, slowing the Chevy as it neared a red light. "Hold on," he said. "This is going to get pretty wild."

Patterson cruised through the light, two cars on his left screeching to a halt and barely avoiding head-on collisions with the dirty white clunker. He then floored the auto and sped down the street. The brakes remained spongy, so he gave himself extra braking time for what became a series of sharp turns, the Malibu fishtailing with each sharp cut of the steering wheel. Glancing in his rearview mirror, he saw that the SUV was two blocks behind them—and gaining.

"If only I could get us into a traffic jam so that the SUV can't maneuver." Patterson said.

"I think we've got more trouble," Sela announced as she looked over her shoulder. "There's a second SUV following us."

Patterson exhaled in frustration, swung the car around the next corner, dark smoke pouring from the tailpipe. Up ahead he saw a group of cars blocking the road.

"That's just great," he said. "I don't think we can get by. Hold on to the dashboard. I'm about to brake hard. Then we run for it."

The car came to a halt just feet from the rear bumper of a late-model Toyota hatchback. Patterson and Sela sprang from the vehicle and ran for a building on their left, where dozens of people were entering in their Sunday finest. Worshippers were being dropped off for services at St. Matthew's Catholic Church.

"Did you maneuver this just to get me into church?" Patterson said as he grabbed Sela's hand and pulled her forward.

The pair pushed their way through the crowd and entered the large church. Patterson stopped momentarily before advancing up the main aisle. Everyone on the right was wearing red garments. Everyone on the left was wearing blue.

"Good Lord!" Patterson exclaimed. "Is there partisanship even at Mass?"

"At least they're under the same roof and talking to each other," Sela replied breathlessly. "That's more than most Republicans and Democrats are doing in the country right now."

Patterson and Sela walked into the sanctuary, circled behind the altar, and entered the sacristy, where a priest was putting on his vestments.

"This is not the time for confession!" the priest whispered.

"Just passing through, Father," Patterson said. "But we'll be back if things work out!"

The couple exited the church through the rear door of the sacristy and began running down an alley.

"Damn," Sela muttered when she spied the second SUV approaching. It was going the wrong way down a one-way street and, braking hard, blocked the exit from the alley, leaving skid marks on the road.

The rear window of the SUV was lowered. In the back seat were Audrey Dickerson and the First Lady. The vehicle was being driven by a Secret Service agent.

"Get in!" Dickerson shouted. "Quickly!"

Patterson and Sela tumbled into the rear of the vehicle, the back door of which had mechanically swung open. The SUV then sped away as Patterson saw that a second Secret Service agent was in the front passenger seat.

"Thank you, ma'am," Patterson said.

"My detail has been keeping an eye on you," the First Lady said. "This is probably Hart's doing. He's the head of—"

"*Etiam Electus*," Patterson interrupted. "Yes, I know all about them."

"You'll have to come with us," Dickerson said.

"Where are we going?" Sela asked.

"The last place Hart or my husband would look for you," the First Lady said. "The White House."

Chapter One Hundred Six
Removing a Figurehead

MAXWELL HART AND LUCILLE RAINES RODE THE ELEVATOR DOWN TO THE THIRD BASEMENT BELOW THE HARRY S. TRUMAN BUILDING, WHICH WAS THE HEADQUARTERS FOR THE UNITED STATES DEPARTMENT OF STATE. Both wore black business suits, which was part of a decades-old custom whenever the thirteen administrative members of *Etiam Electus* met to discuss an issue of sufficient importance that dictated the leadership convene in secret. They stepped off the elevator, walked down a long corridor and entered an unusually large round conference room. They seated themselves at a highly polished mahogany table and remained silent. The only illumination came from dim recessed wall lighting that ran the circumference of the room just below the ceiling. The effect was to keep the faces of those in attendance in semi-shadow.

When the last member of the thirteen was seated, Secretary Hart spoke quietly.

"We are meeting for one purpose," he said. "No other business shall be conducted except that for which you were summoned."

There was no reply from any member.

"Do you swear allegiance to the United States of America?" Hart asked.

"We do," the members replied.

"Do you swear allegiance to *Etiam Electus* and its goals?" Hart asked.

"We do."

"Very well. Let us begin. It is known to all present that President Herbert Chase Hastings brought the country to the brink of nuclear war for no valid reason. No terror threat ever existed in Pakistan. We also know that President Hastings is mentally ill and that the events described in the article by Jay Patterson, which has somehow made it to the Internet and major television networks, are factually correct. Is there any disagreement as to these points?"

The room was silent.

Nick Scarabelli spoke next. "Removing the President is desirable but risky. It makes the Republican Party look weak and almost ensures that a Democrat will be elected in the next presidential cycle. I can make sure that TINN discredits Patterson's report."

"I agree," said a prominent CEO of a large petroleum company. "I think the country will swing back towards Hastings even if some are not willing to publicly admit it, which has always been the case."

"I don't believe Patterson is going to give up," Raines said. "There will undoubtedly be follow-up stories, and we failed to successfully prevent his article from reaching the Internet."

"I have operatives making sure that Patterson and his immediate circle of friends and colleagues shall meet with tragedy very soon," Hart said reassuringly.

"He and his friends have escaped before," Raines noted, "and there are others like him. Many won't believe Patterson's report, but over time it will be proven to be true. The damage is done. Hastings lined his pockets with the aid of a petty Third World dictator while allowing Iran to control our electoral process. Hell, the entire world knows what Hastings did. There can be no foreign policy as long as he's a sitting president. We must face the fact that Jay Patterson brought this administration to its knees. We have to give the country a change in leadership to temporarily placate the press, as much as it pains me to say so."

"I respectfully submit to this body," General Sutherland said, "that the president's mental incapacity trumps everything. What happens the next time his borderline symptoms show themselves? What country does he try to annihilate then? Next time, there will be no America."

A woman with a low voice was next to express an opinion. She was a vice president from a previous administration and was widely respected in the country and among The Elect. She was in her late sixties and spoke with a gravelly voice after undergoing treatment for throat cancer.

"I regard the President as an extreme liability," she stated. "We agreed some years ago that he would be the nominee of our party because he was going to be—how shall I put it—pliable. He possessed the correct conservative principles, albeit he expressed them in a rather unorthodox fashion, and all of us believed that he would follow our lead when it came to specific policy issues. That has not proven to be the case. Removing him from office may be the expedient thing to do to save face, even if it costs us the next election. As the old saying goes, we may need to live to fight another day."

"I think we may be underestimating Cal Quint," remarked a retired rear admiral. "If Hastings is removed, it may show that the party has the wisdom to properly assess a situation. And remember that Quint is very popular in the country. He polls well with women and younger voters."

At the end of a lengthy discussion, six members of The Elect had spoken in favor of keeping President Hastings in office, while six others adamantly believed that Hastings should be removed from office by whatever legal means necessary."

"It appears we have a tie," Hart said. "But we have yet to hear from our newest and youngest member. His opinion will break the tie. I now yield the floor to him."

"Thank you," Todd Hastings said. "It is my privilege to be here."

Todd Hastings had indeed been looking weary for the past several months, but it had not been solely because he was trying to boost the sales of Sailor cigarettes, which he now knew were laced with nicotine, a fact that had been kept from him by his siblings. He'd been under great stress, as Maxwell Hart had spoken with him on many occasions, grooming him to become a member of *Etiam Electus*. He had found Hart's overtures to be appealing, since he'd not enjoyed being a small player in a company that had once known greatness. His father, brother, and sister represented the real power at PB Enterprises, and he had begun to see that he would never be their equal. By becoming a member of The Elect, he could grasp real power and make a difference in the future of his country.

"I've listened with great interest to all of the opinions expressed here today," he said, "and while I respect them all, I must state unequivocally that my father should be removed from office. He's too much of a liability for the party and the nation as a whole."

There was silence in the chamber for several moments before Maxwell Hart spoke again.

"It's time to vote," he said. "I ask for a show of hands from all those who believe that President Herbert Chase Hastings should remain in office."

Six hands were raised.

"I now ask for a show of hands from those who wish the President to be removed from office."

Seven hands were raised, including that of Todd Hastings.

"The motion to remove is carried," Hart proclaimed.

"But how do we do it?" Sutherland asked.

"We ask Quint to invoke the Twenty-fifth Amendment," Raines said.

"And if he refuses?" Sutherland said. "He's been loyal to Hastings from day one."

"I believe that Quint ran to further his career and saw this day as an eventuality," Raines continued. "I'm quite certain he'll do it. If he should refuse for any unforeseen reason, I have compromising information on his personal life that, were I threaten to release it, would surely compel him to do as I ask."

Sutherland's voice expressed concern. "Invoking the Twenty-fifth Amendment is a lot harder than it seems. Evidence must be presented—evidence of an arbitrary nature, I might add—by the vice president to the Speaker of the House and President pro tempore of the Senate that indicates that the president is unfit to hold office, and it must be based on information supplied by the Cabinet."

"Eight members of the president's Cabinet belong to the larger membership of this body," Hart said. "They will back Quint's assertion that the president's actions have been erratic enough to constitute his being unfit to hold office."

"What about Jimmy Finch?" Nick Scarabelli asked. "I heard he struck a deal with the president to start a white nationalist party."

"Quint is a shrewd man behind his folksy cowboy façade," Hart pointed out. "I have every confidence that he can groom Finch to do whatever he wants, even if we have to make some concessions to his movement over time."

Scarabelli was silent before saying, "I tend to agree. Quint has a keen mind."

"It is formally decided then," Hart said. "President Herbert Chase Hastings will be removed as forty-seventh president of the United States. Cal Quint shall become acting president. This meeting is adjourned."

Chapter One Hundred Seven
Reaching a Goal

VICE PRESIDENT QUINT AND MELANIE MASTERS LAY IN BED WATCHING THE NEWS. Masters kissed Quint and stroked his arms.

"Darlin', I'd like to go again, but in light of Patterson's article finally hitting the airwaves, and the president's ludicrous speech in which he said he was secretly working with the intelligence community to rein in Iran's nuclear ambitions, I'm expecting a phone call any minute now. The man has gone round the bend."

Seconds later, Quint's phone chirped.

"Quint here."

The vice president listened for several seconds before speaking.

"I agree, Mr. Secretary. After the scene in the Situation Room, I don't see any other option. I'll invoke the Twenty-fifth Amendment and become the forty-eighth President of the United States. And please tell Lucille that I'll be happy to appoint her as my Vice President. She may have compromising information on me, but I happen to have credible evidence that she's been having an affair with the president. If we can all agree to let sleeping dogs lie, I think we'll all get along with each other just fine."

Quint ended the call and turned to Masters.

"Honey, you're sleeping with the next President of the United States."

"I find power to be an aphrodisiac," Masters said. "Should I stand at attention?"

"No, that's my job, if you take my meaning."

Chapter One Hundred Eight
Thank God for the Twenty-Fifth

REPUBLICAN SENATORS AND CONGRESSMEN RALLIED BEHIND PRESIDENT HASTINGS' SELF-PROCLAIMED VICTORIES IN ORDER TO GET A TAX BILL THROUGH CONGRESS. It had been slightly amended from its previous version, but it was going to give huge tax cuts to the wealthy and raise taxes on the lower and middle classes. Legislators still regarded the president with marked disdain, but they were beginning to look bad in front of their constituents, who were getting angry that Hastings had passed virtually nothing since taking office. They needed to pass a bill, regardless of how harmful it was, so they could claim they were hard at work in Washington.

President Hastings sat in the Rose Garden on a sunny morning, flanked by several dozen legislators, all waiting to receive a pen from the signing ceremony. The vice president was conspicuously absent. The president picked up the first pen, but stopped before beginning his signature.

"Is NewzTracker out there?" he asked. "Jay Patterson?"

"I'm John Taylor," the editor said, raising his hand."

"And what about Beau Bricker and Maryanne Mistretta? Are you here?"

Both raised their hands.

"You're all expelled permanently from the White House," the President said. "Your days of cyber lying and substitute news are over. Someone escort them out so I can sign this great piece of legislation, a law that will put millions of dollars into the pockets of the middle class. I'm declaring a war on the press after the shameless accusations made about me. The world is at peace, and the nation is calm, again thanks to the Loyalty Militia and the American Paramilitary Union. I won't have any hesitation to call up these forces again if I see substitute news or hear that even a single Grass Roots protester is back on the streets."

The reporters were escorted from the Rose Garden.

The president sat with the first pen poised over the bill, when a reporter from the *Political Gazette* asked a question, violating press protocol for a signing ceremony.

"Mr. President" said an African American male in his forties, "the Congressional Budget Office scores this bill as a disaster that will take away jobs and healthcare from fifty million Americans over the next five years. Can you comment, please?"

President Hastings rose and angrily hurled his pen at the reporter. "Get this black man out of the Rose Garden!"

The reporter was grabbed by the Secret Service and summarily escorted from the premises.

The President sat again as if nothing had happened. "What a beautiful day to revive the soul of America with the greatest tax bill ever to be passed in American history."

"What do you mean I've been relieved of office!" Hastings asked his White House Counsel, Maynard LeBlanc.

"The vice president has declared you unfit to serve," LeBlanc replied.

"We'll see who's unfit to serve. You can tell the vice president he's been replaced! No one can remove me from office!"

"The vice president can, under the Twenty-fifth Amendment. He's now acting president until you send a letter to Congress claiming that no such inability exists. Quint will then have four days to challenge you again and bring the issue to a congressional vote."

"Write the damn letter! Now! I'm more mentally fit and physically stronger than anybody else around here. Bunch of misfits is what they are. I'll fire them all!"

"What shall I use as your argument?" LeBlanc asked.

"That I have executive privilege. No one can replace me. I need to get on with running the country."

"And if Congress challenges you?"

Hastings grabbed Leblanc by the shoulders and threw him to the ground. "Congress is in my pocket! Write the letter!"

The President stormed off, leaving Maynard LeBlanc stunned as he climbed to his feet.

Chapter One Hundred Nine
Verdict

THE SPEAKER OF THE HOUSE STOOD IN THE HOUSE CHAMBER, WHICH WAS NEARLY EMPTY AS ITS MEMBERS WATCHED THE FLOOR FROM WALL SCREENS IN THEIR OFFICES. The Speaker was brief in his remarks and wasted no time in delivering one of the most serious comments ever given by anyone holding the office.

"After consultation with various members of the president's Cabinet, Vice President Cal Quint has delivered to me credible evidence that the president of the United States is mentally unfit and should not serve in office any longer. As prescribed by the Twenty-fifth Amendment, the president has delivered his letter of disagreement on the matter of his fitness. The vice president, however, has reasserted his claim to the contrary in writing. There shall therefore be a vote in two days' time in this distinguished body. If two-thirds of the House of Representatives vote to relieve the president under the Twenty-fifth Amendment, and if Senate votes in the same fashion, then according to the Constitution, President Herbert Chase Hastings shall be removed from office and replaced by the vice president."

In the Senate chamber, a debilitated Senator Leland Wallace, President Pro Tempore of the body, was wheeled onto the floor. A microphone was brought to his side and adjusted so that he could be heard as he turned his head slightly. He wore a gray suit, and his hand shook as he read from a single sheet of paper. He coughed, cleared his throat, and spoke in a feeble voice.

"I've been given evidence by Vice President Cal Quint that President Hastings is unfit to serve any longer in the highest office of the land. Furthermore, he has responded to the president's denial by submitting a second claim alleging mental instability. Accordingly, I am scheduling a vote in two days' time, and if two-thirds of the members of the Senate vote for removal of the president, and if the House of Representative concurs, President Hastings shall be replaced by Vice President Calvin Quint. Thank you."

Wallace was wheeled from the empty chamber and taken back to the hospital in a town car. He pulled out a pack of cigarettes and started to light up, but stopped. He only had a few months to live, maybe only weeks, according to his doctor, and he figured that whether or not he smoked was no longer an issue. And yet, he might have to appear in the Senate one last time and cast the most important vote of his career. He wanted to live long enough to depose self-appointed Emperor Herbert Hastings from his imperial throne.

He put the cigarettes back in his pocket and closed his eyes, sleeping the rest of the way to the hospital.

Chapter One Hundred Ten
Last Card to Play Is the Most Important

First Lady Diane Hastings sat in her office in the East Wing.

"The release of the recording of Herbert talking to himself was timed perfectly," she said. "The entire country got to see him pretend to be a Roman emperor. Audrey, it's time you issue my final statement. I trust you have the appropriate press members assembled?"

"Yes, I do," Dickerson answered.

Dickerson stepped to a small briefing room where two dozen members of the press awaited her statement.

"Ladies and gentlemen," Dickerson began, "I've asked you here this morning to deliver a message on behalf of the First Lady. It is with regret that I have to announce that Diane Hastings, who has graced this mansion with dignity for the past year and a half, has decided after careful deliberation to seek a divorce from Herbert Chase Hastings. Since the filing will be a matter of public record, the First Lady has authorized me to inform you that, although she would like to have kept the details of her marriage private, she is seeking a divorce from the president on the grounds of mental cruelty, spousal abuse, and marital rape. I won't be taking any questions at present."

Dickerson left the room, leaving twenty-four reporters looking at each other with open mouths.

Back in the First Lady's office, Dickerson sat in a chair facing Mrs. Hastings' desk.

"Do you think Congress will vote to replace Herbert with Quint?" Dickerson asked.

The First Lady leaned forward and clasped her hands on the desk.

"I don't know if the votes are there. I've done what I can, however, to throw Herbert under the bus. But I'm afraid many members of Congress are afraid to move against Herbert since some of their constituents voted for him in the presidential election. And they just passed his tax bill. I'm not at all sure they're willing to take such drastic action."

"There's someone waiting to see you," Dickerson said.

"Patterson? Show him in."

The reporter and his girlfriend were ushered into the East Wing office.

"We wanted to thank you and Ms. Dickerson for saving our lives and giving us someplace safe to stay," Patterson said. "I only wish that my report had had more impact. I feel like I let my country down."

"Maybe, Jay," the First Lady said, "it's a case that the country let *you* down."

Using a remote control, the First Lady turned on a wall screen mounted in her office. "Take a look."

Both ABN and TINN were reporting that 12,576 illegal immigrants had been shot and killed from the Towers of Freedom when they'd tried to cross the southern border during the nuclear scare. Church of the Heart membership was in the millions, although Muslims, Hispanics, African-Americans, gays, and Democrats had been barred from attending the church. Virtually every member of NATO had condemned the actions of President Hastings, and Americans whose heritage was of Pakistani descent were denounced as being terrorist sympathizers. The president's Red Republican Legion had taken to the streets, denouncing the media as liberal Communist liars. Members of Grass Roots were being hunted by vigilante squads, dragged from their homes, and tortured. Several hundred citizens, all wearing red Hastings tee shirts and caps, had marched on SETI headquarters to protest the belief that extraterrestrials existed. Lastly, both networks reported that an overwhelming majority of senators and congressmen did not intend to vote for the removal of the president on the grounds that he was mentally unbalanced.

"What have we come to?" Sela asked.

"Mrs. Hastings, I'd like to write an article and upload it," Patterson said. "Is there a room here at the White House I can use to do this safely? There are a few things I have to say before posting them to the NewzTracker website."

The First Lady turned to Dickerson. "Take Jay and Sela to the sub-basement where your private office is located, the one where you communicate with the leaders of Grass Roots, and show him how to upload his next article."

"It will be more of a commentary," Patterson noted. "Short but important."

"I look forward to seeing it very soon," said Mrs. Hastings.

Chapter One Hundred Eleven
From the Heart

DICKERSON USHERED PATTERSON AND SELA INTO A ROOM THAT WAS WELL AWAY FROM TRAFFIC, IN SUB-BASEMENT 2B. It was, she said, a place where no one bothered her. She then pointed out Tabs of various sizes and explained to Sela how she could program them to anonymously upload communication to any site she wanted to access, including NewzTracker. Dickerson said she would return in an hour, and then left.

Patterson looked at Sela and sighed. "I thought my last report would be the most important one of my life, but maybe my next one will be the one people need to hear the most."

Sela nodded and Patterson closed his eyes as he prepared what he would say to the nation. He used no notes, nor did he type any text. Everything he was about to say was being written in his heart.

At last, Patterson opened his eyes and set a SmartTab to record mode before he began speaking.

"This is Jay Patterson of NewzTracker-dot-com. I'm speaking to you from an undisclosed location because members of *Etiam Electus*, an organization under the direction of Secretary of State Maxwell Hart, tried to kill me when I exposed the president's mental health issues, his tobacco-growing operation in Garundi, and the purchase of the last presidential election by Iran. I stand by my report.

"I have a few words to say about the state of our country and its political climate. This land was almost destroyed in the last few days because a president suffering from borderline personality disorder attempted to launch nuclear missiles at Pakistan. You may not believe any of the things I've just mentioned, but that's exactly what I want to speak to you about—what we choose to believe or not believe.

"A recent survey showed that over half of all Americans couldn't name the three branches of government. Roughly the same number is unaware that Congress is divided into two houses, the House of Representatives and the Senate. Less than fifteen percent know how legislation becomes law. Ninety percent of Americans have never read the Constitution. We've stopped educating ourselves and have allowed our elected representatives to be the sole arbiters of truth, when learning the truth is in fact the role of every individual in a free society.

"Perhaps NewzTracker is complicit in this ignorance, since news is digested in small bits without any context, and we believe what we see or hear in the space of thirty-second sound bites uploaded to VOX-POP without bothering to see if what we're listening to is true or false.

"We've forgotten that we govern ourselves, and that the United States is a country by, of, and for the people. Everyone in Washington is a paid public servant—*your* servant—standing in your place to represent you fairly. But we can only govern if we inform ourselves with the best information available. Most people believe that the newly enacted tax reform bill is going to lower their taxes. It won't. And many citizens believe that Jimmy Finch and his American Paramilitary Union are part of America's armed services. They aren't."

Patterson paused as he chose his next words carefully.

"President Hastings said that God lives in all of us. Maybe he does and maybe he doesn't. I'm not a theologian. But if this country is to survive, a citizen who is neither red nor blue must live inside of each and every one of us. The laws and principles in the Constitution aren't dead words on a piece of old parchment. But they only live and breathe when we make them do so, and that can't happen if we follow a man who claims that only *he* can fix our problems. We cannot accept a king, tyrant, or emperor in the White House. Our Founding Fathers recognized the tyranny of King George and started a revolution in 1776.

"There are those today who would start a revolution of a different kind, people like Jimmy Finch, who would break apart the country and rule by martial law. They would have us live in a police state, held captive by the lies of TINN and the Scarabelli family. They would have us revolt against the free expression of ideas and honest disagreement, labeling such as social media lies and substitute news. They would even use religion, such as the Church of the Heart, as a screening tool to decide who is patriotic and who is not.

"Herbert Chase Hastings is a sociopath. He's mentally ill, and yet part of America has bought into his illusions, lies, and contradictory statements because the country wanted bread and circuses as well as a quick fix to all of its problems. Like the emperors of Rome, President Hastings sits in an imperial chair in a coliseum so that honest men and women can be mocked and ridiculed and killed. My question for you, America, is this: Who is more mentally unbalanced? President Hastings, or those who sit in the coliseum with him and cheer on his madness?

Today in our country, there are those who seek to control and manipulate, to prevent the dissemination of the truth. There are those who would project their own failings and pathology onto others, change reality, abuse minorities and the innocent, and live in a perpetual state of paranoia and chaos. It is America that suffers from an elected President who has been diagnosed with pathological borderline personality disorder.

"Even in these politically poisonous times, we must deliver a message of endless hope that this chaotic moment is not our hopeless end."

Sela uploaded the message to the NewzTracker website.

Dickerson returned and informed Patterson that television reporting on presidential succession was inaccurate. Congressional votes were not there to support Cal Quint's invocation of the Twenty-fifth Amendment.

Patterson said, "May I have a few more minutes in this room? I'd like to honor the wishes of a dear friend who is about to die."

"Leland Wallace?" Dickerson said.

"Yes."

"By all means, do so," Dickerson said before leaving again.

"I've reviewed the recordings Leland made," Patterson said. "Send his recordings to the sixty-eight senators and congressmen. I've attached a small note to each recording, a personalized memo to each legislator. We'll discuss it later, but right now you need to send the files as soon as possible."

Sela nodded and followed Patterson's instructions.

When Dickerson returned a second time, she escorted them to a tunnel that led to the Eisenhower Executive Office Building west of the White House. John Taylor, they were told, would be waiting for them and bring them to a private residence that Mrs. Hastings had recently purchased in Maryland. Because she was still First Lady, the house was well-guarded by the Secret Service.

Patterson and Sela left the White House, wondering what lay ahead for the country.

Chapter One Hundred Twelve
So Much for Love

PRESIDENT HASTINGS SAT IN THE OVAL OFFICE, HIS FACE TWISTED INTO A FROWN AS HE WATCHED NEWS OF THE IMPENDING VOTE IN CONGRESS TO REMOVE HIM FROM OFFICE. He reached for the phone on his desk several times, but withdrew his hand, knowing he could no longer solicit the advice of Vice President Cal Quint. The man he'd trusted most had turned traitor, seeking to replace him as president. Had this been his plan all along? Had he, Herbert Hastings, been played by the folksy cowboy personality that masked what was, in reality, one of the most calculating minds in Washington? Hastings thought it likely.

He also began to call Maxwell Hart several times, but no one had ever told him about an organization called The Elect, and he felt he'd been played by Hart as well. If some secret club named *Etiam Electus* was the real power in D.C., then it meant that he'd been nothing but a puppet all along. Unable to resist the urge to fathom what was happening to his administration, he succumbed and put in a call to the secretary of state. He was told that Secretary Hart was too busy to take his call.

He summoned Lucille Raines. He could count on her, could he not? His lover and advisor?

"Herbert," Raines said a few moments later as she sat in a chair next to the desk in the Oval Office, "you're worrying for nothing. Congress doesn't have the votes to remove you from office."

"But the country will lose faith in me regardless. My own vice president agrees with Patterson, Rampling, and Rittner. They say I'm crazy, Lucille. I thought I was invincible."

"You are, my love," Raines said, rising and walking around the desk, and kneeling next to Hastings. "You're the president of the United States. The people love you. You saved the entire world and have brought an end to terrorism. Quint and others in your cabinet are jealous of your accomplishments."

Hastings reflected on what Raines had said. "Yes," he said. "That's *exactly* what's going on. I should have seen it. I'll fire them all."

"I think you should," Raines said. "They're not worthy of being led by a great man such as yourself. When this blows over, you'll be able to pass more legislation and become the greatest president in the annals of American history."

Hastings rose, smiled, and embraced the sexy form of his mistress, who now stood, her breasts pressed against Hastings' muscular chest.

"Never forsake me, Lucille. Diane will be gone soon, and we can be together without all the cloak and dagger."

Raines kissed the president lightly on the lips. "I'll never forsake you, Herbert. Now let me get back to work. We have a country to run."

Alone again, Hastings turned on the wall screen permanently set to TINN. He'd been told by Grant Schneider that the network was going to run a special report on the First Lady—an hour-long program that would chronicle her drug abuse and many marital infidelities. No special was airing, however.

"I'll check later," Hastings said to himself. "For now, I need to jog. I need to stay in shape for the upcoming campaign. When I'm finished with my workout, I'll need to choose a new vice president."

He pounded his right fist into the palm of his left hand. He felt great.

/

Raines looked at the latest vote count that had been sent to her by "Cal the Vote Wrangler," who had been busy working the phones, talking to members of Congress in both Houses on why they should vote to put him into the Oval Office. According to Quint's estimate, the Senate and the House were a total of fifty-six votes short of being able to remove the President from office.

"Damn," Raines uttered.

She took out the president's psychiatric file. She would release it, and she would do so under her own name. Legislators might appreciate the fact that the president's own chief of staff, someone who worked by his side closely every day, agreed with the vice president. Scanning the documents from Dr. Ramplings' file into her phone, Raines added a voiceover to the documents, explaining that she, too, had noticed the president's erratic behavior. She sent the entire message to all major networks and news organizations, including TINN. Nick Scarabelli was a member of *Etiam Electus*. He'd voted against removing Herbert Hastings from office, but he would abide by the decision of the thirteen. He would air Raines' message. After all, he'd torpedoed the report on Diane Hastings being a drug user and adulterer. Scarabelli knew the decision of The Elect had to carry the day.

Raines knew it was unwise to assume victory until it was well in hand, and yet she couldn't help but visualize putting her hand on a Bible and taking the oath of office to become vice president of the United States.

/

The president was able to keep his mind focused for only a brief time after Raines had returned to her office in the West Wing. As Jay Patterson's report on his illegal business dealings with Iran and Garundi replayed on NewzTracker and was aired on other networks, he became increasingly nervous. Patterson had also uploaded an op-ed piece that was receiving tens of millions of hits—a piece that went after him on a personal level. The mainstream media was also covering the coming vote in Congress with keen interest, claiming that such a constitutional crisis had not been seen since the days of Richard Nixon and Watergate.

President Hastings was growing desperate. He could think of only one thing to do: Take his message to the people using VOXPOP.

"The First Lady is a whore. She's addicted to heroin. Jay Patterson is a terrorist and follows the Muslim faith. Cal Quint is a traitor, an ex-cowboy with the IQ of a three-year-old. The press corps is receiving money from Israel to bring down a Christian president so the Jews can gain power in the United States. All reporters are cyber liars. I'm the only person left that the American people can trust."

He recorded a thirty-second message every five minutes for the next two hours.

Chapter One Hundred Thirteen

Last Responsible Effort to Right Wrongs

The vote in the House of Representatives took the standard fifteen minutes. Congressmen could vote at any one of forty-seven electronic stations in the House chamber by inserting a card into a machine that then offered the selections of "Yea," "Nay," or "Present." Congressmen walked about the chamber, talked with each other, and the votes were tallied.

When the Speaker of the House, Marissa Gaitan, graveled the vote closed, she leaned into the podium microphone and read, with a smidgen of satisfaction in her voice, "The final vote on the Congressional implementation of the Twenty-fifth Amendment to the U.S. Constitution and removing Herbert Chase Hastings is as follows: We have three-hundred forty-one *yes* votes and ninety-four *no* votes." That was fifty-one votes more than the two-thirds desired by proponents as a way of inoculating a somewhat more Senate. The number of votes needed was three-hundred twenty-six. The margin had not been great, but it had been sufficient to send a message. The House of Representatives was overwhelmingly in favor of having Vice President Cal Quint sworn in as president.

In the Senate, a roll call was taken. With seventy-five votes needed, the senators answered "yea" or "nay" when their names were called. Seventy-four votes had been reached when Senator Leland Wallace, weak but alert, was again wheeled onto the Senate floor. He spoke in a whispered voice and held up his thumb for emphasis, lest there be any doubt as to how he was voting.

"Yea," he said to the motion to replace Herbert Chase Hastings with Cal Quint.

The president would be relieved.

Wallace was taken back to the ambulance that had brought him to Capitol Hill. He was put on a stretcher and loaded into the rear of the vehicle, where medics helped him change from his suit into a hospital gown. His breathing was shallow, and the ambulance had driven only a few blocks before the senator opened his eyes and made a request of the medic by his side.

"May I have a shot of bourbon and a cigarette?" he asked.

"I'm afraid not," came the reply.

"A damn shame is what it is," he said.

He closed his eyes and died a few seconds later.

Chapter One Hundred Fourteen
In the Name of Truth

Patterson met Bobby Thibodaux at Perk-a-Lot, a popular nationwide coffee chain in Maryland, near the residence of the First Lady. He didn't recognize the NewzTracker technician at first due to his clean-cut appearance. Thibodaux was dressed in a khaki military uniform.

"I think I look pretty good," he said as he embraced Patterson, "although I'm just not the military type. I met some really great dudes, though, and more power to 'em. They serve our country and have a lot more discipline than yours truly."

"Good to see you, Bobby. You truly are a wizard. If you hadn't gotten on Air Force One, I doubt that Quint could have received my story."

"All in a day's work, Jay. And I have a gift for you."

Thibodaux handed Patterson a small thumb drive.

"What's on it?" the reporter asked.

"The names of all one thousand members of *Etiam Electus*. I hacked into the private database of Maxwell Hart. Like I said, they have some great toys on Air Force One. There are quite a few lines of communication that go straight to Hart's office, and I found a back door into a private server that he keeps. Thought this might make a good story."

"Good? It will make a *great* story, Bobby!"

Thibodaux smiled as the two men ordered coffee.

"I didn't think there were enough votes in Congress to remove Hastings," Thibodaux said.

"There might not have been were it not for Leland Wallace. He gave me recordings of sixty-eight senators and congressmen confessing how much they hated Hastings. The recordings also contained evidence that every one of the sixty-eight had sexually harassed or sexually abused women while in office. I sent each member a copy of them, discussing their mischief, and attached a note threatening to make their misdeeds public."

"Sounds unethical. Shouldn't you release that kind of information as a matter of principle?"

"Of course. I didn't tie my threat to their vote on Hastings, but that's the way every one of the cowards took it. I intend to out every last one of them. In the recordings, they all seemed quite proud of their misconduct."

"You're damn good at your job," Thibodaux said. "Maybe *you* should run for office."

"It's not in my blood. My job is to report the truth in the news. That's good enough for me."

"And my Abita Amber?"

"I'll make sure you have a lifetime supply."

"Really?"

"Really."

Chapter One Hundred Fifteen

An Emperor No More

HERBERT CHASE HASTINGS RODE FROM THE WHITE HOUSE TO WRIGHT-PATTERSON TO BOARD AIR FORCE ONE FOR HIS FINAL JOURNEY ON THE AIRCRAFT, A CEREMONIAL FLIGHT ACCORDED TO ALL PRESIDENTS WHO HAD FINISHED THEIR TERMS, ONE WAY OR ANOTHER. Some diehard loyalists and a few staff members from the West Wing had gathered to wish him farewell. They were tearful to see their leader leaving in disgrace, a man they had literally worshipped and regarded as America's only hope to get beyond politics as usual since he had assumed office, he said, to sweep the corruption out of Washington. He had often stated on the campaign trail that "A new broom sweeps clean, and I intend to sweep away corrupt career politicians until the national House is in order." Instead, President Cal Quint and Jay Patterson had swept the town clean of Hastings, his family, and a majority of those who had been a part of his inner circle.

Hastings climbed the tall wide rolling stairs that admitted to the front hatch of Air Force One, but didn't look back at his few faithful to wave, smile, or thank them. He wore a frown, brushed past the aircraft personnel and walked to his onboard office where he sat and pulled down the shade of the window. He never wanted to see Washington, D.C. again. He still didn't know all the details of how he'd been relieved of office, and he had refused to meet with Cal Quint in order to accomplish a peaceful transfer of power. What he did convince himself to know that was also symptomatic, was that Maxwell Hart ran some kind of secret society that had encouraged Quint to assert that he was mentally ill. He wasn't interested in reading the

Twenty-fifth Amendment, nor—not surprisingly, had he ever read the Constitution before assuming office.

How was this different from a military coup? he asked himself again and again. *How could an emperor be pushed out of office? By the time of Augustus, Caesars had attained the status of god, and even Son of God. How was it possible that a deity could* be *spurned by lowly people who were poor and from average breeding, people who carried lunch pails and worked on assembly lines, people who wore silly military uniforms with badges and medals, people who didn't know their proper place in society?*

He closed his eyes as Air Force One took off, headed for his retreat in Colorado. Soon he had drifted into a fitful sleep. He was being hit by the headmaster at the Christian Academy of Virginia, but as the dream progressed, it was Hastings who towered over a series of forms cringing in the corner. First, he beat his wife until her face was bruised and swollen. Then he pummeled Jay Patterson until he was unconscious. Each time he had inflicted a maximum amount of pain, a new person took the place of the previous victim. It was Hart, Quint, Wolcott, and many others. When he was finished issuing punishment, he turned and was no longer in the small room where he had been abused. He was standing on the emperor's balcony in the Roman Coliseum, and the crowd cheered his actions as the gates housing the lions were opened to allow their hunger to appease their instinct.

"Would you like something to eat, sir?"

Hastings opened his eyes to see the chief steward aboard Air Force One, asking if he would like lunch.

"No," Hastings said gruffly. "They're not on the menu. Leave me alone."

The steward left, and Hastings turned off the light in his office, staring into the gloom. He thought of how he would resurrect PB Enterprises, would market Sailor cigarettes to everyone who his PR team could legally target. He would allow Brad and Savannah to work on other projects like the Slipstream 7000, but he himself would continue the legacy of Percy Beauregard Hastings and become the King of Tobacco once again. He would kill as many Americans as possible with PB's lethal product, enriching himself in the process. If Americans were stupid enough to smoke, they deserved what they got, which was death.

And yet the money would be secondary to power. Yes, he indeed loved to control and manipulate. As long as he could cajole and persuade and buy off those under his influence, he felt like he had purpose. He needed people to believe what *he* believed, think like *he* thought, spend time on *him*. He wanted to experience the same feeling he'd had when he pulled his children away from their mothers after each divorce, convincing them that the women had been flawed individuals. "Let me tell you who your mother *really* is," he told his children when the dust had settled from each divorce.

Hastings' breathing slowed as he relaxed and turned on the light in his airborne office again. Free from any burdens in Washington, he could once again live according to the one belief that he had held as sacred since his adolescence: He was the way, the Truth, and the life.

Chapter One Hundred Sixteen
For Better or Worse

WITH CAL QUINT ASSUMING THE OFFICE OF PRESIDENT, AND WITH HASTINGS LEAVING IN DISGRACE, THERE WAS RENEWED INTEREST IN PATTERSON'S ARTICLE ON PB'S ILLEGAL TOBACCO GROWING, GARUNDI, AND IRAN'S ROLE IN THE 2024 PRESIDENTIAL ELECTION. The Red Republican Legion was enraged that its leader had been ousted, although many other factions of the Real Right couldn't ignore the egregious nature of what President Hastings had done. The reporting of John Taylor and Jay Patterson was featured on other networks, and both men had been interviewed a dozen times within twenty-four hours of Hastings' departing for Telluride.

Before being sworn in, Quint leaked detailed information to Patterson on the tense stand-off in the White House Situation Room that had nearly led to a nuclear exchange with Pakistan. Through Patterson's follow-up articles, the country was shocked that it had come so close to annihilation. Patterson's face appeared on the cover of *Time* magazine, and he remained in Maryland since reporters had camped out in front of his D.C. apartment building.

With Secretary Hart having been fired by President Quint for his implication in the murders of Tom Chance, Elizabeth Rampling, and Boyce Rittner, news outlets published daily stories on *Etiam Electus*, although no one in the government had any comment on the secret society. Patterson spoke on air at length about the attempts made on his life and the torture he'd been subjected to in the Virginia barn, but TINN, under direct orders from Nick Scarabelli, denied the existence of The Elect. Lucille Raines, named by Quint to be his vice president, was quick to disavow any association with the Office of Government Inquiry under any of its aliases and denied knowing anything about the murders for which Maxwell Hart was accused of committing.

With Hastings en route to Telluride, the wheels of Air Force One hadn't touched down in Denver before Congress deemed it politically expedient to ask for Special Counsel to be appointed by the Justice Department to investigate Hastings, his children, his Presidential campaign, PB Enterprises, and his ties to Iran and Hamid Abbas Faridoon. The Senate Intelligence Committee and House Subcommittee on Oversight and Investigations both decided in short order to conduct their own investigations into the matters.

News organizations were now keenly interested in Brad and Savannah Hastings, both of whom had retained legal counsel before their father left Washington. Major newspapers and television networks looked closely at the travel itinerary and business contacts of Brad and Savannah for the past five years, and documentaries ran nightly on the dealings of Hamid Abbas Faridoon, who suddenly became a household name in America. As for Sedge O'Connell, members of the press were quick to point out that he'd begun working for PB Enterprises shortly after his dismissal from Marsh & Brennan. There was much speculation that he'd been brought into the company at a time when it was introducing nicotine into Sailor cigarettes because of his vast knowledge of food additives, pharmaceuticals, and proprietary products consumed by hundreds of millions of people around the world. His background, it was revealed, included specialties in addiction and subliminal advertising.

President Cal Quint's association with Hastings was not proving to be a liability as far as Congress or the American people were concerned. He was affable Cal Quint, the man with a smile in his pocket, a down-home ex-rodeo rider who had no apparent affiliation with any of the illegal activities that would soon be investigated. His military service, legislative record, and work with the CIA were playing well with almost everyone except Grass Roots, which claimed that anyone affiliated with Hastings wasn't an honorable man. The few detractors that Quint had, however, were quick to admit that the Twenty-fifth Amendment had been the tool used for removing a mentally ill man from the Oval Office, and the same amendment called for the vice president to step into the vacuum of power. For better or worse, they said, that man was Cal Quint.

Chapter One Hundred Seventeen

. . . And May God Bless America

PRESIDENT QUINT DEEMED IT NECESSARY TO ADDRESS THE COUNTRY IN PRIME TIME TWO DAYS AFTER HE ASSUMED OFFICE. From bar room stools to living rooms in rural America, the nation watched its forty-eighth President speak of recent matters and the direction the country would now take.

"My fellow Americans," Quint began as he sat behind his desk in the Oval Office, "The Speaker of the House, the entire Cabinet, both Chambers of our Legislative Branch and I, as vice president, have, with great deliberation, reluctance, and an uncommon amount of agony, relieved Herbert Hastings from office as President of the United States. While such action was serious and grave, it was done in a manner that our Founding Fathers would have approved of, since they wrote a document that has been amended over the years to reflect the nation's changing needs. The Twenty-fifth Amendment was ratified in 1967 to ensure the orderly transfer of power should the president become incapacitated, either temporarily or permanently. Regrettably, President Hastings was proven to be no longer fit to serve as president."

"The offenses of the Hastings children, Sedge O'Connell, and ex-Secretary of State Hart appear egregious in nature, although these individuals must be accorded due process depending on the findings of the investigations being conducted by the House, Senate, and Special Counsel.

"To be clear, I invoked the Twenty-fifth Amendment because I regarded President Hastings' actions to be erratic and a threat to our nation, especially as it pertained to foreign policy and the deployment of the military. I myself witnessed the president as he attempted to launch nuclear weapons at targets in Pakistan, a longtime ally which had nothing to do with any terrorist activity known by our intelligence agencies.

"I was also greatly troubled by the president's actions that, knowingly or not, brought the country to the brink of deep division and civil war. Because the president suffers from a recognized mental disorder, however, I am granting him a full and complete pardon in the hopes that he will find compassionate medical treatment. I make no moral judgment on our former president, which, if you will allow me to speak from the heart, is above my pay grade.

"My first action as your president will be to arrange a summit with Pakistan's Prime Minister Yasir Rafiq to lessen the tension between our two nations and normalize relations. Secondly, I am reinstating the recently fired NASA Administrator so that he may coordinate worldwide efforts to deflect Comet JM-2026A. Finally, I am instructing SETI to work with the world's scientific community to study the signals from an apparently intelligent civilization orbiting Tau Ceti, although I wish to reassure every American and those around the world that there is no evidence that such intelligence poses any threat to humanity.

"The Union stands. The rule of Law prevails. With God's grace, I shall serve you and our country to the best of my ability. Thank you, good evening, and May God bless America."

Chapter One Hundred Eighteen

Appearance of Back to Normality

AMERICA SEEMED TO BE PLEASED WITH PRESIDENT QUINT'S ADDRESS. People were cautiously optimistic that the comet could be deflected and that nuclear war between *any* two nations could be avoided. Indeed, it was hoped that the recent scare might generate renewed nonproliferation talks, as well as serious dialogue about the ever-present danger of an accidental nuclear exchange. News outlets reported that normalcy had, to a large extent, been restored to the country, which was breathing a palpable collective sense of relief.

Diane Hastings and Audrey Dickerson announced the formation of the National Association for Battered Women, an organization for those who had been the victims of sexual violence or harassment, whether physical, verbal, or mental. Cookie McKnight had been hired as the organization's spokesperson.

Jimmy Finch's weekend warriors had effected a complete retreat from urban areas and were once again invisible to the public. Many of their encampments flew the Confederate flag, and Finch declared himself a candidate for a seat in the Tennessee state legislature under his newly formed Supreme White Brotherhood Party. There was argument that Finch should be arrested as having ordered murder in the streets in Tennessee of Grass Roots members, but at the time he had been protected by a sitting president. Still, one has to wonder if people like Jimmy Finch should go free, given his murder history.

Holly Gerard Finch issued a public statement that the Church of the Heart would be open to people of all races and creeds, although she insisted that Muslims be vetted carefully. Several state attorney generals moved quickly to file motions in appellate courts to declare the church's policy of vetting to be unconstitutional unless the Church of the Heart wished to incorporate and forego its tax-exempt status as a religious institution. Even then, many claimed the church's policy was a violation of civil rights laws.

Josh Rollins was being heralded as a hero for defying the Hastings ban against replying to signals from Tau Ceti. The astronomer was in great demand as a lecturer and had been invited to chair an international panel on discussing the ramifications of living in an era when humanity could no longer claim to be the only intelligent species in the universe. He accepted the position, although he decided to devote most of his time to the scientific pursuit of developing a mathematical language to begin a conversation with the alien life forms 12.5 light years away.

Chapter One Hundred Nineteen
Democracy or Survival of the Fittest

PATTERSON SENT A FINAL ONE-WORD MESSAGE TO THE ACCOUNT OF LoneWolf777@qmail.com. The communication simply said, *"Why?"* Although Patterson had a good idea why the new president had sent him messages, he wanted to know specifics. He didn't anticipate a reply, but was invited to the White House the next day to meet with President Cal Quint. He was shown into the Oval Office, offered coffee, and sat on a striped couch facing Quint on the opposite couch, separated by blue carpet containing the presidential seal.

Quint crossed his legs, sipped his coffee, and smiled at the reporter. "I thought you'd be contacting me," he said. "You have questions?"

"Several, Mr. President, but one in particular. Did you give me information to help the country, or to further your own political ambitions? Have I been operating as a member of the free press, or as a political pawn?"

Quint raised his eyebrows and nodded. "A fair question, Jay, although anything I say is off the record. The answer is that the two aren't mutually exclusive. It's no secret that I worked the rodeo circuit in my youth, and I felt a lot of pride if I could stay on a bull for eight seconds. But at the end of the day, I wanted to collect a paycheck. I'm not very good at quoting scripture like my predecessor, but I believe the Bible says that a worker is worth his wages. If I do a job, I want to be compensated."

This wasn't the answer Patterson wanted to hear, and his frustration showed in the knit brows on his forehead.

"Listen, Jay, when I decided to be Hastings' running mate, I knew he was mad as a hatter. But I also knew that he stood a good chance at defeating Harrison DePeche. That meant there was also a good chance that I'd be sitting right here in the Oval Office one day, only not as a visitor, but as president. I wasn't exactly sure when it might happen, but Wolcott and others fed me a lot of compromising information on Hastings, such as his specific psychiatric condition, The Elect, and PB's involvement with Iran and Garundi. I couldn't put such information out there myself because it would have violated all conventional political protocols. How could I succeed Hastings if I were perceived as a traitor to my boss and party? A vice president doesn't bring down the chief executive. I had to orchestrate this so that people would come to *me*, people such as Hart. For the record, I'm not a member of The Elect. *Etiam Electus* are kingmakers, Jay. And while they have an agenda largely unknown to the American people, I knew that Maxwell Hart wouldn't turn a blind eye to Iran buying an American presidential election. It would violate all of his notions of purity and straight-laced governance. Whatever his flaws, which are considerable, he was a general, and I knew he wouldn't cotton to Hastings getting into bed with a country known for its radicalism and terrorist ties."

"Tell me about Pakistan," Patterson said. "Besides the president's illegal business dealings, his attempt to wipe out the nation played a large part in your invoking the Twenty-fifth Amendment."

Quint sighed and sat back against the sofa cushion. "Yes . . . Pakistan. It was a part of my plan that almost went horribly awry. I encouraged Hastings to flex his muscles, knowing that the Joint Chiefs and Maxwell Hart would take a dim view of the president's saber rattling. It was well-known in intelligence circles that there were no terrorist camps near Gwadar, so I thought pushing Hastings in that direction might hasten The Elect to ask me to assume power. I had no idea that his wife was going to ask for a divorce, which is what sent the man off the deep end."

"You knew he was mentally unstable, and yet you encouraged him to threaten risky military maneuvers."

"I encouraged him to talk tough, nothing more. I admittedly explained the command structure to him, but I truly didn't think he had the intelligence to use it, or that anyone in the chain of command would let him get to first base. I was wrong."

Patterson was unsettled by what he was hearing. Quint was obviously not the hero that he or the country thought he was. He was a man who had played a dangerous game to assume power. His claim that he had agreed to be the vice president under Hastings in order to provide his own personal system of checks and balances was believable only up to a point.

"Are you telling me that democracy is now safe and the government will pivot back to the normal business of running the country . . . whatever normal is? And what of The Elect and its agenda to radically alter the structure of the federal government of the United States?"

Quint grinned and shook his head, amused by the query.

"Another question without a clear answer, Jay. Hastings is mentally disturbed, but that doesn't mean I disagree with many of his ideological beliefs."

The color drained from Patterson's face as he tried to assimilate the words of the new president.

"You look like a kid who just smoked his first cigarette behind a barn," Quint said," but here's the deal. The Towers of Freedom will stand. I'm strong on securing the borders, and if illegals won't respect our immigration laws, they'll have to pay a heavy price for their incursions into U.S. territory."

"And what of taxes, the economy, science, and the environment?"

Quint shrugged. "Like Hastings said, it's survival of the fittest. I can't solve the problems of every poor American any more than I can save Bangladesh or a climate that's beyond repair. I deal with today, the here and now. There's going to be hell to pay down the line—I'll grant you that. But in the year 2026, life belongs to people who can stay on the bull. It's been the underpinning of Republican philosophy for generations."

"It's cruel."

"It's history. The country started with a lot of political parties. The Federalists, Jeffersonian Republicans, Jacksonians, Whigs, and too many others to count. Along came the Industrial Revolution and we ended up with a two-party system that revolved around the haves and have-nots. This is the digital age, however. The one thing I learned as a political science major is that technology drives social and political change. Technology always pushes aside the little guy. And you hit the nail on the head in your op-ed piece. Most people can't name the three branches of government. The Internet has dumbed people down, not made them smarter. They'll believe whatever they see on TINN or hear on VOXPOP and a dozen social media sites like Facebook or Instagram. They want to ingest what they call news as fast as they can buy some shiny bauble with their chip implants. And that's why it's time to take the last political step."

Patterson was sure he didn't want to hear what was coming. "Which is?"

"Permanent rule by one party."

"For the rich and powerful. The have-nots need not apply."

"As your friend Leland Wallace would have said, a damn shame is what it is, but yes. What's the old saying? Pull yourself up by your bootstraps, right?"

"Some people don't own boots."

"And the Federal Government isn't a shoe company. All this won't happen overnight, mind you, but the trends are irreversible."

"You're wrong, Mr. President. America is better than that. There will always be resistance to your philosophy of government. Grass Roots isn't the only opposition you'll face."

"I agree, but if I snap my fingers, Jimmy Finch and the American Paramilitary Union will come to my aid. So will TINN, the Scarabelli family, The Elect, and the Church of the Heart. The latter was my idea, by the way. The Real Right is a force that can no longer be dislodged from society. It's a sociological reality as much as a political one. O brave new world that has such people in it. *The Tempest*. Act Five, Scene One."

"Hart will go on trial as a murderer," Patterson countered. "It will be a wake-up call to the country."

"And he'll be convicted. But members of the judiciary are members of The Elect. Hart won't stay in prison for long, and he'll remain Head of *Etiam Electus*. And don't think for one minute that people will disapprove of The Elect. It's now America's fourth branch of government, one that saved the country from Armageddon. They'll accept the organization as easily as they accepted chip implants."

Patterson lowered his head. He knew Quint's analogy to the chip implant made a lot of sense. Leland Wallace had said that the country was dying. Maybe he'd been right.

"It's my job to try to stop you," Patterson said. "It's the job of a free press. I won't give up trying to expose the truth and prove that America is still a viable democracy."

President Quint extended his right arm in a sweeping gesture, as if to motion to the world that lay beyond the Oval Office. "Be my guest, Jay. No one will try to hunt you down anymore. I've seen to that. Go where you want and write whatever you please. Time will decide which one of us is right."

"Thank you for your time, Mr. President," Patterson said tersely.

Quint rose and extended his hand. "Think about what I've said, Jay. I picked you as the one I would share information with because you know how to analyze a problem. You'll come around."

Patterson turned and left without taking Quint's hand.

Chapter One Hundred Twenty

Hope for Social Responsibility for All

Patterson, Sela, Taylor, and Thibodaux gathered in the NewzTracker transmission room. Bobby Thibodaux sat drinking an Abita Amber, cases of which were stacked in the corner.

"I've begun contacting the women named in the recordings Leland gave me," Patterson said. "Not every senator or congressman mentioned specific names when they were bragging about their sexual conquests, but a surprising number of them did. Some women have already come forward, and more will undoubtedly emerge from the shadows to make public accusations, since there's strength in numbers. Diane Hastings has agreed to raise money through her organization for the legal fees of women who accuse the men Leland recorded. I think there will be a great many resignations in the months to come—or denials, as the case may be. Leland was a gentleman who detested the behavior he heard his colleagues discussing, and he had the guts to do something about it."

"What about the thousand names of the members of *Etiam Electus* I gave you?" Thibodaux asked as he tilted his head back to bring the dark bottle of beer to his lips.

Patterson looked at his editor.

"In time, Bobby," Taylor said. "The country has a lot to process. The Elect's membership cuts through all levels of the federal government, the military, and industry. The Government is too fragile right now. Jay and I agree that the story must eventually come out over and above what Maryanne Mistretta wrote, but with so many congressmen expected to resign because of Leland's recordings, there might be nobody left to mind the store."

Sela grabbed a beer and sat on the edge of Bobby's desk, clanking bottles for a beer cheer for NewzTracker's wizard.

"It's scary as hell to know that The Elect," she said, "the fourth branch of government, as Quint put it, is out there somewhere making decisions outside of constitutional boundaries of a Democracy."

"Not any scarier than everyone having a chip implant in their arms," Patterson noted. "Like the Internet, it was a mistake to forsake privacy for convenience."

"By the way," Thibodaux said, "if anyone is interested, Felix Ogo is still riding around in his Jeep every day as he surveys his country's fields of yams and tobacco. He seems unfazed by the negative publicity he's receiving."

"I doubt he needs the help of Hastings anymore," Taylor noted.

"Point well taken," Thibodaux said. "Hell, Faridoon arrived in Garundi a couple days ago and hasn't left Jumba Ogo since. I guess the Iranian mafia is all the dictator needs."

"By the same token," Patterson said, "I don't think President Muhammed Al Assad is very pleased with Faridoon for getting caught and bringing Iran's nuclear program under worldwide scrutiny. Jumba Ogo may be Faridoon's permanent residence from now on."

The four friends raised their beer bottles in a toast.

"Here's to justice for the little guy," Patterson said. "And to the Atlanta Falcons and a simple day at the ballpark. It's American."

/

Patterson and Sela stood outside and gazed at the stars. The night was clear, and the dark heavens were filled with thousands of points of light.

"The aliens at Tau Ceti could teach us so much," Patterson said philosophically, as he put his arm around Sela's waist and drew her close. "If they're advanced, that is. Maybe they're just like us."

"They're probably more advanced, since the odds of their developing technologically at the exact time we did are pretty slim. As Rollins pointed out, it might take decades—maybe hundreds of years—to start even a rudimentary conversation with ET. That twenty-five-year round trip to complete a simple message is pretty daunting."

Patterson remained quiet for several minutes.

"What's wrong?" Sela asked. "Something's on your mind."

"Yeah. It's everything Quint told me. Maybe he's right. Perhaps the paradigm shift in modern culture can never be reversed. Quint's view of the future is positively dystopian, but have we sacrificed so much to technology in the last two hundred years that we've lost our souls? Is there no turning back to a bipartisan America?"

"You've invoked the soul," Sela said, "which is a spiritual concept."

Patterson laughed. "I suppose I have. You know, in the time we've known each other, you never told me *why* you're religious in a world that has very little use for God anymore."

"It's because of a story my grandfather told me when I was a teenager and questioning everything, which I suppose is normal for an adolescent who doesn't have much use for church doctrine. But what he said might apply to Quint's pessimism about the country as much as it does to questions about God and spirituality."

"Do tell."

"A young man approached his pastor after a Sunday service and said, 'Reverend, you're aware that I'm not a believer, but I'd like you to humor me and participate in a little thought experiment about the existence of God.' The pastor usually didn't engage in debates about the existence of the Creator, believing faith wasn't something that could be tested, but he told the young man to go ahead.

So the man turned around, cupped his hands, and then faced the pastor again. 'Okay, Reverend,' he said, 'I have a sparrow in my cupped hands which I captured this morning. Pray to God right this minute to let you know whether the bird is alive or dead.' By now, many parishioners had gathered to witness the conversation between the pastor and the young man, who believed that there was no way the pastor could pass the test.

If the pastor said the bird was alive, the young man would crush the bird and show its lifeless form to all present. If, on the other hand, the pastor said the bird was dead, the young man would simply open his hand and let the bird fly away. It was a no-win situation for the pastor. Either way, God and the power of prayer would have been disproven.

A hush fell over the crowd as the pastor closed his eyes for several seconds. 'Well,' said the young man, 'is the bird dead or alive?'

The pastor smiled and said, 'I can't answer your question, but what I can say with certainty is that the answer is in your hands.' "

Patterson smiled. "What you're saying is that the answer to Quint's claim that American democracy is dead lies in the hands of the American people."

"Precisely. You said in your op-ed that you wanted to talk about what people choose to believe or not believe. It's up to Americans, Jay. Where people put their faith is up to them, but serious decisions need to be *informed* decisions. That's where a free press comes into play."

"And God?"

"It took my grandfather a while to become a believer, but he got there. He said the answer had been in his hands the whole time, but that he'd forgotten to look."

Patterson kissed Sela on the forehead. "Your grandfather was a pretty smart guy. Mine was, too."

"What was your Grandfather's name?"

"Emanuel. In Hebrew it translates to *God is with us*. Do you think that's a nice name for a son?"

"It's a beautiful name, Jay," Sela said smiling. "But what if he is a she?"

"Then her name might be Emuna, meaning *faith*."

Smiling and overcome with feelings . . . "I love you so much, Jay,"

"I love you too, Sela, and that's why we're going to the J.P. first thing in the morning."

Still sensing Jay's need to be alone, she kissed him and walked back inside.

Jay wandered off into the dark. He sat in the grass and looked at the sky again.

Informed decisions. One had to do due diligence and think matters through. Comets, emperors—humanity could save itself from them or allow itself to be destroyed.

Somewhere beyond the solar system, intelligent beings were communicating with Earth. He couldn't see them, feel them, or touch them, but he knew they were there. He didn't have to see to believe.

He thought of his recent discussion with Cal Quint. He knew in his gut that things didn't have to play out as Quint had asserted. There was a different path open to the country if its people knew where to look, but the nation had to make a choice: Do business as usual, or become a government by, of, and for the people. If American democracy, a voice for all. Its people had strayed, there are two roads with two different outcomes. America can't have it both ways.

Using his phone screen for illumination, Jay opened his old dog-eared Bible, turned to a random page, and read:

"No man can serve two masters. He will either hate the first and love the second, or he will treat the first with respect and the second with scorn."

Patterson glanced into the heavens and cupped his hands, knowing what he was holding. He'd found a master he could follow.

Acknowledgments

I want to express my appreciation to those who made significant contributions to this, my first fiction endeavor, hopefully a page-turner. First I must thank my very knowledgeable and experienced collaborator William Hammett for his sage advice and assistance throughout. My sincere gratitude also goes to former United Nations writer Di Finch for her helpful edits. Finally, a big thanks to my wife, Dianne, for her positivity and just-in-time secretarial support.

About the Author

Emanuel Cleaver II is a United Methodist pastor, American politician, and a member of the U.S. House of Representatives. Cleaver currently represents Missouri's 5th Congressional District, where he's served since 2005. He regularly makes appearances on *Meet the Press* and *Face the Nation*, as well as *Oprah* and *Good Morning America*. Keep up with Congressman Cleaver at https://cleaver.house.gov/